<u>Early Acclaim For *The Cantora*</u>

"*The Cantora*, an utterly transporting reading experience.
…immensely skilled setting and scene building… Brazil during the
1500s—a vivid life for the reader."
　　　—*Carina Guiterman, Editor, Little, Brown & Company
Publishers*

"If You Enjoyed *The Book Thief*, You Will Fall In Love With
Cantora"
　　　—Hailey Zwanzig, Illustrator, *Left Hand Tree* by Jay
Gunter

"A Lyrically Stunning Novel . . . A 16th Century Jackie Evancho.
5-Stars!"
　　　—Justin Haldeman, Author of the forthcoming novel *The
Duke's Jubilee*

"The Cantora, Remarkable Story, Breathtaking In Scope, A Cadre
Of Unforgettable Characters"
　　　—William T. Goodman, Author of *Desert Sundays, An
Obvious Slam Dunk,* & the forthcoming *Go With The Night Wind*

"Great historical fiction - enthralling from the first page to the
last! 5-Stars"
　　　—*Barbara Jane Anderson*

And From *The Cantora*: "Yema's voice filled the church, and
some felt it filled the world… An ecstasy upon the ear, a vital
singing, the honeyed perfume of song."
　　　—Page 23, *The Cantora*

Edited by Naïma Msechu
Cover Artwork by Nicole Brauch, http://www.nicolebrauchart.com
Website Design & Cover Layout by Dan Gayle
Business Management & Website Support by Lynda Makara

Ordering Information:
Ingram Book Company
Print Edition ISBN: 978-0-692-86261-2
eBook Edition ISBN: 978-0-692-86297-1

First Edition, March 2017
Book II of *The Cantora* Series

Books I of *The Cantora* Series—

São Tomé   *Rapto em Lisboa*

Publisher's Cataloging-in-Publication data
Cohn, Paul D.
The Cantora— The Native Singer of Colonial Brazil
Ingram Book Company

Burns-Cole Publishers, https://www.thecantora.com/
burnscolepub@aol.com

Printed in the United States of America

Dedicated in loving memory to Laurie Batchelor and Sonny Shaffer

The Cantora
♫ *The Native Singer of Colonial Brazil* ♫
(Book II of The Cantora Series)

The Cantora

Standing alone on her balcony above the abbey's courtyard, a nun stares at the workers finishing the construction below. Bathed in the yellow light of the late afternoon sun, two structures extend their grim silhouettes across the rough cobblestones, a gallows where she will die in the morning, and a burning stake for her ward, the little girl known as The Cantora.

One of the workers notices the nun and calls to his fellows. At the same time he makes a circling motion around his neck and jerks an imaginary rope upwards, lolling his head to one side. The others laugh. She looks away from this familiar taunt as her thoughts turn to the child. *What must it be for Cantora imprisoned two stories below in a cell where no light enters? The little girl has never known such cruelty in her short nine years on this earth. And now before morning prayers we are to die.* She considers further, knowing that life without this child is truly no life at all. *If I die to save her, so it will be.*

The nun goes to her desk, retrieves her journal, and places it on the wide wall of the balcony. The fading sun now partly hidden behind the jungle canopy at the west edge of the settlement briefly illuminates her features revealing a pleasant oval face with a fringe of black hair ringing the wimple at her forehead and temples. Her light blue habit—that of the Portuguese Coimbran Order—compliments the sister's fair skin and penetrating brown eyes. She is a woman who often shows a generous and welcoming smile, but someone equally capable of a contentious, censoring frown.

As she routinely does before Vespers, the sister pulls a stool forward, opens the journal and begins to record the day's events, her Hebrew script flowing evenly across the page.

> I write of this, perhaps my last evening on earth if I fail to save the child. Then tomorrow I will inhabit Heaven with Cantora, we two condemned by the very Church I serve and she so wished to serve. Surely she will serenade at the throne of God, and I will swell with pride.
>
> Are these Catholics fools? Secretly, I've always suspected thus. There is no one here, not even Bishop Damião or any of the wretched tribunal who can read my Hebrew. They may send my journal to Lisbon, but I do not care.

Tomorrow I will no longer need it.

She gazes to the east, across the courtyard wall to the bay and the docks usually littered with people waiting in turn like insects to deposit their shards of wood bound for Europe. But today, for the first time in her memory, the harbor is deserted. There is smoke too, smoke rising from biers in the death yard and the remains of native huts burned in the uprising. The nun wonders, *what is the significance of two more deaths after so much killing?* She sighs and turns to a journal entry recorded the evening following her first visit to the docks, an entry nearly two years old, written shortly after her arrival in the New World.

> Ours is a land of chaos and death, of rapacious commerce and a Church equally so. God must look away from this hateful Brazil coast, for if He knew this sad and lonely land, surely what happens here could not. Perhaps He is never among us, or in His disgust has made this place Inferno Novo.

The nun turns a page and reads her account of that first visit.

> Noon passed an hour back. I view a cluttered dock crowded with African and Indian slaves and free Portuguese, each burdened with dyewood bundles bound for weighing and then to the ships. At the end of the tally line a ship's officer sits at a makeshift desk under a canopy recording the weights. He has two sets of ledgers, one for the slave owners, the other for free Portuguese. The officer doles out a few copper reis to each Portuguese. The slave overseers will receive their pay at day's end.
>
> A brief rain has drenched them all. Each wretched soul in the line is stained from the dyewood, bodies running red, or orange, or black, the garish colors mixing at their feet and through the slatted dock into the waters below. The wash of waves stains the shore itself.
>
> Eyeing the Indians, the spoilers wait at the fringe. Many of the natives are near death from the coughing sickness. A woman staggers a step

and goes down. She has a baby wrapped at her breast, the infant now screaming under the mother's weight.

These Indians are a handsome people, and may have enjoyed good health until we Portuguese arrived. Now they stoically endure sickness and pain to the moment of death, standing without complaint, a corpse shuddering from fever and cough, the last sign of a life at its end until they fall. Two spoilers rush forward, one holding the still woman with his foot, the other stripping the dyewood bundle from her. No one moves to help. In a moment someone rolls her over the dock's edge, the baby's cries silenced in the water. Even from this distance, I can see several bodies in the stained swirl, each writhing under the assault of the countless vicious fish that inhabit this stinking bay.

There is more, but she cannot read further. She remembers the bishop warned her to not go near the harbor and docks, but she had to see for herself. The sister closes the journal. "What's the use?" she says to the evening air. "What's the use?" In a moment she returns to the current day's entry and signs her name, not her Catholic name, but her family name, Leah Anna Saulo, her Jewish name, the name she possessed years ago in Lisbon. She again sighs and lays the bound volume aside.

The memory of the visit to the docks forces it way back into her thoughts. A ship's captain approached her that day, requesting a blessing for his voyage. "Sister, we sail for Spain at first light. Will you bless our journey?"

It was a strange request, asking a nun for a blessing. She suspected this Spaniard had other motives, but she answered kindly. "I will bless your sailing sir, if you carry no slaves. I do not bless slavers."

The man took a step backwards and made an unctuous bow. "Of course not, dear sister. Both Crown and Church prohibit the taking of Indian slaves. I carry only dyewood for the clothiers of Spain and the Vatican."

The captain and his backers stood to make a fortune if the voyage proved successful. With a shipload of dyewood sold in the markets of Europe, particularly the red color, the same paste-rouge the Indians applied so casually to their faces and bodies—when refined, more precious than gold—this captain could buy a fleet of ships. "Cardinal red," as the Europeans now called it, was extremely rare and expensive until the discovery of dyewood trees in the New World. Prior to this find, only the highest church clergy and wealthy nobles could afford the red pigment previously imported from the far east. The first Portuguese explorers called the trees yielding the red dye *brasa,* the word for ember, and soon the coast, with its abundance of *brasa* trees, became known as Brazil. The Indians called the pigment *Mbóia tuguy,* blood of the Devil.

"You will be a rich man once you arrive in Spain with your thoughtful gifts for the Holy Father," the nun said.

"God willing, dear sister, if we live to make the crossing. *And* avoid the English and Dutch corsairs that plague our seas. Please believe me, I carry no slaves."

Either the man was a dolt, she thought, *or too clever to register her jibe about the Holy Father. And what hypocrisy!* Everywhere she looked there were slaves. "Point out your ship, dear captain."

There were four ships in the harbor, and he gestured to the farthest, a three-masted schooner anchored several hundred yards off shore. "So please give us your blessing. She is the Santo Tomás."

The name brought her up short. "Did you arrive here from São Tomé?" she asked. All vessels arriving from Tomé Island carried African slaves. "Perhaps your ship's name is just a coincidence."

"Of course, dear sister. As you say, the name is simply a coincidence, an unhappy coincidence."

She gave him a withering stare. "Captain, you are lying. I know your ship. My name is Sister Mãe da Doçura, and I arrived here just last month from São Tomé. On that sorry island I was the chronicler and principal scribe for Bishop Henrique Cão." The man looked stricken. The nun shook her head. "Your drama is overblown. Your vessel is a dedicated slaver and you will not get my blessing." He began to protest. She raised a hand to silence him, but he pressed on.

"Tell me Sister Doçura, when you look at the spectacle on the docks, the sick and dying Indians, these pitiful souls perishing from disease which we brought, why is there no priest there to offer salvation, or at the very least absolution?"

What a stupid and mean-spirited question, she thought, and likely the man was pandering to her. No matter, she again chose to respond in a kindly manner. "This question I now ask myself. You see, I arrived here on a Sabbath morning, captain, with the docks mostly empty. Even the bodies had been removed. Not like it is now. This is my first view of the true situation. But you know the answer as well as I." She extended her arm and drew a boundary in front of them. "Because of the moneyed influence from the slavers, we clergy are prohibited from ministering to those who toil on the docks. And sadly it is the Church's position that slaves, both Indian and black, are property and thus not worthy of His Grace."

"The Indians are vicious heathen cannibals," the man responded. "If they die like vermin, it is God's will."

Doçura looked around, making sure there was no one to overhear. Then she said, "May I remind you of our Savior's words in John 6, Verse 54 which admonishes us to the Sacrament, '*Whoever eats My flesh and drinks My blood has eternal life, and*—' "

The captain shrunk back in horror. "*Surely* Sister you do not equate our Blessed Sacrament to cannibalism? The Sacrament is —"

Although she had sufficiently shocked him, she raised her voice and continued, "and then following in Verses 55 and 56, '*He who eats My flesh and drinks My blood abides in Me and I in him.*'"

The man simply stared at her, his mouth open.

"Let me point out, sir, that many of the natives are cannibals, but not all. Certainly none that live here in our little settlement of Luís. My life on São Tomé taught me the valued lesson of tolerance, tolerance of other people. Is it not Christ's purpose that we bring salvation to these Indians? Is it not improper that our mission is denied to those enslaved? Where in the volume of God's Law are we directed to enslave?"

Suddenly she'd grown weary of this pretentious Spaniard and the hateful docks. "Please do not think me rude sir, but I must go." She gathered the skirt of her habit, turned and walked quickly away, her thoughts painfully confused. Ever since arriving in this New World, Doçura found herself plagued by heretical thoughts—thoughts so alarming that she pushed them to the very back of her mind, forcing them into retreat each time they began to gnaw their way forward.

***

The afternoon fades to evening. The nun returns to her desk and the first pages of her journal, pages left blank from the onset. When she began the volume, she knew there would be something important to record on these pages. On this evening, her last on earth, they come to her.

She unfastens her collar, reaches inside and unhooks a gold chain from around her neck. She places the necklace next to the journal. The sight of the precious strand brings her to tears—this sacred chain that once was hers, the chain that held the amber kamea passed down from her grandmother, the chain she gave to her brother the night they were kidnapped, the very chain which was returned to her on São Tomé after her brother's death, this chain that connects everything from her past. She wipes the tears on her sleeve and considers the journal's first page. With hands trembling, she begins to write.

> I am a nun of questionable origins, having lived my life until the age of sixteen as a Jew and a member of the family Saulo in Lisbon. Eight years ago on the first day of Tishri, our Holy New Year, my brother and I were kidnapped along with two dozen children from our synagogue. The Crown soldiers who stormed our lovely place of worship took most of the children down to the harbor for shipment, conscripted to work the sugar plantations on São Tomé Island. A few girls, including me, were given kidnapped infants and sent to the convent at Coimbra. There the nuns trained everyone in the Catholic faith and taught us to care for the children. Almost five years later I had the chance to accompany a shipment of children to Tomé. Hoping to see my brother, Marcel, I embraced the opportunity, although I'd had no word of him for years. Happily, sadly, I found him dying in the hospital at Elmina, a two days' journey from São Tomé.

Later on that dreadful island, Bishop Cão (the
Church's first black prince) who greatly
admired my brother for his opposition to
slavery, assigned me the task of translating
Marcel's journal from Hebrew to Portuguese.
The bishop told me he believed my brother to
be a Just Man, a Saddiq.

In that first year I became acquainted with
my brother's large family, including his
intended wife, Ariella, and their children. (It
seems my brother fathered or adopted a
significant number of children.) Two years
later, after Bishop Cão was forced from the
island and I prepared to depart Tomé for Brazil,
Ariella graciously gave me the gold chain. It
remains the dearest gift I have ever received.

The sister stares at the remaining blank pages. If there is
something else to write, she does not know. She goes to the balcony
and sees that the work in the courtyard is finished, the place
abandoned except for a guard in the shadows by the outside gate. A
fragrant breeze touches her skin, one otherwise refreshing, though
tonight it feels as cold as the January winds of Lisbon. There is a
single torch atop the gallows illuminating the space and casting
restless and bizarre shadows.

The Vespers bell rings. Sister Doçura crosses herself and
kneels to pray. She cuts the prayer short and stands up, again making
the sign of the cross. "God well knows my devotion," she says aloud.
"Prayers may come later. Now I must do something to save Cantora."
Earlier in the week she'd prepared a note for Father Julian, still not
knowing if he was alive or dead. She gave it to the child acolyte,
Agato—a young boy who admired the girl—when he brought her
food that evening. Now, days later, the hour of Vespers is at hand,
and still no one comes to see her.

At the little girl's bedside, next to her own, she considers the
child's meager belongings, a bracelet and a necklace, both made of
twisted animal sinews and strung with a single ivory clam shell ribbed
with clay-red stripes. There is a shabby stick doll with arms of
bundled grass, and a woven headdress dyed orange with a circle of
blue feathers, the same headdress worn by the child on the day of

their first meeting. Sister Doçura settles the child's necklace over her head and around her neck, tucking it next to where her gold chain had been. She thinks of Cantora imprisoned in a cell somewhere beneath the abbey, a cell dark as night itself. She puts a hand to her breast. In the year since she has known the child, the little girl has captured her heart.

Doçura turns to a blank page in her journal and, with her left hand pressing against her forehead, pens another note. Next she retrieves the dagger kept by her bed, placing it over the gold necklace on the table. She paces for a moment, then returns to her desk and uses the dagger point to pry open a link, effectively cutting the strand in two. The nun tears the note from the journal and folds half the necklace inside it. The other half she drops into a handkerchief which she pushes into the tight sleeve of her habit.

If Agato would only come. He is her last hope.

Ever since her abduction in Lisbon eight years before, hopes—those outcomes always illusive yet so wished for—remain more fragile than the slender veils of mist at morning's first light. Now any outcome other than death for her and Cantora seem completely out of reach. Regardless, she has to try.

***

It all began with a rumor: an Indian girl who sang with the voice of an angel. A tiny girl, perhaps only nine years old. No one believed it at first, but the rumor persisted. Finally one day a runner arrived bringing news. Fr. Julian from a Caeté Indian village to the north would travel to the settlement next week with the child and her family. Bishop Damião immediately sent the runner back with instructions that when they were a few hours travel from the abbey, they should camp and await his emissary. Damião, a priest who struggled furiously against the daily chaos that surrounded him, summoned Sister Doçura to his office.

Ushered inside, she found the bishop sitting behind his desk. As usual his tiny dog looked up from the man's lap and over the desktop. The bishop immediately stood, placed the dog on his desk, walked around and offered her a chair. He returned to his chair, retrieved his pet—settling the animal in his lap—and explained the situation. "You see, Sister Mãe, there is no telling what heathen apparition these Indians may send us. I must have someone see first and prepare them, and perhaps prepare us for this visit." The bishop tried to like the sister; he did admire her intelligence and direct manner, and he often called her Mãe to make her feel more comfortable in his presence. If the truth be known, he felt intimidated by Sister Doçura; but what the bishop found even more troublesome was her Jewish birth and refusal to go to confession.

Bishop Damião continued. "Since Fr. Julian endorses them, I must assume they are members of his church, Christian converts." He made a face. "Hopefully they are no longer cannibals."

The nun found it curious that the bishop chose the words "Christian converts," thus avoiding the more common Novos Christãos, the term reserved for converted Jews and Moors—words now part of the Inquisition's list of epithets so often hurled against those souls persecuted and tortured. After a moment's hesitation, she asked, "Am I to believe these rumors, that this child can sing the Latin Mass? If so, that is truly remarkable."

"Indeed that is what we hear. According to Julian's letter, this little girl may be a miracle, The Almighty's Grace among us." He ran a hand over the large silver cross that lay on his desktop. "Supposedly she is no ordinary singer. Could it be that this is the first miracle of our New World? Surely I have heard of no other." He stood and paced the room, the dog following at his heels. He gestured to the balcony and the forest beyond. "Could God in His wisdom produce such a blessing from this primal wilderness, this diocese in nowhere? Everyone knows the Latin Mass is reserved just for priests and perhaps acolytes, but certainly never a girl." He shrugged. "Julian says this child sings to him with a voice from Heaven. So he lets her sing at Mass."

The sister admired the native people, and she felt a swell of pride. A chill quickly replaced it. She wondered at the source of this sudden dread. "Perhaps it is God's wisdom to send us a girl," she said.

"It might seem so." The bishop sighed. "And an Indian girl at that." He returned to his chair and spoke in somber tones. "You see sister, the unsettled nature of this forlorn place, the jungle, these naked devils, how can this be God's creation? How am I to bring order here? Back home in Aveiro I was an assistant inquisitor. I led a simple life, cleansing of the faith. Purification of the flock, if you will." He clenched his fists. "What burdens us here is unimaginable! We indeed *need* a miracle."

Sister Doçura rose to her feet and began to speak. Damião interrupted her. "I know, I know sister, I have introduced an uncomfortable subject." He gave her a cold smile, knowing how distasteful she found the topic of inquisition. He wondered why he'd mentioned his Aveiro activities to her.

Bishop Damião stood with the intent of escorting the sister to the door, but she took a step back and gave him an angry look. "With all respect, sir, I have seen enough inquisition on São Tomé, and heard enough of its horrors in Portugal and Spain. My parents fled inquisition and now live in the Ottoman. As they are in a new land, so are we. God has given the Church and each of us the opportunity to do good work here, *His* work." Sister Doçura walked to the entrance and paused. "And I intend to do that good work."

Once she was gone, the bishop went to the balcony and watched her cross the courtyard and enter the hall below her residence. He imagined her walking angrily up the stairs. He considered this argumentative female a problem, but since she was so well-connected to the Tomé Colony—the source of his most needed supplies—he resolved to tolerate her presence. At best, she remained a difficult asset.

***

As the time of the visit approached, everyone at the abbey and the surrounding settlement grew excited. Again Sister Doçura— summoned with urgency—found herself in the bishop's office. A tall priest stood next to him, a thin man with deep-set blue eyes that gave his unshaven face a haunted look. His clothes were dirty, and he appeared exhausted. "Sister Mãe," Bishop Damião said, "you know Fr. Julian, the one who will deliver this fabled cantora to our humble abbey."

The sister gave a slight curtsey. "Fr. Julian, yes. It is good to see you again." She turned to the bishop. "Did you say 'cantora'?"

Julian, who had been holding the bishop's dog, placed him on the floor and crossed himself. "You must first hear her sing, dear sister. Then it will be *The* Cantora."

The bishop broke in, nodding to the priest. "I have instructed this deliverer of miracles to take his rest for today. Tomorrow, Sister Doçura, you will accompany him to their camp and bring the treasured singer here."

"Where are they? How far?"

Fr. Julian smiled. "Not far, Sister, two hours north by mule, camped by the Rio Jacu."

The nun gulped. "I have never before ridden, neither horse nor mule."

Bishop Damião gave a short laugh, then stood and walked to the door. He opened it for Sister Doçura. "I will send someone over this afternoon with a gentle animal for you to learn. It seems this child singer provides us all with new experiences."

Chapter 2

As promised, a soldier from the garrison arrived with two mules in tow. He placed a small stool on the cobblestones and assisted Doçura into the sidesaddle on the smaller animal. She found the riding uncomfortable but tolerable as the soldier first led her around the courtyard before mounting his mule to demonstrate the fine art of controlling the animal.

Next morning, as the sun first colored the eastern sky, she went to the chapel where Bishop Damião and Fr. Julian conducted the Lauds sunrise devotion. The bishop's participation in this service was unusual. "...but today is special," he declared in his brief sermon. Afterwards he asked Julian and Doçura to join him for a breakfast in his private quarters. Two acolytes stood by as the three of them settled around the bishop's small dining table. The acolytes served a fine breakfast of boiled hen's eggs, maize biscuits and honey, and steaming yerba buena.

"Am I expecting too much from this child?" the bishop asked.

Fr. Julian, looking much improved from the day before— clean shaven and wearing a newly-laundered robe—answered, "We shall see, Excellency. At the very least she will be an extraordinary asset to the Mass."

After further speculations and casual talk, and the breakfast concluded, the bishop stood and gestured outside. "Well," he said, "you two must start your journey. I am eager to experience this momentous day for our little diocese in this backwater of Christendom."

They set off, led by an Indian guide on foot and trailed by two armed soldiers from the garrison. The forest at the border of the settlement had always loomed mysteriously to Doçura, but only because she had not much considered it. Once inside she began to savor the sights around her.

Fr. Julian commented on her composure. "I had thought, dear sister, that you would regard the jungle with trepidation."

"Oh, I'm quite familiar with jungles from my time on Tomé Island. The many creatures, the thousand greens, the sights and smells, they fascinate me. Perhaps The Garden was something like this." She pulled herself upright, trying to ease her discomfort. "I cannot say the same for riding this poor animal. His gait is uneven, and the saddle was certainly not made for a woman wearing a nun's habit." And then, with a wave of her hand and a quick smile, "But in service to Our Savior, I will happily survive."

To their astonishment, a large cloud of delicate butterflies, small and of the palest green, descended from the trees and hovered everywhere, alighting on the mules and around everyone's eyes. "They steal salt from the animals' skin and from the eyes," Fr. Julian explained, brushing several from his face. "The Indians call them *hapoo jeyurã*, tear drinkers." As if the priest had commanded their leave, the myriad *jeyurã* took flight, rising and falling around them with wind-like sighs. Doçura found the swirl of butterflies remindful of the early spring snowfalls in Lisbon, and she grew quiet and thoughtful. But then, as if the forest wished to further its welcome, they entered a small clearing where stood an immense fig tree from which a steady rain of vermillion flower petals cast loose by a flock of noisy birds feeding in the highest branches, drifted to the jungle floor.

Having noticed Doçura's long silence, Julian said, "You appear thoughtful."

"I am," the sister replied. "Just thinking of home." In an effort to not be questioned further she asked, "Do you miss Portugal, Fr. Julian?"

"Yes," he answered. "What I wouldn't give to see my home again."

"Where was that?"

"Way to the south. Portimão." He paused for a moment. "Would you believe that my father was a priest?"

She gave him a quizzical look. "I've heard of such things. Did you live with him?"

"Oh no. He was the vicar for the southern diocese. But he

took very good care of my mother and me. Everyone in town knew he was my father, and no one seemed to care." He raised a hand to his ear. "Hear that? We're getting close."

Within minutes they arrived at the Caeté camp on the south bank of the Rio Jacu. Doçura found herself surprised by the number of people, adults and children, about a dozen in all.

The Indians began an excited chatter as Fr. Julian helped the sister dismount. "They've never seen a nun before," he explained. The priest introduced the adults, the singer's father and mother, two aunts and an uncle. One of the aunts—the only native fully clothed—stood apart from the others with her arms crossed and stared unblinkingly at Doçura. The woman wore a twisted red cloth encircling her head, and a vest decorated with vertical strings of black beads. With her heavily tattooed face and forearms, she presented an imposing figure.

Fr. Julian paid particular attention to her. "This is Janaína," he said. "She is the tribe's medicine woman, the *turguy kuñã*."

The nun acknowledged her with a quick smile, but the woman remained impassive. "Is she angry?" Doçura asked.

The priest shrugged. "Perhaps, but it's complicated. I'll explain later."

Doçura eyed the children. "So who is the little girl with the miraculous voice?" she said, then felt silly, knowing none of them understood her.

To the nun's amazement, a beautiful youngster stepped forward. In distinct Portuguese she said, "I am the girl who sings in church." The child wore an orange headdress with a ring of blue feathers, but was otherwise naked. She had a round face, lovely olive skin, and dark eyes that danced as she spoke.

In reflex, the sister crossed herself. "Oh my," she said, "How unexpected!"

"She is quite remarkable," the priest offered. "Yema would have introduced us all if I had not. The Indians encourage their children to speak freely to anyone."

"Yema, that's her name?"

"Yemanjá, actually," the priest answered. "Though everyone calls her Yema." The little girl smiled and curtseyed.

"Yemanjá?" the nun repeated. "I've heard that before."

"No doubt you have. It's one of their pagan gods, the Goddess of the Sea. The natives invoke her name all the time. Some carry little carved statues of her."

Yema spoke up. "Yemanjá is also the..." She searched a moment for the words. "—the guardian of children."

In that instant, Doçura had known exactly what the girl intended to say. Her throat grew tight and she stifled a gasp. Here was the same fear she'd felt in Bishop Damião's office when they first talked about the child. It took her a few seconds to regain speech, though she could not voice her feelings. Instead she said to Fr. Julian, "But the quality of her Portuguese?"

"Ah yes," he answered. "Yema's gift goes far beyond song. She seems to remember everything, and her propensity for language now extends to rote Latin. Besides the singing parts, she has learned the full liturgy of the Mass just by listening."

"Should it bother us that this rite is limited to priests and acolytes? Certainly not a female."

Julian shook his head. "She does not recite the Mass, but only sings a brief portion, the *Confiteor Deo*. With Bishop Damião's permission, perhaps she can sing more. I pray he will understand, as I know you will understand when you hear Yema sing."

By now the Indians had laid out woven mats in the short grass along the riverbank and set out a meal of yam bread, fruit, and cured fish. They began a singsong chant. Doçura listened closely as Yema chimed in. What she heard was simply a little girl's voice, nothing extraordinary. She decided not to comment, but thought, *What is happening here?* and gave the priest a quizzical look.

Misunderstanding, he responded, "This food is in our honor." Doçura shrugged and settled herself between two of the children, a boy on her left and Yema on her right. The medicine woman, Janaína, spoke to the boy and he immediately moved, making room for her. She next spoke to Yema.

The little girl listened and said, "Janaína wants to know if you are a medicine woman?"

"I am not," Doçura answered. "Simply a woman of the Church. We are called nuns."

When the girl explained, the woman gave them both a troubled look and spoke in hard, sharp sentences. "Janaína is upset because you are not *turguy kuñã*," Yema said. "She wants someone to give us a remedy for the coughing sickness."

"I wish I could," the nun answered.

"The Indians blame us for bringing the sickness," Fr. Julian said. "I suppose they are right." He swept his hand around. "None of these people appear ill, but several at the village have died, and many more are stricken. That's why Janaína's husband is not here. He is gravely ill."

The nun turned to the little girl. "Tell her I wish we had a remedy. I truly wish we did. And I am sorry for her husband."

The conversation moved to lighter subjects. The sister asked Fr. Julian, "What are we to do about all this nakedness? You know the bishop dislikes—"

"Indeed he wants his savages clothed," he answered. "And we'll find clothes for them at the settlement before we meet with him tomorrow."

Yema gave the priest a puzzled look. "Fr. Julian, does this bishop think we Caeté are savages?"

"A figure of our speech, little cantora, and you are not savages."

Doçura listened with amazement. She passed her fingers across the child's feathered headdress. "You don't miss a thing, little one, do you?"

***

With the meal concluded, they set out for the abbey. Once more mounted on their mules, Doçura said to Julian, "May we ride ahead? I have many questions." The priest nodded and they moved off. Once out of earshot, she asked, "Are these people cannibals or not? Is their civility just for show? They appear as savage as any people I've ever seen. Certainly more so than the natives around the settlement. All this red paint, tattoos and feathers."

"You certainly get to the heart of the matter, dear sister," Fr. Julian said. "Bishop Damião assured me you would."

"It is my nature to be direct. And that child. She has the same tattoos around her eyes as the witch woman. That's what she is, right?"

"I said it's complicated, and it is. First of all, they were quite recently cannibals. They ate the bodies of enemies captured in wars with other tribes. By eating them, the Caeté believe they acquire the spirit of the enemy, and thus defeat them."

"Disgusting!" she said, but could not help remembering her

conversation with the ship's captain. *In a similar manner we acquire the spirit of Christ,* she reasoned, *the Sacrament of His Person.*

"True," Julian said, bringing her back to the present, "but they also have some rituals I've only heard about, some so awful I cannot even tell you. I hope I never live to see them. For now they have given up the practice of cannibalism because I forbade it. It may be the intervention of our Savior, or it may be the sickness. So many men have died, none have the energy to wage war. I'm sure distant tribes without a priest still war and eat their captives."

"And the woman, Janaína?" Doçura asked.

"Besides being the child's aunt, the name *tuguy kuñã* means blood woman. She oversaw the care, feeding, and eventual killing and eating of the captives." He reacted to the sister's startled look and nodded. "Yes I said 'care.' You really don't want to know the details. So our little girl is the apprentice to the witch woman as you call her. She is a *tuguy kuñã* in training. That's why she has the face markings at the corners of her eyes. Makes her look like a cat, doesn't it?"

The two of them looked back to see the natives following in the trail a distance behind. "And as you've seen," he went on, "Yema's talents are considerable. She and her aunt are the only females allowed to go along when the tribe trades with others who do not speak their dialect. Our cantora has the skill to listen to a language and quickly translate it. She has little trouble with the native languages since most are similar. They regard her as a treasure in the village."

"How long did it take her to learn Portuguese?"

"Oh, quite a while," Fr. Julian answered. "At least a year. She was very insistent, following me around, yammering constantly. But she can also be quite charming, so I put up with it. Even before she knew much Portuguese, maybe after a dozen or so church services, she began to recite Latin and sing some of the Mass. I was astounded."

"Her speech seems almost cultivated."

"It is, dear sister, at her insistence. You will have plenty of time to find out how insistent she can be."

"What do you mean?" Doçura asked.

"I should not have said that," the priest answered, appearing shocked by his own words. He crossed himself. "Oh my goodness." They rode in a tense silence, broken only by loud calls of birds in the treetops and the chatter of Indians following in the trail. Finally he said, "Bishop Damião believes that if Cantora lives up to expectations, the Church will adopt her and you will be her guardian."

Doçura felt a sudden chill and pulled her mule to a stop. "That is not right. What about her family?"

"I don't know." The priest shrugged. "We shall see. It will likely be the end of my mission with these people."

"Adopt? Don't you mean steal? Do you know the Hebrew word *khateefat*, Fr. Julian? Well I do! It means stealing children. This is a dangerous thing we do. Besides, the girl sounded quite ordinary when she sang back at the camp."

"I should have not have said what I did, Sister Doçura. But regarding her singing just now, that was because she sang with the others. By herself, it's quite another matter."

The nun turned the mule and rode back to the Indians who had nearly caught up and trudged just a few yards behind. She wanted to be alone with her thoughts, but Yema ran up, grabbing at a leather strap that hung from the saddle. She began asking questions. The nun pulled the strap away from her. "Little one, don't. I'm afraid the animal will step on you. Have someone lift you up here and you can ride with me." Someone did, and in the next moment the child was riding on the sidesaddle in front of Sister Doçura, one hand resting on the saddle's rim, the other on the nun's arm which encircled her waist. Yema's hair smelled of cinnamon, and the touch of her hand and the feel of the child's gentle weight as she leaned back against the nun made Doçura's heart melt with affection.

As they neared the settlement with Yema slumped forward, fast asleep, Doçura's dread grew. For the past half-hour she had entertained the idea of warning the Indians, telling them to go back to their village. What would she do then? Gather her few belongings and return with them? An exile with a native tribe in the jungle? Excommunicated? The thought was nearly as terrifying as what lay ahead. But it struck her that it might all work out once the bishop heard Yema sing. Her voice would sound like any other child's. He would simply shrug, chastise Fr. Julian, and send them all home. Then she could go back to her usual churchly duties, ministering to the native women and children of the settlement. This is what she always wanted to do, work with women and children and little babies. Help them deal with the rigors of the dyewood trade. Help them with salvation, salvation here on earth, and salvation from the pain of disease and injury. And for those enslaved, salvation from their lives of misery. Her brother's lifelong mission had been a fight against slavery, and she wished to do the same.

***

The next day, Saturday, began with violent thunderstorms that delayed their meeting with Bishop Damião. Fr. Julian remained quartered in the abbey, while the newly arrived Indians took shelter with their brethren in the settlement's thatched huts called *ógas*.

When the group finally assembled in the afternoon, they found the bishop in an unsettled mood, irritated at the weather's effect on his schedule. The natives were also unsettled, having to wear clothes, many of them for the first time in their lives. Bishop Damião was surprised by the number of people—too many for his office—and allowed only Yema and her brother, her parents, Fr. Julian, and Doçura into his inner sanctum. He gestured for everyone to take a seat, then walked around the room, greeting each person as Julian made the introductions. To the great amusement of the children, his dog watched the goings-on from his perch atop the bishop's desk. After the introductions, the bishop knelt in front of Yema and extended his hand. "So you are the little cantora?" he inquired.

"Yes," answered Yema, placing her small hand in his. "I am the girl who sings in church."

"My-oh-my, child, your Portuguese is indeed excellent. Fr. Julian has so informed me."

"Bishop Damião," Julian asked, "would you like to hear Yema sing? I can recite a brief liturgy to the *Confiteor Deo,* and then provide the cadence for her to sing the *Confiteor.*"

Perfect, thought Sister Doçura. *She will sing, the bishop will be disappointed and he will send them home. That will be the end of it.*

To her distress, this did not happen. The bishop waved his hand. "That won't be necessary," he said, looking at Yema. "I am sure your voice is most special. We shall hear your charmed singing in church tomorrow morning."

Julian protested. "But Your Grace, her voice is also most unusual for a child. It would—"

Bishop Damião stood. "Fr. Julian, my day is much too crowded." He walked to his office door and opened it. "There will be

many opportunities to hear her sing. Tomorrow, Julian, tomorrow."
As the group filed out, he motioned to Doçura. "Will you stay a
moment please?" He closed the door, then turned and said, "Dear
Mãe, have you come to know this child?"

"A little, sir. Just on the trip from the Jacu encampment. Her
intelligence seems remarkable."

"So it would seem. Have you heard her sing?"

"Yes, with the other natives. She sounded like any other child.
Nothing unusual. I wish we had listened today. Tomorrow may be
disappointing."

"I see." The bishop wrung his hands and gave a series of
nods, for a moment unable to find the words. Finally he said, "Well,
would you spend some time with the girl this afternoon? Find her
something suitable to wear, not those rags she had on today. Take her
to that woman in the settlement."

"Yes," she said, "Fr. Julian and I intended to do so this
morning, but the storm kept us inside. I'll see to it this afternoon."

"And one more thing," Bishop Damião said, "if these people
want to be all painted up for Mass tomorrow, that's fine. But can
Yema please have a clean face?"

Doçura assured the bishop she would do her best, then left the
office. *It's starting,* she thought. *I will be a party to this kidnapping.*
When the nun caught up with the Indians, she addressed the child's
mother while Yema translated. "The bishop would like your daughter
to wear something special for tomorrow's Mass. There is a woman
here, she and her daughters make clothes." The Indians dutifully
followed Doçura through the settlement, the children playing, running
ahead, the nun silent and lost in her thoughts.

Bishop Damião stepped onto his balcony and watched the
Caeté group as it worked its way through the confusion of brown
huts. After a moment he returned to his desk and picked up the large
silver cross. He went to the altar in one corner of his room, knelt, and
held the cross aloft. He gazed at the crucifix on the wall behind the
altar. "Oh Mighty Lord Jesus, Light of the World, Savior of Mankind,
bless us tomorrow with Your Grace. Grant that this Indian child shall
be your first miracle of The New World. I plead this as Your most
faithful servant at the very frontier of God's realm."

Chapter 3

The sun rose from the Atlantic into a beautiful sky strewn with small clouds extending to the horizon, and a soft breeze from the ocean promised a temperate morning. Doçura woke at first light and went to the abbey's kitchen where she drank a hurried cup of tea, then walked to the nearby chapel for the Lauds devotion. An acolyte conducted the service for the few souls in attendance, a soldier from the garrison, a half-dozen sailors, and a young Indian woman who Doçura knew to be a prostitute.

After the devotion, she walked to the church and found it already surrounded by a talkative crowd eager to hear the little cantora. It appeared that a good number of the Indians had spent the night sleeping on the ground around the building. Soldiers were stationed at each entrance to keep the crowd from overrunning the place. It was a simple structure, fifty feet long by thirty wide, and covered with a peaked, thatched roof that overhung the sides of the building to less than three feet above the ground. This design, which the settlers copied from the native huts, afforded dry shelter even during the heaviest rainstorms. The building's interior had four rows of finished wood benches directly in front of the altar for Europeans, and a series of log benches to the rear for the natives.

Doçura, concerned about the day's events, had not slept well. Her worries continued through Lauds and her brief visit to the church, and now stayed with her as she entered the small dining area next to the abbey's kitchen, a space reserved for church workers. There were several people there, all of whom she knew, including the settlement priest, Father Paulo—unusually drunk for a Sunday morning—and his assistant. Sitting at another table were two young Indian women, sisters in training, who met frequently with Doçura in preparation for their voyage to Portugal and formal schooling at the Convent Coimbra. The last thing the nun wanted was to be around people this morning. Nevertheless, she greeted each person, then seated herself with the two women.

"Are you excited to hear this fabled child sing?" one of them asked. But before Doçura could answer, Fr. Paulo, having overheard the question, rushed from the room followed by his assistant. The young woman frowned and said, "I think he's upset that he is not conducting Mass today. It will be Fr. Julian? Is that right?"

Doçura nodded. "That's only because the child knows him. Her name is Yema. And hopefully for Fr. Paulo's sake, I think it will be Julian just for today." A slave boy brought in the usual breakfast, thick maze gruel and yerba buena tea, setting the plates in front of the women. They said a brief grace, then poured goat's milk on the cereal and sweetened it with black syrup. In an effort to avoid the subject of Cantora, she tapped the syrup pitcher with her spoon. "Do you know where this came from?" she asked. "What it is?"

The two novitiates looked at each other. The young woman named Sincera said, "I know it comes from Tomé Island, but I have no idea what it is. It's one of my favorites." In fact, black syrup was a favorite with all the natives, and often used as a trading currency. While the Indian population knew sweet foods—flower nectar, ripe fruit, and honey in moderate abundance—the thick, black syrup from across the sea was particularly suited to their taste. It had the subtle flavor of roasted figs, and the myriad of ants suspended in the liquid gave it a unique sharpness. Honey on the other hand was sweeter, though the wax and broken bodies of bees gave the local honey a somewhat bitter flavor. Honey from Portugal and even that from São Tomé was filtered through gauze and did not have the bitter undertones. But gauze was in short supply in the settlement, and used primarily for insect netting around sleeping areas.

Doçura held up the heavy pitcher. "This is why our Church can afford to send you to Portugal— sugar. Indeed the syrup does come from Tomé, and it's produced from the sugar mills. It drains into basins beneath the drying bins and slaves collect it. Most likely that's why our priest was so drunk this morning. It makes a very strong beer." Then in a hushed voice she said, "Never doubt for a minute, ladies, our Church is devoted to commerce almost as much as to our Beloved Savior." Before the subject of the child singer could be raised again, the nun stood and excused herself. "I must return to my quarters and prepare for Mass." She quickly retreated from the room, leaving her companions exchanging puzzled looks.

***

Although no one needed a reminder that day, a half hour before nine, the bell atop the abbey rang, announcing Mass and summoning the faithful. The bell, just above Doçura's room, startled her. She had been drifting in thought and prayer, asking for guidance and understanding for the events that lay ahead. The nun waited a few minutes, then left for the church. She'd found no one in the courtyard and scarcely anyone along the way. Everybody was already there, the church nearly filled. From the size of the mob, it appeared to be the entire settlement, and most of the congregation would have to listen from the outside. A soldier motioned to Doçura from a side entrance, escorting the sister to her usual seat on the front-row bench. She was pleased to see Yema and her companions sitting there, including Janaína who appeared as stern as ever.

The child, her eyes dancing, patted the bench and said, "Please sit here." Doçura settled herself next to the little girl, smiling at how pretty she looked in the blue shift dress they had found for her the previous day. "See," Yema said, plucking at the nun's habit, "we are almost the same color."

Once settled, Doçura turned to greet the people who sat behind her, and was met with a line of sullen faces. These were privileged citizens of the settlement, accustomed to sitting in the front row. Merchants, slave traders, dyewood brokers, and others irritated not only by the change of seating but by the presence of the Indians in front of them.

The congregation turned silent, standing as Bishop Damião— gently swinging the smoldering incense thurible—took his place in front of the altar table. He faced east, his back to the congregation. Next Fr. Julian joined him and stood with his hands clasped in prayer, then turned briefly and smiled at Yema, who nodded solemnly. Fr. Paulo's assistant took the third position next to Julian, providing the required Trinity. Doçura speculated that Fr. Paulo was likely too drunk to attend, much less take the third position. Two Indian altar boys came forward, one taking the thurible from the bishop, the other handing him the veiled chalice. Julian took the sanctuary bell from the table and rang it three times, accepted the chalice from the bishop, and placed it next to the Missal. The bishop retired to his chair to the left of the altar table.

Fr. Julian crossed himself, and gazed at the crucifix above the table. He recited, *"In nomine Patris, et Filii, et Spiritus Sancti... ."*

And thus began the Mass.

Paulo's assistant and Fr. Julian worked their way through the *Ordo* and Psalm 42. Julian delivered the priest's introduction, and concluded with *"Dominum Deum nostrum."* Next, the assistant chanted the brief *Misereatur Tui Omnipotens,* bringing the Mass to the *Confiteor.* He stepped back and nodded to Yema who by this time was already standing. Doçura gave her hand a squeeze before the little girl ascended the pulpit and took her place next to Fr. Julian. Without prompting, she faced the crucifix and made the sign of the cross. Then, her features radiant, Yema turned to the congregation, and began to sing.

♫ *"Confiteor Deo omnipotenti*
beatae Mariae semper virgini
beato Michaeli archangelo ... "

Churchgoers and clergy alike gasped in unison at the sound of her voice— Suddenly gasped as if struggling for air. Many slid from their seats and knelt or prostrated themselves. Outside listeners fell to their knees, for there was no room to lay flat. Likewise Bishop Damião slid forward from his chair and prostrated himself on the altar, his hands clasped prayerfully in front of him. The three figures on the altar remained standing. Doçura listened in spellbound amazement. The Indians around her displayed satisfied grins, for they had heard their magic Yema sing many times before.

Her voice filled the church, and some felt it filled the world. They heard a powerful grown woman's voice, not that of a child's. A vital singing, the honeyed perfume of song, an ecstasy upon the ear.

And at the end, ♫ *"... orare pro me ad Dominum Deum nostrum,"* Yema left the pulpit and took her seat next the Doçura. Julian waited a few moments while people collected themselves, then continued. The bishop returned to his chair, visibly shaken and with tears in his eyes, tears shared by many in the congregation.

For the worshipers now, the rest of the Mass seemed to take forever, the child's singing having changed everything. Finally Fr. Julian chanted the last words, *"... Patre, plenum gratiae et veritatis,"* and the assistant responded, *"Deo gratias."* A quiet settled over the congregation until Julian, looked directly at little Yema, repeated the last phrase in Portuguese, "Thanks be to God," and then, *"Me'eng kũ Túva veve,"* the language of the Caeté. The congregates repeated the phrase, the two languages mixing in strange dissonance.

At that moment the cold fear again gripped Sister Mãe da Doçura. Her own kidnapping replaying itself in this new land.

***

Immediately after Mass, the Sunday festival began. The bishop, in his efforts to entice the multitudes to the ranks of the faithful, scheduled frequent festivals of food, entertainment, and celebration. All morning the delicious odor of roasting meat, both goat and pig, had drifted across the settlement. The food, prepared in the garrison courtyard, now approached the church via a procession of carts drawn by free Africans and Indians and supervised by mounted soldiers in parade regalia.

Soon everyone began to feel the heat of the day. The soldiers discarded much of their suffocating uniforms, and the natives their Sunday clothing. Doçura congratulated Yema, calling her "The Cantora" for the first time, then used the heat as an excuse to retire to her quarters. Once inside, she removed her outer garments and ate some fruit brought from the celebration.

That afternoon a messenger knocked on Doçura's door and passed her a note. She was summoned to meet with the bishop and Julian an hour before Vespers. When the time arrived, she met them in the courtyard, the bishop taking the opportunity to walk his little dog.

Damião began the conversation. "At Vespers tonight I will say a special prayer of thanks for this child singer. She is indeed the miracle I've hoped and prayed for. Fr. Julian informs me that she is anxious to return to her village, that the medicine woman is encouraging this quick departure using the excuse of her husband's illness. I am sure you both now realize this child can be instrumental in converting the natives." Then he added, "Likely more successful than our past efforts." They paused for a moment to watch the dog's antics as it chased grasshoppers strayed onto the cobblestones from outside the courtyard.

When Julian picked up the conversation, the sister had the feeling that he and the bishop had rehearsed all this. "I invited the family to Vespers this evening. Also we must keep Cantora engaged and tempted. So with the bishop's permission, I promised she could sing the *Glória* this evening. She already knows it."

Doçura gulped, trying to understand her feelings. She felt delight at the prospect of hearing the girl's miraculous voice again; and intensely fearful that her involvement to lure this child into the churchly fold was about to be thrust upon her. Julian had said something important, and she'd missed it. "I'm sorry," she said to Fr. Julian, "please repeat that. The thought of hearing her sing the *Glória* overwhelmed me for a moment."

"What I said, Sister, is that I also promised she could sing more of the Mass next Sunday, and that you would be her instructor. "

Doçura nodded gravely as Bishop Damião picked up where Julian left off. "Dear Mãe, I have asked Fr. Paulo to assist you." With a nod to Julian, he continued. "Fr. Julian tells me the child is fond of you. So I want you to sit with her at Vespers, and in the future spend as much time with the girl as you can. I believe she will stay with us as long as we provide new things for her to learn. You can meet with her daily at the chapel to school her in the chants and hymns of the Mass."

Doçura turned and looked at them. "What about her wish to return to the village?"

Bishop Damião answered. "We want you to persuade her to stay. Let that tattooed woman go home without her. We will give the child's immediate family whatever they want." The nun tried to say something, but the bishop continued. "Sister Mãe, this child is an asset beyond our wildest dreams. I have instructed the garrison captain to provide anything they want, a tent, food from the garrison kitchen, and—."

The bishop's dog began growling, then furiously barking as it ran to the courtyard entrance where a large procession of Indians along with a few Portuguese and Africans streamed inside. From what they could see, it appeared there were more than fifty people. At the head of the procession walked an Indian leading a goat with a rope around its neck. The bishop addressed Fr. Julian. "See to that, please. And see if you can catch my dog." Doçura took the opportunity to excuse herself.

A smiling Fr. Julian returned with the squirming dog and set him by the bishop's feet. "They're all here for Vespers," he said. "And the goat's a gift to the Church." He looked around. "Where is Sister Doçura?"

The bishop inclined his head towards her quarters. "Just as you warned, I'm afraid Sister Mãe does not approve of our scheme. But right now, dear Julian, there are far too many people for our small chapel. Pass the word. We will celebrate Vespers in the church. Think of it, Julian, our largest Vespers ever."

***

Sitting at her desk that evening, a large candle illuminating her journal, Sister Doçura recorded the day's events. As the nun contemplated the meeting in the courtyard, she paused for a moment, then started a fresh page.

> Late afternoon brought my most dreaded fear. Bishop Damião charged me with schooling Cantora. He aims to coerce her to stay in the settlement, not to return to her village. Because of the child, the crowds were so large we moved Vespers to the church. Her singing the *Glória* was a supreme treat, but I could not shake my fear. Perhaps she is indeed a miracle. I don't understand how a small child can sing so beautifully. If I am to be her teacher, what will I do when she pleads with me to return home?

Doçura prepared for bed. She removed her clothes and washed herself using the water basin and pitcher in the corner of the room, then rubbed her face and body with a fragrant poultice of flowers given to her by Marét, Yema's mother. Next she donned her nightgown and brushed her hair, sighing as she remembered how long and beautiful it was years ago in Lisbon. The sister had not said a Rosary for her evening prayers in quite some time. But this evening, lying in her dark bed, the gauze net moving softly around her, she said the Rosary twice before falling into a troubled sleep, the *Glória* echoing in her thoughts.

Chapter 4

On Monday morning, Yema's father and most of the visitors prepared to leave for the village. Only the girl, her six-year-old brother, and the mother would stay. Before leaving, the family and Janaína conferred for a half-hour by themselves in the courtyard. Then the children and mother, accompanied by Doçura, followed the Caeté to the edge of the settlement where they said their good-byes. The nun found herself painfully missing her own family as she watched the affection the tribe members showed one another as they bade farewell. Later that day she enrolled Yema and her brother in the settlement school.

The next afternoon, the nun and Fr. Paulo began Yema's religious instructions in the abbey's chapel. At first only the mother and brother attended, sitting quietly in the back with Doçura's young Indian novitiates. Occasionally the two novitiates stood in when needed for the Mass ceremony. After a few days, the attendance grew to two dozen, including the bishop who sat by himself and watched the goings-on.

Doçura hoped Yema's daily involvement and her obvious interest in learning would entice her to stay in the settlement. Fr. Paulo tried to arrange work for her mother, as a maid in the garrison, a helper in the abbey's kitchen, or tending the settlement's large vegetable garden. In every case she turned them down, indicating her lack of interest in staying for more than another week or so, citing her growing fear for the health of her brother, the husband of the blood woman Janaína.

Doçura and Paulo spoke with Fr. Julian who planned his return to the village on the coming Saturday. He responded helpfully by telling Yema's mother that he would send a runner back with news of her brother's health. He also confided to Paulo and Doçura that, "The only reason she remains here are the instructions she and Yema received from Janaína. The blood woman told them that she did not trust foreigners, but also feels we are here to stay, and they must find a way to accommodate to our presence." When Paulo and Doçura appeared taken aback by this, he said, "Even though these natives are a simple folk, they're not stupid. Without cunning, the Caeté could never have survived in this jungle."

***

To the delight of the clergy, services on Sunday were again overrun with worshipers. This day Yema's singing sounded ever more glorious. In addition to the *Confiteor Deo*, her recital of the *Agnus Dei* prior to communion again brought tears to the eyes of many of the faithful. Her exquisite voice seemed to soar to the heavens. Most stirring was the manner in which she raised her lovely face and hands when she began the *Domine Jesu Christe*.

Bishop Damião began making plans for a new church, and determined to provide the Vatican with the first holy revelation of the New World, contemplated a letter to the Holy See requesting the *Consilium de Virtutibus*, the Council of Miracles. He was greatly pleased with the joyous nature of the festival that afternoon, but also concerned about the improvised shrines that began to appear around the church and abbey. He expressed his worries to Fr. Paulo and Doçura. "I understand the flowers and fruit and other trifles. I'll even tolerate the decorated stones, but the little wooden statues are graven images. Pagan blasphemy. How can we tolerate these?" He picked up one from the several left at the church entrance and handed it to Fr. Paulo.

"It's their tribute to little Yema," Paulo said. "I see the Africans making them too. It is a good thing if we can attract more Africans to our church. Everyone speaks of Cantora with great passion sir, and as you've observed, she is a remarkable asset to our mission here." He refrained from telling the bishop the statues also symbolized the native Goddess of the Sea, Yemanjá, but later that day confided his own miracle to Doçura. "This child has indeed inspired me, dear sister. My cravings no longer demand strong drink. I took to drink because of my homesickness for Lisbon. I felt I did not belong here. Now I do."

Each morning Yema awoke excited with the prospects of both school and liturgical training. She felt disappointed that she understood so little of the Latin, but knew it would come in time. This was balanced with her swelling sense of pride and her interest in learning more from the Europeans. The whites had knowledge she thirsted to understand. Each day brought new and intriguing mysteries; they seemed to know so many things. To her delight one day, Fr. Paulo produced a magical instrument called a lute on which he played the notes she was instructed to sing. This was so unlike Fr. Julian's method of singing notes in a lower pitch, and the two of them then striving to make it perfect. Where would she fit this magical lute into her learning— Would Fr. Paulo show her how to play it?

As far as her singing was concerned, she'd always wondered about her voice. The tribe had songs, and the men who sang the chants often gave her a part or two to sing. At first they included her begrudgingly, and only at Aunt Janaína's insistence. When Yema grew older, the men allowed her to sing more. But their chants contained only a few tones, not the soaring notes of the Mass.

All the children, particularly the boys, learned to whistle bird calls for hunting. The girls teased them since they could often do it better, and groups of children would compete to see who could make the best calls. Yema was the champion bird-caller because she sang the calls as well as whistled them, adding subtle vocal variations not possible otherwise.

Yema found the whites' religion puzzling, so unlike her tribe whose beliefs in spirits included both ancestors and persons of the netherworld. Also, these Catholics did not heed the Caeté gods whose presence was everywhere, the sky and sea, the rain, the jaguar, the sun and moon and many stars, even the hordes of ants that sometimes marched through the jungle. She could not be sure if this Jesus person was an ancestor to the Europeans. Certainly he must be since they had so many carvings of him and his symbol, the cross. She preferred carvings of animals, animals like the tapir who provided sinews for bracelets, earrings, and bow strings, food and hides for her tribe, an animal of the night, difficult to hunt and demanding much skill from the hunters. And she treasured the carvings of her namesake, the Sea Goddess Yemanjá.

But the foreigners' religion must be special, she reasoned. It seemed connected to everything they do, from the immense sailing ships to the beautiful lace shawl that Sister Doçura sometimes wore. And of course, there was the music that had added so much to her life, apparently an essential part of their beliefs. The whites had asked the natives to pledge themselves to the Christ person, and a great number had done so for reasons she did not fully understand. Possibly they had accepted the white god out of some kind of fear—fear of all the weapons and ships and mysteries under the Europeans' control.

A few years ago, when she was just a little girl, Fr. Julian baptized many in her tribe and told them they were now part of Christ's family. Aunt Janaína said it was all nonsense, but thought it a good idea to accept their rituals. Yema soon learned that compliance and expressions of faith greatly pleased the whites, particularly the clergy. If that's what it took to continue her musical training and privilege for her family, certainly she could go along with it.

At the beginning of the second week, the Caeté astounded Doçura. Yema's training for the day had just concluded, and her mother and brother came to the front of the chapel. Yema took her brother's hand and prompted him to speak. In halting Portuguese he said, "Sister Mãe and Fr. Paulo, we want to teach you our talk and learn…"

Too shy to continue, Yema finished for him, "and we want to learn Portuguese." The little boy giggled while the mother smiled and nodded.

After this exchange, Doçura hoped this meant that Yema's family would be more willing to stay. But her hopes were short-lived when a runner arrived on Thursday with news that Janaína's husband lay near death. Yema's mother made immediate plans for her and the two children to return to their village. The news sent a chill through everyone involved, though somewhat softened by an accompanying letter from Fr. Julian promising to return Yema to the settlement as soon as he could.

Regardless of Julian's assurance, Bishop Damião summoned Paulo and Doçura to his office. He appeared in great distress. "If they return—" He put his head in his hands. *"When* they return. Well, I was about to send a letter to Pope Julius' secretary, Giovanni de' Medici, requesting they convene the *Consilium de Virtutibus* in our behalf. Now my little girl of miracles has gone back to her savages."

Doçura spoke up. "If we had forced them to stay, sir, there's no telling the outcome. Fr. Paulo and I returned a message to Fr. Julian asking him to encourage Yema's father to accompany his family back here. We promised him work on the docks where he will be well paid."

"Yes. Of course," Damião responded. "You have handled this well. We must all pray for their quick return." He stood and walked to the balcony, staring across the settlement. "And we must pray that church on Sunday is not abandoned because of Cantora's absence."

Indeed Sunday Mass was not well attended. Even to the most faithful, the services seemed bland and uninteresting, and much to the displeasure of the clergy, about a dozen Africans and Indians used the interlude during communion to leave the church. The bishop, who was serving communion at the time, grew so angry that he motioned for Fr. Paulo to take over, returning to his chair at the left of the altar. He glared at the people leaving, several departing with obvious indifference through the entrance closest to the pulpit. He could not help thinking, *I'd wager they'll be the first in line when the food carts arrive.*

Crowds at the festivities that afternoon were in contrast to church attendance. Throngs of people sang, danced, and played games. Small children in noisy groups ran everywhere, chasing one another with grasshoppers or small lizards in their hands. When the food carts left the garrison and headed toward the church, the people cheered, further angering the bishop. A distinct chant began, "The Cantora! The Cantora!" over and over again. Someone had placed a life-sized wooden statue on the lead cart with garlands of flowers around its neck and heaped at its feet. As the cart drew near, Bishop

Damião saw that despite the rough nature of the carving, the face was definitely Yema's. "So now we are worshiping idols?" he said angrily and headed back to the abbey.

***

At the Caeté village the body of Janaína's husband lay on an elevated bier in front of the community house. Beneath the platform a smudge fire burned day and night keeping flies and scavengers away. The body had lain there five days awaiting burial on the sixth, the end of the mourning period. Janaína donned her jaguar cape and raged around the village denouncing everything Portuguese. She blamed the Europeans for bringing the coughing sickness and decried their religion for dividing her people. From the first, she decided her husband would not have a Catholic burial. The controversy left Julian in a most isolated situation. In addition, he found disturbing images scratched in charcoal on one post of the bier, stick figures with severed arms at their feet. He knew what they meant, *"Karu ãva Jekuaa!"* – "Consume the whites." The entire community seemed on the edge of violence, many believing that eating Portuguese flesh would make them immune to the mysterious coughing sickness.

The return of Yema and her family to the village further heightened tensions. Janaína demanded the child sing the burial chant, something the girl had done several times in the past. Fr. Julian pleaded for the soul of the dead, even while sensing this was an argument he could not win. Regardless, he said to the family, "His spirit cannot rise to heaven without a Christian burial."

In the end, Yema's mother negotiated a compromise, one Julian found quite unsatisfactory, yet was powerless to change— Cantora would sing the *Glória* at the graveside. To nearly everyone's astonishment, and to Julian's great distress, Yema's singing of the *Glória* included a number of the Latin words which she translated into Caeté.

As the girl finished the hymn, she noted the upset registering on Julian's face. Afterwards she asked him, "Did you disapprove of my using our language in my singing?"

Janaína stood nearby, and Julian not wishing to aggravate an already tense situation, replied cautiously, "I found it surprising, that's all."

Yema appeared suddenly shy and looked at the ground. "Oh Fr. Julian, it was not my intention to surprise you except in a pleasant way. I thought the more we Caeté hear words we understand, the more we will appreciate our new faith."

Upon hearing this, Julian found himself so flustered that he changed the subject. He felt it impossible to explain the sanctified connection between Latin and Holy Scripture. To add to his confusion, what Yema had just told him seemed wholly reasonable. Yet similar transgressions in Portugal had led to convictions of heresy and burnings at the stake.

***

For Paulo and Doçura, the week following Yema's absence became dreary and uninteresting. In the afternoons during the usual time for lessons, Doçura busied herself ministering to the sick at the hospital. She encouraged Paulo to do the same. "Dear sister," he said, looking desolate, unshaven, and smelling of beer, "I was already there this morning."

"Then go again," she told him. "Or work in the vegetable garden. Anything, Paulo. I am confident little Yema will return to us. And this time she and her family will stay." For Paulo's sake, she tried to sound confident, but secretly had her doubts. *If the girl does not come back, what will I do?* In her confusion, the sister toyed with the idea of going to the village, perhaps enlisting a few soldiers to go with her. *But to do what?* she thought. *Force her back to the settlement?* She found these thoughts as disturbing as the girl's absence.

Fr. Paulo's return to drink ended tragically. One night during the second week he left his quarters in the middle of the night and staggered to the docks. Workers found his drowned body the next morning, his corpse savaged by the piranha. The death shocked the entire community and an air of desperation gripped the settlement. Death was commonplace here—one only needed to visit the growing graveyard behind the hospital—yet Fr. Paulo's presence, drunk or sober, had become as expected as the dawn.

After Paulo's funeral on Saturday, Bishop Damião conferred with Doçura. "We are the only senior clergy here," he said. "I have too many duties to give adequate time to conduct all the services. I am turning everything over to Paulo's assistant with the exception of Sunday Mass." He paused while a long roll of thunder passed by. The rain poured off the roof and splashed onto the balcony outside his office. The bishop's mood matched the grim weather. "I have sent letters to Tomé Island asking for a temporary priest, and to Lisbon requesting a new senior priest and two others so we can expand our mission to the native villages." Damião sighed and picked up his dog, placing the animal on his lap. He gave the nun a tormented look. "In the meantime I need to recall Julian. That means we lose contact with little Cantora and her family. What shall I do? It is a terrible risk."

Doçura considered this. "Is that why no one was sent to tell Fr. Julian of Fr. Paulo's passing? He would have—"

"Yes, sister!" he said angrily. "That is why *I* sent no one."

She stared at him, startled by his outburst. Knowing he could not personally admit this to Julian, and she having put him in a difficult position, Doçura said, "May I suggest, sir, that your request includes a letter from me. I will plead with Fr. Julian, telling him of my desolation, and asking him to bring Cantora and her family back with him."

Damião stood and smiled, the first smile she'd seen from him that week. The burden of not informing Julian of Paulo's death was suddenly lifted from his shoulders. "Please excuse my angry tone, Sister Mãe. Your suggestion is excellent." He took a piece of parchment from a drawer and settled an inkwell and quill next to it. He gestured to his chair. "Please use my desk to prepare your letter. And if you could include a sentence or two... uh ..."

"To explain why we did not notify him of Fr. Paulo's passing?"

"Yes, of course, Mãe. Thank you. As usual you have read my mind." The bishop pointed to Fr. Paulo's lute which rested on a stand next to the door. "I understand Cantora was enthralled with that instrument."

"Yes sir. Unfortunately no one else knows how to play the lute, or even how to tune it."

"Surely someone can learn to pick out a note or two. Let the girl know that it awaits her. Perhaps this will hasten Cantora's return to us."

The nun seated herself at the desk and began to write. Bishop Damião found a leash for his dog. He kneeled and attached it to the animal's collar while the dog jumped and barked with anticipation. "The rain's stopped," he said. "It's time for his walk."

***

Feelings of joy pervaded the settlement when late the following week

Fr. Julian returned with Yema's family. They moved into a tent provided by the garrison, and the children began attending school. Paulo's assistant immediately took Yema's father to the dock to introduce him to the overseer. Doçura visited with the family as they settled their few possessions in the tent. "I am very sorry about your uncle's passing," she told the girl. To her surprise the child crossed herself as did the mother. Then an even bigger surprise: Yema hugged her.

"I am happy to be back," the girl said, "and so is my family, but we are so sad about our friend Fr. Paulo. May we visit his grave?"

My goodness, the sister thought, *how savage can these people be with this kind of sentiment?*

The mother smiled and said in halting Portuguese, "Yema taught me some of your talk." More than anything, hearing this made Mãe Doçura feel that the family was here to stay. She tried to respond in Caeté, but could not find the words.

For the next several weeks the lessons, both liturgical and language, moved forward with pleasing results. The sister learned enough Caeté that she began to practice outside the confines of the abbey chapel, though often stumbling over words that included clicks and grunts. Julian, who knew Caeté well, playfully helped Doçura, frequently repeating whole sentences to demonstrate the unusual cadence of the language.

A conversation during this time with Fr. Julian raised concern about the nature of their work with Yema. The sister and the priest had established a routine of walking around the outside of the abbey after morning services to discuss the day's lesson. On one such morning during their walk he asked, "Shall we tell little Cantora that the bishop has requested a *Consilium de Virtutibus?*"

"I haven't given it much thought," Doçura said. "Even if it's granted, it will be many months before they get here. I think we should wait until the council arrives. *If* they arrive. Do you really think Rome will grant the request? That will be a miracle in itself."

Julian paused to pick up a broken wooden carving, one unfinished and poorly made, perhaps an intended image of Yema. He turned it over in his hand. "There are some things I've told no one." He related the incidents surrounding the uncle's funeral. At the conclusion he said, "It was blasphemous to hear the *Glória* with heathen words mixed in. There was nothing I could do." He threw the carving into the weeds.

"You cannot change things," the nun said. "Put it out of your mind if you can." She thought for a moment. "How on earth did she learn the Latin words?"

He shrugged. "Oh it's my fault I guess. In helping her with pronunciation, I explained Latin in Portuguese, sometimes even in Caeté. Yema is amazing. She remembers absolutely everything."

"So I've noticed. I will be more cautious explaining things to her, particularly Gospel. So did you say anything to her after the funeral?"

"Very little. By then I suspected they were coming back with me. I didn't want anything to affect that." He winced. "There's more." By now they had reached the entrance to the courtyard.

Doçura walked ahead, starting another circuit. She turned and cupped a hand to her ear. "I hope you're going to tell me how you got them to return here."

"That's certainly part of it," he said. "To start with, I mistrust their easy compliance. Little Yema is still a pupil of the blood woman. I am positive that loyalty to the tribe is stronger than her bond to us. Much stronger. I further believe they are here because it gives them some advantage, or they think it does."

"Seems a little far-fetched."

He stopped and looked at her. "Doçura, I have lived with these Indians for the past three years, and I respect them. I want to convert them to the faith of our Lord Jesus." He crossed himself. "But they have a treacherous side, and it should not be underestimated. Their savagery is just beneath the surface. Before I arrived they were eating people as part of their religion. *Eating people!* And I find the veneration Yema receives both here and back at the village unsettling. I believe there is something about this we do not understand."

Chapter 5

Three months after Yema's return, a new priest arrived from São Tomé. He came on a ship full of African slaves, most of whom were desperately ill with a disease that threatened the entire settlement. Doçura had seen this malady twice before on Tomé when vessels from Africa and Portugal carrying the sickness attempted to make port, an affliction considerably worse than the coughing sickness, one that struck Europeans, Africans, and natives alike. The typhus.

A death ship like this would usually be quarantined far out in the harbor, but in this instance the captain and many of the vessel's company were dead. The remaining crew, in mutiny and many crazed with fever, ran the three-masted schooner aground a short distance from the docks. Those on board began to scurry off, climbing down rope ladders from the deck, swimming and wading ashore. When the alarm of disease rang out, garrison soldiers rushed to the waterfront to force the mutineers and escaping slaves back onto the ship.

When the soldiers saw the telltale signs of typhus—red skin splotches and fever madness—they retreated in terror. About thirty desperate souls had made it to shore. Men who were able fled into the settlement or to the surrounding jungle, knowing they would be sent back to the ship if caught. Finally the garrison captain, threatening death to any soldier who did not obey, forced his troops to round up what fugitives they could find and drive them at musket-point back onto the beached vessel.

The one exception was the new priest, Fr. Spadaro. Soldiers found him crawling in the shallows mumbling with delirium. They placed him on a litter, carrying the priest to a quarantine tent hastily set up a distance from the hospital. The sole physician at the hospital, a courageous doctor named Pero Cardim who tended the sick without regard to his personal safety, told the garrison captain that the settlement was probably infected. "Set up two camps," he told him, "one for the Europeans, one for the slaves. Guard them day and night. No one leaves without my say-so. Get the rest of those people off that ship and burn it."

The garrison captain began to object. "But Dr. Cardim, sir, the ship has stores and the safe may contain—"

"Captain, *to hell* with the gold and stores! Burn it. You can search for the gold in the wreckage."

The area around the ship soon became a frenzy of activity. Those who were fit enough clambered down the rope ladders and stood in anxious groups on the shore surrounded by the terrified militia. Others were lowered in rope baskets by their few able shipmates and staggered or were carried to their respective groups by others from the ship. The dead remained on board. Julian arrived and said prayers for the departed. The last items off the boat were two crates of chickens and a half-dozen goats, the latter thrown overboard from the aft deck and left to swim ashore. By this time two soldiers, waist deep in water and wielding axes, had broken through the outer hull. One man shoved his axe through the hole to make sure the ship's side was fully breached. Another threw a flaming torch inside and almost immediately the ship began to heave billows of black smoke. A few minutes passed, and soon the vessel was overwhelmed with flame. The fire leaped into the sails and rigging. Everyone on shore backed away from the inferno as the militia, using the butt ends of their spears, prodded the new arrivals to their camps.

***

Sister Doçura, exhausted from tending the sick, sat on the edge of her bed dressed only in her underclothes. Her room was stifling hot. A single candle burned at her bedside. To the east, the light from the burning ship still illuminated the harbor. She had watched for a while, the dread building inside her. She knew it was only a matter of time before the whole settlement would be infected. The sister started to say her rosary before going to bed, but found herself too tired to continue. A knock came at her door, and Fr. Julian announced himself. "Just a minute," Doçura called out. She quickly put on her cotton cap and a black shift she occasionally wore around the abbey, then opened the door and told Julian to come in. "You look as tired as I feel," she said.

"I am. But we have urgent work to do." She gestured for him to continue. "I've just come from the bishop's quarters. He wants us to meet with Yema's family tonight and encourage them to return to their village until the plague is over. He wants them to leave at first light."

The nun shook her head. "Oh my goodness, I've not even thought about Yema until now. I agree. He's right." She put her hands together. "I pray no one took refuge in their tent." She motioned towards the door. "Wait outside. I'll get dressed."

She found her wool-rope belt and cinched it around her waist, looping her rosary over it in the customary fashion. Then locating a thin veil, she tucked it under her cap so it covered the back of her neck. Next, she slipped on her sandals and went into the hallway.

Julian sat on a wooden bench under the light of an oil lamp set into the brown plaster wall. A pitch torch lay on the floor in front of him. With some effort he rose to his feet and picked up the torch, holding it over the oil lamp until it sputtered to flame. In silence the two walked down the stairs and into the courtyard. Once they passed the main gate and headed toward the settlement, Julian began to talk. "Bishop Damião is in a terrible state. When he visited the sick, one of the seamen told him that Father Spadaro was carrying a letter from the archbishop of Lisbon. Damião thinks it might have to do with the Council of Miracles." He put a hand to his eyes. "I guess it's burned up now."

"Do you think Spadaro knows what it says?"

"We might never know. He may die. In the meantime the bishop wants Yema and her family safely away from here. He views the little cantora as an absolute treasure. He's not willing to risk her dying in case the council is on its way." Ahead they could see the familiar shape of the family's tent near the garrison. "The garrison captain will provide two soldiers and mules for everyone to assure their safe arrival. I am charged to go with them; to look after them."

"But Julian," Doçura said, "you are needed here!"

"I know." He shrugged. "Bishop Damião was very insistent. I'll be gone for only four days, two there, two back."

"Their village is only a day's ride past the Rio Jacu where we first met them?"

"Yes."

Julian and Doçura could see a candle burning inside the tent. The nun called out. Marét, answered and bade them come in. By now the mother, father, and little brother spoke a jumbled mixture of Portuguese and Caeté, as did Doçura when talking with the family. Yema on the other hand—always self-disciplined and wishing to learn more—restricted her speech to Portuguese when conversing with non-Indians. She occasionally lapsed into native tongue after a considerable pause, but only when she was unable to recall the Portuguese word or phrase.

Upon seeing the two clergy enter their tent, Yema and her brother hugged Doçura and Julian, but Marét stood back and appeared quite upset. "Your ship has brought a new disease from your damned world. As if the coughing sickness was not enough."

A tragedy, the nun thought, knowing there would be more in the future. "We are sorry," she said. "That is why we're here." As she explained the situation, Yema began to cry, sobbing that she did not want to leave. Her fervor both pleased and frightened Doçura. She had never seen the child like this before. In an attempt to comfort the girl, she put an arm around her. The family finally agreed to leave, promising to meet in the abbey courtyard at first light.

There was something else that nagged at the edges of Doçura's thoughts, then suddenly took form, making itself fully apparent and adding to her distress—The burning of the ship and possibly the archbishop's letter. *Were there other letters burned?* Perhaps one from her family, from the province of Antalya in the Ottoman? She treasured those letters from her mother and father that arrived once or twice yearly, having made the perilous journey through the Mediterranean and round half a world. Their correspondence was always in Hebrew, and her family had accepted Doçura's fate as a Catholic nun. They understood that this was the likely outcome for many Jewish girls kidnapped by the Church. The use of Hebrew had started with letters they exchanged during her first years on São Tomé. She speculated that her parents found the language comforting, perhaps a sign that she had not fully lost her Jewish identity. Doçura also speculated that possibly she too wished to retain her birthright.

***

In the morning the garrison captain showed up with the family in tow along with two mounted soldiers. The mother and father each sat astride mules with the little brother behind his father, the boy's thin arms circling the man's waist. Yema sat in front of Marét on a cushion wedged behind the pommel. The girl appeared to have been crying for some time, and continued on the verge of tears. An additional mule for Fr. Julian accompanied the group as did two burros loaded with supplies. Most of these were destined for the Caeté village, gifts from Bishop Damião, small casks of black syrup, axes, blankets, iron nails, and hemp rope. With a new disease brought onshore, one that would surely plague the Indians, the bishop hoped the gifts would soften their anger which was certain to come. Doçura had seen them approach from the settlement, while far behind them, smoke continued to rise from the hulk of the burned slave ship. She quickly finished dressing and met the group at the abbey's front gate. Julian had preceded her, and was settling himself in his saddle when she arrived. About the same time, Bishop Damião appeared from the chapel and joined the group as they advanced toward the edge of the settlement and the forest beyond.

At the sight of the bishop in his gray tunic, Yema's tears

began anew. "What happens if all of you die?" she sobbed.

"God willing, little Yema," Bishop Damião said, "we will all be here when you return." She continued to cry, her eyes red and nose running. "Ah Cantora," he continued, "we have delayed Lauds this morning so we could wish you safe journey. I will say a special prayer for you and your family and our brave soldiers, and for Fr. Julian." Hearing this she brightened a little, pulling at the skirt of her shift and wiping her face.

By now they had reached the jungle trail. The bishop patted Cantora, reached up and embraced Fr. Julian, thanked the soldiers, and said, "Safe journey to you all." He made the sign of the cross and knelt to pray. Doçura followed his lead. They looked after the group for a few moments, then turned in silence and walked back to the abbey, all lost in thought—thoughts that for the moment seemed to overwhelm them. Once at the abbey they entered the small chapel and began Lauds. Doçura had never seen Bishop Damião pray as fervently as he did that morning.

***

At dusk a lone figure emerged from the jungle trail and urged his mule forward in the direction of the settlement hospital. Once there, and before dismounting, Fr. Julian called for Dr. Cardim. He had just swung his leg over the saddle when the doctor emerged from the tent. To keep Yema from sliding to the ground, Julian rested his hand on her inert body which was slumped on a cushion ahead of the saddle.

Pero Cardim reacted quickly. "Keep her on the animal and let us move away from here."

The priest appeared confused, but complied, leading the mule while the doctor walked alongside holding the girl in place. "She may have the typhus," Julian said.

"Impossible," Cardim replied. He took the animal's halter and brought him to a stop. "She cannot have typhus because those exposed do not show illness for at least ten days. Of that I am certain. Cantora has something else." He gestured back towards the quarantine tent. "I don't want her anywhere near there."

"Where then?" Julian asked, drawing Yema from the saddle and handing her to Cardim.

The girl straightened her legs and tried to stand. The doctor steadied her, kneeled, and looked into her face. He felt Yema's forehead. Her nose was running, eyes red, and the girl sounded a hoarse wheeze when she tried to talk. "She has coryza," the doctor said, "what they call the coughing sickness, what we call a cold." He shook his head in angry frustration. "I cannot understand what makes us a little sick makes them so very sick. I am completely puzzled why this simple illness is so severe in these people." He studied the priest for a moment, then said, "Do you believe as many others do, that this is the will of God? That this is because—"

A weary Julian raised a hand to silence him. "Of this, doctor, *I am certain*: The vengeful God of the Old Testament gave His Son to lead us to charity for all. Regardless of what anyone says, Our Lord Jesus is not vengeful. And no-longer is The Father. That is the true lesson of Christ."

Cardim nodded in agreement and pointed towards the abbey. "I want you to take her to Doçura. I am sure our dear sister will be most willing to care for this special child." He paused. "Wait here, I'll send some medicine with you."

He walked to the hospital and returned carrying a brown earthen pot. He set the pot on the ground and stirred the contents with a wooden paddle. The dark green, leafy mixture gave off the scent of mint. "This is an herb the Indians use. It's like our mint back home, but considerably stronger. Sister Doçura should give Yema a few spoons of it each day, and also rub it on her chest. It helps loosen the cough and may reduce her fever." He again felt Yema's forehead. The girl began to cough and wheeze, trying to talk. The doctor patted her cheek. "Save your talk for later, beloved child. When you are feeling better." He lifted Yema onto the saddle while Julian held her in place.

Dr. Cardim tried to sound cheerful, but Julian saw desperation in the way the man wrung his hands. "Is she going to be all right?" the priest asked.

In a quiet voice the doctor said, "Your prayers will help."

"How is Fr. Spadaro?" Julian asked.

"Still with fever," said Cardim. "Nothing he's said makes any sense. Bishop Damião visited him twice today. He told me about the letter. It's quite a mystery."

Yema began to shiver, her teeth chattering. By now it was well into the evening with only a thin line of daylight showing along the jungle's edge. "You better get going," the doctor told Julian.

When he entered the abbey courtyard, Fr. Julian found Doçura just leaving Vespers. He called to her and she came running over.

Yema hung onto the saddle, trying to remain upright.

"Oh Heavenly Father!" the nun said, taking the girl in her arms. "Tell me what's wrong, child." Yema opened her eyes and forced a smile. She mouthed a few indistinct words, then shut her eyes and clung to Doçura, her tiny hands pressing against the fabric of the nun's habit.

Fr. Julian explained as best he could. He concluded with the doctor's instructions, and offered to carry the medicine pot upstairs for Doçura. As they hurried across the courtyard, he asked, "Did they have typhus on Tomé?"

"Yes. Twice I think."

"Did it spread to the colony?"

"In a way. It wasn't like the plague. Maybe only one person out of twenty got it. That was bad enough. Both times it came on ships just like now, but we quarantined them in the harbor. None of the infected were allowed on shore. Still some people got it. God only knows what will happen in this situation."

"On Tomé, how many of those infected died?"

"About half. A few people never fully recovered. Even though they appeared all right, some remained befuddled. As if the fever madness never fully left them." Doçura thought for a moment, then continued. "My brother wrote in his journal that his ship from Portugal was infected. Apparently he just had a mild case."

When they entered the nun's apartment, she went to the bed and placed the child on her back. Doçura found a spoon, and Julian propped the little girl to a sitting position, encouraging her to take the medicine. The nun next laid the child flat and rubbed the potion onto her chest. The medicine felt cool to the nun's fingers, yet underneath the girl's flesh seemed to burn. Yema relaxed a little, though her breathing remained terribly labored. Doçura's heart seemed to squeeze into a hard, painful ball, and she began to cry. After a moment she snuffed fiercely, wiping her face on her sleeve. "This is not a time for tears," the nun moaned. Doçura motioned to Julian. "Let us talk in the hall." They stopped a short distance from the room. "What about the rest of the family?" she asked.

Julian looked downcast. "Not great, I think. Marét appeared to be getting ill when I turned back with Cantora. I thought it best if they all went on to the village, yet I fear for the lot of them."

From inside the room they could hear Yema coughing—Short

stifled sounds, the child struggling for air. "I'd better get back," Doçura said, and bade Julian good night. Once in the room she knelt by the bed and began her rosary. In the middle of the third decade she heard footsteps in the hall, then a knock on her door. "Just a moment," she called. Yema had turned on her side and curled into a ball. Her teeth were chattering. Doçura covered the child with a thin blanket and went to the door. There stood Bishop Damião. "Come in," she said.

He walked to the bed and looked down. "How is she?"

The nun shrugged. "I don't know. Yema's a strong girl with a strong will. With God's help she'll survive."

The bishop looked as downcast as Julian. "I've placed such hopes in this child." He made the sign of the cross and turned away from the bed. "I don't know what I'll do if she dies. What will I tell the council? They may be on their way." He looked at Doçura. "You've heard the rumor? About the letter?"

The nun nodded. "Yes."

"If she dies, I guess we have enough witnesses. The *Consilium*—"

Doçura gasped. "I will not have this conversation here," she said quietly. "Not in my room, not in her presence."

The bishop turned to the bedside, knelt and clasped his hands. "You are right, Mãe. The child's health is most important." Damião stayed a few minutes by the bed, praying quietly. Finally he stood and straightened his vestment. "I asked Doctor Cardim to visit you in the morning. Please excuse yourself from Vespers. Stay with Cantora. I think the doctor should bleed her."

She saw him to the door and wished the bishop good night, returned to the bed and stared at Cantora for a minute, then took the candle from the bedside and placed it on her desk. Doçura sat in her chair and put her face in her hands, the little girl's struggled breathing the only sound in the room. *These Christians and their bloodlettings,* she thought, remembering that it was forbidden in her Lisbon community. Why did she recall this one brief sermon? She could not have been more than twelve at the time, but in her mind the rabbi's words sounded clear. "We Jews do not let blood. It is a custom of Christian medicine that borders on the pagan."

"What is clear," she said aloud, "is that none of my worlds fit me, not my lost Judaism from Lisbon nor my Catholic world of

Coimbra and São Tomé, and now this hostile coast of Brazil. We're not helping these natives with our religion, we are poisoning them with disease and commerce. They were cannibals before we came and if we leave, will be so again. No people deserve the kind of legacy we impose." She looked back at the vague figure of Yema on her bed. "This poor innocent child. Perhaps we are cannibals of another sort, not of the flesh but of the spirit."

Despite her fever and confused state, Yema heard these words. She could see Sister Doçura through the gauze of the insect net. Or was it her mother? She could not be sure. The figure changed again, this time Aunt Janaína wearing her jaguar cape, the yellow fangs centered above her eyes. "I must live through this," she called out, her words choking into a violent spasm of coughing.

The nun came to her side and stroked her forehead with a damp cloth. "Yes my little Yema, you *will* live through this. On the promise of my life, dearest child, you will indeed live."

Chapter 6

Yema's condition improved over the next several weeks. During the third week, on her first day out of bed for any length of time, she sat in the shade on the balcony and ate maize gruel with black syrup. She liked the warm mixture as it soothed her throat and eased her cough. "Do you eat this every morning?" she asked Doçura.

"Yes," the nun answered. "That and some of your wonderful guava fruit from the jungle." She was pleased when the girl asked for some. She cut several slices and brought them to her, then carried the stool from her desk and sat next to Yema. They ate from a plate balanced on the rough surface of balcony's waist-high stucco wall.

Earlier in her convalescence—just the second day she could sit up—Yema had sharpened the edges of Doçura's dagger with a small rock she'd asked the nun to bring from the courtyard. Then she used the keen edge to shape each long fingernail to a point, finally using the stone again to make each nail perfect.

"Why did you do that?" Doçura inquired, amazed at how skillful the child was with her hands. "Your nails look dangerous."

Yema lay back on the pillow and examined her fingers. "If I am to die," she said, "I will enter the afterlife as a jaguar. The other animals must recognize me." She lifted both hands, splaying her fingers wide apart, making a low sound in her throat.

"Why a jaguar?"

"That is my *vy'arenda* from Aunt Janaína."

"Heritage?"

The girl considered this. "Heritage. Yes. Each person has a destiny, a forest animal. Or one of the water."

Doçura found the idea intriguing. Taking the child's hand, she pressed the nails into her palm, showing her the indentations and saying, "So little jaguar, I am marked. What would be my *vy'arenda?*"

"I don't know," Yema said. "It depends on what you do in the tribe. I mean what you do *best* in the tribe. I will ask my aunt when I see her."

***

During this time Dr. Cardim visited twice daily, often standing just outside the doorway and inquiring about the girl's health, having explained that if carrying the typhus, he did not want to expose them to it. They were confined to nun's room on orders from Bishop Damião who usually visited in the afternoon. Meals were brought to them from the abbey's kitchen by one of Doçura's novitiates, or sometimes by a young Indian boy about Yema's age in training as an acolyte. He was obviously smitten with the girl, often lingering in the doorway, waving shyly and calling out to her.

"When can we go outside?" Yema asked. "And when will I hear from my family? I'm worried about them."

"I am too," said Doçura. "Let's see what Fr. Julian has to say." She looked over the courtyard until she saw someone she recognized. She called down to the woman, asking her to find Julian. Across the courtyard she could see soldiers stationed at the abbey gate. They had orders to bar anyone from entering who appeared ill.

A half-hour passed, and Julian and Dr. Cardim showed up, both pleased to see Yema's progress. They asked Doçura to step into the hall where she immediately began asking questions, the first as to the health of the colony.

Cardim's steady stare unnerved her. "So-so," he said. "It appears that we have a new coughing sickness more virulent than before. Many of the natives are severely ill. Quite a few have died. As for the typhus, it seems to have slowed."

"What about Yema's village?" Doçura asked. "What news

from there?" It bothered her that the girl was sitting alone in the room and possibly frightened by their private conversation.

Julian shook his head. "We've heard nothing. It's unlikely they got away unscathed. The village could have the same coryza as here. That does not bode well for them. On the other hand, it's likely they do not have typhus in the village."

"So the typhus here is not spreading?" the nun asked.

"Not as bad as I thought it might," said Cardim. "All the same, we still have plague flags flying at the docks, and three ships have turned away. One just this morning after offloading cargo in the bay. What was your experience with typhus on Tomé?"

"It never took a real toll on the colony," she answered. "A few cases, not many."

Cardim stroked his chin. "It seems that typhus more often infects in crowded places, ships and such. We have only a half-dozen residents with it. That's why I think it may be a good sign for Yema's people."

"Is Fr. Spadaro better?" she asked.

"Yes, thank God. But as far as the content of the archbishop's letter, he knows nothing."

"And the *Consilium*?"

Fr. Julian spoke up. "We've asked each new ship's captain, and no one has any news. We've no idea if they're coming."

Doçura inclined her head toward her door. In her usual direct manner she addressed them both. "That precious child in there is going to live. In a few days she might even sing. Julian please, see if you can get something from her village." She turned to Cardim. "Yema's worried, and this isolation is not fair."

"I understand," the doctor said. "In a day or two I will probably have the plague flags struck. I will recommend to the bishop that your isolation is no longer necessary. Since Yema's getting over the coryza, she may not get it again for a while."

The door creaked open and Yema emerged. She'd been listening. "Fr. Julian," she said, "please find out about my family, my mother and father, my little brother. My Aunt Janaína."

Julian knelt. He was face-to-face with the girl. "You have my promise that I will do my very best, dear child. I will send messengers first thing in the morning."

At sunrise the next day, the priest dispatched two Indian

runners to the Caeté village, one carrying provisions, the other with gifts for Yema's family and the blood woman. Ten days passed, and they did not return.

Midway through this period, Dr. Cardim ordered the plague flags lowered. The first ship to dock was a stately four-master from Lisbon. On board were the three members of the *Consilium de Virtutibus.*

Bishop Damião and Fr. Julian, along with the garrison captain and several of his lieutenants, hastily formed a welcoming party and hurried to the docks.

Once there, they found the three men and the ship's captain surrounded by a throng of natives, mostly women and children—their fear of European disease overcome by curiosity—who were fascinated by the visitors' fancy garb and their small mountain of baggage. Garrison soldiers promptly showed up and pushed the Indians away from the new arrivals. The three clergy appeared amused by all the attention from the strange-looking natives.

Dressed in his finest uniform, the ship captain formally introduced the delegation. With each name and title, the bishop's heart soared. The Holy Father had sent the most prestigious of clergy: The Archbishop of Lisbon, Costa da Martina, a man so old and infirm he needed a cane in each hand to hold himself upright; Adrian Boeyens, tall, gaunt, and darkly severe, a Dutch bishop and the Pope's personal representative; and a youthful Spanish priest, Juan Girona, the brutal Chief Inquisitor of Seville, infamous for his relentless prosecution of heretics, Moslems, and *Conversos*— Jews converted to the Catholic faith.

As the party prepared for their walk to the abbey, a ship's officer produced a nurse chair from the baggage pile. Four smartly dressed sailors immediately stepped forward as the officer assisted the archbishop into his chair. They hoisted the poles holding the chair onto their shoulders and headed off, elevating the old man so he sat taller than any in the group.

What joy might have been shared in the community over the *Consilium's* arrival was blunted by the new coughing sickness spreading through the settlement's native population. Fully half were sick, and the number of deaths mounted daily. Dyewood activity shrank to a trickle since the majority of harvesters were Indian and, whether slave or free, most refused association with both Europeans and Africans.

More and more one heard talk of rebellion. The presence of the four-master from Portugal worsened the situation—Most natives believed each ship's arrival brought new disease. Soon the eat-the-whites slogan, *Karu ãva Jekuaa!* spread, reinforcing the natives' belief that consuming white flesh would make them immune to disease. Doctor Cardim had warned Bishop Damião of this threat, and one could see it that morning at dockside where an angry group of about twenty men, most of them muttering and pointing, stood back a distance from the crowd of onlookers.

Bishop Damião had instructed the garrison captain to take the longer route to the abbey, one that avoided the hospital and graveyard behind, a graveyard where the heap of unburied corpses filled the morning air with a hideous stench. The Indian burial crew had disappeared, and soon garrison soldiers would be ordered to assume the grisly task.

As the collection of clergy and soldiers worked their way through the settlement, Damião walked alongside Archbishop da Martina, looking up and congratulating him on his difficult journey. "Your stamina is remarkable, sir. And at your age."

"Ah, Mateus," the archbishop said cheerily, startling the bishop. It had been years since anyone had used his given name. "Everyone told me not to go, that I might not live to see my beloved Lisbon again. But if this angel sings as beautifully as you say, I will happily find my way to heaven from this Brazil coast. She can sing at my funeral Mass."

In the abbey courtyard a delegation awaited the visitors, Sister Doçura and her novitiates, settlement dignitaries, various acolytes, and Dr. Cardim and Fr. Spadaro, the latter remaining seriously addled from his illness. As the introductions proceeded, Doçura noticed the large mail pouch carried by the ship's purser. Perhaps he had a letter inside from her beloved parents. Next she noted—and immediately felt a sickening chill—the name of the priest from Seville, a name feared throughout much of Christendom. She also saw that Julian, who stood to the rear of the visitors, put his hand to his mouth and looked directly at her when Juan Girona was introduced. She was further unnerved when Bishop Damião presented her to the visitors. Though very brief, Inquisitor Girona seemed to give her a baleful stare. *No no,* she thought, *he's here as part of the Consilium, not as*

Inquisitor. You are imagining things. Yet when she saw the man's swagger as he circulated through the crowd, she could not shake her feelings of dismay.

Immediately after introductions, Bishop Damião asked Archbishop da Martina to bless the assemblage, which he did joyfully. Next Damião announced that lunch would be served at long tables set up in the courtyard, inviting Julian, Doçura, and Dr. Cardim to sit with the delegation at the head table and quickly explaining Julian and Doçura's roles in educating "our little treasure." At this point the sister glanced in the direction of her room, spotting Yema watching the activities from the balcony. Standing next to the child was Cantora's favorite novitiate, the young Indian woman who'd taken the Portuguese name Sincera.

Seeing the little girl gave Doçura pause. She'd not told the child about the *Consilium's* visit, nor its purpose. There'd been no time that morning, and had not told her earlier out of concern as to how it would affect her—All the talk about miracles and such, and with no certainty that the Council would even arrive.

While the gathering dined on an elegant lunch of sliced guava, goat-milk curds, freshly roasted pork, and baked yams with black syrup, Bishop Damião explained that Yema was recovering from the coryza, praising Doçura and Cardim for nursing her back to health.

"When may we hear her sing?" Bishop Boeyens inquired. Everyone looked to Doçura.

She addressed Cardim and Julian. "If the doctor agrees, we would like to practice privately this afternoon in the chapel. Perhaps she can sing the *Glória* at Vespers tomorrow evening. I make no promises. I do not wish to tax her health."

The Inquisitor-priest, Girona, took the moment to move the conversation in a new direction, one that suited his purpose. "Is it not profanation to have a female sing the sacred text? The Church strictly prohibits—"

Bishop Damião, well prepared to defend his decision rose to his feet. Interrupting the priest, he said, "Are not the angels who sing in God's Heaven of both genders?"

"But this girl is not—"

"Father Girona," he said in a mildly demeaning way, "you have not heard this child sing, and I have. She may indeed be an angel."

Girona glared at the bishop and those around him, his gaze settling on Doçura. "Dear sister," he said, "you've barely touched your *marrano*," using the Spanish epithet meaning both converted Jew *and* pig. "Is it not to your taste?" Many around the table gasped.

The sister, though shaken, answered with a firm voice, addressing everyone, "Since Fr. Juan Girona is a long-traveled visitor to our new land, I will excuse his ill manners as fatigue from his journey."

The gathering fell into an awkward silence, the visiting clergy wondering, *A nun, a woman, talking this way to a priest? Could this new world be corrupting the faith?* And next looking to Damião, *Who allows such a thing?*

Girona stood and looked angrily at Doçura, then addressed the Captain of the Guard. "If you would escort me to my quarters fine sir, I'm feeling the need to contemplate all that I've heard here today." He walked a short distance from the table and stood while solders, at the ship captain's direction, sorted out his baggage. The small group headed to the far corner of the abbey, the apartments reserved for the *Consilium.*

The conversation became uncomfortably animated, everyone wanting to avoid thinking about the past moments. The nun left her seat at the table and approached the ship's purser. "By any chance do you have a letter for me? I am Sister Mãe da Doçura."

"I believe so," the man said. He walked to the serving table which by now had been cleared and began sorting things. "I think this is it," he said, finding a thin package and turning it over so he could see the address. Oddly, he then covered it with his hand obscuring the writing, writing that Doçura immediately recognized. She reached for the letter, but the purser slid it away as if in a game of shells. After an awkward moment—he with an appearance of mirth, she with a look of irritation—the purser abandoned the letter and turned back to his sorting. The nun took the package and hurried off, her aggravation quickly replaced by her eagerness to read the letter inside.

In her room she found Yema kneeling with Sincera on the balcony playing jackstraws. The little girl immediately jumped up and ran to Doçura. "Is it true that those people came from across the sea? They came to hear me sing?"

"That is true, little one." She looked toward Sincera, wondering how much the novitiate had told her. This was certainly not the way Doçura wanted Yema to find out about the *Consilium.*

Sincera frowned. "I hope I've not done something wrong, Sister."

"Of course not," the nun replied, not wishing to alarm the girl. "Sincera, I see Fr. Julian and Dr. Cardim are still in the courtyard. Please ask them to come up here. I think our cantora is ready to practice a little, to test her voice." Yema let out a small yell and clapped her hands. Sincera nodded and left the room, relieved to be away from Doçura's questioning gaze. The nun showed the child the letter package. "This came from my family in the Ottoman. I am so excited to read—" To her surprise the little girl looked startled and backed away.

"Did it come from that ship? The new one in the harbor?"

"Yes. So did our visitors. What's wrong?"

"Do they bring more sickness to kill the Caeté?"

Doçura was horrified by the girl's question , but asked in an even voice, "Where did you hear that?"

"Sister Sincera," the child said, not sensing the nun's upset.

She knelt and put her arms around Yema. "I don't think they brought a new illness, sweetheart. These are holy men, priests from the Church. God has protected them, and God will protect you."

They heard footsteps in the hall and looked up to see Julian and Cardim standing in the doorway. The doctor said, "I hear our Cantora may be ready to resume her singing."

Yema smiled and gave her familiar curtsey.

Both men laughed. Her curtseys seemed so out of place for an Indian child. "Well," the doctor continued, "let's hear you sing a little. You certainly look well enough."

"Yema," Julian said, "do you feel up to singing the *Glória* tomorrow evening? That's what we should practice."

Without hesitation the little girl took a few steps backwards, opened her arms wide and—to everyone's astonishment—began.

♫ *"Et in terra pax,*
Hominibus bonae voluntatis,
Laudamus te, Benedicimus te,
Adoramus te, Glorificamus te,
Gratiam agimus ... "

The first notes sounded a bit strained, but then she gathered herself and the power of her voice returned. The listeners stood spellbound.

Cardim motioned her to stop. "I think she's ready," he said. Doçura and Julian crossed themselves.

***

After a successful practice, and with a note sent to Bishop Damião that Yema would sing the *Glória* at tomorrow's Vespers, the child and Doçura returned to the nun's quarters. On their way up the stairs, she again told the girl about her parents' letter. Yema said she no longer feared it. But there still seemed something wrong. *What was it?* the nun asked herself. *Ever since they'd met with Julian and Dr. Cardim, something had been missing.* Her concern left when they reached the door. They quickly went out to the balcony to read the letter.

In her hurry to open the letter package, Doçura failed to notice that the three sealing wax closures on the outer lappet had been broken and repaired with orange wax of a similar color. When she withdrew the parchment letter from the pouch, the repair on the letter itself was clearly evident along the envelope fold, particularly where the opening string—normally sealed in place with wax—hung loose. The nun paused to examine the pouch. Sometimes letters were opened by someone looking for hidden gold leaf, and her letters often showed obvious signs of tampering, but this one was unusual because of the attempted repairs. She shrugged it off and began to read aloud, feeling great delight at seeing her mother's graceful Hebrew script.

My dearest Leah Anna,

"Who is Leah Anna?" Yema asked. "And what kind of writing is that?"

The second question surprised her. She had no idea the child could even recognize characters. "These words are in a language called Hebrew. I didn't know you could read."

"Just a little," the girl said. "I follow along in the hymn book sometimes. I don't know what most of the words mean."

Then it hit Doçura. She knew what was missing from earlier in the afternoon. "Yema," she said, "when we saw Fr. Julian, you did not ask him if he'd heard from your parents. That's the first thing you always ask of him."

"Oh, Sincera told me they are all right. She talked with someone from the village just a day ago."

The nun didn't know what to make of this. Though it satisfied her curiosity, she wondered why Sincera had not offered her the same news. "Good to hear," she said. "Excellent." Pointing to the letter she continued, "Now please let me read on. I am sure you will have more questions. I'll answer them in a moment." The child gave her a series of impatient nods. Doçura repeated the salutation and continued reading.

May my letter find you well. Your father and I send greetings from Antalya. I can report that your sisters Rebecca and Sarah and your brother Yakub are thriving here, as is your father and I. Kalif Mashuud ben Nafid, the region's governor, has been generous to our growing Jewish community, granting work to anyone who wants it and allowing our craftsmen inside his several palaces and fortifications. In that respect, your family now has a brickyard not unlike ours years ago in Lisbon. And just as you and your brother did, the three children all help with masonry casting and other chores. Although they do not indulge in the dangerous mischief that you and Marcel left behind, which likely still haunts the churches of Lisbon and Almada...

Yema began hopping from foot to another. She could no longer contain herself. "What mischief, Mãe? What mischief?"

"Well," the nun said, "you see this letter here, it is Yod-heh. And these two are Heh and Sheen. These are the Hebrew letters which symbolize the Jewish God, Yahweh." She took her quill and ink and wrote them out on the back of the parchment, י׳ה, ה, ש. "My brother and I would inscribe these letters in hidden places on the bricks."

"How could you do that?"

"They were fancy bricks used for ornaments. There were plenty of places to hide the letters in the wet clay. We made them very small."

"Is Yahweh the same God as Jesus?"

"No, Yahweh is The Father of Jesus."

Yema took the letter and pretended to read it. "Why was that mischief?"

"Oh I don't know. Maybe because we weren't supposed to do it."

"Why did your father call you Leah Anna?"

The question unsettled Doçura. She took a hard swallow, considering how best to explain. She did not wish to tell the child about her kidnapping. "My name was Leah Anna Saulo before I took my Catholic name of Mãe Doçura. A woman who is studying to become a nun takes a Catholic name."

"Like Sincera did?"

"Exactly." Doçura felt a sudden need to say more to the child. "I will tell you about Leah Anna. That name was also my grandmother's." She took the letter and pointed out two characters. "This is the letter *Lamed*, and this is the letter *Alef*. In Hebrew they are written like this." Again she used her quill, לא. "Backward from the way we write in Portuguese. These are my grandmother's initials." She handed the parchment back to Yema and walked inside. "Let me change out of these hot clothes and I'll show you something interesting."

Doçura returned wearing her black shift. She reached inside the neckband and unhooked her gold chain, handing it to Yema. The child's eyes became enormous, and for a rare moment she was speechless. "This was once my grandmother's. And at one time it held an amber amulet called a *kamea* with my grandmother's initials on it."

"What happened to it, Mãe?"

"Amber is quite fragile. It just broke off one night, and I lost it." And again in her thoughts, *Tell her nothing of the kidnapping!*

Chapter 7

The new coryza spread through the Caeté village like floods after the spring rain, first a trickle, then a torrent. Janaína wore her jaguar cape day and night, believing it would protect her. Indeed it seemed so, as she remained healthy while many around her grew sicker each day.

Earlier in that week, two Indian runners had arrived from the European settlement. They bore food and gifts for Yema's family and Janaína. The runners were young men from the tribe whose families still lived in the Caeté village. At first they felt no concern, assuming they would return the next day, and everyone listened eagerly to the news of Yema and the settlement. Hearing of Yema's likely recovery brought some cheer, but the stories of many Indians dying there from coryza gave Janaína the excuse she'd sought—to rid her tribe of Catholic influences. She appealed to the runners. "Stay in our village with your families. You are better protected here." And to the whole crowd, "What have the white men brought us, disease, slavery, the ruin of our forest, and the loss of our sacred animals?"

"But *Tuguy Kuñã,*" one said, using her formal title, "we promised Fr. Julian that we would return."

"Return to what? To catch the coughing sickness and die?"

"Many are dying here. At least the settlement has the white doctor Cardim." He motioned to the half-dozen funeral biers smoking around the village, the nearest one containing both a mother and her child.

"Who has he saved?" Janaína asked. She did not intend to lose this fight. She gestured to their burdens. "They send us bribes. Let me see what you've brought?" The two laid out the gifts and food, two polished brass mirrors, a dozen beeswax candles, black syrup and packages of highly prized salt pork. Marét and husband Jégeuro examined the gifts, then stood back, confused as to what to do. They desperately wanted to be with their daughter, but feared going to the settlement because of Janaína's warnings. Even more, the blood woman wanted Yema back in the village. The child was the tribe's treasure and her spiritual progeny. She briefly conferred with Jégeuro and Marét, then turned to the two young men. "Take half the salt pork and syrup, and most of the candles. Share them with your families and do not return to the whites until I tell you to." She surveyed the crowd of Caeté, many of them suffering from the coryza. "I have a plan. One that will rid us of the diseases the whites bring. Follow me."

She led a group of people, mostly men and boys, into the large hut used for the village church. "Get rid of these Catholic ornaments," she said. "Add them to the smudge fires of your loved ones. And half these benches too. Bring the sick from your huts. Make places for them, grass mats and robes. One useful thing we can copy from the whites is their hospital." She clearly knew the second part to her plan, but it was not yet time to disclose it. Janaína smiled to herself. She'd known two days earlier about Yema's recovery through word from her *mangea,* the young woman at the abbey whom she'd persuaded to spy for her; and because of the constant flow of persons between the Caeté village and Portuguese settlement, Janaína received reports almost daily.

***

Friday arrived in the settlement. There was much excitement among the clergy, and the Africans and Indians, when they heard that Yema would sing at Vespers. Many of the Indians believed this was a sign that the coryza epidemic would soon be over. As on other occasions when Cantora sang at Vespers, the service was to be moved to the church to accommodate the crowd.

That morning Doçura, feeling both excited and fearful, found Yema to be in good spirits. The little girl, happy to be away from the confines of the nun's apartment, played with other children in the courtyard while Doçura and Fr. Julian looked on.

"Does the child know the Trinity for Vespers will be the *Consilium de populi?*" the priest asked.

"No!" the sister said, "nobody told me that."

"Bishop Damião wants them to conduct Mass on Sunday, so he thought he'd start with Vespers. It's quite an honor for our little church."

"Oh Julian, I don't know. We've got to tell Yema and maybe introduce her to them."

He thought for a moment, then called out. "Yema! Would you come over here please?"

The child ran up, out of breath, her face wet with perspiration. A boy about her age followed, tagging her several times. Yema kicked at him playfully. "Stop it, Agato." The boy— one of the acolytes in training and often serving in the Mass—continued his pestering until Julian told him to stop. Yema turned to the priest. "Yes, Fr. Julian?"

"Are you looking forward to singing this evening?" She smiled and nodded, still not quite able to catch her breath.

Doçura spoke up. "I think our three visitors will conduct Vespers, and they will also serve Mass this Sunday. What do you think of that?"

The girl seemed unconcerned. "Oh that would be fine."

"Would you like to meet them?"

"Yes, yes," she said, hopping and clapping her hands.

The nun turned to Julian. "Alright, Father, what next?"

Fr. Julian had already considered the idea and had an immediate answer. "We've been taking meals with the *Consilium* and Bishop Damião in the front of the chapel. You've probably noticed tables are missing from the kitchen area." Doçura nodded. "Why don't you and Yema sup with us?"

Sooner or later, she thought, *I'm going to have the spend time with these people. It might as well be this afternoon.* She put an arm around Yema. "Well, little Cantora, let us get cleaned up and into our Vespers clothes. You will be the guest of honor." The child gave a little yell and ran across the courtyard for the abbey stairs. Doçura shrugged and smiled at Julian. "Every day that girl surprises me." The nun headed for her room.

When Doçura got to her quarters, she found Yema standing over the wooden wash basin, attempting to fill it and trying not to spill the heavy pitcher. The nun took the pitcher from her and poured the basin half full. Immediately the girl pulled off her clothes and stepped into the water. Doçura began to wash her, admiring the flawless texture of the child's olive skin. "Look how dirty this water is. Hop out, we've got to start over." Yema giggled and did as requested. The nun took the basin to the balcony, looking first to make sure no one was underneath, and dumped it over the side. After the second washing, she dried Yema and had her put on some muslin underclothes she'd recently procured from the Indian seamstress.

"What are these?" asked Yema. "They'll be too hot."

"They are special underclothes for church," the nun replied. "You won't be too hot. You can wear your blue shift."

Yema, acting more like a three-year-old, put her arms in the air and held them up until Doçura dropped the dress over her head. "Get your sandals," the nun told her, "and I'll fix your hair." She found her woven grass sandals and pushed her feet into them, then stood patiently while the nun combed her dark hair. Next Doçura took a narrow red-and-blue twisted ribbon and wrapped it over the child's forehead, tucked it behind her ears, and tied it at the back of her head.

The child looked angelic in her blue shift dress with the ribbon across her forehead, the remainder disappearing under her glossy shoulder-length hair. "Now," Doçura said, "I have to show you how to greet our visitors. You've seen how we kiss Bishop Damião's ring from time to time?" The child nodded. "Have you ever done that before?"

"No."

"All right, let's practice." She slipped the silver ring off her left hand and moved it to her right. "Now, the Bishop's ring is larger and on his right hand. So are the rings of our visitors. You kneel like this, and each visitor will extend his hand." Yema did as instructed. "Then you take his hand and kiss the ring." The child smiled and kissed the nun's hand. "That's all there is to it." She moved the ring back to her left hand.

"May I also curtsey? I like that." Yema picked up a brass mirror, turning it one way and another, admiring the nun's handiwork.

"Afterwards you may curtsey. That would be fine." Doçura took a few minutes to change her habit, then went to the balcony and looked to the end of the courtyard at the entrance to the chapel. She saw Agato and the other altar boy standing on either side of the steps. "It appears we should go down. I think they will start serving soon."

The two descended the stairs, Yema leading and excited. Once outside she skipped her way to the chapel and began to tease the boys. They stood impassively, not wishing to abandon their posts. Before Doçura could get there, the *Consilium de populi* emerged from their quarters close by the chapel and greeted the children. Yema immediately knelt, and one-by-one the *Consilium* members extended their right hands, and child kissed their rings. Then she stood and curtseyed. The three clergy laughed heartily. By the time the nun got there a few moments later, priests and child were engaged in animated conversation. As Doçura arrived, they all turned to her.

To her astonishment, it was a smiling Fr. Girona who spoke first. "Dear sister," he said. "This child is schooled so thoroughly in manners and speaking, you are to be congratulated. Her Portuguese is better than mine."

"I would happily take credit for that, Fr. Girona, but it is Fr. Julian who deserves your praise." The nun put an arm around the squirming girl and drew her close. "Yema's speech, manners, and singing are almost as polished as when Fr. Julian brought her here from the Caeté village over six months ago."

Girona continued. "Well then, it is to your credit, dear sister, for nursing her back to health. The doctor has shown us how hard the coryza is on the Indians." He gestured towards the hospital. "Our visit to their sickbeds was quite disturbing. First the typhus, now this deadly coryza. We have prayed that our Lord will ease the natives' anguish. It is sadly remindful of the plagues back home."

Doçura wondered why this inquisitor was so unexpectedly friendly. Her instincts told her to beware. Still, he went on in his pleasant manner, this time addressing Yema with the other clergy looking on. "So am I to understand that little Cantora will participate in our Vespers this evening?"

Yema answered him. "Doctor Cardim said I may sing only the *Glória* tonight. Then more on Sunday if I do not cough."

The three clergy nodded gravely. Doçura wondered if they really believed this little girl could be the fabled Cantora.

Fr. Julian, Bishop Damião, and Dr. Cardim, who had been standing a short distance away enjoying the scene, announced dinner. The group moved toward the chapel entrance. Little Yema instinctively understood her role, paying particular attention to Archbishop da Martina, chatting and walking slowly with him as he labored his way inside. His Eminence seemed to greatly appreciate her attention.

Once everyone was seated, servers from the kitchen brought steaming plates of baked yams sweetened with black syrup, fried manioc, roast bullock on platters heaped with sliced guava, and pots of yerba buena.

Next the servers poured goblets of Rabo de Anho for each diner, and the group prepared for a round of toasts. Bishop Damião led off, again thanking the *Consilium* for their presence, and declaring his appreciation for the special red wine and the bullock, "… things we have not savored for a long while, and all the way from our home in Portugal."

Yema had never tasted bullock before, and found it much to her liking. As for the wine, Cardim seated next to her cautioned, "Drink very little so as not to affect your singing." Despite its sour flavor, the girl found the drink gave her a pleasant feeling, like someone gently lifting the back of her head, a sensation similar to the effects of *pohã,* the potion used by Aunt Janaína to summon spirits of the departed.

As the dinner wore on, Yema became bored. "If it is true that we will have Vespers in the church?" she asked Doçura. "May I wander around the altar here and look at all the holy things? I've never done that before."

"Yes," the nun told her. "Ask those two novices from out front to show you. They're familiar with everything."

Yema slid down from her chair and ran outside before Doçura could finish her sentence. The boys' empty dinner plates lay on the chapel steps. A short distance away the two were catching the small yellow-and-brown lizards that often scurried around the west-facing walls in late afternoon. When a boy caught one, he would throw it at the other. At the moment Yema arrived, each boy had a lizard and was prepared to throw; and at her sight they froze, then quickly recovered. "If you children can behave yourselves," she said, "you've been invited inside to show me—" Her words cut short as she dodged two lizards tossed her way. *"I'm* not inviting you," she continued, "it's the *Consilium.*"

With this news the boys stopped laughing and dusted themselves off. "Why?" they both asked.

"Because they want you to show me around the altar. You two serve Mass and know what all those things are."

Agato, who was quite smitten with Yema, bowed and extended his arm. Rolling his r's like a Spaniard, he said, "I will be happy to show the famous *La Cantora* around."

She brushed his arm away and walked ahead of them up the steps into the chapel. As they approached the front, he considered offering false instructions as a joke, then looked back at the dignitaries and changed his mind. The three stopped in front of the altar. Agato said, "When not part of a service, you must stop before going up the stairs. Boys bow and cross ourselves. Girls kneel and cross themselves."

She did as instructed, then noticed they'd attracted the attention of the adults. "Don't speak Caeté," she told the boys. "Speak Portuguese. They mustn't think we're uncivilized."

As the boys began to point out and explain things, Yema found herself drawn to the Crucifix and the agonized figure of Christ. Though she appeared to be paying attention to the two novices, her gaze kept returning to the Crucifix and the pedestal on which it stood. The pedestal was covered with a white cloth, and she wondered what it looked like underneath. *What does that hide?* she wondered. The white cloth interested her as much as the cross itself. She remembered Aunt Janaína explaining that except for woven grass and leaf mats, cloth had not existed before the Portuguese arrived.

She thought about the supposed mystery of the Catholic faith. *Why would they honor a man killed by some people so long ago? A man not killed in battle?* If Christ were an ancestor, that she could understand. Instead she felt a stronger bond to the mysteries of the Caeté; those beliefs seemed more compelling than what the Catholics believed. Though when her thoughts returned to the beautiful chants of the Mass and the wonderful lute that Fr. Paulo had played, that was magic enough.

Sooner than expected, the gathering finished dinner and called to the children to leave. Outside they found many of the ship's company waiting, including the captain, purser and other officers, along with a compliment of sailors carrying the archbishop's nurse chair and ready to escort everyone to Vespers. As Archbishop da Martina seated himself in his chair, the captain addressed the group. "It is our honor to accompany the *Consilium* on our last evening in the New World. In the morning we sail for Lisbon with a cargo of precious dyewood." He settled his gaze on Yema. "Of course we have come to hear the fabled voice of The Cantora. We also ask the assembled clergy to pray for our safe voyage."

The sun sat low on the western edge of the settlement. A light breeze from the ocean carried the graveyard's sickening odor, and in the approaching twilight one could see the smoke and some flames rising from the place. It appeared that some of the poorly tended funeral biers had caught fire.

As the group set out for the church, an officer approached Doçura. "You are Sister Mãe da Doçura?" he inquired. He held his red officer's cap in both hands, wringing it nervously.

"Yes?"

"I am Arneldo Pãiva, the ship's navigator. I also occasionally serve as the captain's scribe for important documents." His uneasiness continuing, he glanced around. "I must speak with you about a most important matter."

Doçura found herself put off by the man's insistence. "Senhor Pãiva, as you know we are heading to Vespers. This will be the first time the *Consilium* will hear Cantora. Could this wait until after the service?"

"Dear sister, the ship's company will return to our vessel immediately following Vespers to prepare for our voyage. We leave tomorrow, and many days late. With the Indians refusing to work and all the sickness, we—"

"Alright," she said impatiently, "tell me now while we walk."

As they moved towards the abbey gate he glanced at Yema who was holding Doçura's hand. "Dear sister, this matter is urgent and *very* private." The man suddenly appeared terrified. "Please!"

Doçura squeezed Yema's hand and pointed ahead of them. "Go walk with Fr. Julian. I'll be along soon. Right behind you." She turned to Pãiva. "Now what could be so important at a time like this?"

"Sister Mãe, you received a letter from the Turkish Ottoman when our ship arrived? A letter from your parents?"

She felt a sudden panic. "Yes. From the purser. What about it?"

"I was asked to translate the letter into Spanish."

Doçura's blood turned cold, and she found it hard to breath, nearly stumbling at that moment. The officer seized her elbow to keep her from falling. "You read Hebrew?" she wheezed.

"Yes, yes. I am a *Converso*. Just as you."

"Who requested that?"

"The captain. He—"

"Why? I don't understand."

The man slowed his pace to keep them well behind the rest of the group. "The purser, who is a religious zealot and suspicious of everything, found the letter in the mail pouch and gave it to the inquisitor Juan Girona. He in turn gave it to the captain asking if anyone on board could translate it."

Doçura continued her troubled breathing. She stopped to catch her breath, put her head down and pushed her hands against her knees. "Go on."

"The captain and I have sailed together for many years. He was protecting me and refused to tell Girona who made the translation."

Anger began mixing with fear. She quickened her pace so they would not arrive at the church too far behind the others. "Girona could not denounce you just because you are a *Converso* and read Hebrew?" she said. "Not on a Crown vessel. He's a Spaniard. And our guest."

"Don't be so sure. His zeal for inquisition knows no bounds. Many times on our voyage here he drank all night with the crew, then slept through the day. I'm certain he recruited a number of crewmen to his cause. *Believe me*, even the other two *populi* fear him. Since the Crown's religious alliance with Spain, Girona's malevolence permeates Portugal as well."

By now they were only a short distance from the church. The dignitaries were seating themselves inside, and she saw Yema standing with Julian by the entrance waiting for her.

Arneldo Pãiva continued. "You notice the inquisitor does

most of the talking. They defer every discussion to him. It was that way on the ship, and I see it here also."

Doçura thought back to when Juan Girona used the word *marrano* at their first meeting. At the same time she saw Fr. Julian summon a soldier and point her way. The soldier took a torch from a stand beside the door and headed for them through the crowd of Indians seated outside the church. "They want me to go inside," she told Pãiva.

"Be warned, dear sister. Given the opportunity, Girona will use your parents' letter against you." Then he whispered, *"Sholom aleichem,"* and stepped away.

She'd not heard this beloved Hebrew salutation in years, the last time from her dying brother Marcel. She whispered after Pãiva, *"Aleikhem shalom,"* and hurried into the church, her heart pounding so hard she could feel the blood rushing in her ears.

Chapter 8

For Sister Doçura, the first part of Vespers became a blur as she fought against the fear that threatened to overwhelm her, responding mechanically to each ritual exercise until Yema walked onto the dais.

The child's voice sounded angelic when she sang the *Glória,* seeming more resonant than ever, carrying with it a slight hoarseness from the coryza and providing the subtle quality of lamentation.

Yema's impact on the *Consilium* was immediate. Archbishop da Martina serving *Trinitas duo,* weakened and lost his balance. He sat down in a nearby altar chair gripping his canes in one hand, his forehead with the other. Fr. Juan Girona, serving *tres,* appeared dumbstruck. Bishop Boeyens who was leading Vespers, paused as Yema finished the sacred chant and returned to her bench—Paused so long it appeared he'd forgotten the Mass, finally stammering the continuing phrase, *"Dominus Vobiscum..."*

When the girl seated herself next to Doçura, she took the nun's hand. It startled Doçura from her thoughts as she began to consider the *Glória's* effect on the *Consilium.* Surely Inquisitor Girona would maintain his appreciation of The Cantora and hopefully her role in guiding the child. Indeed that was the case. Following Vespers, the first to congratulate Yema and Doçura was Girona. Even Boeyens, not given to much conversation because of his limited

Portuguese, heaped praise on them all. The nun's fear lessened as the group returned to the abbey, the visiting priests looking forward to Sunday Mass two days hence, eager to convene the *Consilium de Virtutibus* and consider the prospect of a sanctified miracle.

When they arrived at the abbey, everyone congregated in the chapel, returning to the dining table and sharing toasts from a keg of spirits given to them by the ship's captain. Doctor Cardim poured a cup for Cantora. "Sip this slowly," he said. "It will soothe your throat and help you to sleep." Indeed that was so. Within minutes Yema was asleep, her head resting in Doçura's lap. The nun carried the child upstairs, put her to bed, and returned to the chapel.

It was Archbishop da Martina who greeted her first. The strong drink had enlivened the old man. "Dearest Sister Doçura," he said, "we are most astounded at what we heard this evening. Although none of us understand how a mere child can sing with a mature woman's voice." He acknowledged her by raising his cup, then continued. "Doctor Cardim tells us he thinks Cantora can sing both the People's *Confiteor* and the *Glória* on Sunday. Do you agree?"

"I think so," she answered. "Let's see how she feels tomorrow."

"With that possibility," the archbishop continued, "we intend to convene the *Consilium* Sunday afternoon." He crossed himself. "And if we conclude this child and her divine voice are true miracles, then we request that you and Bishop Damião consider the possibility of her returning to Rome with us when we present our findings to the Holy Father. Presenting a living miracle would be most unusual, perhaps the first in Cristian history."

The suggestion caught Doçura by surprise. "I've never considered such a possibility," she said. "I assume you would want me to go with her. Perhaps her parents and little brother also?"

"Yes, of course. Her family if necessary. I would like to meet them."

She looked to Bishop Damião and Fr. Julian before she continued. "Isn't there the possibility of a serious controversy here? A dangerous precedent, a female singing in church? That could be an *iurgium maior.* The child would be caught up in it."

Juan Girona answered. "Oh yes. We've considered that. Remember we came knowing the child was a female. If we declare a divine miracle, then it is God's judgment and it must be considered."

Doçura wondered if it was the drink's influence that brought them to this dangerous subject. Did they propose this because they had not considered it thoroughly, or because they were testing her in some way? The *Consilium* could order her and the girl to Rome if they wished, and she would have to comply. Doçura knew if the petition was denied or fell under suspicion, there could be accusations of witchery, even heresy for questioning Papal doctrine. Finally she said, "May I suggest we put this off? Perhaps after Sunday and the results of your deliberation?"

***

At the Caeté village Janaína announced her plans to the tribe. They would set out to find some whites, kill them, and have the tribe feast on their hearts, brains, and limbs, just as they had done for generations with their native enemies. But this time, rather than bringing them back alive and fattening the captives before killing them, they would eat the whites immediately, thus acquiring the spirit that protected the foreigners from the coughing sickness. The other part of her plan was to return Yema to her tribe and end the Christian nonsense. For this she recruited Jégeuro, the child's father. Impatient with his daughter being absent for so long, he eagerly accepted.

When they left the next morning, she told him, "Bring what weapons you need. I bring only my knife and cape. The jaguar will keep me invincible."

After a day's travel and their arrival on the north bank of the Rio Jacu, they spotted two settlement soldiers wading in their direction. The Caeté stepped into the jungle and waited. The soldiers carried muskets along with chains and neck collars. Janaína assumed they were chasing runaway slaves. They let the men pass on the trail, then stepped behind them, their sounds drowned out by gusts of wind preceding an oncoming storm. Yema's father raised his blowpipe and felled one of the soldiers instantly, the man falling so his comrade saw the red dart protruding between the man's shoulder blades. Janaína shouted, "I will kill this one," and charged the man with her knife. He raised his musket and shot point-blank, then reached for his companion's musket. Before he could lift it to fire, Jégeuro hit him with a second dart, causing the man to fall to the jungle floor.

At that moment the storm broke with bursts of thunder and a torrent of rain. Both soldiers were nearly paralyzed and fighting for breath, their bodies writhing in the muddy leaf litter. In the ceremonial way and with a single motion, Jégeuro seized each by the hair, put one foot on the man's chest, pulled the head to one side, and cut their throats, nearly severing the heads.

He raced back to Janaína, shocked to see that she was dead. Kneeling and sobbing, he pulled the bloody cape from beneath her body and buried his face in it. The Caeté had no word for vengeance, so he used the Portuguese, *"Vingança."* He stood and shook his fist in the direction of the settlement, the rain running down his face and body. *"Vingança!"*

Jégeuro knew he must rescue his daughter before the killings were discovered. He dragged the bodies into the jungle and covered the two soldiers, then pulled Janaína's body a short distance away, and covered it as well. Then he struck out for the settlement. After a night in the forest, chanting and praying and chewing shards of *pohã* bark, he emerged from the trail at the hour of Sunday Mass. He carried Janaína's cape rolled under one arm. Jégeuro waited until the path to the church looked clear of people. In the distance behind the hospital, a grim sight greeted him. More than a dozen funeral biers smoked into the morning air at one end of the cemetery. He could not recall ever seeing a bier in the settlement. Perhaps the Portuguese permitted this to ease the Indians' concern about the new coryza. There were obviously too many dead for the biers and grave-diggers. He could see red-hooded vultures feeding among the corpses, ungainly hopping from one body to the next.

As Jégeuro approached the church, few paid him attention. Those who did, acknowledged him with gloomy looks that matched the forbidding landscape around them. He found it unusual that so many people—all of them natives—crowded around the church, yet it was fairly vacant inside. It was not immediately evident to him that the crowd was there to hear Cantora, and the Indians were clustered outside to avoid contact with the whites. Jégeuro found a space on a bench just behind the Europeans. Four rows ahead of him he spotted his daughter sitting with Doçura, Fr. Julian, and Bishop Damião.

Three unfamiliar priests in fancy garb occupied the pulpit. It surprised him when the second priest, a man who supported himself with two canes, finished his shaky Latin chant and Yema rose to her feet. To her father, his daughter looked transformed into a Christian angel, very much like the winged children in the illustrated scripture that Fr. Julian once showed him. The child ascended the pulpit, faced the congregation and began to sing.

🎵*"Confiteor Deo omnipotenti,*
beatae ..."🎵

Jégeuro intended to stand for only a moment, just to let Yema know he was there. But when he stood, having forgotten the jaguar cape, he dropped it. As he picked it up, the cape unrolled, exposing the bloody pelt. In a state of distress and without thinking, he made the death sign.

Yema paused for an instant, startled. Now she put a hand to her mouth, shocked to see the orange-and-black cape, but without Janaína. Her aunt's not being there meant only one thing. From the age of five, ever since the tribe discovered her gift of song, her aunt had shared the secrets of the netherworld with her. Yema understood she would someday inherit the Caeté's sacred garment and wear the mantle of the tribe's mystic. In this instant her path became clear. She raised both hands to her cheeks, dug her sharpened nails into the flesh and raked four bloody lines down each side. Then Yema began to sing anew, now in her native tongue, voice shrill and eyes blazing, her small hands making signs in the air, the blood visible on her fingers and streaming down her cheeks.

🎵*"Ixé téra Yemanjá, Tembireko pupé Paranã!*
Ixé 'am pu 'ã japete
Me 'ẽ paraguasu tata ... "

The moment Yema paused, everyone knew something was wrong. Doçura looked to the rear, but by then Jégeuro had sat down, dropped the cape to the floor and bent low, burying his face from view. She turned back. The Caeté words suddenly registered. She could not believe what she'd heard. "I am Yemanjá the Sea God. I will strike you down. Turn the waters to fire."

Jégeuro fled to the back of the church and motioned for his daughter to follow. He held the open cape above his head. The Indians jumped to their feet and began to shriek, some in Caeté, others in Portuguese. "Eat the whites!" The chant repeated by the larger throng outside. Bishop Damião rushed onto the dais and pleaded for silence. Everyone ignored him. Yema ran through the screaming crowd to her father. The many Portuguese in attendance, sitting mainly on the front benches, crowded fearfully onto the platform with the clergy. Someone knocked Archbishop da Martina off his feet. He clattered to the floor along with his canes. The

Europeans who ran from the church immediately found themselves assaulted by the Indians.

The twenty or so soldiers attending the service and those stationed by the doors took action with their lances and swords. Though none carried muskets, they quickly drove the Indians away. The few natives armed with knives attacked the soldiers, but they were no match for the steel weapons and were soon cut down. Yema and her father ran from the church toward the abbey and the jungle beyond. After a short distance, the girl was unable to keep up, so Jégeuro threw her over his shoulder and continued running. He gasped out the story of Janaína's death and his killing the two soldiers. He felt his daughter sobbing, tears mixed with blood from her face, staining his chest and arm.

A soldier whose horse was tethered near the church took chase. He caught up and ordered Jégeuro to stop. When he did not, the soldier grabbed Yema by one foot and hoisted the child out of her father's grasp, then dropped her onto the ground. He again came even with Jégeuro and killed him with a single thrust of his lance. After dismounting, he caught the sobbing Yema, got back on his horse and forced the child face down across his saddle. The soldier galloped in the direction of the garrison.

In the midst of the turmoil, Doçura rushed onto the dais to help the archbishop struggling under the crush of people. Pushing her way through, she met the fierce eyes of the inquisitor Girona. *"Marrano!"* he said, "You are the agent of this blasphemous child and will pay with your life."

She ignored him and reached to help da Martina. He glared up at her with the same hatred. "Leave me," he wheezed. "I would rather be trampled than helped by a cursed nun who has schooled a heathen witch."

Doçura handed the canes to Fr. Julian who helped the archbishop to his feet. Rising to the nun's defense Julian shouted, "The child was startled to see her father. She simply completed the *Confiteor* in her native tongue."

"Nonsense!" Girona shouted back. "Someone already told me what she said." He gave Julian a malevolent stare. "If you wish to further this fraud, Julian, we can certainly include you in our holy inquest. I intend to convene a tribunal to expunge this sacrilege."

By now the chaos had lessened as the remaining Indians were

driven from the church. Many of the Europeans left the platform and either sat exhausted on the front pews, or crowded to the entrances, watching the natives as they retreated into the settlement. Girona summoned two soldiers. He pointed to Doçura. "Take this purveyor of heresy to the garrison and put her in chains." The soldiers hesitated. The sister was much loved by nearly everyone in the community.

At this moment Bishop Damião attempted to intervene. "Let us not be so hasty," he said. "We need not rush to judgment."

Hearing this the soldiers stepped back, now joined by the Captain of the Guard. In a loud voice the captain announced, "The child is captured and the father killed. We have confiscated the blood woman's jaguar skin and are moving to restore order."

Girona addressed the nearest soldier. "Give me your lance," he demanded. The man hesitated for a moment, then handed it over. The inquisitor seized the opportunity to fully take control, turning the lance and pushing the butt end into the captain's chest. "In the name of the Holy Inquisition," Girona said, "arrest this woman and put her in chains." He turned on the rest of the group, leveling his gaze at Bishop Damião and Fr. Julian. "Anyone who supports this blasphemer is also suspect and will stand trial." Next he addressed the Dutch priest. "Bishop Boeyens, you are the senior cleric here. Should this woman stand trial?" When the bishop hesitated, the inquisitor continued in a most demanding way. "Adrian Boeyens, you are the *Pope's representative*. We did not come around half a world to listen to the voice of Satan. I ask you to head the tribunal as *Inquisitio Consilii*. I will be the chief prosecutor."

Boeyens nodded gravely. "Put her in chains," he said to the soldiers. They seized Doçura and led her away. Bishop Damião motioned to Fr. Julian. The two left the church and walked back toward the abbey. They turned to see Sister Mãe da Doçura being prodded at lance point in the direction of the garrison. At the same moment a series of commotions in the settlement demanded their attention. Not far away, groups of Indians were fighting with small knots of soldiers, the latter greatly outnumbered. Here and there native huts began to erupt into flames, figures running from dwelling to dwelling, setting them afire.

The two men hurried towards the abbey. Bishop Damião spoke first. He had tears in his eyes. "I am ruined as bishop. After this

I am sure the Church will replace me. This is tragic. Our settlement is being destroyed."

Julian put his arm around his bishop's shoulder, something he'd never done before. "We have been through so much together, sir. If we are to fail, then I will fail with you. We must save Doçura and little Yema."

"But my God, what she said. And in the *Confiteor Deo*. That damnable Caeté monkey talk. Who would have thought?"

"Girona is intentionally plotting against Sister Mãe. Do you know he has a copy of a letter she received from her parents in the Ottoman? Apparently the letter was in Hebrew."

"Someone translated it?"

"Yes. Arneldo Pãiva, the navigator on the ship that brought the *Consilium*. He's a *Converso* and they forced him to translate it."

"Something blasphemous in it?"

"I don't think so. But the fact it's in Hebrew is—"

"Nonsense. Everyone knows Doçura is a *Conversa*. On São Tomé she translated the Saulo Chronicle for Bishop Cão. That was in Hebrew."

"Sir, you were an inquisitor. I understand this new inquisition in Spain suspects all *Conversos*. You must know how Girona thinks."

"Unfortunately I do. All the same, I've come to greatly admire Sister Mãe. We must do something." Neither said anything about Yema. Both knew she was doomed.

Just before they reached the abbey gates a Caeté woman ran up to them, a dead child in her arms, a likely victim of the coryza. "Eat the whites," she hissed in her broken Portuguese, her teeth remarkably white against her taught lips and dark skin, her face a mask of anguish. Bishop Damião made the sign of the cross and reached to touch the child. The woman recoiled and began shouting curses.

Nearing the courtyard, the bishop's dog came running to greet them, someone having freed him from Damião's office. The bishop shrugged and picked him up. They kept walking, the safety of the abbey a few yards distant, both men feeling very alone.

Chapter 9

Once at the garrison, the two soldiers with Doçura in tow paused. The gates stood open and the confusion of people inside appeared near riot. At one side of the large enclosure lay a dozen black slaves face-down in the dirt, their feet shackled to one another and collars around their necks. Several untethered slaves lay on the ground next to the group. Three soldiers struggled to attach and extend the chains to those not manacled. Two other soldiers, panic evident on their faces, stood guard with muskets ready. At the far side of the garrison, against the high timber barricade that made up the outside perimeter, a group of fifty or so Indians—men, women, and a few children—a number of them grievously wounded, sat on the ground screaming epithets at the soldiers standing guard. Doçura looked for Yema but did not see her.

More captives rounded up from around the settlement were streaming into the garrison prodded by soldiers and Portuguese and Spanish seamen pressed into service. From shouted fragments, Doçura heard accusations blaming the Africans for torching the native huts. The chaos in the settlement had become a full-fledged revolt, the disparate groups fighting the garrison troops and each other. Doçura's captors still did not know what to do with her. Confused, they looked around.

Gesturing to the natives against the timbers on the far side, the nun said, "Take me over there. I'll tend to the wounded. You go restore order." Relieved, both soldiers pointed in the direction and abandoned her. Doçura saw several individuals she knew and greeted them, then waded into the group, sorting out the wounded and directing some women to help her. She tore strips of fabric from her habit, handing pieces around, encouraging everyone to assist those most injured.

"Has anyone seen Yema?" she asked. None had. She wondered if the child lay dead somewhere. She eyed the piles of bodies inside the garrison. *The child is alive,* she told herself. *Do not think otherwise.*

Doçura worked feverishly for some time when suddenly those around her turned silent. A shadow loomed over her. She looked up to see Girona and the garrison captain. The priest looked fearsome, now wearing his inquisitor's garb, a full length black cloak with a high collar and red-fox lapels. A thick gold chain bearing a jeweled silver cross encircled the priest's neck, the cross pinned to the left side, over the heart. Despite the heat of the day and his heavy clothing, he appeared unaffected.

"Why is this woman not chained?" he demanded. "Instead I find her consorting with these natives?"

"I am doing God's work. Helping the wounded," she said.

Girona glared at the captain. "A heretic cannot do God's work. I want her locked up."

The captain hesitated. He admired Doçura for her good works around the settlement. Reaching for her hand, he intended to help her up. "Sister, please come with me."

To the shock of everyone, Girona pushed him aside and jerked the nun to her feet, then shoved her at the captain. "Hear me, captain! No 'sister.' No 'please'! This woman is a heretic, a blasphemer. She will be treated as such." With these words he stalked away, heading for the garrison gate.

Doçura brushed at her arm, curious to see the inquisitor stop and talk with two soldiers guarding a group of prisoners, one of them a large brutish man whom she'd noticed before. She found it even more curious when the two bowed and crossed themselves as Girona left.

"I am sorry, Sister Doçura," the captain said. "A woman should never be treated in such a—"

"Where is Yema?" she asked. "That's my only concern."

The man shook his head. "We don't know. The soldier who captured her is dead, killed before he could deliver the child here. His horse is missing, and we suspect the Africans." He paused. "You know the soldier killed Yema's father?"

"Yes I know. It's a terrible thing."

"They were fugitives," the captain said, "and had to be stopped. Still it's a shame." After a moment of thought, he nodded in the direction of the garrison's living area, a cluster of grass *ógas*. "I've no idea where to house you. I'll find a vacant hut, but we do not have any facilities here for white women."

"Put me with the whores," she said. "I know most of them."

The captain shook his head, then gestured to a sergeant who stood nearby. "Take Sister Doçura to her quarters in the abbey. Post a guard and allow no one to enter. If the inquisitor-priest shows up, send him to me."

***

Fr. Girona walked directly to the abbey from the garrison and summoned his fellow *populi*. They agreed to meet in the chapel, first closing the outside door and looking around to make sure no one else remained in the sanctuary. The two younger priests assisted Archbishop da Martina to the front and helped seat him at the communion table. Bishop Boeyens took the seat next to him, while Girona sat across from the two.

The inquisitor cleared his throat and began. "My esteemed servants in Christ. I have come to this accursed colony prepared for the sort of deviltry we saw at Mass this morning." The two others gave him puzzled looks. "Oh gentlemen, I have never underestimated the Devil's cleverness in his efforts to deceive and misguide us. It is my sincere belief that he rules this place." He waited a moment for his words to sink in, then excused himself to the rear of the sanctuary where the wine and spirits from the previous Friday remained stored in an ornate chest. "Now," he said in a loud voice, "I must briefly digress before I return to the sacrilege at hand."

He brought three clay goblets, a bottle of wine, and the nearly empty cask of spirits from the back and set them in front of the clergy. Before continuing, he poured each of them a drink, wine for Boeyens and da Martina, and a mixture of wine and spirits for himself. "As I said," Girona went on, "I have come prepared. Thus *we* have come prepared." He took a drink from the goblet, the black fines from the wine speckling his teeth and lips. "The ship that brought us to this hellish place will return in a week or so to transport our prisoners and take us back to our homes in Europe."

"How can that be?" Boeyens asked. "And what prisoners?"

"As much as that Captain Torres dislikes me," Girona said, "he will do my bidding. The Church financed his voyage here, and his cargo will make him rich back home. He merely sailed down the coast a ways to Fortaleza to take on more dyewood. The paucity of labor and supply here made it impossible for him to fill the ship's hold." He poured more spirits into his goblet and continued. "Ten of the ship's crew now pledge their loyalty to me. They stayed behind and are currently taking measures as I have directed."

Girona was suddenly distracted by a commotion outside the chapel. He went to the door and swung it open. He could see four of his men leading Bishop Damião and Fr. Julian away, their hands bound, blindfolds over their eyes, the bishop's dog yapping at their heels. "Fr. Boeyens," he called, "come see this."

Boeyens came to the door and looked out. "This is indeed extraordinary," he said.

Girona took his arm and pulled the door shut. He led the bishop back to the table where da Martina was seated. "Please tell the archbishop what you just saw."

Boeyens did so, concluding with, "Based on what we saw at Mass this morning, I concur with these arrests."

Archbishop da Martina nodded in agreement and said, "How can we keep them arrested? They have the garrison captain's loyalty. And in a way we are Bishop Damião's guests. Although I am his superior."

"Indeed true," said Girona. He drained his goblet and poured more wine for himself and his companions. "Seeing these two men arrested means the garrison captain is now also in chains or dead, and my men have taken over." He extended his hand to the archbishop. "You, sir, are now in charge of this colony." Since da Martina said nothing, Girona continued, "May I summarize what I think our actions should be?"

The Lisbon archbishop seemed befuddled. Finally he said, "I know what we need to do, Fr. Girona. Give me a minute to collect my thoughts." He excused himself and hobbled up the aisle. "I need to visit the privy."

Boeyens rushed forward and propped the outside door open, then returned to the communion table. "We are likely of the same mind," he told Girona, "but tell me how you think we should proceed."

The inquisitor laid out his plans. This was the moment he'd most looked forward to, yet wishing he had a larger audience, but that would come soon enough when they returned to Europe. "The Holy Curia stipulates that clergy accused of profanation must be tried by fellow clergy. Thus Damião and Julian must be returned to Portugal. That will leave no priest here except Fr. Spadaro who is useless at the moment. I suggest we elevate the assistant to that dead priest Paulo, and give him a provisional position. He seems competent enough to conduct Mass and serve until we can send a replacement or two."

"And Doçura and the child?"

"With the archbishop's approval, I suggest the following. Having seen the evidence for ourselves, we need not convene a tribunal. Further, there are no mitigations to consider. The crimes are evident and clear. If we can agree, and I think we can, I propose the nun be hanged and the child burned. She is too small to hang effectively, and I want to make sure nothing of her remains."

By now Archbishop da Martina had returned, moving slowly down the aisle towards them. Boeyens rose and assisted the old man to his seat, then outlined Girona's proposal.

Da Martina considered for a moment. "I concur. Except why should we not also burn the woman?"

Girona answered. "The nun suffers from *corrupto de sangre.*" He translated for Boeyens, "Corruption of the blood. She should not receive the cleansing benefit of fire, but must die with the corruption inside her. For our Holy Inquisition in Spain, this has become our customary method of dealing with *Conversos.* "

They agreed the plan was sound, but when they returned to Lisbon, there would be other difficulties. Archbishop da Martina's personal judgment would come under question, and because the supposed miracle had turned out to be a fraud, he would be burdened with defending the three of them.

The archbishop said what they all had been thinking. "We cannot arrive in Portugal without something to show for our journey. The potential embarrassment requires a remedy. I believe that prosecuting Damião and Fr. Julian there will provide that remedy." He grew quiet, pondering his next thought. At last he said, "As far as what we do on these shores, disposing of the cantora child here is the logical choice. If by any chance she was heard to sing back home, that could change everything."

***

Doçura spent two days in her room without visitors except for Agato who brought her meals and emptied the chamber pot. Though her door was unlocked, a guard remained there day and night. Each time she asked Agato about Yema or any news, he said he knew nothing other than the rebellion was still going on. That she could see from her window.

On Tuesday Doçura asked, "What about Bishop Damião and Farther Julian?" She had at least expected them to visit.

"I've not seen them since Sunday," he said. "After the riot, I ran home from the Mass and hid in the kitchen."

"But what about Sincera or Dr. Cardim?"

The boy shrugged. "They've tried to come see you," he said. "But there's a guard at the bottom of the stairs too. No one is allowed up here except me."

"And your parents?"

"Sincera said they left for our village as soon as the riot started. They were afraid to look for me." Tears welled in his eyes. "Sincera said she is going to leave too. Soon. But I promise I will stay."

At that moment the guard opened the door and poked his head in, directing his words at Agato. "Enough talk. Leave."

The nun's and the little boy's eyes met. In one way or another, their daily talks always ended like this. Agato gave her a hurried smile, said, "I'm sorry, Sister Doçura," and left.

The next morning, the light just coming up in the sky, and awakened by the bell announcing Lauds, Doçura went to the balcony curious to see who would be in attendance. She spotted the three *Consilium* at the same moment they saw her. Inquisitor Girona held a parchment rolled under his arm. Upon seeing Doçura, he unrolled the single page, holding it in her direction. He said something, but he was too far away, and she could not hear him clearly. She went to her desk and drank a cold cup of yerba buena left from the day before. Suddenly she knew what Girona had said and the nature of the parchment. It was a warrant for her execution. *No trial,* she thought. Somehow, ever since she had seen the inquisitor at the garrison on Sunday, this was what she suspected would happen. "For the love of Christ's charity," she said aloud, "and for all the Jews condemned back home, I will kill that man if I get the chance. Then my death will have some meaning."

She watched the few souls leave Lauds; and as she did every day, looked without result for Fr. Julian and Bishop Damião. The last to exit the building were the three *populi*. They conferred briefly, then looked her way. Archbishop da Martina hobbled in the direction of his quarters, and the other two headed for the stairs. Doçura pressed a hand against the dagger hidden under her wool belt. She felt the handle against her skin, knowing this might be her only chance to kill Girona, briefly wondering about Yema and remembering how the child had carefully sharpened the edges of the dagger.

Was it something the inquisitor had seen in her that brief moment this morning before Lauds, or a thing he'd planned all along? She didn't know, and it made no difference. In a few moments the men barged into her room, the two *populi* accompanied by the brutish man she'd seen before at the garrison.

Girona, without a greeting of any kind, said in an even voice, "This is Diego. He is now captain of the garrison. He will be your hangman." He unrolled the parchment and handed it to him.

Doçura realized there would be no opening to stab Girona. Perhaps if she could get the other two to leave?

Diego looked over the parchment and shrugged. "I cannot read," he said in Spanish, *"No puedo leer,"* and handed it back to Girona.

The inquisitor, appearing to have known this from the start, took the document and smiled. He stood very erect and began to read slowly, pausing after each sentence. "By order of the Holy Inquisition: At dawn, Friday April sixteen, Year of Our Lord fifteen-hundred-and-seven, the Conversa, Sister Mãe Doçura, known also as Leah Anna Saulo, will be put to death by hanging. At the same hour, her ward, the child devil known as Yema will be—"

"You found her?" Doçura asked. "You found Yema?"

Girona did not answer, instead he paused, wishing he had his torture apparatus from Castile. *How dare a woman, a corrupt marrana, interrupt an Inquisitor? This woman cannot die soon enough.* He glanced at Boeyens, then resumed reading. "At the same hour, her ward, the child devil known as Yema will be cleansed by fire and die at the stake." He rolled the parchment and placed it under his arm. "May God have mercy on your souls," he said and walked out. The other two followed, the guard pulling the door shut as they left.

Doçura's heart soared. Yema was alive! That's all that mattered.

***

That evening she was alarmed by Agato's appearance. One side of his face was covered with a red bruise and his eyes were swollen. He'd been crying. When she asked what happened, he did not answer, just set her tray of food down and backed toward the door. "I must get your yerba buena," he said as he left. When the boy returned, he appeared to trip, the earthen pot smashing to bits on the floor.

The guard looked in, the door grinding against the broken pottery. "Clean that up," he said, and pulled the door shut. Agato knelt and began gathering the shards of clay. Doçura joined him. "They have Yema," he whispered. "In a cell below the abbey. I'm bringing her food. The guard kicked me when I tried to talk to her."

"Did she say anything?" the nun asked. "Is she all right?"

"I don't know. There's only one opening just above the floor. I can't see her. She took her food yesterday but said nothing. Today she did not take her food. It just fell inside." He began to cry again.

By now they had gathered up the pieces and dumped them into the chamber pot. "Go empty this," the nun said. "I'll dry the floor."

When he returned, the guard followed him inside the room, suspicious of all the activity. Doçura spoke in Caeté. "Agato, they will kill us Friday before dawn. We have only tomorrow. You are a brave boy. You must save Yema."

"Sincera might help," he said. "She is still—" The guard seized Agato up by the hair and threw him into the hallway, then reached back and slammed the door.

***

Yema sat on the cold floor of the cell, shivering. The cuts on her face were throbbing, and her neck and face were hot to the touch. The day before she had felt much better, her wounds not so painful. Now she was sick as ever. The Africans—the same ones that killed the soldier who had first captured Yema—held the girl for what ransom they might get. They'd treated her wounds with salt water and the same herb that Dr. Cardim had used for the coryza. Without constant washing, the cuts again became infected. Early the previous morning, the militia had raided the *óga* where she was held, killed all the adults, and set the hut ablaze, leaving the children screaming for help.

In her delirium Aunt Janaína came to her, describing the heaven she would inhabit. "You will be free to roam," she said. "Queen of the forest." Yema stroked her arm and felt the coarse hair of the jaguar. "Day or night you may wander the forest, sleep where you may, sun where you may, and all the animals will honor you. The Caeté do not live here, nor does any man."

Yema knew what she must do to prepare for death. In the pitch black she felt about the floor, finding a bone or two, the clay bowl from yesterday's meal, piles and lumps of smelly filth. Then she found it, a smooth stone the size of a guava fruit. She held the stone against her body, rocking back and forth, reciting what her aunt had told her. *"Ché porãite mano."* "I welcome death." *"Che ñiã kuimbe itá."* "My heart becomes stone." *Death is so common,* she thought. *I've seen so much of it. This past year has been about singing, but it has also been about death.* She tried to sing a few notes, but could not.

Yema remembered asking Janaína, "Will I be able to sing in Heaven?"

Her aunt had considered the question for some time, then put a hand on either side of the child's temples, her fingers covering the cat lines she herself had etched there, recalling when she did so, the two of them drunk and hallucinating on *pohã,* conversing with ancestors long passed. She gently pressed the skin back, drawing Yema's eyes open and unfocused. "I see the jaguar in there my beautiful niece, but I don't know if she can sing." She let go the child's face and tickled her chin. "As you often do little niece, you've asked me a very puzzling question. I will give it much thought."

Yema rolled over onto the stone floor, the cold providing some comfort against her painful flesh. She saw her father, mortally wounded and crying out for her. She could not recall what animal he was now in death, but she would meet him soon. Then Yema clearly saw all the dead from her village, her uncle and so many others. "They are somewhere in the afterlife forest," she mumbled. "At peace. Away from people and all their cruelty."

Part II

Chapter 10

I've spent nearly a week imprisoned in my room. Except for Agato who brings food, I have seen no one but the guard stationed outside my door. Bishop Damião and Fr. Julian must have been arrested; the last time I saw them was Sunday. Earlier in the week I gave Agato a note for them, but he says neither clergy can be found. Maybe Dr. Cardim has also been arrested. The boy's not seen him either. Now it's Thursday, the hour of Vespers passed, and Agato has still not appeared. A new note lays folded on my desk. Coiled inside is half of my precious gold strand, but there is no one to give it to. And Yema and I are to die at dawn tomorrow.

I must do something, anything. I take my supply of water and pour it into the wash basin, then go to the door and pull it open. The guard glares at me. "I'm out of water," I tell him, shoving the pitcher his way. "Have Agato bring me some. And my food too." He grabs the pitcher and disappears down the hall. At this moment I could flee, but there is still the guard at the base of the stairs, so I have nowhere to go.

In a few minutes he returns with my water. "Where's Agato and my dinner?" I ask. The man gives me a grim smile and turns his back. I close my door and go to the balcony. Nothing has changed, the torch atop the gallows, the burning post nearby, a sentry at the courtyard gate. I consider the few scraps from last night's dinner and brush the flies away. So this wretched food will be my last meal, and I will die hungry. On the bed are the white penitent clothes I'm supposed to wear tomorrow. To hell with them. Let Girona hang me in my nun's habit.

I'm thinking about knotting the penitent garb and my bedclothes together to make a rope, climb down to the courtyard. A stupid idea with the guard ever-present at the gate, and another at the stairs. A man would do this, carry a club or a knife and kill them, or die trying. There's my dagger on the desk. If it weren't for the faint hope of saving Yema, I would risk escape, welcome death in failure.

But now the door is thrust open and here is Agato. He leans into the door and closes it. I speak to him in Caeté. He sets my plate of food on the bed. It doesn't look like much, some sliced yams and something else. Handing him the folded paper, I say, "Here's a note for Sincera or—" I'm having trouble thinking. Panic. This is my only chance. "Agato," I say at last, "inside this note is half a gold chain." I pull the handkerchief from my sleeve and show him the other half. "Take the note to Sincera to give to Yema's jailer. The message says he will get the other half when I know Yema is freed."

He is silent for a moment, then finally mutters something, tears running down his cheeks. "Sincera fled back to our village. I'm the only one left."

I push the note at him. "Then *you* give it to the jailer."

"I can't," he says. "He's the man who kicked me."

"Ah Agato," I say, "but gold speaks its own language to thieves." I'm desperate for anything new to tell him, to give this boy a man's courage. I unbutton my collar and lift Yema's shell necklace over my head. "Look here." His eyes grow wide. "This is Yema's." I dangle the ivory shell with its clay-red stripes in front of him. "This will keep you safe. It carries the spirit of Yemanjá."

He takes the necklace and slips it over his head as the guard steps into the room. "Get out," the man says in Spanish, "or you will die with this witch in the morning."

Agato answers, "I must get her yerba buena," and dashes past him. I can hear him running down the hall, his sandals slapping the stone floor.

Over an hour has gone by, and the boy has not returned. Perhaps that's a good sign. I ate my dinner, and despite the tasteless yam slices and a mash of boiled onions, my stomach demanded the food. Now, with nothing else to do, I take my journal and look for a hiding place. Finding none suitable, I put the dagger to use. It's a good thing Yema sharpened the edges. I slice and tear broad strips of cloth from the penitent garment and also from my bedclothes. I'll make a rope and wait another hour or so. Then I'm going over the side into the courtyard. Dagger in hand, I'll take my chances. The guard outside my door is asleep, snoring loudly. He's most likely draped in a chair blocking my doorway because I can see the shadow of what must be chair legs beneath the door. I doubt there's a chance of leaving that way.

***

I must have fallen asleep. For how long I don't know, but I'm awakened by a thumping outside my balcony. My God, there is Agato standing by himself on the gallows platform, the ladder used in construction tilted against my balcony wall. Immediately I signal him and rush inside. I wrap a wide strip of the penitent material twice around my waist and shove my dagger into it—a good use for this offensive cloth. Back on the balcony, I raise the skirt of my habit and climb over the side. It seems impossible to me that Agato could have moved this heavy ladder.

My question is answered the moment I step onto the gallows platform. There is only a sliver of moon, and the gallows torch lies on the ground, sputtering a weak flame. In the poor light, I see a man step from below with Yema under his arm. He's carrying her as one would a sack of maize. He sets the girl next to Agato who steadies her upright. It's obvious she's unable to walk. I climb down and join them.

"Where is my gold?" the man says.

"Carry the child outside the gate and strap her onto my back. Then you'll get your gold."

Yema makes a noise and points at the burning stake. I don't understand her words, nor can I see what she's pointing to. But Agato does. As we move towards the courtyard entrance he catches up. He has the jaguar cape. "She wants this," he says. *How strange,* I think, since earlier in the day I'd not noticed it by the burning stake. Perhaps Girona put it there after Vespers.

"What is your name?" I ask the man. "I want to thank you."

He just grunts.

"You must be the jailer?"

"Yes," he says.

"Where is the sentry by the gate? And the one by the stairs?"

"I found women to keep them occupied," he tells me. Now we are outside the abbey walls. He puts out his hand. "Give me the gold chain."

I unwind the cloth around my middle; my dagger falls to the ground. Agato whispers he'll pick it up, and does so. "Put the child against my back," I tell the man. "Strap her on with this cloth." She is filthy and has obviously soiled herself, but I don't care. Despite the circumstance, I've never felt so joyous—We are escaping with this precious child. Now I feel Yema's arms around my neck, her face against my shoulder. Even through the fabric of my habit her flesh feels remarkably hot. She's burning up. I ask the man, "What will you do? You helped us escape. They will hunt you down."

He steps in front of me, very close to my face. He smells of drink, and in an angry voice he says, "With your gold, blasphemer, I will pay someone to hide—"

Yema pushes hard with her legs, tipping me forward against the man. She lets go of my neck and grabs the jailer's shirt with both hands. "Go with us," she sobs. "You saved us."

He reaches up to dislodge her. "I want my gold, you heathen—" He gasps and falls back. With both hands, Agato has driven the dagger deep into the man's side. Yema's arms are again around my neck as I watch the jailer writhe on the ground. I'm stunned to see him reach out, grab Agato by the leg, and pull him forward. The boy comes easily, falling to his knees. As he does, he uses his weight to plunge the dagger into the man's throat. The jailer gurgles blood and goes silent.

"Here," Agato says, and hands me the dagger. I let the knife drop to the ground, afraid to touch it. Without hesitation he searches the man's clothing, quickly coming up with the gold chain. He gives me the strand, picks up the dagger, and wipes the blood onto the man's shirt. "Come on," he hisses. "I know the way."

In just a few minutes we are in the jungle. So far we've traveled the same path that everyone takes when heading north to the Rio Jacu and the Caeté village, but once inside the forest, I feel lost. I call out to Agato who is running ahead. "Do you know where we're going?" I ask. "I've traveled here only once. Quite some time ago."

Yema answers for him. "He knows the way."

"How are you feeling?" I ask. I've no thought of putting her down. She feels light as a feather, and we're making fast progress.

She hugs me hard. "I feel terrible, but I think I can walk. You saved us."

"Agato saved us," I say, a little out of breath. "Stay on my back. You can walk later, and I can take a look at your face then." A thousand questions race through my mind. But I ask the one that still leaves me in shock. "How could Agato kill that jailer?"

"He is the fellow that kicked Agato."

"I know all that. Still, a boy killing a grown man? A large and dangerous man?"

As we trot along the jungle path, Yema tells me a horrific story. How the children of the Caeté village watched the adults kill their captives. How they dismembered and gutted them. How they roasted human flesh over their fires and feasted afterwards. And then the frenzy of a pohã-crazed celebration. All of this she tells me as casually as one recites a school lesson. Finally she says, "Will they come looking for us?"

I tell her I think so, and the village is the first place they'll look. "But we need help," I continue, "so that's where we're going." She mumbles something about her mother and brother, then slowly goes limp. She's still burning up, and I'm thankful that she is sleeping. Agato has slowed down and is directly in front of us. Finally we come to the clearing where almost a year ago I marveled at the giant fig tree. "I've got to rest," I tell him.

He holds Yema while I untie the cinch around my middle. She slides to the ground and we both kneel next to her. I run my fingers over the scars on her cheek. They feel hot, raised and swollen. "What are we going to do?" I ask him. "I've nothing to treat her with."

"Maybe at the village," he says. "Her aunt was the one who knows those remedies. But Yema told me she's dead." Now for the first time I've made the connection— That's why Jégeuro had the jaguar cape and why Yema went so crazy at Mass.

The sky is covered with a carpet of stars, and I can see Agato in the dim light. I can't decide if he looks silly or ominous with the cape over his shoulders and the animal skull with its ferocious teeth resting atop his head. He shows me the sinew necklace with its single shell. "Yema told me I could keep this. She said I'd be more powerful than Jesus if I could save her life." He flashed a smile. "I guess I am."

How interesting, I think. *Was our pending death a crucifixion? Are we somehow saved? A resurrection? For what purpose in this trackless jungle?* I tip forward. "Put Yema on my back. We must keep going."

She awakens as we move her. "I can walk," Yema says, trying to stand. The child barely lifts herself before she falls back. Agato helps her rest against me as we strap her to my waist. She puts her arms over my shoulders and I stand up.

"Do you want your dagger back?" the boy asks me.

Although I can barely see, it appears he's commandeered a man's belt—perhaps the jailer's—and has it strung across one shoulder over the jaguar cape, the dagger thrust through a slit in the leather, its handle held in place with a thong. He begins to untie it.

"Keep it," I tell him. "You know better than I how to use a knife." In truth, I don't want to handle the thing. Never in my life have I touched something that has brought death to another. Once on the trail I say, "Let's get as close to the Jacu as we can, maybe by daybreak. Then I've got to look at Yema's wounds." He says nothing, just trudges ahead of me. "What are we going to do for food?" I ask.

He glances back. "When we can see, there is food everywhere in the forest."

After an hour or so, and Yema restless with fever, she begins to mutter words that make little sense. Attempting to keep her spirits up, I say the first thing that occurs to me. "What can we do for your wounds?"

Initially she does not understand. But then she says, "Oh Sister Leah, the Africans washed me with seawater and *jehe'a*. It seemed to work."

"*Jehe'a?*"

"The stuff you call mint."

My God, I think, her words sinking in, *am I now Leah? Leah Saulo? Meaningless if we don't survive.* "Where do we find *jehe'a?*" I ask.

Agato answers for her. "It grows along the river banks. We'll find it."

Fatigue begins to overtake me. My feet hurt, as does my back. I don't want to rest until we reach the river. I'm searching for thoughts to distract me from the pain, finally seizing an image of my father in Lisbon as he headed off to work each morning. He seemed most always in a pleasant mood, wearing one of the many knitted caps my mother made for him. So today he's getting up and going to work in the Ottoman, in the little town of Antalya, working for the sultan, and he owns his own brickyard.

It is my understanding that the sun rises earlier there since it comes from the east. That's what I've been told. Oh how I miss my parents. Now I'll never hear from them again. So which cap is he wearing today? In Lisbon he had more than we could count—tightly-knit wool caps for the cold months, and those loose-knit silk ones for the hot months, most full of colors like Joseph's coat in the Bible.

On São Tomé my brother Marcel had a son named Joseph. But now I recall when we first started work at my father's brickyard in Lisbon. I was perhaps twelve and my brother ten. Ten, about the same age as Agato. My father was a leader in our Jewish community, but he received much criticism for allowing his daughter to work in commerce. Girls were restricted to the home, to learn chores of the house, to be trained by mothers and older sisters. I remember how excited we were to work there among all the clay and brick molds and kilns.

And now I know why I've grown so fond of Agato. If his skin were a few shades lighter and his hair curly, he would look much like my brother at age ten. Those same lively eyes, always curious, the quick smile and wit, the boy's thin frame—tall for his age—and his confident manner. Though as far as I know, Marcel never killed anyone.

The sun is beginning to come up, and I've felt something strange about this trail all night. In the new light it becomes apparent.

First, the trail is much wider than I remember, but it's the tracks that get my attention. "Agato," I call out. "Look at all these tracks."

He stops until I catch up. He's already figured it out. He must feel as much dread as I do. "Sister Mãe, I've been looking at them a while." He stoops down and traces some with his fingers. "These are mules and these are men. The newest ones are on top, heading back to the settlement. That means they've been to our village."

"How long ago?" I ask, though I have no idea how he might know.

He points ahead of us. "A few days, Sister. See how leaves have fallen on top of them. No leaves have been stepped on."

"That means they're not looking for us," I say. I know it's a stupid comment. Neither of us want to speculate on the fate of the Caeté village. Also, it is likely the village no longer holds refuge for us. Agato says nothing, just gets up and continues walking.

My exhaustion returns. Within a short time the hoped-for sound of the Rio Jacu greets us. We arrive at its bank, and I see the river is much higher than before, and quite muddy. Agato plunges right in and swims the short distance across. "Could you touch bottom?" I call to him.

"Yes," he shouts back. "You can wade it."

I can't possibly do it with Yema on my back. "Come back here," I call. "I need your help." On top of everything else, it's started to rain. I find a grassy spot away from the muddy trail and kneel down, loosening the fabric around my waist. Yema releases her grip and leans against me. She appears barely awake, and struggles to stand. I see the full damage to her face. There are four thick tracks down each cheek, raised and inflamed. I almost cry out at the agony of seeing this; but these two children have shown such bravery, I must do likewise.

"There is *jehe'a* on the other side," Agato says.

Surprisingly Yema speaks up, "It's no good without the seawater." The boy helps steady her.

I point down the river. "How far to the ocean?"

"A few hours," he says. "There is a trail on the other side."

I put my hand out. "Give me the dagger." With a strange look, he unties the thong, pulls the knife from his belt, and hands it to me. "Now," I tell him, "Grab the edge of my habit and hold it out." The lower half of my skirt is wet and muddy, and has almost tripped me several times. I take the knife and saw at the fabric, then tear it across. "Pull the back around here so I can reach it," I say, then cut the rest away, turning to the left, then to the right. Yema is the first to laugh, and Agato joins in, the both of them wild with laughter.

"Your legs are so white," they howl. "How can they be so white?"

I throw the muddy fabric at Agato. "It's because they've never seen the light of day," I tell them. "Now, let's get across the river." It begins to rain in torrents and has us completely soaked. I pick up the cloth from my habit and tie it underneath Yema's arms. Next I tell Agato to find me a sturdy walking stick. He spots a jumble of flood debris, and quickly returns with a stick that will work. We help Yema down to the river and into the water. I walk in the lead, using the stick to steady myself. With my other hand I hold the girl by the yoke I've made with the fabric. Agato supports her feet. Thus we work our way across the river, Yema's head and feet above water, her seeming to enjoy the ride and splashing water on her face.

When we get to the other side, I collapse from exhaustion. Yema crawls a ways and begins pulling up some low-growing plants.

"Jehe'a," she says, carefully rubbing some on her face.

I crawl next to her and take a look. How strange the grass feels on my knees and legs, something I've not felt since I was a little girl. The mint-like smell of the *jehe'a* reminds me I'm ravenously hungry, and thirsty beyond measure. Yema returns to the edge of the river and begins to drink. I do the same. Another new experience for me.

"Roll over," I tell Yema. I shield her face from the rain and rub the wounds with *jehe'a,* running it along each line of proud flesh until it oozes blood, something I've seen Dr. Cardim do. Obviously this hurts, but she does not cry or turn away. I wonder if this simple herb can possibly cure her infection. Then I remember Dr. Cardim saying that, while the Indians are vulnerable to our European diseases, they have a remarkable ability to overcome infection. I can only hope this is true.

My worry about the Caeté village nags at me. I know how Yema yearns to see her mother and little brother, and wonder if she heard my conversation with Agato about the soldier tracks. I decide to say nothing.

Agato calls out, "I've got food." He's coming back from the

jungle, holding something in the jaguar cape. When he gets closer, I see a brown mass of sticks and rotted wood. Wriggling within this jumble are white grubs as big as my thumb. He eats one and offers me the cape.

He knows what my reaction will be. "I do not eat worms," I tell him. Yema takes one, bites it in half, and chews up both parts. The two of them begin to gobble the grubs as if eating berries from a vine. I cannot watch and turn my head away. Within minutes they eat them all. Agato goes back for more. "I guess I'm going to starve," I say. He returns with a new batch which they consume more slowly than the last. "What do they taste like?" I ask.

"Pretty awful," Agato says, "unless you're really hungry. It's something we eat while traveling. They're better cooked."

"You roast them over a fire," Yema adds.

"I'm not eating worms," I say again. "Can you find some fruit, guava or something?"

"There's no fruit around here," Agato says. "Guavas grow on the hillsides."

"What about *yva* vine?" Yema says. "You can eat the blossoms."

Agato goes searching, this time along the forest trail that leads to his village. He's gone quite a while, and when he returns, he shows us the cape nearly full of beautiful pink flowers, some almost as big as his hand. Curiously his young face is drawn with anguish. "You can eat these," he says, then sets the cape on the ground and wanders off. I taste one of the blossoms. It has a fleshy texture, a mild perfume smell, and a bland flavor, but at least it's food. Yema partakes also. Finally I eat a couple of handfuls, then turn my attention to Agato. I see him a short distance away by the river. He's walking slowly along a flat, kicking bits of sand ahead of him with the toes of his sandals.

Our situation is exceedingly grim, but this is the first time I've seen Agato so distressed. I walk over and thank him for the *yva* flowers, then say, "The only time I've seen you like this is back at the abbey after the jailer kicked you. Can you tell— " He gives me a sorrowful look and starts talking.

"Back there I found three dead people in the forest," he says. "Hardly anything left of them, but one must be Janaína. I found her bead vest. I would have brought it back, but it's in pieces. I think the two others were whites from the settlement." He opens his hand and shows me a few black beads, small and oval in shape. There's no doubt where they came from. I reach to touch him, but he pulls away. He looks at me, his sorrow replaced with anger. "Why have you Portuguese brought us so much sadness?" I can see he wants to throw the beads at me. Instead he hesitates, his eyes filling with tears.

I answer as best I can. "Agato, I don't know why things happen as they do. But I do understand we are alone in this jungle and need each other to survive." I look back at Yema lying in the grass, her hands covering her face, protecting herself from the rain. The wind picks up and lashes the downpour against us. "Please don't tell Yema about her aunt. At least not now."

Agato answers me with renewed anger. "I am a Caeté, and I will go to my village." He turns and starts for the trail.

"Stop!" I shout. "Stop!" I follow him and catch up as he enters the forest. Then I step in front and block his way. He does pause, his head down. "Agato, hear me. I know you are worried about your family. I am too. Right now we must take that trail downriver. Find saltwater so we can help Yema." He says nothing and tries to shove past me. I grab his arm. He struggles and tells me to let go. I persist. "I will let you go if you will hear me out." I release my grip and he stays. "You have saved Yema and me by your brave acts. We will go to the village after she recovers. I do not know how to survive in this jungle. You children do, but Yema is too ill to help. If you leave us, we will perish. Is that what you want?"

He does not respond. Now he turns and trots back towards Yema. As he does, I see him toss the beads onto the ground, then dust his hands together. I assume Agato will keep his secret.

Chapter 11

Walking the trail downriver takes most of the day. Finally near sunset, we get to the ocean. It's been sunny for the last two hours, so we're mostly dry. When we started, Yema walked a little, then I had to carry her, cinching the child onto my back with the sodden cloth around my middle. Along the way, Agato found enough for us to eat, more *yva* blossoms and another horde of grubs which he and the girl ate. These grubs were smaller than the earlier ones, yellow in color, and just as disgusting. Best of all, he discovered a cache hidden by some animal, and from it gathered an impressive pile of *upi'a* nuts.

These were dark brown and large—I could barely hold three in my hand—and had a thick shell. Agato and I broke these open by pounding them with rocks. The meat was quite delicious.

Now it's nighttime and we sleep huddled together, all of us grateful that we're dry. I consider the torrent of rain earlier in the day. If this were Lisbon, we would be nearly frozen by such a soaking, and likely catch our death of cold. Here in the tropics, one can be soaked and still not chilled. We'd walked in the downpour for at least four hours, and towards the end, I had almost forgot the rain. I began to perspire as soon as it stopped.

I was able to treat Yema twice with the mixture of *jehe'a* and saltwater. It may be my imagination, but I think her wounds look less inflamed. Before falling to sleep, she said she felt better. Her fever feels diminished, and I'm confident she will survive, more from her fortitude than whatever treatment I've provided.

This place where the Jacu greets the Atlantic is actually a small bay. To the east, one can see the surf breaking on a line of sand and then the ocean beyond. In other circumstances this setting could be beautiful with its tranquil waters, the broad shore peppered with small plants sprouting from the sand, and the surrounding forest with trees growing to the sky.

During our journey so far, we came across a few animals, many different birds of course, and a several groups of noisy monkeys high in the treetops. On this shores, and for the first time, we encountered a quarrelsome water lizard the children call *y 'teju*. These animals are similar to the crocodiles that prowled the waters of São Tomé, though considerably smaller, the largest no more than three feet long. I label them quarrelsome because there are always two or three nearby, often rushing at us, their jaws agape and hissing. They never get very close, and do turn and scurry away if we charge back at them. The children say they are harmless, and I now find their antics humorous. The children also say they are good eating, but we lack the necessary fire to cook them.

By no means are we going hungry, although I found the fare difficult to eat at first, mostly mussels, and several kinds of clams and oysters. One particular clam has a ribbed shell like the one on Agato's necklace. The oysters come in many sizes, most having a pearl-like appearance to their inner shell. We ate all of these on Tomé Island, but cooked of course. Eating them raw takes some getting used to. I tell the children that these shellfish are forbidden by Jewish dietary law. That in our Lisbon community we were not allowed to even touch them. Yema and Agato find this laughable, reminding me that the Caeté make food from nearly anything and everything.

***

Four days have passed since arriving at this bay, and Yema's health is much improved. Only the edges of her wounds are slightly red, her fever is gone, and so is the swelling on her face. We continue to treat her with the *jehe 'a* mixture, but gently so as not to make the scratches bleed. It is my fear that once healed, Yema will have four permanent scars down each side of her beautiful face. Today, both children began nagging me to go to the village. I distract them with a request to repair my gold chain. It's an easy task. We simply pry open the link I cut through, and using the butt of the dagger, close it over the adjacent link. It feels good to have it around my neck again. My habit is in shambles. I discarded the yoke because it kept me stiflingly hot, and I lost my coif and wimple along the way. So now I go bareheaded, something I've not done since I was younger than Agato and Yema.

The children leave to collect more shelled creatures for dinner, using the jaguar cape as they have every day to carry them. While they're gone, I tidy myself up a bit. We were fortunate to find a freshwater pond a short distance away from our camp, and I go there to drink and wash myself. Next I clean up our camp, if one could call it that. We have a bed of leaves to sleep on, and a fallen tree of some age on which to sit. We are at the edge of the forest, with a thick canopy of trees overhead, but we quickly discovered that even this cover does not keep us dry during rainstorms. So we built a shelter over our sleeping spot using tree branches interlaced with an abundance of broad leaves from plants we found around the pond.

Today it's sunny, which is a blessing when Yema and Agato return. We set the clams and mussels in the sun, and in an hour or so the shells open a little. Then we pry them full-open with our fingers. I still find them unpleasant to eat, and try to imagine they're cooked. The children consume them with great zeal. We throw the empty shells to the *y'teju* with amusing results. The lizards quickly crunch them to pieces with their long jaws, all the while quarreling with their fellows. Once they discover the shells contain no meat, they violently shake their heads, flinging pieces everywhere. Yema calls them "stupid" because they never learn that the shells are empty. The children again complain that we have no fire to cook them.

Agato describes how these lizards are cooked by the Cąeté, then asks me when we can go to the village. Neither he nor I have told Yema about the tracks by the Rio Jacu. I glumly speculate about the rebellion at the settlement. Did it give the new garrison commander an excuse to attack the village? What else could those tracks mean? If we go, I expect to find only ruin. I've shared none of this with the children, saying rather that the longer we stay away, the more likely the soldiers have looked for us at the village and left. Agato knows this is foolish, but keeps quiet.

The boy has not kept silent about finding Janaína's vest. To my astonishment, yesterday he told Yema about what he found, and showed her a short string of beads he'd not shown me. I don't know what to think about this child's deceitful nature, which at times seems full of purpose. Did he and Yema scheme to kill the jailer? It's outrageous that children could plan such a thing. And Agato having the dagger was certainly happenstance.

Yema's reaction to the news about her aunt surprised me; it was completely matter-of-fact. "That's why we have her cape," she said. "I see Janaína in my dreams. She told me what happened to her." Then she lost her composure and began to cry. "I see my mother and little brother," she said. "My father too. But they are still people. I don't know what animals they're supposed to be."

***

In the late afternoon with Agato looking on, I examine Yema's face. The child's scars are red, but healing. I'm fairly sure she will carry these the rest of her life. "We'll go to the village tomorrow," I tell them, then add, "I think we should say a prayer for our journey." They both give me indifferent looks and wander off.

Now after all these days of running it occurs to me. I've not prayed since Thursday, and have hardly thought of it. To whom shall I pray? Am I Leah Saulo or Sister Mãe? The children seem not to miss prayers at all. For me, and maybe for them, this seems strange; just a few days ago we were praying daily, many times daily. Are we abandoned by God? I think not since we've survived so far, and Yema has recovered. How can I encourage these two resilient and resourceful children to pray when I find myself unable to? And to a religion that meant to kill us? In this life no one questions God's purpose. How then can I? Yet was it God's intent that I forgot my rosary and cross at the abbey?

The next morning we prepare to leave, eating a large meal of shellfish, along with a delicate and delicious water plant which the children harvested from the freshwater pond. The *"ka'apetãi,"* as they call it, has a pepper flavor and a crunchy texture, quite unlike anything I've ever tasted. As we start out for the village, I am burdened with my despairing thoughts for what we might find. Yema walks in the lead with a long stick which she uses to probe the ground and surrounding foliage for snakes. This is a precaution we've not taken before. But yesterday the children came across a large snake, perhaps twelve feet long, which had devoured some kind of animal. One could see the creature still kicking inside the snake. The children call this serpent a *"kuriju."* Many natives in the Luís settlement kept smaller versions of these as pets, but I suspect at some point they turned them into food.

As we trudge along, I examine our situation. It seems impossible—two children and a woman alone in this New World jungle and without resources. Will we ever savor bread again, or the orange flavor of yerba buena? Will I ever again sleep in a bed? And the other thought that troubles me, *Are there other lost souls like us in this wilderness?*

My thoughts turn back to the events at the abbey gate. With Agato walking just ahead of me I ask, "What led you to stab the jailer?"

"Yema told me how much you love that gold chain. So we decided to get it back."

"How?"

"I was going to hug him around his middle and steal the chain from his waistband. When he read your note with first half of the chain inside, that's where he put it. We guessed he'd put the other half there too."

"That doesn't explain why you stabbed him," I said.

Agato shrugs. "Your dagger was there on the ground, and stabbing him seemed the easiest thing to do." He shrugs again. "Anyway, he kicked me. I hated him." The little assassin gives me a boyish grin, jumps around, and begins walking backwards in front of me, gesturing with his hands. "I knew I could kill him when I picked up the dagger." He twists and runs a distance ahead of me, looking back when he stops. This exchange leaves me speechless. *While this boy is brave beyond measure, now like so many men, he is corrupted by violence.*

Around mid-afternoon we near the village. First we spot the clearing ahead that marks the boundary of the Indian settlement. Next we see many vultures circling in the air. The children run ahead. There's nothing I can do but hurry after them. We come upon a scene of complete devastation. Every *óga* is in ruins, many of them burned. There are dead everywhere, men, women, and children, their bodies and pieces of such piled up and scattered like remnants of a flood. The animals, vultures and time have done their hideous work, and it is impossible to tell one person from another.

The children begin to shriek and moan, pounding each other with their fists, wailing with tears streaming down their cheeks. It's obvious the Portuguese did this. If it had been an attack by natives, they would have taken the women and children. Yema and Agato run from ruined hut to ruined hut, all the while screaming and crying. I am just numb with pain, though I expected this all along.

I catch up with Yema and stand in front of her. She glares up at me. *Does she blame me and my white brethren for this massacre?* I take both her wrists and pull her hands up. "*Do not* scratch your face again," I say. "We need each other more than ever." She wrenches away and continues to run. I catch her a second time and hold her close. Yema kicks me in the shin, though I think it hurts her more than me. The upper half of her body hugs me while the lower struggles to run away. She is heaving with sobs. I lift her off her feet and hold her as tight as I can. "Listen to me," I say. "I love you like my daughter." This little bundle of sadness goes limp and lets me stroke her head. "I am so sorry for what we found here." She looks up at me and I see a sorrow in her face more intense than I've ever seen.

Agato has quit running. He's just wandering around, dragging the jaguar cape. The boy lets it drop and I go over and pick it up. He finds a gourd rattle that somehow survived the fires, and gives it to Yema. The rattle is yellow and covered with bumps. These bumps are painted and connected in a way that shows rough animal pictures, and its elongated end serves as a handle. Yema hands it to me and begins to cry for her lost family. Agato does the same. I take their hands and we stand there and weep. The vultures have lost their fear of us, and a good number have descended from the trees to feed on the bodies.

The smell is horrific.

I pick up the cape, tucking it and the rattle under my arm. I again take their hands and we walk towards the trail leading back to the Jacu bay.

As we enter the forest, Yema takes the cape and hands it to Agato. "Wear this," she tells him. "I —" Words fail her. She runs ahead to retrieve the stick she carried earlier, then continues in front of us, again rapping the bushes for snakes. The light begins to fade, but the sky is sufficiently clear with a bit of moon; we have no trouble finding our way back. It's well past dark when we arrive at the bay. We are exhausted and starving. Huddled together in our bed of leaves under the rough shelter, we fall asleep.

In the morning with hunger gnawing our innards, Yema and I go to the shore and collect mussels, prying them from the rocks with sticks. We are too impatient to dig for clams, but she decides to wade out a ways, and comes back with a few oysters. Agato went to the freshwater pool to gather *ka'apetãi*. We have several pounds of mussels in the jaguar cape when Yema finds a mound of seaweed floating in the shallow water.

"Now I remember," the girl says, and drags the mass of weeds onto the shore. She starts loosening sheets of the stuff—brown with curled edges—and rinses them in the seawater. "We ate this when I went trading with the men and my aunt."

The child grows silent and looks at me with tears in her eyes. I put an arm around her shoulder and pull her close. "I'm sorry, sweetheart," I say. "Somehow we'll get over this." We add handfuls of the glistening brown weed to our shellfish and head back to the camp. Yema runs ahead of me and I take the moment alone to say Kaddish. This is the first time I've done so since my brother died.

Agato has returned from his foraging. As we get closer, he appears green from head to foot, having draped long strands of the *ka'apetãi* over his shoulders and around his neck. We feast on seaweed and the *ka'apetãi* until the sun warms our shelled creatures enough so we can feast some more.

With our bellies full, we walk to the freshwater pond and spend some time refreshing ourselves. I tell the children we need to make baskets for carrying things. The jaguar cape is now tattered, dirty, and smells dreadfully. Yema knows how to make baskets and directs the activity. We use the dagger to strip green stalks from the bushes and cut them to length. The girl ties them together with pieces of vine so a good number cross in the middle. Agato and I next bend the twigs into a bowl shape while Yema weaves vines around the edges. She cleverly secures the end of each vine into the twigs to anchor them. We line the bowl with leaves and congratulate ourselves. It's so easy, we make another.

I'm at a loss as to where we should go next. Are we to spend forever in this wilderness? I ask Yema who's traveled some, "Is there a friendly tribe up the coast who might take us in?"

"I don't think so," she says. "They all seemed hostile. Only traded with us because we had many warriors. Janaína told me most other tribes feared us."

I suggest we travel up the coast anyway, adding, "… get as far away from the Luís Settlement as we can."

We agree this is a good idea and decide to leave in the morning.

Chapter 12

We've been traveling three days now, making good progress the first two, but yesterday it rained so hard we sought cover in the forest, finally settling under the ruins of a giant tree that must have fallen years ago. We stayed reasonably dry, though spent the day hungry and discouraged. There is one advantage to the rain. The hordes of insects that regularly pester us mostly disappear during rainstorms.

There's a strong sun this morning and we head to the beach in search of food. The tide is full, so all we find is seaweed. Grateful for anything, the three of us sit on a log in the sand and eat until the salty taste of the brown weed begins making us sick. We wander up the coast until almost midday when Agato, who is in the lead, spots a stream running from the jungle. The shallow stream is thick with darting fish. After drinking our fill, we crawl on our hands and knees to catch the fish. As usual the children eat them with great zeal, heads, guts, and all. I am slightly more restrained, biting the heads off and shaking the innards loose before I manage to choke the fish down.

Our landscape has changed from the gently sloping beach that reached to the trees with the forest behind it, mostly uniform and level. Now we encounter beaches with steeper slopes ending against low cliffs with frequent runnels cut into them, many flush with streams of fresh water. The headlands above these cliffs continue for a ways higher, and the trees appear to be different from those in the low forest; they are shorter and quite sparse, not at all stately. The land between them is grass and brush, most of it appearing dry despite the frequent rain.

Agato has taken up running to the top of these headlands and keeping pace with us from afar. We often see him dashing among the scrub, occasionally stopping to examine something, then charging forward again. In the afternoon, Yema and I stop by a stream to drink and catch more fish. Agato joins us, sliding down a sandy cliff from above. There is a small tree by the stream where it joins the beach, and we decide to rest a while in its shade. All three of us fall fast asleep, and wake only after a breeze rustles the branches overhead. We drink our fill and continue north.

For some reason I'm anxious to keep Agato with us, so I engage him in conversation. "If Yema's selected to be a jaguar," I ask, "what will you be?"

He shrugs. "I don't know. Yema is a jaguar because her aunt made her so. Most children don't get a *kuarahy'ã* until their thirteenth year."

"*Kuarahy'ã?* I don't know that word."

Yema, who is a little ahead of us and listening, stops and turns. She points to her shadow. "That's my *kuarahy'ã,*" she says. "My shadow. It is always with you. In the light it strays a little, but at night, in the dark, it hides inside of you. It becomes part of your dreams."

Agato slows and looks down. "My shadow looks just like me, only longer."

"No it doesn't," the girl points out. The boy wears the jaguar cape over his shoulders with the skull hanging loosely behind him. She takes the skull and settles it on his head. "What do you see now?" she asks.

"I see a Caeté boy with a jaguar skull on his head."

We all laugh. Then Yema takes him by the shoulders. "I see a boy as brave as the jaguar. I see Agato who saved Sister Leah and me. Give me my necklace, and you can keep the cape. It is yours."

Agato slips the shell necklace over his head and hands it to Yema. Their conversation continues while I try to decide my view of this. If we were back in the settlement, I would dismiss their jaguar talk as pagan nonsense, but with the three of us alone on this unknown coast, I find some comfort in their strange beliefs.

Much later in the afternoon we arrive at a bay considerably larger than the Jacu's. We walk to the edge of the forest where the river empties into the bay via a short stretch of rapids. A little further up, the river is running evenly, but is much too wide to wade or swim. Further still, we can see more rapids flowing from a distant headland.

"If we are to continue up the coast," I tell the children, "we must find a way to cross." There's only an hour of daylight left, so we turn back to the bay.

We forage for food and find nothing. Thus we spend the night huddled together, hungry and occasionally dozing, but mostly kept awake by restless monkeys chattering in the trees above us. In the morning we are blessed with a low tide and find large quantities of clams in the tidal flats. We eat our fill, leaving plenty of shellfish for our next meal. After these many days, my habit is in shreds. So I strip off the lower part to make a cloth sling from what's left of the pathetic material. Into this sling we load our next meal.

The children comment about my grimy undergarment, and I'm certain they're wondering when I'm going to go as naked as they. Neither has worn a stitch of clothing since we left the Jacu. Agato wears only the jaguar cape and the jailer's belt, and Yema her necklace and the gourd rattle. The rattle hangs around her neck, suspended by a cord she fashioned with woven grass and threaded through a hole at the small end. She found it uncomfortable hanging in front, so now she fusses to keep it over her back between her shoulders. Whenever Yema's doing anything—even sleeping—it's always in her way. I suspect she will soon discard it.

We set out upriver to look for a crossing. There is a floodplain with easy walking until we get to the rapids at the headland. There is a flood path here also, but many large boulders that we have to work around. On the plateau above we find the river broken into numerous small channels, many only inches deep. "Maybe we can work our way across," I say as we traverse a few of these shallow streams. Then we get to one that's only a few feet wide and perhaps a foot deep. We can see the main part of the river through the trees. From where we're looking it's impossible to tell if it can be crossed. At this stream, Agato comes up short and points into it. A closer look shows it swarming with piranha fish. It is common knowledge that these savage creatures are the scourge of many rivers in this New World.

Agato does a childish thing. He jumps into the water and attempts to stomp on the piranha. He gets several vicious bites and leaps from the water howling in pain. One fish is still hanging on. He kicks it loose and it flops in the grass. His leg is bleeding, the blood running down his ankle and over his heel. I make him sit down and cut a bandage from the top of my habit. He keeps trying to get at the fish so he can kill it.

"For the love of God," I shout, "sit still." He's startled by my outburst, and does as I say.

Yema takes the dagger and jams it through the piranha's eyes. Hanging thus, she presents it to Agato. "Even the most stupid jaguar," she says, "knows not to do that. Perhaps you are a turtle." She lays the fish in the grass, runs the knife edge along both sides, and peels off the skin. Next Yema slices it into several pieces and hands us the meat. For perhaps the first time in his life, Agato is speechless. He sits there patting his wounded leg while slowly chewing her offering. I find the raw fish surprisingly good, and eat a second piece.

Agato says what we all know. "No matter what, we cannot wade that river."

We eat a few clams, save the rest for later, and travel back towards the bay. On the way, we speculate as to what we should do next. I suggest we build a raft, but have no idea how to do so. Agato says we can use the dry wood along the bay's edge as floats and kick our way across.

Perhaps he's lost his mind, but I respond kindly. "How are we going to do that when the piranha will chew us to pieces?"

"We'll wait for the tide to come in," he says. "They won't swim in salt water." Yema disputes this, and they argue back and forth. We're about a mile from the bay when Agato spots a beehive. *"Eirete!"* he exclaims and starts looking for a pole to knock the hive loose.

"What are you going to do when you get it down?" I ask him.

"I'll stick it with my pole and carry it to the river. Then I'll drown the bees."

"We've plenty to eat," I tell him, "and there will be more in the morning. Why risk getting stung?" He persists, so Yema and I leave him and continue on our way. About a hundred yards from the beach we stop, alarmed at what we see. It appears there's a small group of Indians sitting in the sand and several men with spears surrounding them. We promptly turn and start back up the trail. We've gone only a short distance when two fierce-looking warriors step from the forest and confront us. The men are quite tall, have long straight hair, and are covered from head to toe with elaborate patterns of black and red paint. They threaten us with their spears, indicating that we should head to the beach. As we get closer to the others, the two warriors call out excitedly.

"Who are these people?" I ask Yema. The children and I have been speaking a mixture of Caeté and Portuguese, and when I ask her the question, she puts a finger to her lips.

"Speak only Portuguese," she says. "They may understand Caeté."

"Who are they?" I repeat.

"I cannot say. They will know I recognize them." A moment later she whispers, "They are Caribs."

Hearing this I feel intense panic. The Caribs are the most feared of all Indians, murderous cannibals who raid other tribes, carrying off captives to be fattened like cattle. I try to glance back, hoping to spot Agato. One of them jabs me with his spear. It penetrates my habit and feels like it may have drawn blood.

At the beach, the Caribs force us to sit with the captives, five men, four women, and four children. Their ornaments and tattoos indicate they are from different tribes. One of the men speaks to Yema in a language that sounds familiar, yet I can understand only a few words.

"Half of these people are Potiguara," Yema tells me. "The others are from a band I've never heard of. That man knows me from when we went trading."

Yema and the man jabber on. Two more join in. Meanwhile I've become a subject of much curiosity from the captives. They ask me questions, but not understanding, I only shrug. Our captors on the other hand pay me little attention.

I keep looking toward the headland, hoping Agato is safe, terribly worried how he'll survive. I reach behind and feel the wound on my shoulder. My hand comes away stained with blood. I press harder, but there is little pain. Hopefully the wound isn't deep. That brings me to focus on the Carib spears. The tips are iron. That means they've seen whites before, either traded or perhaps made war against them. I also note that many carry curved knives that appear to be made from metal barrel hoops. Each knife is suspended by a hide band strung around the warrior's waist. Otherwise, these men are completely without clothes as are the captives. The tattoos, the body paint, the nakedness, our flight from the abbey all fully strike me—I am in fact beyond civilization. And live or die, my life is forever changed.

The Caribs split the captives into groups and force us into canoes. I'm in the second one. A man in front and one in back paddle us across the bay, and it takes only a few minutes. On this new shore, several Caribs stay to guard us, while two canoes return for the rest of their fellows. It is near dusk now, and we're herded toward the forest. One Carib removes a clay pot from a covered portion of a canoe and brings it along. Wisps of smoke rise from the pot, and it is obviously too hot to carry without the wood handles that protrude through holes on either side. This is their fire-carrier. When we get to the forest, we are directed to gather dry wood and moss for the cooking fires.

Yema shows me what to look for—dry moss and branches sticking underneath fallen logs, protected from the rain. While we work, she tells me what she's learned. "These Indians were captured a few days ago from somewhere down the coast. Yesterday the Caribs ran across our tracks, and knew they'd catch us sooner or later. They know there were three of us. Some are returning tomorrow to look for Agato." She cries briefly, repeating his name, angrily dabbing tears with the back of her hand.

Yema and I are tied together at our ankles, and watched closely by a warrior. We work our way back to the encampment with our load of fire material. "Why did it take so long for them to catch up with us?" I ask.

"You'll see why tomorrow," she says. "We will have to march up the beach while most of the Caribs paddle beyond the surf in their canoes. That's why they move so slowly."

I am filled with despair. "I hope they don't find Agato," I say. "Perhaps he can survive alone."

"Me too," she says. "I hope they don't catch him. When they get the boys to their village, they will *kapõ* them."

"I don't know that word."

She makes a motion at her genitals. "Turn them into girls," she says.

My blood runs cold. I've heard this practice attributed to the Caribs. They castrate boys to make them fatten quickly. I'm sure there is a quaver in my voice when I ask, "What will happen to us?"

Yema gives me a fearful look. "We'll be safe until we get there. It's the women's job to fatten and kill us for food."

"How many days to their village?"

The girl shrugs. "No one knows."

I recall Fr. Julian telling me of the Caeté's practice of fattening, then ritually killing and eating captives caught in war. And this was the so-called familiar tribe we tried to civilize? Possibly my view of these Indians—all these New World natives—is naïve to the extreme. Many times I heard the curse of disease was God's punishment for their heathen and cannibal ways, for their worship of idols and magic, and that God tinted their skins brown as a caution to us. Perhaps these views are correct and I am the one in error. How could people behave in ways so savage, so beyond reason?

The Caribs have two fires going, both with several earthen pots steaming into the air. A while ago, when the last canoe arrived with the remaining warriors, they brought three nets full of fish ashore, apparently caught in the bay. These they dumped into the pots now boiling on the closest fire. I'm enticed by the smell of cooking food, and wonder if they will give us any.

Now the most extraordinary thing happens. The Caribs slide the vessels from the fire, add enough water from the river to cool them, and bring two pots to us. After eating raw things for so long, this cooked meal tastes unbelievably good to me. The fish are so simple to eat. One just strips off the loose skin—discarding the scales and all—and eats the flesh down to the bone. I'm so eager to eat my fill, I fail to notice the fish are not cleaned until I discard my second carcass. *What else did I expect?* Soon we captives are surrounded by cast-off fish bones.

My pleasure lasts only a moment when one of the captives remarks, *"Ha'e kyra guarã jejuka."* Yema explains: "They feed us well so they can kill us soon."

I've been thinking about, and dreading what happens next. We are bound in groups of three, each by an ankle to another person. Yema's and my companion is one of the Potiguara men whom she seems to know; his name is Cabeço. People begin to shuffle a short distance into the dark to relieve themselves, and we do likewise. My embarrassment is somewhat lessened by the fact it's nighttime. Tomorrow I'll just put up with it; I've no other choice.

I suppose I should be prepared for one insult after another, but I'm frightened when the Caribs pass among us to tie our hands behind our backs, and lash our feet individually. I'm scared of what's coming.

Yema reassures me. "They'll get drunk on *pohã*," she says. "Cabeço told me this happens every night."

Though the light is poor, I can see well enough to examine the ropes on our feet and hands. They appear to be of Old World origin, those typical of ship's halyards or unraveled hawsers. These ropes, along with the iron spear points, convinces me that I am not the first European they have encountered. An encounter that surely favored the Caribs and brought death to the whites.

A while back, they took a steaming pot off the second fire and set it to cool. They eagerly gather around the it, mixing the contents with a stick. One of the men tastes the mixture and declares it's ready. Now they dip out portions using sticks carved like wooden spoons. The Caribs heap more fuel on the fire, then begin to sway and chant. One man—perhaps the chief—throws a heap of wet moss onto the fire which makes a cloud of steam and smoke. The Caribs face the fire, breathe the smoke and link arms. Next they dance in a circle, first to the left, then to the right. Over and over. One by one, the dancers break from the circle and stagger in many directions, most of them talking, mumbling, gesticulating, apparently conversing with long-lost friends and ancestors.

This goes on for quite some time. Finally a few lie down where they are and go to sleep, while others sit together talking and laughing, revisiting their visions and recounting stories. At last they let the fire die, and all but a few of them fall fast asleep.

***

In the morning we eat the remainder of last night's fish. The Caribs allow us to cleanse ourselves in the river. Very early, one canoe returned to the far shore in search of Agato. Yema and I pray that he is now far away from here, that he is free and will somehow survive. And we are saddened for ourselves and our miserable situation. The remaining three canoes fill with Caribs who proceed to paddle downriver and towards the sea. We captives start a forced march up the coast. They've removed our tethers, but keep us herded together like sheep. Eight men with spears and blowguns guard us, compelling us forward with shouts and threats.

Within an hour the hot sun begins to take its toll. The children in particular are complaining they're thirsty and hot. Two more hours pass without a freshwater stream. The Caribs have skins of water, and up to this time have offered us none. Finally they call a halt and pass the skins around. We've had nothing to eat since morning, and I assume we will see no food until much later. We start off walking again, and I sense the adults are slowing their pace to ease the children's distress. The Caribs curse and bully us, so we take turns carrying the smallest youngsters on our backs. We're walking in the wet sand, close to the water. It's much easier than further up the beach where it's dry. Yema plods along, never complaining, often talking with the adults. They recognize the *tuguy kuñã* markings on her face and treat her with great respect.

At least three more hours pass. We are parched with thirst, exhausted, and starving. Finally we come to a freshwater stream and everyone throws themselves into it, cooling and drinking at the same time. The stream is shallow, about a hundred feet wide, and fans out into small rivulets on the nearly level beach. We wade across and rest briefly. The Caribs urge us to our feet and we prepare again to march. We go only a few hundred yards when they shout for us to stop. We spot the four canoes coming through the surf near the shallow river. As we turn back, Yema and I strain to see if Agato is in one them. To our relief, he is not.

Yema looks toward the jungle, pointing to the sloping highlands that rise inland from the beach. "Do you think he's following us?" she asks. "Maybe he's right about the piranha and crossed the bay in the saltwater."

I think of the vicious fish in the saltwater bay at the Luís Settlement and doubt the possibility. I know we share the same hope—if we are to be saved, he is the one to do it. But how against a force of twenty Carib warriors?

We return to the river bank just as the Caribs drag their canoes out of the water and onto the sand above the high tide mark. Then they order us to the edge of the trees. They are hungry too and plan to hunt, having caught very little in their nets. We appreciate the shade and rest, and despite our hunger, most of us fall asleep.

Our rest is short lived. One of the younger Caribs, a boy about sixteen, tells our guards he's discovered a patch of *pohã* bushes. They supply us with baskets and harvesting tools—flat sticks with one side honed to a knife-edge—and send us to gather the bark. The branches are thin and flexible, so we work together, one holding the branches while another scrapes the bark loose. As we work, Cabeço describes the attack on his village. I'm beginning to understand some of his words, but Yema translates also. "The cannibals came before dawn, just as we were waking. We were completely unprepared. Hardly put up a fight. They herded us together and looked everyone over, taking six of our most healthy people. They already had nine captives from somewhere inland, although two of them escaped the next day."

Both Yema and Cabeço are chewing *pohã* bark, explaining it helps with the hunger. I try a little and find it bitter and unpleasant. I'd briefly forgotten my hunger, but now it's back, gnawing at my insides.

Then, when the guard has his back turned, Cabeço whispers something that gives us hope. Yema excitedly tells me in Portuguese, "They know a friendly tribe north of here. Two or three days up the coast. Many warriors. Maybe we'll run into them. They might rescue us."

"Don't you think the Caribs know about them?" I ask.

At the next opportunity she asks Cabeço. He says he is not sure, telling her that he only knows of these people from their trading visits to his village. Yema considers this, her hopes obviously fading. Nevertheless she says, "I'll listen and see what they know."

While the Brazil coast abounds with tales of the Carib, Yema next tells me something I've not heard before. "You see," she says, "we are simply food to them. They hunt people like deer or peccary, never taking more than they need. Only with people you don't have to kill them, you take them with you."

It's now late afternoon, and the hunters return with nothing. They are angry and arguing among themselves, gesturing at us. Finally they start a fire and cook the few fish caught earlier, impaling them on roasting sticks which they hold over the flames. The smell of cooking food drives us mad, but they offer us none. As night falls, the Caribs build up the fire and begin a sing-song chant. We note there is no *pohã* boiling on the fire. I try to sleep, wondering if they plan to kill one of us for dinner. My hunger is so intense, so constant, it becomes like another person, an attached twin, a hideous companion that I cannot shed.

Our guards continue to talk and argue loudly, and it's almost a relief when Yema shares the bad news with Cabeço and me. "They know about the tribe north of here," she says. "They have some kind of plan."

"What?" I ask.

In the dim firelight her eyes glisten. "I don't know," she says. "I don't understand them as well as I thought."

***

Morning brings no relief from our hunger. We've taken to drinking as much water as we can, filling our bellies with something. Our march starts again, our miseries magnified from the day before. As the heat of the day bears down upon us, I descend into a stupor, walking as if in a dream. The Caribs are angry and demanding, prodding us at every opportunity. We can only hope the canoes launched early this morning will bring something back to eat. Yema and I have a cheerless conversation about Agato and her village which only furthers our despair.

Sometime in the forenoon a woman points out a line of trees on the north horizon that appears to extend into the ocean. The waves of heat dazzle against us and the view is so distant, it's hard to judge what we're seeing. The image persists, so it's no mirage. Then we see something else, a column of smoke. The Caribs begin to talk with great excitement, and soon a single canoe comes through the surf, the occupants shouting and waving their hands.

We wade about in the shallow ebb and flow of the surf, cooling off as the Caribs confer. Yema listens. Her face changes from curiosity to dread. Soon all we captives know, and everyone is terrified. They prod us forward, our worst fears realized. Ahead lies the camp of the Caribs. The column of smoke is a warning—Their village cannot be far.

Chapter 13

As we march toward the trees, I recover from my stupor. The sense of dread settles in my stomach, and despite having nothing inside me, I feel I'm about to retch. But now there's a subtle change in mood among the captives. The camp ahead is far too small to be part of a village. From what we gather listening to the Caribs, this is an advanced group. Their main tribe is still some distance away.

As we get closer, the people at the camp become clearly visible. They already know we're coming because we see the other canoes being hauled through the breakers. And now they come to greet the warriors. All of them are women, some accompanied by children. They bring manioc cakes and, to my surprise, they give food to everyone, captors and captives alike. Cabeço cautions us, "Do not be deceived by this kindness. They know people fatten better if calm and well fed."

The new Indians swarm around, appraising us like cattle and congratulating the warriors. The Carib men turn arrogant and puffed up, slapping each other on the back and some of us on our behinds. A tall woman who's been giving orders to everyone, and perhaps is their *tuguy kuñã,* studies each captive with interest. Her eyes are cruelly objective as she pays particular attention to me, putting her hands all over my body, shoving them under what's left of my tunic and feeling my breasts. I push her hands away, and she does not persist. Yema says, "Because your skin is so white, she thinks you will make a good *ñami kuñã.*"

The words translate "milk woman," though I'm certain she means nursemaid. Interesting since I've never had children. But this gives me an idea, one which might save us. The woman is visibly pregnant, so I pat her belly, then move a hand to my breast. I smile and nod, trying to look pleased.

Yema immediately picks this up and clings to me, "*Sysy,* " she says, the word for mama. The woman frowns in disbelief and moves to examine a Potiguara woman nearby. Though all of us are terrified, Cabeço gives me a knowing smile— To what purpose, I have no idea. How much longer any of us will remain living is a question; yet despite this peril there is a grim irony to my circumstance. Will this former nun, a Jewish woman and accused heretic, become a nursemaid to cannibal children?

My thoughts are interrupted when one of the captive boys begins screaming, struggling to break free from the two Carib children holding him. A Carib girl stands in front of the trio making profane cutting motions at his private parts, then pointing to hers. A warrior intercedes and separates the children. The captive boy throws himself against one of our women, sobbing and clinging to her. She glares hatefully, hurling curses at the Carib children.

The inspection process goes on. My musings return. *Why has God sown this New World with so many things monstrous? Burning and hanging for Yema and me, a Caeté village destroyed, deadly illness rampant, warring natives and cannibals, children mutilated? Both Old and New, are people the curse of this world? Without we Portuguese and these natives, this place would be near paradise— abundant water and creatures thereof, food, lush forests and wild beasts, a countryside of generous beauty and temperate clime.*

It turns out the line of trees behind the camp occupies a rise of rocky land only a few hundred feet wide. The prominence appears to extend past the surf and more than a mile into the ocean. A few stretches are barren with only rock outcroppings and breakers surging along them. All four of the canoes are resting on the sand, and the Caribs instruct us to carry them through the trees. The dugouts are frightfully heavy, and it takes eight of us to carry a single one. As we emerge from the forest and the tangle of brush, we come across a broad, slow moving river which empties into an immense bay, a body of water so wide that the distant shore is barely visible. We see a more organized Carib camp. Pulled up on the river bank are three canoes considerably larger than the ones we've carried. These have short masts with a reed sails rolled and lashed to the crosspieces. I've seen seagoing canoes like these before in the harbor at Luís. Supposedly they can travel great distances.

Everyone ends up on the river side of the tree line. There are several fires burning, all of them with fish drying on long poles suspended in the smoke. The Caribs continue their ghastly hospitality, offering us as much as we want to eat.

There is a sense of relief among the captives, and it seems our fate as dinner fare might be postponed. Yema explains why, confirming the rumors I'd heard about the Caribs living on an island some distance away. "I guess we'll not get eaten here," she says. "Those canoes will take us to their village someplace out there." She gestures seaward.

"We've got to come up with a way to escape," I say. This suggestion seems foolish. Even the night-before-last when the men were intoxicated with *pohã*, they guarded us closely. And despite the sentries also being drunk, they stayed alert to us. Nothing makes any difference—With our hands and feet tied, no one can do anything. Now, with almost twice as many Caribs, escape seems impossible.

Cabeço says there's talk about another celebration tonight. With their women present, I wonder if it will be different than before. I look around their camp and am astonished at what I see. The women have a number of iron tools, axes, a large chisel, and several knives which appear to be the same as the ones Portuguese seamen carry. I'm puzzled why the Carib men don't have these, but then I see they've taken a keen interest in the tools.

Yema listens intently. Finally she says, "I can't tell if they got hold of the tools in a trading expedition, or were taken from a ship. Maybe the women attacked it while the warriors were away."

Next the women unveil their most prized possession, one they'd kept covered until now. It's a large iron kettle at least four hands wide, one typical of those found in a ship's galley. Their *tuguy kuñã*—indeed the woman who inspected us—takes up a hand axe and begins banging on the pot. The men gather round feeling the rough, black surface, cooing in admiration. They dance to the rhythm of the banging and bring forth the *pohã* bark gathered from the night before. They dump it into the kettle.

I decide to make an appeal to the *tuguy kuñã*, pleading my desire to become her nursemaid. I must come up with something to save Yema and me from that iron pot. I'm also wondering if the child's singing could help us.

Before I get a chance to do anything, the Caribs march us back through the tree line and onto the beach on the south side. Once there, they tether our feet as before and provide us with sticks for harvesting *pohã*. We're led a ways into the jungle and begin to collect bark. These bushes are larger than the previous ones, and we rapidly fill our baskets. Once a basket's full, we leave it on the ground, and someone hands us a new one. Several Carib children circulate around, taking the baskets to a clearing nearby. There's no chance of escape here, as each trio of captives is guarded by a Carib adult brandishing a club or a knife.

We have the clearing partly in view, and I can see the children stack several baskets together and disappear towards the beach, presumably taking them to the encampment. I notice a movement near some baskets of *pohã* left on the ground. My heart stops. There's Agato. He's painted himself with the same red and black patterns as the Carib children. Our guard is too close and I can't say anything to Yema, but she senses my shock.

"What is it?" she inquires.

"Not now," I say as calmly as possible. I mustn't attract attention to anything. Out of the corner of my eye I see Agato pause by each basket. He does something with the *pohã*. I've no idea what. He's crouched low and appears to be limping. In a few seconds he's gone.

I'm unable to relate any of this to Yema. Without warning we are rudely pushed by our sentry and two others who've joined him. The Caribs order everyone back to the beach. Their manner of dealing with us has changed, leaving us puzzled and afraid. We're in the lead group, and Yema listens to the Caribs as they talk and gesture wildly. She continues for a moment, then turns to me. The color is drained from her face; she's choking, unable to catch her breath.

"They're going to kill some people tonight," she gasps. "They'll cure the meat before going home."

Unfortunately she's said this in Caeté. Immediately a few captives understand. The word spreads. People begin screaming and crying, struggling against their tethers, throwing themselves to the ground, refusing to move. In the midst of the turmoil the *tuguy kuñã* appears, pointing a hand at Yema. A man seizes the child while another cuts her loose. They loop a rope around her neck and drag her off. At the same time I see one of the captive women treated likewise, and then Cabeço.

As they're hauled away, it occurs to me that the Caribs have chosen the captives who most threaten them, Yema with her blood-woman markings, Cabeço who seems to know everyone, and the woman who has been most protective of the children. The terror overwhelms me and I start screaming hysterically. I'm unable to control myself, tearing at my hair, pounding my fists against my legs, finally falling to the ground and rolling into a ball, holding my knees to my chest. I am cast into a living hell.

I feel a sharp pain in my side. A Carib man stands astraddle of me, an animal look in his eyes, his spear jammed against my ribs. He commands me to stand. I struggle to my feet and join the other captives as we march back to the camp by the river.

Once there, we have our feet tied fast together. Then the Caribs knot a common rope around each captive's neck and snug it tightly between two trees. Thus we are forced to sit upright in a way that any movement by an individual tightens the rope around those on either side. The coarse rope chaffs painfully against my throat. They've left our hands free so we can steady ourselves against the ground. I'm terrified they will keep us this way all night. Those to be slaughtered, poor Yema, Cabeço, and the woman are roped together with their hands tied. They sit against a tree about fifty yards distant, too far for us to call to them. Any who try are clubbed viciously by Caribs. These inhuman savages have sunk to the absolute depths of depravity.

We sit in a line like this for what seems an eternity. The sun sinks behind us in the jungle, and I estimate we have only an hour of daylight left. In the meantime, the Caribs have built a dozen more fires and gathered two sizeable piles of sticks, one stack of long, thin poles with their bark removed for skewering meant, and a pile of forked sticks to support them around the fires. On the fires closest to us, the largest one, the iron kettle steams into the air. Earlier the Caribs dumped it full of *pohã* bark. I keep thinking about Agato, wishing I could have told Yema, and wondering how he could possibly help us. My thoughts were so disordered at the time, perhaps seeing the boy was only my imagination.

Now comes a grisly prelude to the slaughter. A hunting party has killed a gigantic snake, at least fifteen feet long, and they drag it into camp. The upper part of its body is distended just like the one the children encountered a few days back. They cut the snake open exposing the remains of a capybara. It must have been swallowed head first, because the front half is partly digested revealing a disgusting slime of gray meat, matted hair, and white bone. Most prominent is the animal's skull and large front teeth. Two Caribs hang the remains on the same tree where Yema is tied and begin salvaging the meat.

A group of women and children continue to butcher the snake. The adults cut and loosen the skin while the Carib children pull the skin down the body to reveal the animal's pink flesh. Strips of meat are sliced from the carcass, pierced with a knife, and threaded onto the long poles. Soon half the fires are covered with drying meat.

There is a captive woman sitting a few spaces away, one that has shown a friendly interest in Yema and me. She says something I mostly understand—that the Caribs may have so much meat to cure, they might spare our people. I glance her way and force a smile, grateful for any hopeful word.

As the butchery continues, a large earthen pot is placed nearby. Into this go some of the snake's innards and handfuls of her eggs. The children seem particularly adept at stripping and cleaning the innards before putting them into the pot, often using their teeth to pull loose and discard unwanted pieces of offal.

By now almost all the fires are occupied with poles of drying meat. The Caribs briefly eye Yema and the others and start four more fires. Their abject barbarism continues as they bring us food—dried fish from one of the fires—and a water skin to pass around. I eat because, just as I did at the abbey, I need to stay strong and alert to any possibility of saving Yema and the others. The Caribs eat also, many talking in excited tones and gesturing at the three against the tree.

I assume the killing will be put off for a while because the *pohã* kettle, which was earlier taken from the fire to cool, is now surrounded by Caribs with their wooden ladles. At the same time, three men pass among us, tying our hands behind our backs.

It appears the Caribs will work themselves into a passion of drunkenness before the killing starts. Night has come too quickly, and I try to make out Yema through the gloom and smoke. All I can see is her body slumped forward, her head down. Never in my life have I felt so helpless and afraid. The savages have built up the central fire and form two circles around it, the women and children in the inner circle, the men on the outside. They start the same sing-song chant we heard before. The men circle in one direction, the women in the other, the adults often breaking from the group to drink *pohã*. This goes on for perhaps a half-hour, the circles alternating directions. As before, individuals begin to depart the dance in groups or by themselves, talking and waving their arms, a few assuming bizarre postures.

But then something strange happens. Many of the Caribs sit down and seem to fall asleep, soundly enough that they just slump over. Some struggle not to do so, convulsing on the ground, laboring to stand up. This is very different from what happened the prior evening when those who slept calmly lay down before dozing. Even our guards are affected. They end up like the others. We captives struggle to free ourselves. Two of our men try to get back-to-back so they can untie their hands, but their movement is impossible because the neck rope is so taut. The Carib children run around screaming, frantically trying to rouse the adults.

Then from my left our neck rope goes slack. I see Agato sawing on a man's rope with my dagger. His hands come loose and the boy gives him the knife. The man quickly frees himself and others. Agato crawls over to me. He's unable to stand, so weak he can't work my knots. But soon one of the women releases me, and now Yema is at our side.

There is chaos everywhere. The captive men and women move from Carib to Carib, cutting their throats, stabbing the pregnant women in the belly, cursing and screaming. Briefly seized by the bloodlust, my voice joins them. But then the killing becomes so ghastly I cannot watch— The women are mutilating the bodies in unspeakable ways.

I come to my senses and pay attention to Yema and Agato. "You are the bravest person I have ever known," I tell the boy. His legs look awful, covered with deep cuts and gouges. Behind one knee I see a tendon exposed. "What happened to your legs?" I ask.

He gives me a wan smile. "I kicked across the bay and had no trouble. Not until I got near the other side. I hit a patch of fresh water and the piranha got me."

"You followed us for two days like this?" Yema asks.

Despite his feeble state, the boyish grin returns. "I put *mborasy* sap in their *pohã.*"

The girl looks horrified. "You touched it?"

"No choice," he says. His eyes seem to cloud.

Yema puts her face in her hands, her body shaking with sobs. "You should have let us die," she wails. "You stupid boy!"

"I don't understand," I tell them, terrified over what I might hear.

Yema slides next to Agato, holding his head against her, rocking him back and forth. "*Mborasy* is what we use on our arrows," she says mournfully. "More deadly than the *curare*. No one ever touches it. The men collect the sap, but always use tools and bowls. There's no cure."

It's impossible to comprehend, but Agato seems to have accepted his fate. He looks at me, then to Yema. "I lost the jaguar cape."

"You kept the dagger," I say. "You saved us all."

The word gets around. Agato becomes the center of attention, many voices raised in his praise. Yema explains what's wrong and the talk softens to whispers and prayers. I guess she's right about the poison because no one offers advice. Cabeço and another man return the dagger to us, thanking the boy in the process.

Agato complains he's cold, so we move him near the fire, making him as comfortable as we can. We're close to where Yema and the others were tied. I look over to see three Carib children lashed to the tree. None are older than four. They're terrified beyond all reason. "What will happen to those children?" I ask. I'm speaking in Caeté because I want at least some of these natives to understand me. Yema turns to Cabeço. Before she can speak I say, "Are any of you people cannibals? Potiguara or the others?"

I'm pleased that Cabeço seems to know what I said, though I don't understand his answer. Yema translates, "The children will not be harmed. They'll become slaves to the band that takes them in."

I don't like this, but I must attend to Agato. The fate of these children can wait. Still I ask, "What happened to the other Carib children? The older ones?"

Yema seems to know. Apparently it's been a topic of discussion. "They're hiding in the forest," she says. "They think we eat people like their tribe does. We'll never see them again."

She is kneeling next to Agato and begins a soft chant, allowing some of her charmed voice to come through. Everyone stops to listen. A little life returns to his face. Yema takes the necklace from around her neck and carefully lifts the boy's head, settling the shell on his chest. She leaves her hands there, rocking forward and back, gently pushing against him. "You will be the jaguar," she tells him. "The bravest of all." Then she goes back to her chant. The people press around us, captivated by her voice. I take Agato's hand. As usual I feel helpless.

After a while Yema says, *"Che hayhu nde Agato ... "* She's telling the boy she loves him. That she will be his bride in the afterlife. That they will roam the forest together, and all the animals will know their names. In the firelight Yema's eyes flicker yellow as the jaguar's. The boy is breathing quietly. He seems to be at peace.

I stand and take her hand. We leave Agato and spend a few minutes walking through the camp. The first thing I do is take snake meat and water to the three Carib children. Though they remain terrified, one child—a little boy—manages a smile. The natives have dumped the dead Caribs into the river. I'm pleased it's still dark. The last thing I want to see is more carnage when the piranha and water lizards tear the bodies to shreds. We check on Agato, then walk a short distance upstream, wash and refresh ourselves, and return to where the boy is laying.

There's a faint light in the eastern sky, the bay still black with its reflection of night. Agato says he's cold, and we feel him shivering. The fire's warmth seems not to have helped. Yema and I lie down on either side of the boy, pressing him between us. Dr. Cardim once showed me how to hold a person's wrist to feel the heartbeat, so I feel Agato's, then my own. In contrast to mine, his is fast and very faint. I'm lying on my side, my head resting in the crook of my arm, the other across his chest with my fingers touching Yema.

How much time passes, I'm not sure, but it's daylight now and I'm awakened by the girl's soft crying. Agato is dead.

It just seems impossible—this brave, beautiful, precious child is lost to us. Our companion in so many days of wandering. Our savior twice. More if one considers all the food he found. There are no words to express my sorrow. We carry his body to the edge of the camp and cover it with leaves. I can't think of anything else to do right now. Most everyone has followed us, and each person pays his respects. Yema and I sit on the ground nearby, both of us lost in grief.

Yema says only one thing. "I am the last of my tribe."

Chapter 14

Shortly after sunup the next day, we bury Agato in the clearing where he gave his life to poison the Caribs and save us. His grave remains shallow because of the hard ground beneath, so we cover it with rocks gathered from the riverbank. Yema and I erect a small cross to mark the spot and pledge to visit him again if we ever can. Then I explain the Hebrew tradition of placing small stones on a grave as remembrance. We search and find a few with some color, selecting the best two for our memorial. The natives watch all this with great interest, Yema explaining they think Agato was a truly clever boy. They are particularly impressed that he painted himself like the Carib children. If he were seen at a distance, he was likely ignored.

For the second time in a week, I say Kaddish. First in Portuguese, then in Hebrew. I speak slowly, pausing after each phrase so Yema can repeat the line, realizing that I have never said these prayers in Portuguese before. Next I explain to her about *Nahala,* the ceremony of remembrance on the anniversary of someone's death. "… and when you bless the candle," I continue, "this is how you hold your hands." I show her the *baraka,* the v-shaped hand position with thumbs spread and hands touching. "This forms the Hebrew letter, *Shin,"* I say, "the first letter in our word for God." I try to trace it in the dirt, but only come up with a couple of rough double-u's.

She arranges her small hands in the same manner and asks, "But how will we know when a year has passed?"

"I will keep track," I tell her. "I know what day it was when we fled the abbey."

***

We spend the remainder of the morning and most of the afternoon sorting through the treasures captured from the Caribs. The iron tools and spear points are of most interest, as is my dagger and the coils of rope. Yema sharpens the dagger and shows everyone how to do the same with the spear points and knives. There are more canoes than we can use, so it's decided the smaller ones will be hidden in the forest and retrieved at a later date, perhaps on a trading expedition. Additionally, the seagoing craft are simply too heavy to remove from the water, and everyone wants to return to their home villages with these Carib canoes, prizes of great significance.

Cabeço and several others ask me what iron is and how white people came to have it. I try to explain that the metal is smelted from a rock called ore, but finally give up because the idea of melting rock is beyond his belief.

It becomes obvious to Yema and me that the two captive groups intended to return south to their villages. We tell them travel in that direction is impossible for us, that we must continue north. Perhaps we could connect with the friendly tribe up the coast? In most cases the Indians would have insisted we come with them, or else leave us behind, but Yema and I have the weight of Agato's courage on our side, and they agree to honor our wishes.

The Carib booty gets evenly distributed between the two tribal groups with one exception, the iron pot. They decide to hold a wrestling match to determine who keeps this prize, Yema explaining that acquiring this kettle will impart great prestige to those who own it.

Body painting is the order of business before the wrestling

match can start. Painting is an important ritual for these natives, one denied to them the past few weeks. The women decorate the men, and the women decorate each other and the children, everyone standing around, commenting on the painters' artistic abilities. The two tribes have somewhat different markings, though all in black and red and made easy by the Caribs' large store of paint. The men of Cabeço's tribe, the Potiguara, prefer broad red and black stripes alternating across their torsos, extending over the arms and laddered down their legs. The women prefer thinner, alternating color stripes vertically down their bodies, with decorations only above the knees. Faces are painted the same for men and women, solid black foreheads, a gap for nose and mouth, and red from the edge of the mouth across the cheeks to underneath the chin. The children receive decorations similar to the adults and specific to gender, but no face paint.

The second tribe—I finally learn they are called the Inanbá—decorate their faces with crescent moons and circles, the moons black, the circles red. The men's bodies are painted horizontally with nested black waves like those on a pond, the women with the same pattern but red and running vertically. Their children are not decorated at all except for an occasional crescent or circle on one cheek.

Personally, not that my opinion matters, I view the decorations as vulgar and unpleasant. Perhaps Yema senses this because when one of the women asks her if she would like to be painted in her tribe's pattern, she declines. I'd hoped the child would retain some of her civilized ways. Perhaps this is a measure of that.

With the body painting finished, the wrestling contest begins. A man was chosen from the Inanbás and likewise from the Potiguara. There are only two men from the latter tribe, both smaller than the Potiguara wrestler. It seems Cabeço's tribe is bound to win in a match like no other I've seen. Despite its seemingly mild form, it turns out to be surprisingly brutal. The contestants are given a rope about four feet long with a knot at each end. Each man clenches the rope in his teeth with the intent of dislodging it from his opponent. They cannot touch the rope in any way, nor can they touch their opponent.

At first the fighters, amid much growling, snorting, and slobbered breathing, jerk and tug each other, wrenching their opponent's head this way and that. The Inanbá fighter, a man named Guasu, falls to the ground and is dragged several yards before he grabs a bush, stopping his progress. He struggles to his feet and charges his adversary. The man does not budge, knowing if Guasu runs into him, the Potiguara will be declared winner. Both men are bleeding from the mouth and appear in great distress. At the last moment Guasu veers off, circling his opponent with the intent of wrapping the rope around the man's neck. The Potiguara is prepared for this move, and spins in the same direction, planting himself firmly, then jumping backwards, jerking Guasu completely off his feet. He lays on his back, exhausted, his head being twisted in every direction, but refusing to let go of the rope.

Up to this time the two tribes had been cheering their men on. But now they call for a halt, deciding everyone's needed for a safe voyage home. Guasu stands up, congratulates his opponent and says, *"Che naháñiri guahẽ ...,"* "I must not arrive home with a broken neck." Everyone laughs, the two men embrace, and the matter is settled.

***

As it turns out, the natives have discussed what to do with Yema and me. Shortly after dawn the next morning, Guasu, his face swollen and bruised from yesterday's contest, comes to sit with us. He speaks passable Caeté. "We will take you across the bay," he explains, "and leave you on the other side. The tribe that lives there is the Tupi. They stay only during the dry season. That is now, so they should be close by."

Yema, who knows the etiquette for such things, says, "If we are to arrive in favor, we must bring gifts."

Guasu looks surprised, and others who have been listening respond with murmurs and nods. As usual, the child has made her mark. I wonder, as I have so many times before, *where in the world does this child get her wisdom?* Guasu consults with the others. This is decided quickly, and I get the impression it had been resolved long before the conversation began. "We have the following gifts in mind," he says. "Two of the Carib dugouts and one axe."

Yema address them, saying rather formally in Caeté, "That will be acceptable." Then to me, "Having two of those canoes will be very high-status for the Tupi. And they're going to be amazed by the axe."

This seems like the moment to make my point about the Carib children. Intending to be perfectly clear, I speak in Portuguese and Yema translates, "I want those little ones painted like Caeté children.

We will take them with us to be adopted by the Tupi."

Yema shakes her head, saying to me, "You cannot ask this. Young slaves are quite valuable. They are a prize of war."

"I don't care," I tell her. "The sins of the parents must not burden the children."

The girl tries to explain, but Guasu and the others completely disagree. As far as I can tell, they simply don't understand this notion of morals.

"We have already decided," Guasu says. "We Inanbá get the children because we did not get the iron pot."

I stare at him, struggling to control my anger. *"Mito mba'eve voña!"* I say. "They will not be slaves!"

After more arguing and with no way to resolve this, I walk over to the clearing and sit by Agato's grave. Yema and a few others follow. For the most part, these Indians solve conflicts via group consent. But they've never encountered a stubborn white woman before. Yema sits down next to me, both of us silent and brooding. The others drift off. *"Ta'arõ Agato,"* I call after them. "Honor Agato." I'm determined to get something positive from this tragedy.

We linger here for perhaps an hour. A thunderstorm passes through and Yema shelters under the trees. I sit by the grave, letting the water run down my face. It's not long before I'm soaked from head to foot. When the rain stops, she returns to my side. "What do you think?" I ask.

"Sister Leah, you are right and you are wrong. Right by the way you do things, wrong by the way Indians do things."

"And which are you?"

"I agree with both," she answers, tears coming to her eyes. "But don't you see, poor Agato and I, we are your children. I go along with whatever you do."

Only a few minutes pass before two women and Guasu appear. They have the Carib children in tow, and the women carry the paint pots. Guasu still looks terrible from yesterday, but I think I detect a smile, and now there is something quite pleasing about his manner. He nods to the women and says to Yema, "Show us how you want these children painted."

The Carib youngsters brighten as they're decorated. I doubt they even recognize the patterns, but that's not important, it is the attention from the women that pleases them.

I'm most interested in what Yema will do. As always, she has the right instinct. Besides the body paint, she's directed the face painting—for the girls, a red circle on each cheek. For the boy, a black arrow point on his forehead. Then she has the Inanbá woman paint a red circle on one of her cheeks, an arrow point on the other. Yema kneels in front of the children, telling them something and pointing to her face, turning her head so they can see the painter's handiwork. Then she gestures in my direction. Whatever this dear child said, it must have worked; without hesitation the little boy takes the two toddlers by the hand and leads them over to me.

* * *

Everyone spends the afternoon preparing for tomorrow's voyage south; though first thing in the morning, Guasu will take us north across the bay. We'll ride in one of the large canoes, and tow two smaller ones behind. If we find the Tupi and they accept us, Guasu and the others will return to join their fellows for the trip south. If we don't find them, we've decided to travel to either the Potiguara or the Inanbá villages. Both tribes live a ways inland, so perhaps we can stay hidden from the Portuguese—a terrible choice, but there's no hope for Yema and me alone in this wilderness. Since these tribes hold us in high regard, perhaps things will work out better than expected.

That evening, the Carib children are a pleasant distraction from my worries about tomorrow. Yema spends time playing with them, teaching a few words of Caeté. Nonetheless, I find myself unable to sleep.

At first light we eat a hurried meal and, after many good-byes, tears, and expressions of gratitude, we load ourselves into the large canoe. We have four paddlers, Cabeço and Guasu in front, two women in back, plus a third woman steering. I get the impression they've never worked one of these large canoes before, but they seem to pick it up quickly.

About hundred yards from shore the breeze picks up. I stand and unfurl the sail, letting it roll down the short mast and tying it in place. I hold one corner and Yema holds the other, adjusting the sail to catch the wind. Much to the delight of everyone, the canoe is pushed along at a pace faster than we can paddle. I wouldn't say we exactly tack, but the direction of the wind varies enough that the woman steering from the rear finds her skills tested.

Since they have no loads, the two canoes towed behind float

high in the water. Ours does not. Soon there's seawater splashing over the bow, drenching all of us. Yema and I get to work bailing. But then the breeze becomes so strong that we begin to overtake the waves, striking them with such force that I fear we might swamp. We roll up the sail and resume paddling, riding with the waves without crashing into them.

I ask Yema, "Do these Indians have the skill to take dugouts like this into the ocean?"

"I think so. We always paddled just outside the surf, then came in when we had to."

We'd been so busy staying afloat, I'd failed to pay attention to the far shore. Now we are more than halfway across. I can see a sandy prominence sticking out into the bay directly in front of us, and a beach curving away farther to the north. There's no surf, so the bay must extend to somewhere beyond where we are able to see. None of us can spot smoke or any evidence of people. I say a little prayer, hoping the Tupi will be somewhere nearby. I do not want to repeat this voyage back across the bay, and certainly don't want to venture into the ocean in this, or any canoe.

The Indians begin an animated conversation, apparently deciding what to do next. As we turn more to the west, towards the hills that step their way inland, Guasu explains. "There are two rivers that empty into this bay. The Tupi will be camped farther inland, where there is fresh water. I have not been here for years, but I think that is where we found them before."

Yema says to me in Portuguese, "He hasn't been here since he was a little boy," then gives a doubtful shrug.

As we proceed inland, the color of the water changes, and there seems to be a slight current. One of the men tastes the water and declares it less salty than the bay. I guess this is progress, and whatever this river is, it has to be immense. About the time we bring the sail into play again, someone spots smoke. Sure enough. We see it rising from behind a forested peninsula about two miles ahead— A great deal of smoke.

Rounding the point we view a large Indian camp on the shore a mile distant. There are canoes in the water just in front of us, and they immediately haul in their nets, frantically paddling for shore, alarmed at seeing a Carib canoe in full sail coming at them. But then Cabeço and Guasu both call out while motioning for us to stand. We raise our hands in the sign of friendship, crossing arms at the wrists, our palms open and facing outward.

Yema points to the high ground above the peninsula and gives me a wry smile. "Their sentries must be taking a nap."

The occupants in the canoes ahead look back at us. By now we're a half-mile past the peninsula's end. I assume that since they see no Caribs behind us, and we've made a friendly gesture, they will accept our presence.

We pass the two canoes and the Tupi look into the ones in tow. Guasu calls out in an unfamiliar language, letting them know these are gifts captured from the Caribs. Yema translates for me. The Tupi shout back, obviously not believing. Guasu points out that we're riding in a craft with the same markings. One of the men jumps into the last canoe and inspects it. His companion throws him a paddle. The man moves to the bow intending to untie the rope. He works the knot for a few seconds, then pulls his hands away in surprise. He's never seen anything like this rope. He begins jabbering and gesturing to his fellows.

We in our canoe find all this very funny. And it is a relief knowing our gifts will most likely make us welcome. Finally the Tupi untie the canoe and paddle ahead of us towards shore, all the while calling out to the crowd gathering at the water's edge. A number of people have waded into the water, including children. Apparently there's no piranha.

Yema and I count *ógas*, concluding there were at least forty, most of them elongated versions of the Caeté's and the ones we had at Luís. This means the village consists of more than two hundred Tupi, and it appears to me that all have assembled to meet us. A portly man with many tattoos, sagging belly, and a yellow feathered headdress catches the bow of our canoe as we land. He introduces himself as the *a'kã kuimba'e*. According to Guasu, a phrase that means head man. It pleases me that his title does not include the word blood.

The Tupi swarm over us, nearly overcome with their curiosity— the canoes, the rope, this white-skinned woman wearing clothes made of cloth, Yema and her facial tattoos, and most of all the iron hand axe which Cabeço presents to the headman. Yesterday Yema sharpened it to an edge as keen than my dagger's, and the chief is very impressed, showing it to everyone. He introduces himself as Tendotapavê, adding that his people call him Pavê. He appears to be about forty, with a round face and deeply cleft chin. His hair, decorated with narrow strands of red liana, hangs in a thick braid to the middle of his back.

Questions fill the air, but since Guasu is the only person who fully understands Tupi, it will be a long time before everything can be explained. The conversation goes on, mainly between Guasu and Pavê, but with numerous people interrupting. Yema struggles to keep me informed. Everyone's attention turns to us when Guasu relates our capture and Agato's bravery. I'm already surrounded by women and children who are feeling the fabric of my clothes, touching my skin— not quite so white after all the sun—looking under my habit's ragged skirt, and pestering me to bend down so they can touch my hair. I'm not sure why, because my hair is not much different from theirs.

With all the people pressing closely around me, the attention becomes quite uncomfortable. Pavê notices this and pushes his way through the crowd, taking my hand and Yema's. She in turn takes the Carib boy's hand, and Guasu and Cabeço pick up the toddlers. Despite his bulk, the chief carries himself in a dignified manner, beckoning for our women paddlers to follow us. They leave the canoe and we trudge up the beach, taking refuge from the crowd.

We go inside one of the long *ógas*, and we're greeted by two women, a very old man, and several children. As close as we can tell, these are Pavê's wives and children and a grandfather. The women ask us to sit on mats arranged around a steaming clay pot. The children look after the Carib youngsters. Yema remains with us to translate. It's become apparent over the past days that she prefers the company of adults over those her own age. I'm certain the loss of Agato has much to do with this.

Our hosts treat us to bowls of the minty *jehe'a* tea, and although it's not yerba buena, it still tastes delicious. They also pass around woven bowls heaped with slices of fresh fruit, smoked fish, and dried meat. I skip the meat since I'm unable to determine its origin. It's at this point that Pavê inquires about our being captured, and then our defeat of the Caribs. The more Guasu goes on, the more admiration Yema and I receive. I finally remind Guasu that we were helpless at the time, and it was Agato who saved the day. Interesting that the boy's legacy remains beneficial Yema and me.

Outside the Tupi prepare a welcoming ceremony. It appears so elaborate and high-spirited, I think it's more for them than for us.

They've a narcotic stronger than *pohã*, and used by men and women differently. The women pass around bowls of the stuff, snuffing it into their noses which causes fits of sneezing, watery eyes, and intense drooling. With the first sniff the recipient's head jolts back as if they've been slapped; with the second, the user becomes incoherent. The men, on the other hand, smoke the substance, drawing it into long wooden tubes. Once the smoke is in the tube, they hand it to a friend who, with a great puff of breath, blows the smoke into the man's nostril. The men react just as the women do.

For adornments, the Tupi cover themselves head-to-foot with a sticky resin, then douse each other with baskets filled with red macaw feathers. This is followed by a cacophony of drums, wooden paddles slapping together, and a chorus of saw-toothed sticks drawn against a frame that emits a frightful buzzing sound. The frenzy of dancing that follows is as macabre as anything I've ever seen. Dancers of both genders simply whirl around in circles by themselves, filling the air with red feathers, crashing into one another, falling to the ground, babbling and drooling.

Maybe this is supposed to be entertainment for the children. While they do not take the narcotic, they mimic the adults, then dissolve into fits of hysterical laughter.

***

It's late into the evening now, and after all the merriment we retire to an *óga* next door to Pavê's. Having never slept in a hammock before—though that's all the natives used in Luís—I find it most comfortable. But I do miss the insect netting from my abbey's bedroom. I ask Yema who's next to me, "What did you think of the celebration?"

I'm surprised by her answer. "Guess I've become a little too Portuguese," she says. "It all seemed insane."

Chapter 15

Early in the morning, as they prepare to leave, we see our friends to the water's edge. Cabeço explains they've told the Tupi that the Carib children, Yema, and I are Caeté refugees. Further, he says he's done this as a favor to me, "... if they knew the children were Carib, the Tupi would either kill them or brand them as slaves."

I ask if he understands that offspring should not fall victim to the misdeeds of their parents.

He shrugs and looks eastward. "Just as you are from across the sea," he says, "that idea is as foreign to us as the land from where you came."

"Will you at least consider it?" I ask.

He nods. "I will consider it. That is because you seem to have special knowledge about a great number of things."

At the shore, the two gift canoes are still there next to each other. We make our farewells and thanks, and one of our female paddlers unties the rope and begins to coil it up. An argument breaks out. The Tupi have assumed the rope was part of their gift. In fact, I think they value it more than the canoes. Native rope is usually made of green liana vines that grow everywhere. They're strong, though not at all flexible. The hemp rope must be quite a novelty to the Tupi.

Guasu is reluctant to step into the argument, but since he's the only one who can communicate, he does. He handles the situation in a very Solomon-like fashion, not intervening, instead turning to Pavê. As best I can understand, he says, "The rope is really two. Tied in the middle. May I untie it and give you the longer half?" Pavê agrees, and that settles it.

Just as they push off, Yema nudges my elbow, showing me two colored stones she found. "Yes," I say, "let them know what they're for."

She wades into the water, handing the stones to the woman who steers. "These are for Agato's grave," she tells her. The woman nods and takes them.

I wonder if we'll ever see these Indians or Agato's resting place again. *"Lnvch vshkt hchvr hktn shlnv,"* I whisper in Hebrew. "Rest peacefully our little friend."

***

In the two weeks just past we've become part of the Tupi village, taking our meals with Pavê and his family and sleeping in the *óga* where we spent our first night. A daughter a few years older than Yema and a son about eight share our hut. Pavê's family took in one of the Carib girls. The boy and other girl are with a family close by. We've learned this village is the Tupi's permanent settlement, not just one for the dry season.

I'm happy to be safe, and have adjusted to the daily activities, mostly work relegated to women and children. For me, it appears that boredom comes with safety. But I do miss the conversations with my peers, and it is difficult to work side-by-side with these Indians without some manner of discourse.

There are also many things I find remarkable about the Tupi, though one truly stands out. Their children are the happiest youngsters I've ever seen. They mind their parents, are never disciplined, and almost never get into trouble or argue among themselves.

Everyone's been patient with Yema and me as we've struggled to learn Tupi. The clicks and grunts are quite different and more varied than the Caeté's, and getting the words right is daunting.

Yema's interests in learning continues, so we practice Portuguese and Hebrew words, writing them inside oyster shells using the black face paint. I then present her with the shells mixed up, and she matches the Portuguese shell with the Hebrew one. For a while this attracted some attention. I've tried to explain school to the Tupi, but they dismiss it, reminding me that children learn everything from watching and working alongside adults. At some point I might try teaching them Portuguese, though impossible until I can master their language.

Yema and I suspect Pavê, and likely some others, doubt my connection to the Caeté. When he asked me, I told him I was a refugee from across the ocean, living in the village when the soldiers attacked, escaping with the children. Perhaps he is accepting this just out of courtesy; and if he's suspicious about the Carib youngsters, he's not let on.

Little Yema's ability to impress everyone remains undiminished. The children had a bird-calling contest of sorts. Since in this tribe only the males are allowed to hunt, the boys ran the show. Several of the children have pet toucans and work at mimicking their calls. The men kill these beautiful birds for their colorful feathers which they use in their headdresses.

The Tupi youngsters go to the forest edge with their pets and encourage them to call, imitating the sound to see if they can attract wild toucans. The children whistle "too chee, too chee." A couple of wild birds did show up, hopping on the branches high in the treetops, looking curiously and calling back. Neither were close enough for a poison dart or arrow.

Yema took up the call, "too chee, too chee." The wild toucans swooped down from the trees and circled the children, then fled back to the nearest branches. At the same time the tame birds tried flying to Yema, struggling to the ground because of their clipped wings. All the children looked at her in amazement. She shrugged, picked up the nearest bird and returned it to its owner. Then she strolled over to where I and a few others had been watching.

When she gave me a smile that appeared somewhat excessive, I reminded her of Proverbs 16:18, saying, "Pride goeth before the fall." Exactly as I expected, her smile broadened.

For a week or so I've struggled with a terrible infestation of lice, bathing every day when the tide was in—thus in saltwater—to rid myself of the damnable things. To no avail. The pests have also infested my clothes, and no amount of washing seems to get them out. I guess that's one advantage of going naked. The natives bathe once or twice daily and only have lice in their hair. Sometimes, if just for a few days, they get rid of them completely.

"Sooner or later," Yema teased, "you'll shed your clothes. Then your skin will turn brown as mine, and you will be one of us."

"I am one of you already," I told her, "and I'll do it without exposing myself to everyone."

I found a solution to the problem, though it turned out to be temporary. Many women in the village weave a sort of cloth out of dry grass, using it mostly to cover themselves at night, or to protect food and other things from flies. Yema and I worked out a way to tie pieces together making a rough shift. I'm sure it looks ridiculous, but at least I'm not without some kind of covering. I hung the remainder of my tattered habit on the south wall of our *óga*, hoping the sun would kill the lice so I can again wear it.

So I wore this pathetic garment of woven grass for a few days, though it drove me nearly as crazy as the lice did. The thing itched all the time and was frightfully uncomfortable. I took to sleeping without it at night, and Yema said I'm halfway there. More likely halfway going out of my mind.

Today I have the pleasure of wearing what remains of my ragged habit, and gratefully it feels free of lice. Yema and I, along with several women and children, are wading in a freshwater pond about two miles north of the Tupi settlement. We're gathering frog eggs from the shallows. It seems the frogs lay their eggs in folds of new grass that grows at the edge of the pond. Everyone's been eating this seasonal feast for the past several days, usually boiling the eggs and grass together. The result is surprisingly tasty, though not nearly as good as the hens' eggs and onion greens my mother used to serve for breakfast. But Lisbon is so far away, and surely I'll never see it again.

The walk here reminded me of my time in the jungle when Fr. Julian and I ventured to the Jacu to first meet Yema and her family. Just as then, today is bright and sunny, with fretworks of sunlight decorating the forest floor. The patterns bring back memories of the intricate façades on the few mosques that remained in Lisbon after the Crown expelled the Moors. Seemingly more numerous than the time when I first met Yema, hordes of pale green butterflies— *hapoo jeyurã*, the tear drinkers—hovered everywhere along our path.

We finish egg-gathering a little after midday. Most of the women return to the village, but a few of us remain. We take our baskets down the trail to the beach, planning to search for turtle eggs. The trail winds through the forest and crosses the pond's outlet stream several times.

One of the women describes this place during the rainy season. "You can't find the stream at all," she says. "The entire forest is flooded for almost half the year. The pond is a leftover from the flood." She points to the high water mark. It's about at eye level, easy to spot because of clusters of dead grass, sticks, and fish skeletons wedged in the branches.

As we get closer to the beach, the wind picks up, driving the treetops this way and that, casting showers of leaves upon us. Just as we're able to see the bay, the wind pauses as if holding its breath. Yema and I are in the lead, and what I see out there stops me short. It's a waterspout stretching down from a black cloud into the water about a half-mile distant. All of us crouch behind a rocky outcrop at the edge of the outlet stream to watch. I guess we're spellbound, because no one turns back to the forest for shelter. Then we see something else. At first it looks like one of the many large rocks that dot the shore of this bay. But it's not; it's a ship's boat with men in it. They land just ahead of the looming funnel and flee up the beach. They are black men, Africans.

They've got two hundred yards to cover and there's no way to outrun it. The thing churns onto the beach, a brown torrent of water racing inland, stretching down from a cloud blacker than night. The rain seems to spring from the sand—runnels of it spiking into the air. There's lightning too, crackling, sizzling, the beach sputtering fire. Two of the men tip the boat keel-up and crawl under it, dragging a third man with them. The upswirl catches the boat, spinning it into kindling, scattering the Africans and wood into the air like chaff. The others are about a hundred yards from us, charging for cover, still in the open. The waterspout hits them full-force, the air so thick they disappear. Yema and I throw ourselves to the ground as sand and debris rain down on us.

Within minutes the storm is gone, lashing the hills inland to the north. We look around. The girl and I are alone; the Indians have fled. We see two bodies near the water's edge, four more up the beach closer to us. No one moves except for one in the nearby group. We rush out. The man is dazed and trying to stand. He's bloody from several wounds, face battered, his right arm twisted and obviously broken. As I tend to him, Yema checks the others.

She comes back quickly. "They're all dead," she tells me. "There's one out in the water."

"All Africans?" I ask.

"Yes." She scratches her head. "One man is tied up. He's dead too."

The African becomes somewhat conscious. He's quite thin with woolly hair and nostrils that flair as he struggles to talk. "Who you white whore?" he says. He's speaking Guinea, the common language of West Africa.

"If you're going to curse me," I tell him, "I'll leave you here for the vultures." He's in great pain, but I offer no words of comfort.

"How do you know Guinea?" he wheezes.

"I lived on an island called São Tomé. That's what the Africans spoke."

"Only white slavers on that island speak our language," he says. "That's where we came from."

Yema brings wet seaweed, and we press it against his wounds, tying the long strands over the larger cuts on his legs and arms. He winces, but I'm not very gentle with him. "Who is 'we?'" I ask him, "are you a slave?"

"Not a slave anymore," he says. "My name is Kwasi. I was chief of my tribe." He points seaward. "Planter's boat mine now."

A thin mist hovers on the water from a squall moving inland.

Vaguely I can see a sailing ship a ways out. It's listing. Perhaps run aground or sinking. What bothers me most is another ship's boat rowing for shore. It looks like it has at least twenty men in it.

"My people here soon," Kwasi says. "Then we kill you."

He makes a grab at my leg, but I jerk away. He can't get up, so I guess he's hurt more than I thought.

"Let's go," I say to Yema and take her hand. We run for the forest and begin tracing our steps back upstream.

We've get only as far the rock outcrop where we first took shelter. Here's Pavê, several warriors, and a few women hiding behind them. He's no longer the kindly native chief. His face is painted with two black stripes that form a sideways V, the apex at the corners of his mouth, the upper part extending above the ear, the lower to the edge of his jaw. The women are painting the other men in the same fashion. The Tupi are armed with spears, bows and arrows, and blowguns.

"Who are these black men?" Pavê asks. *"What* are they?"

"Villains from across the sea," I tell him. There's no time to explain. The boat's landed, the men heading in our direction. There are two groups. The forward group runs to Kwasi, and the second bunch trails behind, slower because they're leading five white men in chains. The blacks are well armed— spears, cutlass, and muskets. A few appear to have pistols stuck in their belts. All of them are rain-soaked from the squall, their wet skin reflecting the sun that just now shines through the clouds. They've taken no precautions to protect their weapons, and as wet as they are, I'm certain they won't fire.

One of the women gets our attention and points to the south. Coming up the beach in our direction are fifty Tupi warriors. It's obvious the Africans have also spotted them, and they frantically talk and gesture among themselves, first looking our way, then at the advancing Tupi. They inspect their muskets and pistols, likely deciding they're useless. In the midst of all this, the men in chains start back towards the boat. A few Africans follow them.

I say to Pavê, "I think we have nothing to fear. Let me go talk to them." I ask Yema to repeat this because she's more skilled in the Tupi language than I. The chief answers in the affirmative, and I'm pleased that he understands.

All of us walk back to the beach and stop about thirty yards from the Africans. Two of them level muskets at us. I've never mentioned guns to Pavê, and there's no time now. He's not afraid because he knows nothing of them.

"Kwasi," I call out, "your guns won't work and you're outnumbered. Surrender." He's standing, though not on his own. Two of his fellows are holding him up.

By now the advancing Tupi are almost as close as we. "Tell them to wait," I say to Pavê. He sends a runner over. The warriors pause, their weapons at the ready.

Kwasi remains defiant. "No woman talks to me that way," he shouts.

There's a log on the beach a few feet from us. I go over and sit there, elbows on my knees, chin in my hands. I stare at Kwasi and say nothing. This lasts for about a minute. Despite the tenseness of the situation, a few of his men begin to laugh. Some of the Indians do too. The runner returns and tells Pavê there are canoes on the way with more warriors. The Africans and men in chains who retreated to the water's edge are now back in their boat. They're a short distance out in the water watching the goings-on.

"What is that big dugout in the bay?" Pavê inquires. He means the sailing ship, of course.

"It's from across the sea," I tell him. Quite abruptly I think of the diseases they bring. A shudder passes through me. At the same time I'm eager to find out about the planter from Tomé. Somehow I've got to talk with those white men. I again call to Kwasi. "These natives will kill you and eat you. Put your weapons down."

For a moment the Africans don't move. Then they begin a slow retreat towards the shore, brandishing their weapons, dragging Kwasi and shouting to the boat in the water. The men in the boat call back, pointing to the now approaching canoes. It's quite an impressive sight. Seven war dugouts with six men each, two paddlers, the rest kneeling, ready to do battle with their spears, blowguns, and bows.

Again I caution Pavê not to attack. I know these Indians. If one of their men gets killed or even injured, they will slaughter the Africans and whites and likely burn the planter's ship.

Chapter 16

The men in the boat react to the approaching canoes by rowing ashore and joining their comrades about halfway between us and the water. We move in their direction as does the larger Tupi group. Pavê motions for the canoes to stop at the water's edge. The warriors pile out, half of them forming a line along the shore, the other half blocking the Africans from the north. There's lots of speculation among the Indians about these strange, new men, but no one drops their guard.

Again I call out to Kwasi, "Your situation is hopeless. Discard your weapons. The Indians have promised not to hurt you." I have no idea if this is true, but it's my best hope to avoid bloodshed.

If Kwasi is their leader, he's not very effective because the Africans just mill about, arguing among themselves and shouting curses at us. The whites are saying something, though we're too distant to hear. At last a few of the blacks step out from the group and lay their weapons on the sand. Others follow, including the men holding Kwasi. The whites spot me and start our way.

I put up my hands and yell, "Stop!" They do. Then I take Pavê by the arm and lead him aside. Whatever savage intent these Indians might have, I must keep it from happening. All eyes are on us. I speak slowly, making sure Pavê understands every word. Yema stays next to me, listening carefully. "We should not harm these people. They have many iron tools like the axe you have. And—"

He interrupts. "We should kill them and take what we want."

"Allow me to finish," I plead. "They also have skills that can help us defeat the Caribs." And next, if ever there was a lie, I say, "These men and that ship may be good luck for us."

"What will we do with them?" he asks.

"I don't know. Let me find out who they are." He looks at me with suspicion, and I know what he's thinking. "Pavê," I say, "I will not betray you. Yema and I will translate every word so you know what's going on. Whatever comes after is yours to decide."

He tells me to go ahead. The situation is dangerously complicated. But since the whites are chained and no longer a threat to us, I decide to talk to the blacks first. "Kwasi," I call, "come over here so we can talk." He's walking better, and needs only one man to help him.

When he gets closer he says in clear Portuguese, "What do you want slaver whore?"

Since I'm completely stunned, I ignore this insult. "How is it you speak Portuguese?" I ask.

Despite his injuries, he now has a superior manner about him. "Why don't you just kill us," he says. "We will not be slaves."

"I do not support slavery," I tell him. "I oppose it here, and I opposed it on São Tomé."

He seems to soften. "So will you hear my story?"

"Of course."

"My people came first from the Congo. About twenty years ago, slavers kidnapped most of our tribe and shipped us to Cape Verde for the sugar plantations. After about ten years we bought our freedom. We had our own plantation, and it was prosperous. All of us are Portuguese citizens. Freedmen."

"Then how did you become slaves?" I ask.

"Several months back, the slavers raided our plantation and took as many of us as they could. They figured we were valuable because we knew sugar farming. A slave broker from Tomé sold us to that damned planter over there." He gestures at the white men.

"Does the planter know you are freedmen?" It's against Crown law to enslave freedmen of any color.

"He knows now. It makes no difference. The Tomé slave pens are full of Portuguese citizens. No one cares as long as they're black."

Kwasi is speaking loudly now, and the whites are reacting with disbelief. One of them shouts, "We didn't know any of this. It's all a lie!" If this is the planter, he's an interesting looking man, tall and broad-shouldered, with a full beard of red whiskers. Quite imposing. To me, he looks very un-Portuguese.

"You didn't tell them after you commandeered the ship?" I ask Kwasi.

"Well, yes," he says, "but before that we had this scheme. Once we knew our destination was Brazil with a shipload of supplies for a sugar farm, I decided it was our chance to break free in a new land. We agreed to speak only Guinea so the whites wouldn't know we understood them."

"Who was the man tied up?"

"A white man in a black skin. A free African. He was going to be the planter's foreman."

"Why was he tied up?"

He glances around at the Indians. "Can they understand us?"

"Assume they can," I say.

"We heard these natives are cannibals. We planned to offer him as something for them to snack on." Kwasi looks at the Europeans. "And we planned to make those fools our slaves. See how they like chains."

I turn my attention to Pavê. "What do you think?"

Apparently Yema's done a good job of translating, because Pavê displays some sympathy towards Kwasi. He gently takes the man's arm and examines it. "Get a splint on this," he tells a woman next to us. He nods towards the whites. "Let us hear their story."

"Who's the planter?" I ask Kwasi.

"Red beard," he says, and produces an iron key. He calls two of his men over. "Go unlock the planter."

As soon as the man's unlocked, he rushes over, protesting all he's heard. He has a strange accent and struggles with his Portuguese. Regardless, his voice is resonant and his blue eyes are intense with anger.

"I'll hear your complaints in a minute," I tell him. "What's your name?"

"I am Lars Orlund from the Netherlands. I paid ten thousand reis for these Africans and their families. They are my property."

I give him a level stare. "It seems to me, Senhor Orlund, that right now you are their property."

Despite Kwasi's obvious pain, he laughs. One woman is holding his lower arm straight while another applies a splint using sticks and a liana-vine wrapping. It's rough, but looks effective.

"Who are you to talk to me like this?" Orlund demands. "Some kind of vagrant white woman with these savages? And those clothes, shreds of a nun's habit? And what female wears a man's belt and carries a dagger?"

"At this moment, senhor, I am the one who is keeping you from getting slaughtered." I'm quite irritated with this fellow and in no hurry to hear his demands. I turn to Kwasi. "You probably want to bury your dead," I say. "If our headman gives you permission, will you act peaceably?"

He nods "I will. Some of them have wives and children on the ship."

Pavê—understanding Yema's translation—gives permission and sends a few of his men to help the Africans. They have no tools to dig with, so they will bury the dead as we did Agato.   The

Dutchman's cooled off some and describes what happened. Apparently it's accurate, because Kwasi raises no objection as Orlund continues, "... and as soon as we sighted land they seized the ship. We were headed for the Luís Colony, but they forced us into this estuary. The storm drove us aground."

"I have something to add," says Kwasi. He looks squarely at the Dutchman. "Did we kill any of your men when we took over? Only one serious injury. Correct?"

Orlund shrugs. "I have to admit," he says, "they were well prepared. Caught us completely by surprise. Only—"

Pavê is getting impatient and signals for them to quit talking. He asks a question. Yema translates. When she speaks her perfect Portuguese, both Kwasi and Orlund cannot believe their ears. "He wants to know what's on that ship," she says. Then smiling, "He calls it a 'big canoe.'"

After a moment the Dutchman says, "Tell him we carry supplies for a sugar farm. As for people, most of my men are locked in the hold. The Africans allowed only a few of the operating crew on deck." He looks out to the bay. "That waterspout missed us. But we still suffered considerable damage."

"How hard aground?" I ask. "On what?"

"A sandbar. Our captain said the ship will float if we offload the cargo. I don't think she's taking on water."

Pavê is still restive, so I suggest we move to the log where I previously had stared at Kwasi. One of his wives comes along, as does Yema. Regardless of how things work out, I think we're stuck with these new people. "A number of things that can happen here," I tell Pavê. "Here are the possibilities. They will need to stay a few weeks to repair the ship. Then you can send them on their way." I'm struck by the fact that if they sail to Luís, Yema's and my whereabouts will be known. I decide to promote a second option. "I think that having them here will keep the Caribs from raiding your village. They want to start a farm to raise a crop called sugarcane. It's used to make a sweet food like honey." I point at the sloping hills to the north. "Do your tribesmen hunt or gather food up there?"

"Not often," he says. "We get more from the jungle along the rivers."

"Those flat areas on the hillside are ideal for sugarcane. There's nothing like that near the Luís Colony." I pause while he thinks on this. "If there's a third possibility," I say at last, "I can't think what it might be."

He stands, extending a hand to his wife. The two of them wander down the beach.

"What do you think?" I ask Yema.

She looks straight ahead. "I think the coryza will return and kill half these people."

"And if they go to Luís," I say, "Girona and his soldiers will come for us and bring the coryza with them."

We watch Pavê and his wife as they mull things over. Finally they head back our way. "I have decided," Pavê tells us. "They can stay twenty days, long enough to fix that boat. Right now these newcomers are at war with each other. If they can get along, perhaps the farm is a good idea. So we shall see." He looks at the ship. "Tell them I want iron weapons and more of those axes."

***

Pavê certainly knows there's nothing like food for hungry people to settle an argument. He orders most of his warriors home and tells the women to bring food for "*ñande mbohupa,*" "our visitors," as he calls them.

A short while later, the Africans and the whites are sitting a distance apart, both eating stew from communal bowls. "What is this stuff?" one of the blacks asks me. His Portuguese is also quite good. That convinces me that Kwasi has been telling the truth.

"Frog eggs and grass," I tell him.

"It needs some red chilies," the man says with a grin.

I address Kwasi. "I want you to come with us to talk with Orlund."

He struggles to his feet, aided by one of his fellows. "Bring him over here," he says.

"It's better if we talk with him over there," I tell him. "I want the other whites to hear what we say."

He's skeptical but goes along, bringing three of his men. Once there I say, "Senhor Orlund, I want you to hear my proposal for regaining your freedom and your ship full of goods."

"What is this insanity?" Kwasi shouts. "They and the ship are now my property."

I put up both hands. "You will hear me out! Do you understand?" When they say nothing, I continue, "The headman has agreed to let you stay long enough to repair the ship. If you insist on fighting among yourselves, you are doomed. He expects you to settle your differences." I look to Pavê. He nods, so I keep going. "If you continue to displease him, these natives will kill you, take what they want from your ship, and burn it." The headman smiles at everyone. There's nothing pleasant about this smile; in fact it's quite chilling.

"Go on," Orlund says.

"These Africans cannot be slaves," I tell him, "because they are Crown citizens. If this case were brought before a magistrate, he would deny your ownership and tell you to file a claim against the Tomé broker." I can see this pleases Kwasi and his men. The whites for the most part give me vicious looks. Regardless, I continue. "I assume you obtained a license for cane-growing?"

The Dutchman nods. "Of course," he says.

"Well, if you kept the blacks as slaves and produced a crop, when the Crown authorities found out you used enslaved citizens, they would seize any payments for your product and put your ship and properties into forfeit."

It's obvious that Pavê understands little of this, so Yema and I take a few minutes to explain.

When I ask Kwasi, "Is the ship's captain Dutch or Portuguese, or something else,"

Orlund answers for him. "Dutch. My countryman."

"So it's clear," I say. "No excuses remain. Your captain knows the law. Thus he would be complicit and put in prison."

"And who would bring such charges?" the Dutchman asks. "Africans are enslaved everywhere, citizens or not."

"*I* will bring charges."

"A woman cannot bring charges in a Crown court," he says. "That much I know."

I respond in my most sarcastic voice. "In that case, I will leave it for you gentlemen to work it out with Senhor Pavê and his warriors." I take Yema's hand and we walk away. Over my shoulder I say, "Perhaps start with where you'd like to be buried. Or better yet, does the ship have a large stew kettle suitable for—"

"Alright!" Orlund yells. "What do you want me to do?"

I stop and stare back at the Dutchman, "It's not what I want you to do. It's what you want to work our with Kwasi and his people. As I said before, otherwise the lot of you are doomed."

Kwasi and Orlund exchange glances. One of them says, "What do you suggest?" Yema and I rejoin the group. Perhaps this is an opportunity to do something about slavery—at least in this little splinter of the New World.

"To begin with," I tell Kwasi, "release your captives and help them repair the ship." Then to Orlund, "Put the Africans to work and share the plantation profits with them. Now that your foreman is dead, they are the only ones who know cane growing."

They gawk at me as if I'm spouting nonsense. "What plantation?" the Dutchman asks. "This is not Luís."

"Has your captain seen the Luís Colony?"

"No."

"If he had," I say, "he'd know there is no suitable land for a sugar plantation anywhere near Luís. My family grew sugarcane on São Tomé, and I lived on that island for several years." I point at the hills to the north. "Those level flats are ideal for cane farming. And I think there's water. That line of trees probably hides a stream's course."

Kwasi asks, "Will the chief let us start a plantation?"

I take a few minutes to make sure Pavê understands. Finally I say, "He's giving you time to repair the ship. So in the meantime, cultivate these natives. Give them some tools and weapons. No guns. They know nothing of guns. But give them a few shovels, axes, knives, and copper, brass, and iron for spear and arrow points. Show them how to work metal. If you have a spare cooking pot, give them that. They will prize a metal cooking pot above all else. If you manage yourselves well, he may grant you permission for a plantation."

Orlund addresses Kwasi. "As crazy as this woman sounds, I agree to all of it if you will release us." The men clasp hands, and Kwasi gives the key to Orlund. He immediately unlocks his men. They walk around, shaking the feeling back into their legs. Orlund introduces his second in command, and says to the man, "Take the boat back to the ship with an equal number of our crew and Africans." He hands the shackle key back to Kwasi. "No more chains for anyone," he says.

Kwasi selects four of his people to go with them, including a lieutenant whom he tells to release the whites from the hold and unchain the captain and on-deck crew. "Bring the empty water casks," he adds, then looks at Orlund and nods towards Pavê. "And let's give the headman here one of our pigs."

"A fine idea," says Orlund. "Give him that damn boar that's raising so much hell. Tomorrow we'll start unloading and bringing people ashore."

When Pavê understands about the gift, he instructs several of his men to lend a hand; but he wants to know what a pig is. Yema has described it as a "fat peccary."

I try to explain that Portuguese ships often carry domestic livestock, but get nowhere with this. Anything domestic to him is a pet, such as the gray sloth that prowls the ceiling of his *óga*.

"A peccary cannot be a pet," he says.

"And neither is this pig," I tell him. "It's something your tribe can feast on."

By now the ship's boat and canoes are ready to set out, and Kwasi and Orlund stand at the water's edge giving instructions. It appears the truce is holding.

Kwasi returns first, still aided by one of his fellows. "I'm going to lie in the grass over there," he says. "I am exhausted, and I believe things will work out for the best."

Pavê confers with several of his warriors, finally deciding to leave twenty or so here to keep an eye on the newcomers. The rest of the Tupi begin heading back to their settlement.

When Orlund joins us, he asks me, "What is your name, and who are you? I think you are a nun or perhaps a novitiate. Your manner is too—"

"My name is Leah," I tell him. "In time you will know the rest." At hearing my own words, my heart sinks. I should never have said "Leah." Only Jewish girls are so named.

"'Leah,'" Orlund repeats, "how interesting." He gives me a questioning smile. "Tomorrow, when the men return from the ship, they will certainly bring Captain Vincent, and also someone I'm sure you'll be eager to meet."

"Oh?"

"Yes indeed. Once we repair our ship, a priest who is destined for Colony Luís."

I struggle to keep my voice level. Out of the corner of my eye I see Yema put a hand to her mouth. "Is he Dutch?" I ask.

"No, a priest of your country," he answers. "Perhaps you've

heard of him—a champion of the Inquisition—Father Armand de Tristamo from Porto."

Chapter 17

With news of this Fr. Tristamo, I tell Orlund we will see him the next day. I'm sure he senses my anxiety despite my attempt to sound at ease. Yema and I return to the Tupi village with Pavê and his wife, this time walking along the beach rather than through the forest.

As soon as we are out of earshot, the headman asks, "You told me the foreigners in Luís made slaves of many Caeté. Did they intend to do that here?"

"I'm not sure," I tell him. "But I doubt it. We have the advantage in numbers."

"And what about these 'guns' as you call them?"

I look at Yema, surprised she translated this. She does not react, and I'm certain she's occupied thinking about the new priest. But her mentioning guns to Pavê makes it clear she wishes to protect the Tupi as much as I do.

I answer his question. "Guns are as deadly as your poison darts and arrows. They make a noise like thunder and give off a puff of smoke. Your weapons have an important advantage. Once a gun is shot, it takes a while to make it ready again. Your warriors can shoot five arrows in that time. Also, as you saw today, they often don't work in the rain."

Pavê's wife begins telling him something, talking so fast I can't understand her. He listens for a moment, then stops. Pavê faces me, gently taking my arms. "Leah," he says, "you provide me with truths that I could never understand. Because just like them, you are *é'póra*. That gives you influence with these strangers. So I want you to be part of my council."

"What is *é'póra?*" I ask Yema.

She doesn't know either, and quite a discussion develops between her and Pavê. He keeps pointing to the back of his hands, then to me. Finally she says, "Since your skin is so white, he thinks you are a ghost."

I find this almost comical. "I am honored," I tell him, "*é'póra* or not."

"Good," he says, and we continue on our way.

Evening approaches, and shadows from the forest edge stretch onto the beach. Soon the sun will be hidden behind the canopy. Yema walks in front of us. She has a driftwood stick which she uses to cuff the sand, each strike sending little sprays of it to one side or the other. It's remindful of how she tested for snakes when Agato was with us. By her way of walking, I know what's on her mind.

I catch up with the child, placing my hand on her shoulder. "Snakes?" I ask.

"Priests," she says, and does not look up.

Just beyond the narrow surf, three Tupi canoes head south towards their village. Apparently they have the promised boar trussed up in one of them, because his squeals are loud enough to hear. "Think about pork for dinner," I say to Yema. "We have the upper hand here. Maybe we'll tie up the priest just like that pig."

"And eat him?" This is not said in jest. She jams her stick into the sand, sending a shower in front of her.

"An unfortunate choice of words," I say. This finally gets a smile from her. "We'll work something out."

***

Shortly after returning, we ate our evening meal. The Tupi had butchered the pig and distributed it around, saving the choicest parts for Pavê and his family, namely the heart, kidneys, liver, and assorted offal. I'd eaten pig liver before, and found it quite tasty. I gladly skip the rest of the viscera which Yema and the others apparently relish. Much to my annoyance, the child makes a show of eating intestine cooked stiff as overdone bacon, breaking off pieces and crunching them between her teeth.

"It's impolite to chew with one's mouth open," I tell her.

"For we natives," she says with a bit of a sneer, "it lets our host know we like the food."

"Ask our host if there's a Tupi word for brat."

She does, and Pavê laughs, pointing a finger at Yema. *"So'o josopy!"* he bellows. Everyone finds this amusing.

With our bellies full, we sit around the fire and go over the day's events. Outside the wind picks up. In the distance thunder booms. Soon the rain arrives, pounding the *óga's* thatched roof. Perhaps the downpour will continue tomorrow, delaying the priest's arrival. Yema sits on the ground, her back against my legs. Pavê sits next to me while one of his wives kneels behind him. She unbraids his hair, cleans it with a comb made of bone, and carefully braids it again, weaving fresh strands of red vine into it. I do the same with Yema's, but her hair is too short for a long braid, so I make two pigtails, tying them off with the red vine.

"We need to explain more of our situation to Pavê," I tell her.

"I must first tell him about Agato," she says.

The Indians grow quiet, giving her their full attention. Yema tells Agato's story, intoning it as legend, allowing a little of her musical voice to come through— Beginning with her father and the jaguar cape, our imprisonment, then our escape, the trek through the jungle, our adventures on the beach, the tragic visit to the Caeté village, and finally our capture by the Caribs and Agato's heroic efforts in saving us. Many of the Tupi run hands along their legs, considering Agato's injuries and what it was like to run through the jungle in so much pain. At the end, Yema sings the first lines of the *Confiteor Deo,* the Indians enthralled by the strange Latin words and the child's enchanted voice.

Yema's *Confiteor* trails off as she elevates her hands over the fire in the Hebrew *baraka*. Everyone, even the men, are moved to tears. The first to speak is Pavê's wife, the one who reworked his braid. She stands up and pats her abdomen. "I am with a new child," she announces. "If it is a boy, his name will be Agato."

"Thank you," I say to her. "That is indeed an honor." Next I next turn to Pavê and say, "So you can see that the priests of the Inquisition wish to capture and kill Yema and me. Thus we must stay hidden when the priest visits."

"If they are here to stay," he says, "that is not possible."

"Well," I admit, "I've not thought this through. Since he's never been to Abbey Luís, he knows nothing of this. Perhaps I can convince him of our innocence."

Yema shakes her head. "Priests are stubborn," she says. "We should just make up some kind of story."

"And when he finally goes to the Luís Colony?" I ask.

The child stands and takes on a defiant posture. I'm astonished at her vehemence. "Then he must never get there," she says.

***

We awake next day to the continuing sound of rain. At our morning meal with Pavê I say, "Maybe this weather will keep our visitors away."

My hope is short-lived when we hear a commotion outside, immediately followed by one of Pavê's sons charging into the *óga*. "The visitors are here," he shouts.

Sure enough. Coming up the river is the ship's boat and a couple of Indian canoes. Most of the people crowd to the water's edge, many of them holding large palm leaves over their heads. Yema and I move to our hut. We'll wait for a better view of the arrivals. One of Yema's friends, Pavê's daughter, comes with us, then decides she wants to see the new people close up.

"You can help us," I say to her. "Do not tell them where we are."

She agrees, and takes off running. All we're able to see is the men alight from the boat. They are under an oilcloth which hides their faces, but two are African, Kwasi and the man helping him. We think we recognize Lars Orlund. It's the other two whites we can't identify. As they walk towards us up the slope, three seamen accompany them, one with a keg hefted on his shoulder, the other two carrying a ship's chest by its handles.

It's obvious that Yema's friend did not understand me. As the group gets closer, she says something to Orlund, tugs at his hand, and leads him directly to our hut. He appears confused until he spots Yema and me in the doorway.

I suppress my panic, doing my best to sound welcoming. I feel Yema behind me as she slips the dagger into my waistband. "Greetings," I say to Orlund. "Who are your new companions?"

"Hello Leah," he says. "I'm going to meet with the headman. You ladies must come next door to interpret." Then in afterthought, "And I'll introduce you to our captain and navigator."

"Not the priest?" I ask.

"No, perhaps this afternoon if the rain stops. This weather is too inclement for him."

What a relief. "Just a moment," I tell him, and retreat into our hut. I pull the dagger from my belt and hand it to Yema. "What was I supposed to do with this?"

The child is unremitting, her voice almost a growl. "Use it this afternoon," she says.

"First hear what story I tell them. I think they'll believe it."

We go next door, through the crowd of curious natives

surrounding Pavê's *óga*. The entire village seems to be looking on. Once inside, it's evident everyone's been waiting for us.

Orlund presents Captain Vincent and the navigator to Pavê, then to me. Pavê sits at his usual spot, the log bench next to the fire pit, a wife on either side. Yema stands behind the headman, quietly translating while the downpour rattles the thatch over our heads. Two of Pavê's advisors—tribal elders, their bodies covered with tattoos and feathered ornaments—sit on a bench across from him. He directs me to sit with them. I guess my appointment to his council is official.

The Europeans exchange questioning glances, but I can see that Kwasi understands what has just happened. I explain briefly, then ask him, "Are you feeling better today?" The African certainly looks improved. His arm is in a sling, with a new splint made of ship's materials.

"I am," Kwasi says. "Thank you."

But I see he's not comfortable standing, so I suggest he sit on the vacant bench next to Pavê's. He's helped by his comrade and settles himself onto it. The man assisting him takes a position standing behind Kwasi. I hadn't taken much notice of this fellow earlier, but now I do. He's an immense man, with broad shoulders and massive arms. A sheathed cutlass hangs from a sash around his waist. It's obvious he's here to protect Kwasi as well as assist him.

I can see that the Europeans find the attention paid to Kwasi—and not to them—aggravating. To soften this, I say to Orlund, "I see you've brought gifts."

"I certainly have," he says. He opens the sea chest and lays three hand axes, three heavy chisels, and bolt of gauze at Pavê's feet, explaining that the cloth can be draped over a hammock and is useful for protecting people from insects. Pavê examines the gauze, looking through it, blowing and feeling his breath on the other side. He comments that it will help him and his family sleep at night.

Orlund presents the chief with the keg, placing it on the bench next to Kwasi. Next the Dutchman produces a copper bowl from his pocket and, using the spigot at the base of cask, dribbles black syrup into the bowl. Interestingly he turns to me. "Should I taste it first?" he asks.

"I'm impressed with your sense of protocol," I tell him, and look at Yema.

She's already asked Pavê. He smiles and reaches for the bowl.

At first, he's more interested in the copper vessel than its contents, testing the rim with his fingers, thumping it with a fingernail. The thump produces a dull metallic sound. His eyes light up when he tastes the syrup. *"Hũ taiírete,"* he says, "Black honey," and passes it to the wife on his right. She's pleased with the bowl and the syrup, then reaches behind her husband and passes it to the second wife. The elders get their turns next.

"Senhor Pavê," Orlund says, "what you taste here is black syrup. It's one of the products that will come from our cane farm. If your people would work for us, in return we will give them with black syrup and other goods." He gestures to the tools at Pavê's feet.

I can't be sure if Pavê understands, because he asks Yema several questions before he responds. Finally he says, "We will consider this."

For the first time Kwasi speaks up, glancing first at Orlund. "We also want to thank you and your warriors for helping us offload our ship."

"How's that coming along?" I ask.

"Quite well," Captain Vincent says. "We should be fully unloaded by evening. Then I think my ship will float again, and we can move closer to shore. This appears to be a truly fine anchorage."

"We had a solemn morning," Kwasi offers. "We brought the wives and children ashore for those who were killed yesterday. Fr. de Tristamo will hold a Mass for them tomorrow."

With the mention of the priest, Orlund and the two ship's officers focus on me. "Well, gentlemen," I say, clasping my hands and settling them on my lap, "I guess we should talk about who I really am." I point to some vacant benches a few feet away. "Please sit down." Outside I see that the rain has stopped. Patchy sunlight begins to appear around the village. Sooner or later I must meet this damned priest.

Before I start, Pavê's two daughters begin serving bowls of *jehe'a* tea. These two girls are nearing maturity, and I'm sure our visitors find the proximity of these beautiful, brown-skinned and naked young women quite distracting. An awkward silence settles over the men which I find amusing. I take the opportunity to fill the copper bowl with black syrup and pass it around. "Try some of this in your tea," I say to the Indians. They do, and respond agreeably.

Orlund says, "Please, Leah, now tell us about yourself."

"To start with, gentlemen, I was called Leah before I took my Christian name. I am both a *Conversa* and a nun, and I will be pleased to assist Fr. de Tristamo in preparation for the Mass tomorrow. It will be the first on this stretch of coast." Yema, who is standing at the edge of the group, looks at me as if I've lost my senses. I smile her way and continue. "Since you have not yet seen Colony Luís, I need to tell you what is going on there. Or at least what was going on there a month ago before we fled."

I address Captain Vincent. "It is my understanding from yesterday that you plan to visit Luís? To take on a cargo of dyewood before returning to Portugal?"

"That is correct," he says.

"The last I heard, Luís is in full rebellion, and no dyewood is being harvested. However there is a port a day's journey south from there that will likely have dyewood."

"What started the rebellion?" the navigator asked.

"The Caeté Indians did most of the harvesting," I say. "They are very susceptible to our routine head colds. For them a cold can be fatal." Yema has stopped translating and is just listening to me. Not informing Pavê about the coryza is a travesty, but I will deal with that later. Right now I must get past the subject of who we are. "Many Indians refused to work, so the dyewood supply dried up. Also, they began attacking the whites in reprisal for the illness. At the same time the African slaves rebelled against both the Portuguese and the Indians. Most of the settlement was burned, and the garrison soldiers could not restore order."

"And you?" Orlund asks.

Nodding in Yema's direction, I say, "This child who speaks Portuguese so well was a student in the settlement school. Since I was acquainted with her family in the Caeté village, we fled there to escape the violence. Unfortunately the garrison soldiers raided the village and killed everyone in retaliation. Only Yema and I escaped. We wandered up the coast for about two weeks before we arrived here. It's very fortunate that these generous Tupi took us in."

The look on Yema's face tells me she likes what she's hearing. The girl begins whispering again to Pavê. I pray she will keep the coryza out of her translation.

"So senhores," I continue, "I am Sister Mãe da Doçura of the Coimbran Order." I move my hands across my skirt. "These rags are what's left of my habit. I came originally from Lisbon, then to São Tomé, and on to Luís. On Tomé, I was the principal scribe for Bishop Henrique Cão. My brother had a sugar plantation there, and I am quite familiar with the culture and refining of sugarcane."

Obviously I've touched on an important subject, because both Orlund and Kwasi begin speaking at once. I put my hands in the air. The hot sun that followed the rain, and the press of villagers around us, has turned the *óga* stifling hot. "Wait a moment," I say. "Kwasi, if you feel up to it, let us move to outside to the shade of the community hut. There's places to sit, and it's only a short walk. It is open and we'll be much cooler."

He agrees, and we say goodbye to Pavê and his family, threading our way through the crowd and into the sunlight. There's a light breeze, and it feels delightful. Kwasi is walking quite well, but his companion—I'm sure the man is his bodyguard—stays with him. The rest of the visitors follow us to the community hut, saying they will wait until we finish our discussion.

As we head that way, Orlund is the first to speak. "Sister Doçura," he asks, "what do you know about planting cane sops?"

"I know how to start sops and ready them for planting. But do you know why they're called that?" Both men shake their heads. "I think they're called sops because the length of cane looks like a little mop after the roots sprout. Or maybe it's because they are sopping in wet sand to sprout. Anyway, when they are fully sprouted, one puts them in the ground and keeps the canes watered. Is there something more to your question?"

"Yes there is. My foreman, God rest his soul, supplied enough cane starts for twenty acres. At least that's what the poor fellow told me. Now Kwasi claims we may have enough for forty acres."

"Explain please," I say to Kwasi.

"I've been taking care of the starts ever since we left São Tomé. Each cane is about three feet long. They have at least a dozen buds each. We unloaded the sand beds this morning, and I got a good look at them."

We've reached the community hut and find places to sit along one wall. A few Indians have followed us, but nothing like the crowd at Pavê's. Yema's stayed behind, so I assume she is satisfied with my story. Once we're settled, I say, "That's curious. Usually a sop is three buds long. How many are rooted?"

"From what I saw," Kwasi says, "almost every bud that's been wet has roots. And nearly all have leaf spears. They are quite healthy."

"And what do you propose?"

"We had the experience on Cape Verde that if a node is rooted and has leaves on a node above it, it will take root in soil. So if I cut canes to shorter lengths, but each with both roots and leaf spears, we will have more than enough sops for forty acres."

I turn to Orlund. "Do you object to this?"

"It's not that I object, Sister Doçura, it's just different from what I understand. If Kwasi is right, we could have a substantial sugar harvest in the first year."

"I've seen this practiced on Tomé," I tell them. "I think that individual cuttings with roots and leaves will indeed grow. If there are no leaf spears, then I suggest three nodes in length for each start."

I rise to my feet. In courtesy, they stand also. "Now you must please excuse me. I have chores here that need my attention. I will come over to your unloading area in the afternoon to meet Fr. Tristamo."

***

After the men leave, I walk back to my hut and change into my reed garment. The lice have returned, and I desperately need to bathe and rinse my clothes. It doesn't take long to find Yema. She's playing with some children, and all of them laugh and make fun of me when they see what I'm wearing. "The tide's in," I say to her, "I'm going to bathe and wash my habit. The lice are driving me crazy. Come with me. I need your impressions of this morning."

The two of us walk to the bathing area, and I can see that the tide is high by the water's level on the stick barricade. The barricade is essentially a fence made of sticks woven tightly together. It's an ingenious way to avoid the perils in this river. When the water's fresh, it keeps the piranha out. When the water is salty, it keeps the *ipirã ijoguahaỹ* at bay. I've never seen a large specimen. The small ones look like catfish, and are quite good to eat, but the Indians say the fish can grow to monster size, perhaps nine feet long, supposedly able to kill a person with one bite.

Yema splashes around in the water, ducking her head under to cleanse her hair. I wade in, still wearing the reed garment, and proceed to rinse my habit. There are a few women and children bathing, and they find my wearing the tent-like outfit into the water hilarious. Ignoring them, I finish with my habit, hang it on the barricade, and take my bath. That brings more hilarity from the onlookers. When I get to my knees on the sandy bottom, the water just comes up to my chin. I pull the stiff tent over my head, allowing it to float on the surface while I wash, never revealing more than my shoulders above water. Oh what I'd give for even a fragment of soap!

My gold chain catches sunlight, glinting just under the surface. I press it to my heart as my eyes settle on Yema. I whisper, "Someday you will wear this dear child. You are my daughter."

At last I say to her, "If you are through making fun of me, what did you think of my story this morning?"

"I liked it," she says. "I explained what's going on to Pavê." Her look turns serious. "Why did you offer to help with Mass tomorrow? They said that priest admires the Inquisition."

"I will be courteous to him. That is, until I need to be otherwise."

Chapter 18

I wait until mid-afternoon, then take the trail to the beach from the freshwater lake where we harvested frog eggs. Yema, who is unwilling to meet the priest, refused to come with me. I pause at the vantage point where we took shelter from the waterspout, and look over the unloading area. There is more equipment and people than I ever imagined. The first thing that gets my attention is a swine enclosure that was obviously brought from the ship. It's made of tar-oiled planks and is nearly five feet high. Every now and then, accompanied by a series of loud squeals, a pig bangs into the side of it.

Several fires burn at intervals along the beach, and it appears that meals are in preparation. The adults, black and white, remain in separate groups, but the children, all of them African, run everywhere. I'd hoped there might be a woman among the Europeans, but I see none, only sailors and ship's officers. A small knot of Tupi warriors remain. They appear at ease, sitting together on boxes of goods from the ship, and occasionally trying to communicate in sign language with the new arrivals.

Finally I locate Lars Orlund and Captain Vincent and head their way. I pull at the ragged hem of my habit, quite uncomfortable that my legs are bare almost to the knees. When I step into view, I get numerous stares from the sailors, and I'm sure they see me blushing despite myself.

"Ah Sister Doçura," Captain Vincent says. "You have come just in time. We hope you will sup with us."

"Go ahead. Enjoy your meal," I say. "I'll stay for a bit, but I must get back before nightfall."

"The same," the captain says. "We don't want to get caught in the open if the rain comes again." He gestures towards the bay. "We'll return to the ship for the night."

"Oh my goodness," I say, looking in that direction. "Your ship's much closer." *And the vessel is much larger than I first supposed.*

"A blessing indeed. She is anchored in thirty-five feet of water, and only fifty yards from shore. This is an excellent harbor, the best I've seen."

"So what are your plans after you deliver the new priest to Luís?" I inquire.

He briefly considers this. "I had planned to pick up a load of dyewood at the Luís colony. If it's still in rebellion, then I'll venture south to see if I can find a supply. On the way back, I do plan to stop here before sailing to Lisbon. If we can find them at either port, I've got a list of additional items we could use here."

As we're talking, a tall, brown-robed priest strides towards us. He has a full head of hair drawn taut and held from behind by a leather collar that circles his neck. A silver cross dangles from the collar and rests at the hollow of his throat. He has a close-cropped beard and intense gray eyes. Before either Orlund or Vincent can speak, the priest says, "And this must be Sister Mãe da Doçura." He gives me a grim smile. "These men cautioned me that you are a woman not to be trifled with."

His comment sounds fatuous in the extreme. Certainly not what I expected from an inquisitor. "This New World imparts wisdom in substantial measure," I say. "One can only hope that all who travel these shores will so benefit."

Orlund and the captain erupt with laughter. One of them says, "We warned you, de Tristamo."

Without reaction, the priest extends his hand. "Sister, I am Armand de Tristamo. I wish to commend you for your skillful rescue of us, and your ability to strike peace with the Africans."

I take his hand and say, "Thank you, Father. May I help you prepare for the Mass tomorrow?"

"Your offer is greatly appreciated, dear Sister. However, we do not have a Trinity. So I will conduct a simple graveside service for the departed souls." Then he asks, "So these Indians are not cannibals?"

"I think not," I say, shifting my focus to all three men. "Nothing I've seen indicates they eat human flesh. Also, the Tupi cultivate several crops, and they tend these gardens with great skill. It is my belief their work in your cane fields would be of value. Truly, your project is off to a good start. If the peace holds, I believe the Indians will welcome a sugar plantation. By the grace of God, you have encountered one of the few friendly tribes on this coast."

"Dear Sister," Tristamo says, "It is my belief that God placed *you* in our path. That He created the storm to bring us here. Perhaps even the waterspout to smite those who seized our ship?"

This might be a clumsy attempt to test my faith. "So it would seem," I answer. "God's wisdom is present in all matters."

"Then you must—"

I interrupt him to put an end to this nonsense, saying, "Please excuse me, gentlemen. I must pay my respects to Senhor Kwasi," then crane my neck, making an obvious effort to spot him. I don't see Kwasi, but do recognize his bodyguard and immediately walk off in that direction. I'm feeling some pleasure in seeing Fr. Tristamo left in mid-sentence.

When I approach the Africans, I see Kwasi sitting on a box of ship's stores. He's eating his dinner. *"Abari mtu Kwasi,"* I say, using the traditional Guinean greeting, "I trust you are feeling better."

"I am, Sister. Thank you." He stands and takes a few steps. *"Harba uduze anmuntu,"* he says— "Walking on my own."

I notice that most of the African women wear long wraps of black or brown cloth that go around their middle and down to their ankles. Yet from the waist up, they are as naked as the Tupi. "Kwasi, may I ask a favor?"

"Certainly. Please tell me."

"My current attire is not appropriate for a nun. I see most of your women wear wraps of cloth. Do any of them have one to spare?"

He asks the women in his group, but none has an extra, so he tells his bodyguard to see if he can find one. The man trots around to the other fires and returns empty handed. He bows to his chief and says, *"Ninkoso* Kwasi, we will have an extra cloth in the morning."

"Excellent," he tells the man, and says to me, "I will have someone deliver it to your village tomorrow."

I thank him and start for home, walking up the beach to the lake trail, purposely avoiding the Europeans.

***

The next morning a ship's boat appears with Orlund and Captain Vincent. There are four oarsmen, and two of them are Tupi warriors. When I express my surprise to Pavê, he informs me that he ordered his men to learn every skill they can from the visitors. Yema and I meet Orlund and Vincent at the water's edge. The planter hands me a folded black cloth. "Compliments of Kwasi," he says.

I unfold it partway, gaging the length. "This will do nicely. Where is Senhor Kwasi?"

"He and others are surveying the hillside. This afternoon he will tell me if it is a good place to grow sugarcane."

"So you trust him?"

"I have no choice. If we are to succeed, he has the knowledge we need."

"A plantation is a large project," I say. "Did you also get funds from the Church or Crown?"

Orlund says, "No, I did not want them involved. I am a wealthy man back home and I am financing two-thirds, Captain Vincent the rest."

We're walking slowly toward Pavê's hut when Vincent says, "We have related matters to discuss with you. Some of a sensitive nature." He looks at Yema. "Could the three of us talk in the community hut where we did yesterday?"

I stop and take the girl aside, speaking to her in Caeté, "I've never kept anything from you, and I will not now. But perhaps I'll learn more from them if— Sorry, that's not what I meant to say. They want to talk privately, and I'll tell you everything that is said. Is that all right?"

Yema is wise beyond her years. She curtseys and says, "Gentlemen, good seeing you," then takes off running.

Both men shake their heads. Captain Vincent says, "Is there something about that child you're not telling us."

"In time, gentlemen, in time."

Once seated at the community hut, Orlund begins to talk. "We must ask you some uncomfortable questions, Sister Doçura, and I hope we can reach an understanding." He looks with concern at the several Indians gathered around, three of them sitting on the bench right next to us. They appear to be listening to everything we say.

I smile at the two Dutchmen. "The Indians can't understand a word. One has to realize that these natives do not have our European sense of the individual. Their community is almost always put ahead of personal needs, even ahead of their families. They share everything. For instance, if they have a dispute, the Tupi resolve it with a group discussion. So they see themselves as part of us, or we part of them. That's why they're here, even though they don't know what we're saying."

Orlund shrugs and says, "That's an example of why we must rely on your guidance if we are to succeed here. So we need to know where your loyalties lie."

"What do you mean?"

"To the Church, Portugal, these Indians, little Yema, something else?"

Most likely I can trust these men, but I'm not quite ready to do so. "Why is this important?" I ask.

Orlund looks at Captain Vincent and says, "I told you we wouldn't get a straight answer from her." He pauses, searching for what to say next. At last he says, "Well then, we think your handling of Fr. Tristamo yesterday was brilliant."

"He's not what I expected," I say. "Not from 'a champion of the Inquisition' as you called him."

"Oh he's a champion all right. Just hides it well. The man's jollity is his way of getting people to open up to him. Obviously you weren't fooled."

"Ah, my first impression of Tristamo was correct."

Vincent clears his throat and asks, "Because he's a man of the cloth, do you feel a loyalty to him?"

"As a priest, yes; as an inquisitor, no. I believe inquisition is a corruption of faith. I don't hide that opinion from anyone."

"Just so!" Vincent says. *"Een verbastering van het geloof.*

The same as we Dutch call it, 'a corruption of the faith.'"

"So we must tell you, Sister, Tristamo believes that all Conversos are suspect. A corrosive influence that should be expunged from the faith. He knows about your time on São Tomé with Bishop Cão, that you opposed slavery and had disputes with both Crown and Church."

"Why are you telling me this?"

"Because your influence with the Tupi benefits our efforts to grow cane. We need you as an ally."

"Thank you. Your project benefits me also. But why—?"

"You are in danger, Sister Doçura!" Vincent says. "The priest has a group of followers on my ship, but we have a spy among them. It is Tristamo's intent to denounce you."

"He's only one man. If you two don't support—"

"No, no," Orlund says, "he'll wait until he gets to Colony Luís. When he's surrounded by cronies."

I shake my head. *If they only knew.* "What cronies? Did you tell him that Luís is in chaos? He may find nothing there. Perhaps the Portuguese have fled?" *I can only hope. Regardless, this situation is perilous.*

"He knows about the rebellion," Orlund answers. "Still, he wants to go."

Vincent speaks up. "As captain, I am bound to take him there. The Diocese Tomé paid me for his passage, and he is my obligation. This deviltry of his surfaced only after we set sail."

"When will your ship be ready?"

"At least two more weeks. There are many repairs to do."

I get up and pace around. At last I say, "Gentlemen, what is it you want to do? Is there something you want *me* to do?"

Orlund says, "We thought you might have some ideas. Anything other than doing away with him."

"Why not offer Tristamo a share of the plantation in return for his silence?"

"We thought of that. It won't work. Since you've been gone from Europe, the Inquisition has become a monstrosity. He would denounce us and have the Crown seize the plantation and Vincent's ship. The legions of inquisitors now use their power to acquire as much wealth and property as they can. They are greedy beyond imagination."

I return to the bench across from them. "There has to be more to this than your concern for my welfare. What haven't you told me?"

"Only that the man's suspicions extend to everyone. We know Tristamo thinks we Dutch are not sufficiently doctrinaire. And now since the Africans are free, he can go after them too."

"The Africans are Catholic."

"He distrusts the blacks even though they are Catholic. That's because they still follow some practices from the Congo."

I raise my hands in exasperation. "That's no secret. On Tomé, they openly mixed their traditional beliefs with our faith. I'm sure it was the same on Cape Verde."

"That's just it. Tristamo saw all this while we were on São Tomé. And you know as well as I, Bishop Cão was driven from the island because he allowed blacks that freedom."

"I've never believed that. It's because he was African and opposed to slavery."

"Our point is," Vincent says, "that Fr. Tristamo has plenty of excuses to come after you, the two of us, and the Africans. Greed always finds a way."

I stand and shake out the cloth, testing to see how it fits me. It wraps around my waist nearly twice, and reaches to my feet. "This is exactly what I needed," I tell the men. "Please thank whomever supplied it. Next time you see me, I'll be wearing my African habit."

Both men get to their feet. Orlund says, "How can you be so unconcerned after what we've told you?"

"Please excuse me, gentlemen. I have chores that need attention. When you come up with a plan, I will gladly assist you. In the meantime, I will also try to think of something."

***

By the time I get back to our hut, my head is spinning. My hope that Yema and I would remain safe in this village now seems impossible. I keep thinking the only solution is to kill Tristamo, or have the Indians dispose of the priest by selling him to another tribe as a slave. He would not last long that way.

My *óga* is deserted, so I drape the insect gauze over my hammock and climb under it, staring up at the timbers that support the roof. *This is what I need, to be in a cocoon, wrap myself up and emerge a different person in another land. A land without conflict.*

I wake up in a little while, hungry and wanting to talk with

Yema. I'd dreamt of writing my family, and decide to ask Captain Vincent for paper and a quill and ink. Perhaps he even has a spare ship's log that I could use for a journal.

I go searching for Yema. The child is always easy to locate. All I have to look for is a crowd of children, and she will be at the center. I find her in the community hut, kneeling on the ground with two other youngsters while several more look on. She's made a set of jackstraws and is teaching them how to play.

My stomach growls, so I go looking for something to eat. My conversation with Yema can wait. A family of Indians have a smoky fire at the far end of the community hut, and I walk over to it. These people are so generous and easy to be with. They have a harvest of oysters roasting on the coals, with many more cooked and open, cooling on a bench. A woman asks me if I'd like some. I thank them and sit down to eat. The adults are having an animated exchange with the children, and I try to understand what they're saying. But they are talking so fast I can hardly fathom a word. It makes me appreciate how Pavê and his family slow down when I'm in the conversation.

Yema comes over and sits next to me. She's chatting with the Indians at almost same pace as they. I am amazed. "How have you learned this so quickly?" I ask her. "We've not been here that long."

"It's been almost a month," she says, then puts a hand to her mouth. "Have you kept track of when Agato died?"

She knows I haven't. "I am sorry sweetheart, I forgot." I pick up a few oyster shells and, using each one as a week, count the days by making charcoal marks inside the shells. We recall each day by remembering events to jog our memories. I think we get pretty close. Next I count back to when we fled Abbey Luís. I use my dagger to make a fine point of a charcoal stick, and write down the dates. As I figure this, I explain what I'm doing. "We fled the abbey on August fifteen, we lost poor Agato ten days later, that makes it August twenty-fifth." I write down 8, 15 and 8, 25. "That makes today—" I pick up the last two oyster shells, "September fourteen. See, we've only been here three weeks."

Yema shakes her head. "You wondered how I learned Tupi so fast? How in the world did you just do that?"

"Remember my telling you that girls weren't allowed to go to school in my community? Well, my parents didn't believe in that, so they schooled me at home. They taught me how to use the calendar.

It's important in the Jewish religion. Then, when I was trained at the convent, the Christian calendar is equally important. Scripture too, it's full of numbers, dates, and anniversaries."

"So what day of the week is it?"

"That I don't know. We left Luís on a Thursday, so we can figure it out later. Or we can find out from Captain Vincent. His navigator must keep a careful record. They use the calendar, along with charts of the stars, moon, and sun, to reckon the ship's position."

I stand up and take her hand. "Let's go outside. We've much to discuss."

The two of us walk from the hut into the bright sunlight. Downriver, far out in the bay, there are lovely clouds building on the horizon. Varied in hue and extravagant in shape, they look like animals, people, faces and mythical creatures, even castles. I'm not quite ready to relate the morning's conversation, so I say, "I'm going to ask Captain Vincent for quill and ink so I can write my parents. If he has paper to spare, we can continue our lessons."

"What did you grownups talk about this morning?" Yema asks. "You promised to tell me."

Chapter 19

Nearly ten days have passed. Yema and I stayed close to the village and away from the ship's unloading area. As best we can figure, one or more Sundays came and went without Fr. Tristamo contacting us. He's probably curious about my absence from services, but at least he's not come looking for me. That was until this morning.

Yema and I are sitting with Pavê and his elders while I explain about sugar farming, refining, and what they might expect from the Europeans and Africans. So far no one has caught the coryza, and I can only hope that continues. We hear the usual commotion outside that signals the arrival of visitors. Sure enough, we see Captain Vincent and Fr. Tristamo just as their boat glides up to the river bank.

I turn to Yema. "There's no avoiding him now," I tell her. "Let's make the best of it and see what we can find out."

We're standing in front of Pavê's *óga*, and here comes Tristamo, striding toward us in his usual manner. Today he's wearing a shortened black robe and a broad-brimmed friar's hat. The captain stays at the riverbank, talking with the oarsmen and several Tupi who've crowded into the rowboat to examine it.

"Well, well," the priest exclaims, "it is good to see you, Sister Doçura." His eyes fix on Yema. "And this must be the amazing Indian girl I've heard so much about."

Tristamo extends a hand, expecting her to take it in greeting. Instead, she crosses herself, makes a brief curtesy, then takes the priest's hand and kisses his ring. The child's demeanor is like nothing I've seen before. She appears suddenly shy and embarrassed, turning on her heels and fleeing back into the *óga*.

I go along with this likely charade, and say, "She's often bashful around new people."

It's impossible to judge if Tristamo is perplexed. If so, he's hiding it well. "I'll take your word for it," he says, "but that's not what I've heard about her."

"One can never be certain with children," I say. "In any case, Father, it's a pleasure to see you. I hope the New World is treating you well."

He squints at the sun, then peers into the hut. "May we go inside?" he asks. "I've yet to get used to this tropical sun."

"Of course," I say, and take him inside, introducing him to Pavê and the two elders, explaining who they are. The chief tells one of the women to get the priest a bowl of *jehe'a*. I go with her, returning with one for myself. "This is the Indians' mint tea," I tell the priest, "not one of the narcotics they're so famous for."

He takes a sip and nods to Pavê. "Thank you, *A'kã kuimba'e Tendotapavê*," he says.

I'm impressed he's made the effort to learn the chief's title and full name, but I don't let my surprise register. To me, it seems that everything Tristamo does is intended to curry favor for himself. I refuse to be drawn in by this, yet I must acknowledge that he is clever and resourceful.

"Sister Doçura," he says, "this is the perfect opportunity to explain my mission for this New World, both to you and these most senior tribesmen. Will you translate for me?"

"Yema is more fluent in Tupi than I," I tell him. "Let's see if she'll do it." I nod in her direction, a dark corner of the *óga* where she appears to be hiding. I speak to her in Caeté, quite unsure as to what reaction she'll give. "Yema, please come translate for us."

The child shuffles forward timidly and speaks Portuguese in a submissive tone, "Yes, Sister Doçura. I will be most pleased to translate for Fr. Tristamo."

To my relief, she does not make another curtsey. Yema's pushed this behavior much too far, and I've no idea what Tristamo would do if he should catch on. I say to her in Caeté, "This priest is an inquisitor. We are in danger already. Don't make it worse with this strange act of yours. *Just* translate."

Yema walks over and stands behind Pavê, suggesting the two elders move next to him so they can hear the translation. When the men have seated themselves, she gives me a thoughtful look, and then in a deliberate manner, says to the priest, "I am ready Fr. Tristamo, go ahead."

Tristamo gets to his feet, interlacing his fingers across his middle; and just like a theatrical presentation, he begins to pace. "Senhor Pavê and tribal leaders, I have come to this New World bringing the Gospel of our Lord Jesus Christ, the Savior of all mankind. I have arrived from lands to the east, from across the broad ocean. And from each and every one of these Christian lands, a fresh wind sweeps through, a cleansing wind called the Holy Inquisition."

I'm wondering if this overblown speech is more for me than for Pavê. Yema's speaking quietly and rapidly, and I'm not fully understanding her, but from what I can gather, her translation has little to do with what Tristamo is saying.

What he says next is truly ludicrous, made more so because many of the words are simply nonexistent in the Tupi language. I struggle to appear somber and engaged as he drones on. "When we left my home in Portugal to sail along the coast and across the equator to Africa, we had fortunate winds that hastened our voyage." He unlaces his hands and makes a dramatic gesture, waving his index finger beside his head. "And then! The full force of God became known to me when these same winds grew stronger and sent my ship directly west, bringing me here."

Yema puts up a hand and asks him to pause. "Fr. Tristamo, this is complicated. Please give me a moment to catch up before you continue."

This child constantly amazes me. Here she is, playing a minor role, yet able to assert her will at a time of her own choosing. Since Tristamo is silent for the moment, I can hear her translation: "This man comes from a country where they kill people who do not believe as he does. He is a dangerous person who intends to bring this holy war to our shores. Fortunately, he will be leaving for the Luís Colony as soon as the sailing ship is repaired."

Pavê and the others smile and nod at this last sentence. Yema tells Tristamo that they understand, and he can now continue.

The priest raves on, citing the favorable trade winds as a manifestation of God's Holy Inquisition. Finally he's through with this frippery and says something of interest, "As you may know, Senhor Pavê, several of your tribe have embraced the Faith of Christ Jesus. In return, I have blessed them with the task of helping me build a chapel on the hillside at the base of the plantation. And I want to thank you for your permission to proceed with this venture. After I depart south, the chapel will be a monument to our one true belief. It will guarantee many bountiful sugar harvests."

Fr. Tristamo kneels to pray. Yema and I cross ourselves and kneel also. He recites 1Corinthians 9 verse 10, the blessing for those who till the soil, and he does so in Latin. The natives look on, likely puzzled by this strange ritual.

I explain the prayer to Pavê and the others, then to Tristamo I say, "Father, I told them yours was a prayer for farmers and the plantation."

He stands and straightens his robe. "Thank you, Sister Doçura." He says this with an agreeable smile and a tone of genuine sincerity. I have to remind myself that he is an inquisitor, and to not be taken in by this feigned pleasantry.

Captain Vincent had joined us a little while back, and now comes forward to greet everyone. When he's finished with his greetings, he says to me, "Sister, since we've never ventured south of here, could you come visit the ship this afternoon and help us with our charts?"

"Your navigation charts?" I ask. "I know nothing of that science."

"Right now," he says, "all we have is a blank space between here and Fortaleza. If you could provide us with landmarks, that would be most helpful."

"I've seen some of the land between here and the Rio Jacu. The Luís settlement is just a few miles south of the Jacu. Beyond there, I have no idea. As we discussed before, Fortaleza is where you may find dyewood if Luís is still in rebellion. I've heard it's a two-day journey south from there."

"That is precisely what we need," the captain says. "So can you come over this afternoon? I think in about four days we'll be ready to sail."

"How about first thing in the morning?" I ask. "I'll have the Indians bring me."

"Yes, that will work." Vincent turns to Yema. "Have you ever been on a sailing ship? Why don't you come too? A new experience."

"I would be delighted," she answers.

Fr. Tristamo says, "That suits me also. Tomorrow I'll be working at my chapel. In the afternoon, will you ladies visit me there?"

Yema steps forward and takes my hand. She smiles sweetly at the men. "Senhores, Father, we will be there." Then she giggles and runs off.

"Well, gentlemen," I say, "I guess that settles it. We will see you tomorrow." I excuse myself and go look for Yema.

I find her next door in our hut. She appears quite pleased with herself. "What has gotten into you?" I ask. "I've never seen you act like this."

"Did you like what I told Pavê?"

"Yes, that was the right thing to do. I'm proud of your quick thinking. Now answer my question."

"Sister Leah," she says, "I'm just copying you."

"What do you mean?"

"One time you used the words 'two-faced.' I didn't know what that meant, but now I do. We must be like the curare, sweet to the taste, and deadly."

"What do you—?"

Yema's lovely face contorts with a mixture of rage and sorrow, the vertical scars standing red along her cheeks. Suddenly she's screaming at me in Caeté, "They are leaving here in four days! You've got to kill that priest!"

"There must be another way," I say.

She throws herself against me, sobbing, her small body trembling. "There's no other way," she wails. "You don't understand! They killed my father, my mother and little brother, they intended to kill me too. Agato died because we had to run away. My aunt is dead.

I was supposed to be the *turguy kuñã,* not die in some filthy cell or burned alive. I am the last living Caeté! The last, Sister Leah, the very last!"

I take the child in my arms, rocking her back and forth. "Alright, alright," I say. "What do you want me to do?"

"I don't know," she moans. She looks up at me, her voice still choked with sobs. "Do you realize Pavê considers us his daughters?"

I shake my head. "I did not know that."

"I've told him everything. How much peril we face. His cousin is the chief of a tribe far upriver. Pavê says he will take us there. That the tribe will take us in." She pauses for a moment, her young face etched with fear. "If that priest leaves here alive, then I will go up the river whether you do or not."

I set Yema on her feet, then kneel down so we're eye-to-eye. "As you already know, Orlund and Captain Vincent also feel threatened by Tristamo. When we meet with them tomorrow, we'll figure something out. If not, then I'll consider Pavê's offer. No matter what, I intend to keep us safe. I promise."

***

At our morning meal with the chief and his family, Yema and I tell him what we plan for our meeting with Captain Vincent. Pavê explains more about their fellow tribesmen upriver. "It's a three-day journey," he informs us. "Twenty or so families, about one hundred people. They are the Támoioj."

I thank him, but can't imagine they will be as accommodating as the Tupi. Nevertheless, it's far enough inland that I doubt we'll ever be found. I really don't want to live my life this way, yet there may be no other choice.

We finish our meal and trudge down to the shore. Two warriors and a canoe await us. Yema and I climb in and we head off, soon rounding the point where the full bay comes into view. A little further on, we spot the sailing ship anchored close to shore. I look to the distant hillside where I can see Tristamo's chapel. I notice it has a peaked roof, more like a Caeté design than the usual Tupi house with a domed roof.

As we near the sailing ship, Captain Vincent, his navigator, and Lars Orlund greet us. They lower a rope ladder and we climb aboard, I in a hesitant manner, Yema scampering like a monkey up a tree. She and I decided ahead of time that we would complete the work with the charts before broaching the subject of Tristamo.

By the time I get on deck, the child is already twenty feet in the air, climbing the shrouds of the mainmast. She points to the crow's nest. "What's that basket up there?" the girl asks.

"That's called the crow's nest," Captain Vincent calls out. "Where we post a lookout. We've posted none today, so go up and take a look."

She climbs quickly up the net-like shroud and ducks into the hole at the base of the platform. In a moment she's peering over the edge, calling down to us. "What should I look for?"

"Anything you want," Orlund shouts. "Whales, ships, dolphins, dragons, birds. Anything." He turns to me. "Oh to be agile like that."

"She's had lots of practice," I tell him. "The Indian children spend half their lives in the trees. It's amazing how they climb."

It's a beautiful sunny morning, and we follow Captain Vincent up the quarterdeck stairs to the wheelhouse. The enclosure has been mostly dismantled, only the four corner posts remaining. The canvas roof and sides are rolled up and stacked against a nearby railing.

On a table next to the ship's wheel, the navigator has a parchment chart of the Brazil coast rolled out. Using a lead pointer, he indicates the equator, then traces down the coast to a rough sketch of our bay. He says, "Here we are at 1.5 degrees south, and about 49 degrees west. You mentioned a second river coming into this bay on the south end." He circles the area. "Does this look about right?"

"Almost," I say, "but there's a rocky spit of land that extends northwest into the ocean on the south bank of this river. It's at least two miles long." While he's sketching this lightly onto his map, I think about Agato's resting place and our terrible experience with the Caribs. I touch the parchment at the imagined location.

He jars me out of my reflections when he says, "So we've got Colony Luís located here at 2.5 degrees south and a little further east, and Fortaleza at 3.7 degrees south and slightly more east. How does that look?"

These latter points and parts of the coastline have been drawn in with black ink and appear much more established than I would have guessed. "Yes," I say, "I've never been to Fortaleza, but the map appears correct." I reach for his ruler and lay it on a line between our bay and Luís. "How far is this?" I ask.

"About a hundred miles," he says.

I run my hand along the ruler. "So each inch is about ten miles?"

"Yes."

"All right, let's start at Luís. A little less than ten miles north is the Rio Jacu bay. It's not very large, perhaps two miles wide and a mile or so—"

Yema starts yelling from the crow's nest. "I see something."

I'm a little aggravated at the interruption. I shield my eyes and look up at her. "Sorry gentlemen," I say, then shouting at Yema, "What do you see?"

"I see sails. I think it's a ship."

Vincent rushes partway up the nearest shroud and stares east. He calls to his steward who's followed him to the base of the shroud, "Recall the entire day crew and have the other two crews stand by! Do we have a qualified lookout on board?"

"No, Captain."

"Then get someone!"

The steward grabs the speaking trumpet and yells to the shore. Figures scramble everywhere. Vincent climbs down from the shroud and stands atop a raised gun platform. The steward says, "Sir, most of the men are working on the hillside. On the plantation."

"Then send a runner. Who's the ranking officer on shore?"

"The second mate. He's in the water by the ship's boat."

Vincent takes the trumpet and calls to the second mate. "Jozef! Assemble a day crew from what you've got, and send a runner for all men to return. We've spotted a ship. A three-master at least."

The mate gives a hasty salute and begins rounding up men. Yema calls down to us. "What's going on?"

"Come down," I shout back.

"Wait," Vincent says. He yells to Yema. "How many sails do you see?"

She looks again. "Lots. Lots of sails."

"How many masts?" he asks.

I'm not sure Yema knows what a mast is. "I can't tell," she shouts. By now we can all see the ship, just a white speck on the horizon. Yema emerges feet-first from the crow's nest and begins her way down.

Within minutes the first ship's boat arrives and the sailors clamber on deck. Vincent sends a man aloft. As soon as he's in the crow's nest, he calls down. "She's Portuguese, Captain. Four masts. Sails full. Aft mizzen furled. Moving slowly. Not much wind. I'm guessing a half-hour out."

"How is he able to see all that?" I ask.

"He's my best lookout," Vincent says. "I think we should prepare for visitors."

I strain my eyes and can just make out the red Portuguese cross emblazoned on the foresail. "How do you know she's not a pirate?" I inquire. "A captured caravel?"

"I doubt it," he says, "but we'll bring our ship broadside. If she's a pirate, she'll change course and come in at an angle. Then we'll man the guns." By now two more ship's boats have arrived, and the deck is swarming with sailors. The second mate stands by, ready to take orders. "Mr. Jozef," Vincent says, "raise the aft anchor and have the men pull the boat broadside. Bring the port guns to bear, but don't roll them out. Let's see if she changes course. Run up the Portuguese and Dutch flags."

Jozef immediately starts barking orders. In a minute there's a gang of sailors turning the anchor winch. We can feel the boat rock as the anchor releases from the bottom and assumes its full weight against the ship. Yema and I run to the stern and watch the preparations. Two ship's boats have run lines around the anchor chain. The rowers pull the ship crossways to the oncoming vessel. The gunner's mate stands nearby. He uses a compass table, about a foot square and balanced on the rail, to align the guns. When the table's scroll arm points straight at the distant vessel, he gives the command to lower the anchor.

The second mate calls to the boat crews in the water, "Stay sharp, men. We may need to adjust our position."

As Yema and I head back to the wheelhouse, we hear the lookout call from the crow's nest. "Captain, Sir. She's not changing course. And she's no pirate. They just raised the Papal flag."

My heart stops. The girl and I rush to the rail. The oncoming ship is the Vitória, the vessel carrying the *Consilium de populi.*

Chapter 20

We catch up with Vincent, his navigator, Lars Orlund, and the steward as they head below decks to prepare for the visitors. There is frenzied activity all around us as Jozef assembles a welcoming formation of sailors.

"Captain Vincent," I hiss, "that ship carries the Council of Miracles, three senior clergy from the mainland. If they find us here, Yema and I are doomed. Most likely your plantation is also doomed."

The men in the gangway turn and look at me as if I've lost my senses. "Sister," the captain says, "we'll talk about this in my quarters." We descend the narrow stairway and enter the door to his living area. Vincent turns to face me. "What in the world are you talking about?"

I look through the small window on the east side of the cabin. They've dropped anchor and are preparing to lower a boat. I have no idea where the steward or the navigator's loyalties lie, but we're out of time, so I press on. "There's much to explain, and no possibility of doing so now. One of the priests aboard that vessel is Juan Girona, the Inquisitor General of Spain. He has accused me of heresy, and I am condemned by the very tribunal that is likely coming to visit you right now. You must hide Yema and me!" I can feel the child's face pressing against my side. She's shaking and terrified.

Both Orlund and the captain react with alarm. Orlund turns to the steward. "Where's Fr. Tristamo?"

"I don't know, sir."

Vincent shouts, "Find Jozef and get him down here! Right now!"

Orlund looks through the window. "There's two clergy in the boat, and their captain. They haven't quite left yet."

The Captain Vincent opens a door at the back of the room. "You can hide in here," he says to me. "It's my chart room."

As I look inside, Jozef shows up. "Where is Fr. Tristamo?" Vincent asks him. "Where's my first mate?"

"Neither onboard, sir, but I'm sure they're on their way. This morning they were finishing the roof on the chapel."

Captain Vincent pulls himself up to his full height. "Now all of you listen to me," he says. "Each of us have a stake in this plantation. While I have no idea what's going on, I'm taking no chances. Mr. Jozef, take a boat with a work crew for the chapel. Find Fr. Tristamo. Tell him we will conduct Mass for our visitors tomorrow morning at his chapel. Just tell him 'clergy,' no details. Under no circumstances is he to return to this ship. Do you understand me?"

The second mate comes to attention and says, "Yes sir." At the door he pauses and turns. "Sir, shall we stay there overnight?"

He thinks for a moment. "No. When it's time to bring everyone back, I'll strike the Netherlands' flag." Without another word, Jozef charges up the gangway. The captain addresses his steward. "Prepare tea and find my dress hat. I've no time to change clothes." The steward brushes past me and produces the hat from the chart room. Then he leaves for the galley. Vincent next speaks to Orlund who continues to stare out the window. "How close are they?"

Without looking around, he puts up a hand, his fingers spread. "Five minutes. Now there's another man with them."

Yema and I move into the chart room. There's a single oil lamp burning, and I extinguish it. "Gentlemen," I say from the darkened room, "their captain is as opposed to the Inquisition as we. At some point, try to send the clergy back and keep him here. If the other man is Arneldo Pãiva, he's the ship's navigator. He's also sympathetic." My fear is getting the best of me, and I'm having trouble catching my breath. I force myself to slow down, and say, "They probably have three prisoners onboard that ship who we should try to rescue. Innocent men accused by Girona."

Vincent peers in at me. "Sister Doçura, you have a lot of explaining to do. We'll be fortunate to get through this with our skins intact. If we fail, the rack awaits us all." He closes the door and I hear him go up the stairway. Orlund follows him a moment later.

When our eyes adjust to the dark room, it's fairly easy to make things out. There's an oval chart table, three chairs, and a ship's chest that rests in one corner. We can see a framework of partitioned shelves covering the wall behind us with many rolled-up charts stuck into its compartments. There are slats in the door, and while we can't see what's going on, we're able to hear everything.

At first there is the sound of two men entering the room followed by the clatter of silverware and dishes. One is the voice of the steward. I sit down at the chart table and Yema settles herself on the chest in the corner. But very soon, she's behind me. "Stand up," she whispers. The child pulls the dagger from under my waistband and hands it to me. "If they discover us, kill Girona," she says.

I grip the dagger and test its point. I've never thought myself capable of killing someone, but now I think I could. The outer room is suddenly full of men, and despite the jumble of voices, I can pick out some specific ones. The first I recognize is that of Bishop Adrian Boeyens because of his Dutch accent, the next are Arneldo Pãiva and Captain Torres of the Vitória, these latter two because of their clear and scholarly Portuguese. And finally I hear Juan Girona speak in his typically demanding tone, using his careless mixture of Portuguese and Spanish.

"Well, Captain Vincent," I hear the Vitória captain say, "if you intend to take on dyewood, then go south to Fortaleza as I did. Luís is still in rebellion."

"We know nothing of rebellion there. Is it still going on?"

Juan Girona answers for him. "It is indeed. Caused by that damnable nun and the supposed miracle. A child singer. We heard this girl could sing the Mass with the voice of an angel. Instead we heard blasphemy from the brat, cursing us in her monkey language."

One can only wonder what these Dutchmen must be thinking. I hear Orlund say, "You mentioned the Council of Miracles when we were topside. Was the child the subject of your Council?"

I glance over at Yema. She has a hand over her mouth, and her eyes are very wide. It's impossible to tell if she's laughing or frightened.

As usual, Juan Girona continues to dominate the conversation. "Yes," he grunts, "she was the subject. We jailed both her and the nun. Their crimes were so obvious, no trial was necessary. As for their conspirators, we have them in custody. Upon our return home, they will stand trial."

Someone asks, "When we were on deck, you said there were three council members."

"Sadly, that is correct," Girona says. "While our captain was on his errand of commerce, our beloved Costa da Martina, the Archbishop of Lisbon, took ill and passed away. His remains now lie in that accursed ground."

"I'm so sorry," Captain Vincent says. Yema and I can hear the sounds of tea being poured, cups, saucers and spoons clinking, and perhaps the sounds of food being passed around. "So you executed the heretic nun and child?" Vincent asks.

"Oh how I wish we had," Girona answers. "Unfortunately, the night before they were due to die, they escaped. In doing so, the nun murdered one of my most trusted men. Stabbed him twice. A hideous crime."

As we continue to listen, I absently pull a handle on the edge of the table. A drawer slides open. Inside I can feel a pistol. I carefully remove it, holding the weapon to the light. As far as I can tell, it appears loaded and ready to shoot. A sniff of the barrel and flint confirms this. I lay the gun on the table next to my dagger. Shooting Girona will be far easier than stabbing him.

What I hear next from Adrian Boeyens almost doubles me over. "We understand from one of your seamen that you have a priest with you, bound for Colony Luís."

"Indeed true," Captain Vincent says, "and a champion of the Holy Inquisition. That's why Fr. Tristamo is not with us today. He's dedicated his time to finishing his chapel. It's at the base of the hillside where our plantation lies. We expect him to depart with us for Luís by the end of the week. The chapel will be a fine monument to his presence here."

"Does he know about the rebellion at the Colony?" Bishop Boeyens asks.

"No. Thanks to you distinguished gentlemen, this is the first knowledge we've had of it. Please fill in the details for him tomorrow. Perhaps he'll decide to go on to Fortaleza."

There is an awkward pause in the conversation. I look over at Yema. We're both puzzled as to what's going on. The pistol fits nicely in my hand when I aim it at the door. I resolve to shoot Girona the moment I see him.

Finally Captain Vincent speaks up. "I expect Fr. Tristamo back before dinnertime. I will ask him to celebrate Mass for all of us at his chapel. Perhaps mid-morning or so? He will be thrilled that you are here, and to have a Trinity."

"Splendid," Girona says. "I assume it will be the first full Mass on this shore."

"That is so," Orlund responds. "And an undeniable blessing."

We hear the sounds of everyone getting to their feet. There are hearty goodbyes, thanks, and good wishes for tomorrow. In the midst of this we hear Captain Vincent say, apparently to Arneldo

Pãiva and Captain Torres, "Could you gentlemen stay for a while? We need help with our charts. I'll have a boat run you back when we're finished." We don't hear an answer, and soon the cabin is quiet except for the sounds of the steward and his helper gathering dishes. Yema and I remain in the chart room, afraid to make our presence known.

A few minutes later we hear footsteps descending the stairway. I crack the door open and see Pãiva and Captain Torres unrolling the chart from earlier this morning. I have no idea how they will receive us. Perhaps shock is my best device, and I will test these men with my words. As I step out of the chart room, Vincent and Orlund walk into the cabin.

"Merciful God!" Torres exclaims. "Sister Doçura! What are you doing here?"

I first address Arneldo Pãiva, *"Sholom aleichem,* my friend." Then to Torres, "Welcome to the home of the Tupi. Shall we call it *'A Costa do Tupi?'* A land of Indians, murderers, errant nuns, and heretic children." Yema makes her appearance, standing next to me, her hands folded. "Everyone assumed you two were dead," Captain Torres says. "Claimed by the jungle."

"The jungle saved us," Yema says. "That and a Caeté boy named Agato."

Captain Vincent and Lars Orlund remain speechless. Vincent mumbles something, rolls up the chart and takes it into the back room. I hear him return the pistol to the drawer. He hands me my dagger when he comes out. "You were well armed," he says.

"A murderess must be," I answer.

"Did you really kill that jailer?" Pãiva asks.

"I offered him gold because the man helped us escape. We feared he would betray us once he got his payment. I would like to say I killed him, but I cannot. The very brave Indian boy Agato did him in. You may remember the child, a ten-year-old, an acolyte? He served as an altar boy." Both men shake their heads.

"Senhores, we have little time and much to cover. Explanations can wait. Captain Torres, are your prisoners Bishop Damião, Fr. Julian, and Dr. Cardim?"

"The very same."

"And do you plan to deliver them to the Inquisition when you arrive home?"

He slowly moves his head from side to side. "Heavens no. Depending on the wind, we anticipate several stops along the way, Hispaniola, Cape Verde, the Canaries, even Madera. At some point I plan to somehow get these men onto one of those shores."

An idea forms in my mind. "None of those places are as safe as this outpost," I tell him. "Smuggle them aboard a vessel headed our way. They are honorable men, and would be most welcome here."

Torres says to Captain Vincent and Lars Orlund, "Girona accused the doctor and the two priests because he and the other *populi* need something to show for their unsuccessful mission. They think an inquisitional court might be an effective way to distract from their failure." He turns to me. "Thank you Sister Doçura. I will indeed strive to get the three men safely here." Then back to Vincent, "This woman has just taken an immense weight off my shoulders."

"And she's put an insufferable weight on mine," Vincent says. "What to do about Fr. Tristamo."

As I start to speak, the captain raises both hands and cuts me off. "Stop!" he says. "Sister Doçura, Leah, whoever you are, I cannot commit a crime against the Church. I will lose my license, my ship, my life. You are going to take care of this problem."

"A reasonable request," I say. "Do you have some kind of a plan?"

"Will Pavê's men kidnap Tristamo for a day or so? Can you get them to do that?"

I put an arm around Yema. "I imagine the chief will do it. He counts Yema and me among his children."

"All right," Captain Vincent says. He gives me a peculiar smile. "But first of all Captain Torres, when do you plan to vacate this shore of madwomen?"

"Tomorrow after the Mass."

"Excellent," Vincent responds. "So here's what we're going to do. Sister Doçura, when Tristamo returns, I will tell him of the Mass planned for the morrow. He will be thrilled, eager to make preparations. I'm going to also tell him that you will show up first thing in the morning with canoes full of Tupi. That they will help him put the chapel in order and attend the service. And I will tell him that more helpers will follow from here once we finish our morning's work. You will take the priest to the Tupi village and keep him there until the Vitória sets sail."

"What should I tell him?" I ask.

"Anything you want. Just leave me, Orlund, my ship, my men, and the Vitória out of it. Do you understand?"

"Of course. What will you do when he returns here?"

"I don't know. I'll think of something. We're going to leave in a few days. After that, who knows?" He looks at Captain Torres. "At least the Vitória will be gone. "

"What's to keep him from denouncing all of us once he gets to Colony Luís?"

"I must take my chances. Maybe he will. All I know is that I am responsible for his safety. He is not to be injured in any way. Is that clear?"

"A flawed plan," I reply, "but it's all we have. I will get Pavê's permission, and I'll be here in the morning."

Captain Vincent produces a handkerchief and mops his forehead. "Thank you, Doçura. Who would have thought ..." He sighs deeply and does not finish. Then he says, "There's a boat waiting to take you back to the village. I will see you tomorrow."

Yema and I leave the cabin and make our way up the stairs with Captain Torres and Pãiva close behind. Once we're on deck, Torres says, "Sister Doçura, your suggestion for rescuing the three prisoners is truly a blessing. They will be forever grateful to you."

"Perhaps not. They may blame me for the uprising at Luís."

"Regardless, these men do not deserve the harsh treatment they've received, and neither did you and Yema. Know that when these three gentlemen appear on this shore, their loss to Juan Girona and the Inquisition will be sweet revenge."

We say our good-byes and climb down the boarding net to the boat. A short time later we're back at the village. The challenge of tomorrow feels overwhelming to me.

The first thing we do is look for Pavê. One of his wives directs us to a hut on the far side of the settlement. Inside we find him gambling with several men. It's a game the men play with oyster shells. The player is blindfolded, and tries to stack the highest number of shells into a column, one at a time, until it topples over. Pavê seems somewhat annoyed at our interruption until I mention kidnapping to him. He gives us a strange look and suggests we go outside to discuss it. We walk a little ways to a large tree with thick roots that spread in every direction.

Once we settle ourselves in the shade of the tree, Pavê looks at the two of us with disgust. "I cannot understand why you people have so many conflicts," he says. When we explain the situation in detail, he begins to appreciate the danger to Yema and me. Nevertheless, he keeps repeating, *"Tarova, tarova."* "Insane, insane."

Yema asks the chief to recall Tristamo's arrogance when he gave his speech to the elders. "The followers of the Inquisition see Leah and me as criminals," she continues. Given the opportunity, he will denounce us."

"Then we should kill him," Pavê says.

"Tendotapavê," I say, "I have given my word to Captain Vincent that Tristamo will not be harmed. Please leave this up to me. The Corajoso will be leaving in a few days, and this troublesome priest will be gone."

Finally the chief agrees. "I will have the warriors ready for you in the morning."

***

After our evening meal, as we prepare for bed, Yema tells me her doubts about the plan. "It will just make things worse," she says. "As soon as Tristamo gets to Luís, he will send soldiers." She makes a gesture towards the door. "Just as they did at my village, the soldiers will kill all the Tupi. Then what?"

There is much truth in what she says. Killing Tristamo would settle this, but I must keep my promise. "Sweetheart," I say, "there has to be a solution. Perhaps it will occur to us tomorrow."

Chapter 21

After a hurried meal the next morning, we set off in two canoes. I tell the warriors my plan. Yema listens closely, making sure they understand. We ride in the larger canoe. If there's a struggle, this one is less likely to turn over. Once we round the point into the bay, I tell Yema to get into the other canoe. When she protests, I say, "It will keep you safe. You cannot be in this dugout with Fr. Tristamo if he puts up a fight."

She says, "I want to hear what you tell him."

"You're not alone," I answer. "I have no idea what that I'm going to say."

As we near Captain Vincent's ship, we see Fr. Tristamo, the

captain, and Lars Orlund in the bow admiring the morning and likely the view of the nearby Vitória as she rolls in the water, responding gently to the waves sliding in from the sea five miles to the east.

"Good morning Sister Doçura," Orlund calls to me from the deck. "Aren't we blessed with such a beautiful morning?" His tone is uncomfortably eager.

"Fr. Tristamo," I call, "are you ready to join us? We have a small work crew, with more to follow."

"Thank you Sister," he shouts back. "I will in a moment." The captain lowers a package bound in brown oilcloth into Yema's dugout. "My vestments," the priest says. "I'm not conducting the first Mass *Trinitas* on these shores in my work clothes."

"A fine idea," I call back, struggling to keep my voice even.

The priest climbs over the rail, makes his way down the boarding net into my canoe, and settles himself in the seat behind me. He's breathless with excitement. "May we take a turn around the Vitória?" he asks. "You've no idea how delighted I am to celebrate Mass with such important clergy, particularly Juan Girona, the Chief Inquisitor of Spain. What an honor!"

I tell the Indians to circle the Vitória, then head north along the coast. As we pass the ship, Tristamo continues to gush, wallowing in superlatives. He repeats the one phrase which I find most irritating. "Just as the favorable easterlies that brought me here were a sign from God, so is the arrival of this magnificent ship with its papal flag and our esteemed visitors."

I turn and smile at him as our two craft finish the circle and head north. "I thought we'd paddle up the coast," I say, "to the base of the hill. It's faster than walking."

"Excellent idea," he says, and calls to Yema. "Aren't you excited, child?"

She yells back. "I am, Father, I am."

After a quarter-hour of paddling, we come adjacent to the hill. I look back at the anchored ships and can barely make out the figures of Vincent and Orlund still standing in the bow. My stomach turns into a knot and a cold sweat crawls over my skin. I give the order to the warriors seated behind Fr. Tristamo. They quickly slip a noose over him, dropping it to just above his elbows and pull it tight.

He stares at the rope, wriggling this way and that, trying to dislodge it with his hands. Then he smiles at me. "Sister, if this is some kind of joke, I find it not at all funny."

"It is not a joke, Father. We're headed back to the Tupi settlement." I tell the Indians to paddle towards the ocean. My aim is to get nearly out of sight of the two sailing ships before we turn south. Tristamo stands up and begins to struggle. The warrior behind him puts a foot on the priest's buttocks and jerks the rope, painfully bending him backwards. The second man stands and forces him back to a sitting position.

I remind the warriors, "Be careful not to injure him." The priest's face is a mixture of shock and dismay. "Do not struggle," I tell him. "You won't be hurt. The Indians are going to keep you out of sight until the Vitória leaves. Then you'll be returned safely."

"No, no!" he shouts. "This is impossible!" He keeps twisting around to look at his chapel as we move away from it. "I'm due to celebrate Mass this morning! Why are you doing this?" He continues to rant, accusing me, cursing the Indians, and asking if Pavê's aware of this outrage. Finally he says, "We are fellow clergy, Doçura. What are you doing?"

I look at him and say, "I am here to make sure you are treated kindly." Then I turn away and put my head in my hands. I should not have told him that. It would be far too easy for the Portuguese to blame the Tupi, stitch a story together that they feared Tristamo would consort with the new visitors and bring the Inquisition here. Or that the arrival of more Europeans meant an attack on their village. Once this priest gets to Luís, my seeming to blame the Indians would only bring retaliation from the Portuguese. I've got to come up with something else. *Must I be the agent of this abduction? I think so.* Turning to him once more I say, "This will be fully explained when we get to the village." My words enrage him further. He continues to shout, his voice hoarse with anger.

In the far distance I can see the point of land where the river empties into the bay. I've less than an hour to think of something.

***

It's around midday, and Yema and I sit with Fr. Tristamo in an *óga* near the riverbank. Pavê had the family that occupies this hut leave so we could hold the priest here. Additionally, he told his people to leave us alone. Otherwise the Tupi would have swarmed around us when we landed with Fr. Tristamo tied up and being led by warriors. This morning, in his eagerness to begin work on the chapel, the priest skipped breakfast. Following his complaints of hunger, Yema brought him some yam cakes and a small bowl of honey.

"Why are you part of this?" he asked her.

"I cannot say," she told him. "It is a bad thing."

Yema's feeling sorry for Fr. Tristamo, and I am too. So far I've explained nothing; in fact I've barely talked at all. Now a warrior comes by and informs us the Vitória has set sail. There are three Tupi guarding Tristamo, and I tell them to find a canoe so we can take the priest back.

All morning I've tried to make myself angry at this inquisitor. I know what I want to say, and being provoked would make it easier. I cannot summon my anger, so now I'll tell him as if reciting a story. "In a little while we'll take you back to the ship. The Vitória has departed."

He begins to cry, likely relieved that he will soon be freed, but also because of what he says next. "You have deprived me of a blessed opportunity to celebrate Mass with two of the most important clergy in all of Europe. How could you do that?"

"Because I am a fugitive from the Inquisition, and they mustn't know I'm here."

Is his immediate shock real or feigned? "Sister Doçura, how can that be?"

"You will discover that when you get to Colony Luís. It is my understanding that you suspect all Conversos."

"Perhaps, but not all." He pauses, then says, "If the Sacred Inquisition demands it, then you must submit. Your trial will be your salvation. That's what—"

"The way you were trussed up this morning, is that how you treat those accused?" I feel a rush of anger. It's almost a relief. I'm sufficiently provoked that I can continue.

"Sister, you did not let me finish."

"I will, Father. First answer my question."

"Tied up? Yes if it's an individual. We lead him through the streets tethered like a goat. But more often than not, corruption of faith afflicts a family or a group. Then we put them in a cart and parade the nonbelievers to our court of justice. We want the faithful to witness what happens when one turns a deaf ear to God's word." Despite Tristamo's situation, his arrogance is undiminished—

Perhaps residue from Porto where everyone feared him. At my direction, the warriors have just untied him. The priest stands up to stretch his legs.

"Does the court ever find someone innocent?" I ask.

"Sister, you told me I'd be—"

I shout at the Indians. "Bind his hands! Tie him by the neck to the center post." Tristamo struggles, but is quickly overcome by the same warriors who have arrived to take him back to the ship. "Cinch the rope tight around his throat," I tell them. The priest begins to choke, his face turning red.

"Father, you are not free until I allow it. Answer my question. Does the court ever find someone innocent?"

He glares at me, hatred etched across his face. He chokes out, "Only if God intervenes."

"Have you ever seen one of these interventions?" He does not answer, so I tell the warrior holding him to further tighten the rope. I repeat my question.

"No, I've never seen such an intervention."

"Have you ever heard of one?"

He is really struggling now, gasping for air, knees trembling. He's trying to reach the post behind him to prevent his weight from making the rope tighter against his windpipe. "Please, Sister," he wheezes, "untie my neck and I'll answer your question."

"Put him on the ground like a *rendfa*," I tell the warriors. "Foot on his back, a leash around his neck." He's forced face-first onto the floor, one warrior holding the rope, the other with a foot between his shoulders.

Tristamo takes a few moments to catch his breath. He's looking up at me, and I stare back. At last I see fear in his eyes. Finally he says, "I've heard that God has intervened in some cases, but I have never personally witnessed one."

"I have heard that if someone provides sufficient payment to the Inquisition, then he is exonerated."

"Of course. God provides those moneys to the individual or family. It is God who makes that wealth available." He's trying to turn on his side. I tell the warriors to keep him face down. Yema gets up from her seat by the entrance and stands next to me. Her look is pure malice. I believe she's beginning to understand what I'm trying to do.

I ask, "So God provides the possessions of the convicted sinners to the Inquisition when you loot their houses?"

"Since they are heretics," the priest says, "they cannot own property. That is part of Church dicta."

"Could your logic be flawed?"

"God's Word is never flawed."

"I inquire about *your* logic, not God's."

"But they are the same," he protests. *"I know* the Word of The Almighty. If my understanding is wrong, then God would correct me."

My rage boils over. Perhaps I should have him killed. I'm silent for a few moments, then say, "If I tell the man with the rope to strangle you, he will do it. Do you understand?"

"Yes," he chokes.

"Then listen to my words and remember them to your dying day. My parents fled your damnable Inquisition and now live a thousand miles from Lisbon in the Ottoman. I have read accounts of what your ilk does to Jews, Conversos, and Moors. The Inquisition is an unholy perversion of faith, an abomination. How is our faith extended by torturing and killing innocents in the name of Lord Jesus?"

"Please don't do this to me!" When I do not respond, he glances at Yema, then back to me. "Sister, how can you talk like this in front of a child?"

I put a hand on her shoulder. "This little girl has seen her entire village destroyed by zealots like you. Her family slaughtered. She has witnessed travail that exceeds any of your inquisitions. You said your mission is to bring the Inquisition to this new land? That God gave you a sign? Well, by your arrival on these shores, God also gave me a sign. *And a mission* to put an end to this bloody nonsense of yours."

I stare at him, using the force of silence. He turns his head and looks away, his long hair tangled with grass and dirt from the floor. Just like his victims, I want this priest to live in fear, to be haunted by a knock at the door or a gang in the night.

"Fr. Tristamo, hear me clearly. I have been under a threat of death by the Inquisition once. I will never be again. After you are released and gone from here, you will never utter another word about me, this tribe, the sugar plantation, or anything related to your time here. These natives have a web of spies that extends everywhere. If you do not keep silent, the Indians will know about it. They will even know your dreams.

"Senhor Pavê considers me a daughter of the Tupi. If he thinks I'm in peril, his warriors will seize you in the night. They will sell you to a tribe far to the interior. There you'll become a slave, never to be found. They'll strip you naked and castrate you. Then they will work you to near death."

He is obviously terrified, but I must twist the knife further. "Just as you pull arms and legs apart on your rack of torture, when these savages can no longer get work from you, their *tuguy kuñã* will twist a cord around your arm to staunch the flow of blood, hack the limb off, and roast it in front of you. The next night they will take the other arm, then a leg, then the other. On the fifth night, not much different than your burning innocent souls at the stake, they will roast alive what remains of you."

Tristamo is shaking hard, his face deadly pale. He retches onto the floor in front of him, barely moving his head to avoid the pool of vomit. "Help him stand," I tell the Indians. "Untie him, but leave the rope around his neck." When they have done so, I say, "They will take you back to the ship now. If you remove this rope, I've told them to slit your throat."

I take Yema's hand and we leave the *óga*. The two of us watch from a distance as the warriors lead the priest to the waiting canoe. He stumbles along, one Indian supporting his arm, the rope trailing on the ground behind him. We wait until the dugout pushes off, then return to our hut. I'm exhausted and scared.

"Sister Leah," Yema asks, "what led you to come up with such a dreadful story?"

I consider for a moment. "Because I don't want you to leave me and go upriver."

She smiles for the first time this day. "I don't think I'll need to. Now, what kind of story was that?"

"I just took what the Inquisition does to people and put it in the hands of the Indians."

"They do that?"

"The inquisitors have a machine called the rack. It pulls people apart. Do you really want the details?"

She shakes her head. "I'm puzzled by the way he thinks. How

he— " She searches for words. *"Tekojoja tem,"* she says.

I consider that phrase. "'Justifies it,' is that what you mean?"

"Yes, I suppose that's right. In the name of Lord Jesus?"

"That is what the inquisitors tell everyone," I say to her, "but I am certain it's simply an excuse. No God, or Son of God, would allow such a thing."

There's the smell of rain and a cover of clouds. Soon a shower begins, and we hear it patter overhead; the rain takes the heat from the day. "I am so tired," I tell Yema, and crawl into my hammock. Soon I fall fast asleep.

***

Yema and I stayed in the village for the past two days. We've heard nothing from the Dutchmen. Around noon on the third day, Lars Orlund and Captain Vincent arrive in a ship's boat. Both men seem rather jolly. "Senhores," I say, "it is good to see you."

Captain Vincent says "Likewise," and hands me a flexible reed basket. It's ornate, made of flattened reeds, and has an alternating black and light brown design. It even has handles. Inside there is a bound volume, several quills, and a bottle of ink with a cork stopper. "This is our way of saying 'Thank you,' Sister Doçura."

I take the volume and examine it. Stenciled on the outside cover are the words Ship's Log, but inside all the pages are blank. "This is a fine gift," I tell the men. "Thank you so much." I flex the basket. "Where did you get this? I've never seen anything like it."

"The African women make them," Orlund says.

"Must be something from Cape Verde. I saw nothing like this on São Tomé. It's quite handy."

"We'll be leaving this afternoon," Vincent says. "Thanks to you and Captain Torres, our charts are now complete. And tonight we'll have a full moon. It should be excellent sailing. I will go south for dyewood and return in a few weeks." He points to the ship's log. "If you want to give me a letter then, I'll see that it's kept safe and posted from Tangier or Gibraltar. A letter mailed from one of those ports is more likely to get to the Ottoman."

I hand the volume to Yema. "Our lessons can go forward," I tell her. I take a deep breath and ask, "What of Fr. Tristamo?"

Both men shake their heads. Orlund says, "What on earth did you do to him? He's afraid to come on shore, and rarely leaves his quarters. Without our asking, he told us he'll never say anything about you or our activities here."

"I didn't do anything to Tristamo. Just—"

Yema breaks in. "Senhor Orlund," she says, "Sister Leah scared him so bad, he peed his britches."

"The child exaggerates," I tell them. "How did you explain his absence to the *populi*?"

"That he was suddenly taken ill. Didn't want to infect them with whatever he had."

"They believed it?"

"I think so," Vincent says. "We still held Mass. Just on the shore, not on the hillside. Nearly everyone from the Vitória attended, and most from my ship too. You should have been there."

"Does Tristamo know about the rebellion in Luís?" I ask. "Will he stay there, or go on to Fortaleza with you?"

"We haven't told him about the rebellion," Orland says. "I guess he'll decide when we get there."

I take a moment to collect my thoughts, finally asking, "He didn't say anything about what happened here?"

"Not a word."

"Let me assure you gentlemen, I took full responsibility for the priest's abduction. None of you are implicated in any way."

Orlund says, "We get that impression. Thank you so much, Sister Doçura. You took quite a risk."

"We shall see," I answer. "And you must also thank Pavê. I could not have done it without his warriors."

Captain Vincent heads next door to the chief's *óga* while Lars Orlund and I continue to talk. In a few minutes he's back. "We've got to return to the ship," the captain tells us. "So I'll see you ladies in a few weeks." He takes my hand and kisses it.

Orlund does the same. "Please come over to our unloading station tomorrow," he says. "We've moved the last of our things to the hillside, and we're building quite a settlement there. You must see our progress."

I bid Captain Vincent safe journey, and tell Lars Orlund we will be there in the morning.

Chapter 22

The next day at the unloading area we discover that almost everything is gone, even the pig enclosure and the wooden planting beds. I assume most were used for firewood. Pavê, his two wives, and the young son who shares our *óga* are with us. It is strange to see the bay without ships anchored there.

Since there's no one around, we start for the hillside. Kwasi comes running towards us when we are about halfway there. Out of breath, he smiles broadly, finally saying, "Greetings. Greetings. I saw you come up the beach, so I hurried down here."

His arm is still in a sling, but without a splint. "How's your arm?" I ask.

He flexes his fingers. "Still sore, but I can use it a little. Should be healed in a few weeks."

We follow him along the beach to the base of the plantation hill. As Orlund had suggested yesterday, we're impressed with the number of structures we see, mostly domed *ógas* in the Tupi style, and a few with the peaked-roof design similar to those of the Caeté. There's plenty of activity, mostly children of all ages running around, the younger kids looked after by the older ones. The majority of them are black, but there are a few Indians mixed in. This means Kwasi and Orlund have been able to recruit native families to work the plantation.

When I tell Kwasi they've done well recruiting Indians, he says, "Possibly it's because we named the plantation *Yvyty py Eorat.* It means Hill of Honey. The Tupi don't have a word for sugar." He tips his reed cap to Pavê. "At least not yet."

The first thing we do is to go inside the Capela de Tristamo. I'm aggravated the chapel's named after the priest, but since he did convert a number of natives, I guess the name should stay. The structure is neatly done and attractive inside. "Someone's made quite an effort to beautify this place," I tell Kwasi. "Smooth benches, cushions to sit on." I note the cushions are the same material as my woven-reed basket.

"Our women did most of the work," he says. "This chapel is fashioned after ours on Cape Verde."

I cross myself for good luck. Yema does the same. Possibly thinking alike—pleased that Fr. Tristamo is here by name only. When I turn to go outside, I see an interesting display along the back wall. It's a long shelf with a confusion of things, pieces of fruit, small piles of nuts, and scattered among them are beautiful figurines, crosses of several colors with ornate symbols carved into them, heads of men and women, all with African features, and brightly painted flower carvings. Some are made of clay, others from wood. "What is this?" I ask Kwasi.

"It's part of our Candomblé tradition," he says.

"Something from Africa?"

"Yes. We couldn't put it up until after Fr. Tristamo left."

"Candomblé? I don't know that phrase. The Africans on Tomé Island had traditional displays, but none like this."

"Candomblé means to dance in honor of the gods."

"Gods?"

He frowns. "Excuse me, Sister. Previously 'gods' when we lived in Africa. Now that we are Christians, it is to honor The Father and The Son." He walks along the shelf and points out various items. "The holy crosses are in His honor. The food is traditionally for the poor, but since we have no poor here, these are tokens. We have flowers to express our joy, and each adult will place a carving of themselves in the church so a little of them is always in the presence of God." He picks up one and holds it alongside his cheek. "This one is mine."

"It's a fair likeness," I say. "Who did these?"

"One woman and two of our men are traditional Candomblé carvers. It's a special skill." He pauses to arrange the display, turning some of the heads so they face the altar at the front of the chapel. "Come outside," he says, "there's something I want to show you."

We follow him a short distance to where a crew of men are working on two structures, both similar in design to the chapel, and nearly as large. Kwasi points to one, then the other. "This will be my home, the other is Orlund's." He adjusts the sling on his right arm, wincing a little as he does. "As soon as this arm's healed, I intend to start farming. In the meantime, I'm getting these two houses built."

Kwasi tells us he must get back to work, and suggests we take the trail up the hill to the first cane field. "I think you will find Senhor Lars there."

After a bit of a climb, we arrive at the first field. It's easy to spot Orlund with several others in a ditch at the far end. When we get there, we see he's ankle deep in mud. He gives us a welcoming smile, wiping his hands on the grass. "I apologize for not coming to greet you," he says. "This ditch was about to wash out, and we had to fix it before it flooded the field. Anyway it's great to see you."

As we worked our way across the field, Pavê and his son lagged behind, stopping to examine the cane plants, each now about six-inches high. When the chief catches up with us, he asks a question. Yema translates, "How tall must these plants be before you harvest them?"

Orlund reaches up as far as he can. "Twice as tall as a man," he says. "It takes almost a year." Pavê's son hears this and looks disappointed, complaining they've used all their black syrup. "Well, young fellow," Orlund says, "in a month or so we may have more. Likely one of the many stores Captain Vincent will bring back. He's stopping here on his way home."

***

A little more than three weeks have passed since our visit to the plantation, and it's about mid-morning. A ship's boat rounds the point and proceeds towards the Tupi settlement. We recognize it as one from the Corajoso, Captain Vincent's ship. As they get closer, Yema and I see that all the rowers are either African or Indian, and the only European visible is Vincent's navigator. Even from the distance we can hear pigs squealing. We assume he's bringing swine for the village.

Then we see something else. Yema and I are shocked into recognition. Standing on the seat in front is a small black-and-white dog. It's Bishop Damião's. When he spots us, he begins barking excitedly, leaps from the boat, and swims to shore. He's all over Yema and me, wagging his tail, rolling at our feet, jumping on us, finally lying on his back, furiously running his little legs in the air.

"Good morning, Sister Doçura," the navigator shouts as they get closer. "It looks like the little critter knows you." The man jumps from the boat just as it makes shore. "That's the friendliest dog I've ever seen."

We're too speechless to answer. The animal is making frenzied circles around us, kicking up little showers of dirt and sand as he does. In a moment Yema asks, "Where did you find him? He's Bishop Damião's."

"I'm not surprised to hear that," the navigator says. "An Indian girl gave him to us at Colony Luís. She said it was the bishop's dog."

"He was a favorite with the children there," I tell him. "I

figured he ended up in someone's stewpot."

"Does he have a name?"

"Not that I ever heard," I say.

Yema's holding the dog, practically squeezing the daylights out of him. He's licking her face and thrashing his tail. "Let's call him Porõ," she suggests. "It means lucky."

"Fine with me," he tells her. "I'll leave him with you." We chat about the dog a little longer, then the navigator says, "You'll be pleased to know we dropped anchor this morning near the base of the plantation." He extends his hand. "I hope you are well."

I take his hand in greeting. "Sorry," I say. "We were just overwhelmed when we saw the dog." I catch my breath. "How was your voyage?"

"Excellent indeed. We have a full load of dyewood, the majority of it cardinal red. Worth a fortune when we get home." The pigs begin to struggle, squealing and rocking the boat. "I've got to unload these swine," he says. "Then we can talk." They have two pigs trussed by the feet and a pole inserted through their legs. The rowers unload the beasts, laying them on their sides on the riverbank. "Gifts for the Tupi," the navigator says. "We brought back almost thirty for the plantation. We thought the Indians might cook them today. Then we could come over for a feast."

By now Pavê has joined us, and he instructs some men to carry the pigs to the community house. Yema tells him the animals are intended for a feast. The chief thanks the navigator and says it's a grand idea. "We will have a celebration," he adds. As the chief leaves, the dog follows at his heels.

"Go get Porõ," I say to Yema. "Or he'll end up on the roasting fire with the pigs." She runs after them, soon returning with the dog in her arms.

"They eat dogs?" the navigator asks.

"The Tupi eat everything," I say. "To them, I think 'pet' means something to eat. The Indians have no concept of domestic animals."

Yema shrugs. "I'm afraid Sister Leah is right."

"So tell me what you found at Colony Luís?" I ask.

"Not much," the navigator replies. "The place is in ruins, mostly abandoned. Even the garrison. The docks are torn up, the abbey burned down, and there are people living in the church. There's a few huts still standing."

"What people? Any Portuguese?"

"Indians and blacks. Escaped slaves I think. Only Portuguese left are riffraff. All the commercial people moved to Fortaleza. That place is booming." He looks out to the bay. "I'd better get back," he says.

"We'll come with you. I want to hear—"

He interrupts me. His look turns serious. "I am sorry, Sister. Captain Vincent does not want you anywhere near the plantation. It's a matter of safety, both for us and for you."

I give him a level stare. "I have learned to trust the captain's judgment, but I can't imagine what it can be. Please tell me."

"The captain would rather tell you himself. But I assure you that your staying here is for the best." He walks toward his boat. "I must get back to help with the unloading."

"Wait," I say, and take Porõ from Yema. "Give the dog to Senhor Orlund. At least for now. He's not safe here."

They push off, and leave Yema and me standing on the bank, wondering. "See you in a while," he shouts. Porõ stands on the seat next to him, wagging his tail. He seems perfectly content as they row away.

"What now?" Yema asks.

"I guess we'll find out later." I take her hand. "Let's walk up upriver. They're going to slaughter those pigs. Killing things bothers me."

"Can you believe they found the bishop's dog?"

"Perhaps it's a sign," I tell her. "I've been praying each night for the safe return of those men. Someday I hope to see the bishop's reaction when he sees that dog."

A while later Yema asks, "Are you going to give the captain that letter you wrote to your parents?"

"Yes, of course. Why the look of concern?"

"It's just that— Well, what are they going to think when they read that I'm an Indian girl?"

"When they read about what we've been through, they will be proud of us both. Remember, I told you my brother adopted two mulatto children? So now I've added another, the first member of our family from the New World."

"But those mulatto kids were your brother's children. You

told me twins, the children of one of his wives. The woman who was kidnapped."

Yema's got the story a little mixed up, but it's close enough. I hug her to me. "We are also relatives, little one. Always. I promise."

After a while we see two columns of smoke rising from the community hut. I assume the pigs have met their sad end, and are now roasting for dinner. We head back, both of us worried about what we will hear from Captain Vincent.

Once we're at our *óga*, we try not to let the waiting get the best of us. Yema runs out to play, and I spend the time bringing my journal up to date. For some reason I just can't keep my eyes open. I'm sitting on a grass matt and, rather than getting into my hammock, I stretch out on the floor and soon fall fast asleep.

The next thing I know, Yema is shaking me. "Wake up Sister Leah, they're coming."

"All right," I say, and try to focus my eyes. I hear the sound of rain on the thatch. "How long's it been raining?"

"Just started. Wake up."

Going to the doorway, I catch water in my hands, washing my face to revive my senses. I dry myself off with a scrap of cloth left over from my discarded habit. I'm almost finished when Captain Vincent appears in entrance.

"May I come in?" he asks.

"Yes, yes," I say. "Good to see you."

"I've brought you something." He hands me two rolls of cloth, one of uncolored muslin, the other a woven black fabric. "Figured you'd need a change or two of clothes."

"Oh this so nice. Thank you."

"We've got so much to talk about," he says, "but I've not eaten since morning. May we enjoy our meal first, then come back here to talk?"

Yema hands him one of the large leaves we use to shelter from the rain. She and I each grab one, and we hurry over to the community hut. Inside we find a lively crowd of Indians, Pavê and his family at the center. Sitting with them are Kwasi, Lars Orlund, and the Corajoso's navigator. We see no other Europeans or any of the ship's crew. After a hurried round of hellos, we get down to the business of eating. The Tupi have prepared quite a feast. We have fresh guava, and besides the roast pig, they have cooked yams and maize bread. Orlund's brought a small keg of black syrup, and it's been poured into a shallow clay dish. The natives in particular are thrilled with the syrup. They dip almost every bit of food into it except the guava.

"Will you keep that dog for us?" I ask Orlund.

"I certainly will," he says. "He's taken quite a fancy to me. No Indians eating him on my watch."

It appears the Tupi had planned one of their narcotic-driven welcoming ceremonies. Stacked to one side we see baskets of red feathers, pots of their tarry concoction, and the long pipes they use to smoke it.

Everyone eats their fill, all the while exchanging pleasantries. When we're about finished, Pavê suggests the men play the oyster-shell game. Baskets of shells are brought over, and the contests begin. Captain Vincent suggests it's a good time for us to talk, and invites Lars Orlund to join us.

"Go ahead," he says to Vincent. "I know it already. And Sister Doçura and I will have plenty of time later."

The three of us hurry back to our *óga*. Yema stirs the coals in our fire, adds dry moss to make it flame, then enough wood to provide good light.

The captain hands me the bundle of black cloth. "Unroll it," he says.

When I do, I find a rolled parchment at the center and a straw doll about five inches high.

"Read the parchment," he says. "We found it in the rubble of the chapel."

Inscribed across the top in broad letters: WARRANT OF CONDEMNATION FOR CRIMES AGAINST THE HOLY ROMAN CHURCH. Below the heading are two sketches, one of me, the other of Yema. The likenesses are approximate, but sufficient. Below the drawings, we see our names and a list of our crimes. Across the bottom of the document: REWARD FOR APPREHENSION {DEAD OR ALIVE} – 5,000 GOLD REIS.

Vincent says, "You two made quite a name for yourselves."

I spread the parchment on the straw mat and put a stone on each corner. Shaking my head, I say, "Why such an immense sum?"

"Of that I'm not sure, but there's a notice like this posted at the church in Fortaleza. Now take a look at the doll."

It's a simple figure, straw throughout, tied at the wrists, neck, waist, and legs, the binding keeping it together and providing shape. Two things stand out. The features are drawn in black, just dots for the eyes, a slit for the mouth, another dot for the nose. Radiating from the eyes, towards where the ears might be, are three lines like cat whiskers. A simple 'y' is inscribed on the chest. "Yema?" I ask. "Yemanjá?"

"Both. Most everyone who fled Luís ended up in Fortaleza. You and Yema— That's all anyone talks about."

I hand the doll to Yema. As if it were poison, she holds it by one errant straw. "That's the ugliest doll I've ever seen," she says.

"Ugly or not, they're everywhere in Fortaleza," says Vincent.

"I thought they concluded we died in the jungle?" I say.

About then we hear an uproar from the direction of the community hut. Moments later the navigator joins us followed by Orlund and Kwasi, the latter two laughing so hard they have to hold each other up. "The Indians have gone insane," Kwasi informs us. "They're snorting that black stuff, and—"

He chokes laughing and Orlund has to finish for him. "They're covered with red feathers and completely out of their minds. Two of them fell into the fire."

"I hope not Pavê," I say.

"No. Two warriors I don't know."

Kwasi studies the wanted notice on the floor. "I just heard about all this today. I think I'll have our women make some of these dolls. Yema, I see you already have one."

She gives the African a sour look and tosses the doll to him. "It's yours, Senhor Kwasi. Put it in the Capela de Tristamo."

By Kwasi's expression, it's obvious he's irritated by Yema's behavior. To avoid further words between the two, Vincent responds immediately. "All right gentlemen, ladies, this is serious. Sister Doçura, you wonder why the reward is so much? I think the Church is taking no chances. The clergy there are desperate to quell the rumors. It seems every African has one of those dolls, and most of the natives do too. I suspect many Portuguese also have them. The 'ys' are scribbled everywhere, mostly sides of buildings, one even on the church until they scrubbed it off."

"It's turned into some kind of hysteria," the navigator says. "One rumor, particularly among the Spanish, claims that Yema was crucified, that she's *la Nueva Niño Cristo,* the New Christ Child." He glances over at Yema. "Is it true you can sing like an angel?"

The girl does not respond. She's just standing in the shadows, dazed and brooding.

Finally Vincent says, "Listen Doçura, besides your so-called crimes being the talk of Fortaleza, there's a mercenary element there, and they're forming gangs to go look for you. A reward that size is a big incentive."

"I imagine it's only a matter of time," I say, "before Fr. Tristamo joins the mob."

The captain looks surprised. "You didn't know he stayed in Luís?"

"My goodness. No one told me. Seems so unlike him. Why did he do that?"

"Tristamo's a changed man. I've never seen anything like it. Said his mission was now with those less fortunate. I'd still like to know what you did to him."

"As I told you before, I did *nothing* to him."

Vincent shrugs. "Back to Fortaleza then. Unfortunately I arrived there short of crew, so some seamen I hired may be of the mercenary type. That's why we don't want you over by the plantation until we leave. That's also why I've let no one go ashore. All the unloading this morning was done by men from the plantation."

"I appreciate your diligence," I tell him, "but what about the sailors who were here last month? They certainly know about me."

Vincent sighs and looks away, then makes an angry gesture at the parchment. "Once we found this in Luís, I cautioned my crew to say nothing about our time here at the plantation. Only a few of us knew about the reward until we got to Fortaleza. With money like that, some of the sailors may be unable to keep their tongues from wagging. We were at Fortaleza for nearly a week, so everyone in my crew knows about the reward now."

I pick up the notice and roll it up. "May I keep this?"

"It's yours," Vincent says.

Yema walks past us and out the door. Once outside she pauses, then returns to the doorway. "All you people are given to madness," she says.

We continue to talk until evening approaches. The rain persists, but at a moderate pace. "We'd better head back," Captain

Vincent says. "We're leaving in the morning."

I hand him the letter for my parents. "Thank you for posting this. I told them to address any reply to you at your station in Amsterdam."

"If we get a good price for our cargo, I'll likely be back before you hear from them. Maybe as soon as four months. There's an excellent dyewood supply at Fortaleza."

After the men leave, I go next door to Pavê's and find Yema staring into the fire. The headman and his two wives are on the floor sound asleep, obviously too impaired by the celebration to get into their hammocks.

"Maybe I should start sniffing that black narcotic," Yema says. "Then I'll be permanently out of my mind."

"That might work," I answer. "Then you can join the rest of us."

"It's not funny."

"I didn't say it was. Anyway, once Vincent is gone, I don't think we'll be in much danger."

"What's to keep some gang from coming here and killing us?"

I sit down next to her. "We're so far from Fortaleza, I doubt if anyone will bother. Besides, they will have to come via the bay, and I'm sure someone will spot them. Pavê will protect us. So will Orlund and Kwasi." She leans her head against me and I pull her close.

"Yema," I say, "I believe you were very rude to Kwasi this afternoon."

"I'm sorry. I was angry."

"You should not have told him to put that straw doll in the chapel. Those figures are part—"

"I hate that chapel. *Tristamo!*"

"It's only a name, sweetheart. It is still God's house. Are you going to let me finish?"

"Yes," she sighs.

"Figures are part of their Candomblé tradition. So one should not make light of that. Anyway, I think Kwasi was trying to be funny by suggesting the women make more dolls."

"I didn't mean to insult him. It just made me mad." She stands up and extends a hand. "Come on. I'm ready for my hammock."

We go back to our hut and prepare for bed. I admire the cloth that Vincent gave me, then roll the wanted notice backwards so it lays flat. I wedge it between a strut and the thatch wall. The girl asks me if I'm going to leave it up. "For a day or two," I say.

We're talking quietly because Pavê's daughter and son are already asleep. Yema crawls into her hammock and says, "Should I apologize to Kwasi?"

I give it some thought. "That's probably not necessary. But I can think of a treat for all of us. Have the African women teach you their songs. I know everyone wants to hear you sing."

Chapter 23

The next morning I get a pleasant surprise. After our meal, Yema says to me, "Unroll the muslin cloth you got from Captain Vincent." She's all smiles.

The cloth is rolled around something, but I'd paid no attention to it; there was simply too much going on yesterday. The material is at least four yards long, enough for two wraps, and perhaps even a top of some sort. At the center I find a package tied with string and wrapped in oilcloth. Untying the string, and to my absolute delight, I find five soaps, each about the size of a clam, and a ball of heavy black thread. There are two needles inserted into the thread.

"Oh my goodness," I say to Yema. "Why didn't someone tell me about this yesterday?"

"Captain Vincent assumed you would unroll the cloth. When you didn't, he asked me to tell you after he left."

"You both are scoundrels for not letting me know. What a nice gift." I hold the cloth up to my chin. "I can even make a dress out of this. What do you think?"

She's already gathered up the morning's dishes, preparing to wash them at the river. "Why bother," she says, and walks out the door. The child waggles her little backside at me as she departs, knowing I find the gesture particularly irritating.

***

Over the next several weeks, Yema and I spend more and more time at the plantation. I've grown bored with the work at the village, mostly gathering and cooking food, or laboring in the vegetable plots. I find the plantation activities more interesting, likely because it reminds me of times at my brother's farm on Tomé. Also I miss conversing with Europeans. If I can't have a woman or two to talk with, Lars Orlund will have to do. He's educated and witty, and I find his accounts of the Netherlands most intriguing. It would seem the Dutch are a tolerant people, certainly more so than the Portuguese. To Yema's delight, spending time with Lars allows us to see Porõ. The dog has become his constant companion. "I'm not surprised," I told him, recounting what I'd noticed in Luís. "The animal prefers the company of men rather than women."

Orlund has told me little of himself. It sounds like he's quite well off since he has a large farm across the bay from Amsterdam near a town called Almere. He's said nothing about his family, and I'm curious if he has a wife and children. At one point he mentioned a village called Maarssen, a day's ride south from Almere. "There's quite a Jewish community in Maarssen," he tells me.

I find this hard to believe since the Portuguese Crown controls all the Dutch provinces. "They worship openly?" I ask.

"Oh no," he says, "any worship there is done in secret. The Portuguese would like to keep us all under their thumbs. But their unending war with the French insulates us in a way. Crown forces around Amsterdam are minimal at best."

"That's not what we heard from Archbishop Boeyens," I say. "To hear him tell it, he's the Holy Emperor of Amsterdam." In any other company, what I just said would be blasphemous. I scrutinize his features, but all I see is agreement—rather pleasing agreement, though I suspect he might be pandering to me. Yema says I'm too suspicious. She's taken quite a liking to this burly Dutchman.

Yema and I spend our days working in the cane fields, pulling weeds, hoeing, stripping insects from the spiky leaves and canes, and making sure the irrigation water flows evenly. With my several changes of clothing, soap, and a freshwater stream for bathing, I'm able to stay mostly free of the damnable lice. There are a few vacant huts because some workers decided to sign on as seamen with Captain Vincent and return to Europe. Yema and I found one complete with a fire ring, benches, and hammocks, and we've made it into a comfortable home.

We frequently take our morning meals with Kwasi and an Indian woman he's taken up with, and very occasionally an evening meal with Lars Orlund. The Dutchman seems to be working all the time. He's up before dawn, never eats at midday or takes an afternoon nap, and is back in his hut after dark, usually eating cold soup before climbing into his hammock.

I insisted on fixing him a proper dinner for one evening, and he accepted. Yema and I decide to make stew, something that will last him a few days. We use oysters and clams, cut-up yams, and the *ka'apetãi* greens that grow in great profusion along the banks of the stream that works its way down the hillside plantation. We thicken it with maize flour. I decide to wear the new dress I made from the muslin. Yema says I look like one of the grand ladies I've told her about. "The grand ladies wear silk," I tell her, "not muslin."

She asks me, "What's silk?"

"It's a fabric more delicate than a breeze," I say, then tickle her. "As smooth as the skin underneath your chin."

She does a little sashay. "I might like to wear silk."

"As much as I'd like to see you wear clothes," I tell her, "I doubt if either of us will ever wear silk."

On the day when we made dinner for Lars, we insisted that he arrive at least an hour before dark. He does not, but shows up when the light is almost fading, Porõ trotting beside him.

He has an excuse, though. "I was filthy from work," he says. "So I stopped to take a bath. Unfortunately I had no way to dry off. If you ladies would excuse me, I'd like to change my clothes." We step outside his *óga* while he changes.

When we go back inside, he says, "Speaking of clothes, Sister Doçura, you look quite elegant in that muslin dress."

Yema puts a hand over her mouth, and I am sure I'm blushing a little. Hopefully it's dark enough that he doesn't notice. "You're late," I say. "Let's eat dinner."

He's very pleased with the fare, and eats zestfully, thanking us over and over. We use oyster shells to scoop up the broth and yams and toss the empty shells through the doorway. Porõ chases after them, hunting for scraps. Yema recounts our time on the shores of Jacu Bay when we encountered the *y'teju* lizards. She laughs about their antics, then gets teary-eyed when she thinks of Agato.

"Sweetheart," I suggest, "tell Senhor Orlund about Agato. How he saved everyone from the Caribs. What a brave boy he was."

"I can't," she says. "You tell him."

I sigh, feeling as much sorrow as Yema. "Lars," I say, "we'll tell you some other time."

It's dark outside, and the girl goes to the door, calling for Porõ. He comes scampering inside, a brown lizard in his jaws. The dog stretches out by the fire and eats his dinner while we look on with disgust. Lars asks, "So you think Bishop Damião will be pleased to get his dog back?"

"Pleased?" I say "No. Overjoyed." I'm trying to sound hopeful when I continue. "We've done what we can to free those men from the Inquisition. The rest is up to God, but if somehow they make it to these shores, you will find them admirable company." This conversation goes on for quite a while, and I sense that Lars hopes for their rescue as much as we do.

"Senhor Lars," Yema asks him, "why do you work so hard? You never seem to rest."

He turns thoughtful, then says, "Well ladies, I am given to fits of melancholy. A poverty of spirit, if you will. I find that hard work keeps those demons at bay."

Yema asks me what melancholy is.

"Sadness," I tell her. "The Caeté word is *vy'ave'y.*" Then I say to Lars, "I hope the success in the cane planting has raised your spirits."

"Certainly so. We've planted nearly twice as many acres as I expected. Kwasi showed us how to split the sprouting stalks, and get two or more starts from one."

Porõ begins making frightful crunching sounds, breaking lizard bones. Yema picks up what's left and leads the dog out of the hut. She's back in a minute or two. "I put it over by the chapel," she tells us. "Maybe he'll finish before he comes back."

"Speaking of the chapel," I say to Lars, "it would be a joy to see Bishop Damião and Fr. Julian again, to have worthy priests here to conduct the Mass."

"Kwasi and I, well really a number of us, would like to have services there now. Could you conduct them?"

"Nuns are not allowed to conduct services per se. In fact, we're not even allowed on the pulpit unless given permission by a priest. But I could stand in front and recite scripture."

"Latin or Portuguese? I always thought Latin seemed a waste of effort, since only clergy can understand it."

"Either," I say. "Even Heb—" The word sticks in my throat. I feel a rush of panic. No one on this earth except my parents know I can recite Old Testament scripture in Hebrew. No one! The Church considers it the utmost heresy. Lars and Yema give me strange looks.

"What's wrong?" Orlund asks.

"This may seem off the subject," I say, "but it is not. You mentioned the Jews of Maarssen. I must know how you regard them?"

"With respect, of course. They are the givers of the Old Testament."

His answer is almost in reflex, and I believe he is quite sincere. I ask, "Do other Dutch people feel the same way?"

"Many, yes. For the same reasons we oppose the Inquisition."

I stand up and begin to pace, at the same time asking Yema to make tea. She puts a clay pot on the fire, and places a few sticks of dry wood around it. I produce my pouch of yerba buena. "My supply of buena from Captain Vincent is running low," I tell Lars, "but we should drink to our new church service. I'll be pleased to conduct it."

"So your mission continues?" he says.

"What mission?" I ask, my voice rising. "Why on earth do you say that?"

"Why? Look at the response I got from you. It was just a simple question, Doçura. You are a woman possessed."

Yema offers an agreement. "It's in her nature," she says, repeating my words from an earlier conversation.

I stare into my cup, deciding how to explain. "In Jewish tradition, it's called *Ha Tsorekh Goral*. In rough translation, 'the requirements of one's destiny.' But it's much more than that. Each Jew is given the life-long task to better the world. As one would expect, God doesn't just go around assigning tasks; they are only revealed in the midst of trial. The more extreme the trial, the more formidable the task. In my case I've had several, each one more daunting than the last." I glance at Yema. She's watching me intently, her face isolated in the firelight, eyes yellow, the cat tracings focusing her stare. I find it unnerving, and must remind myself, *when the child is most interested, this is how she looks.*

"So as you already know, at sixteen I was forced into the Catholic faith at the Convent Coimbra. As part of this ordeal, the nuns assigned me the responsibility of caring for some of the infants who were kidnapped with us. Whether as a nun, or in the guise of a nun, that seemed a worthy *Tsorekh Goral*.

"But on my travels to São Tomé, I found that God wished to try me further. At the port of Elmina, I discovered my brother on his deathbed, dying from a failed mission to expose the evils of slavery. Once on Tomé I worked as the principal scribe for Bishop Henrique Cão. The bishop was black, totally opposed to slavery, and he told me about my brother's heroism, how he died helping him gather evidence against the slavers. I take up the battle, but before I know it, the Church banishes Bishop Cão back to Africa. As far as I can tell, the slave owners bribed the Curia to get rid of him. I'm so disgusted, I leave for Brazil before the new bishop arrives. It's the same blasted thing at Luís. At the behest of the slavers, the Church restricted us from ministering to those enslaved.

"As if this wasn't enough, God placed Yema and me in the path of the most dreaded inquisitor of all, Juan Girona. So now I must oppose slavery *and* the Inquisition. And once we're on the run, many times my *Tsorekh* runneth over. First I'm able to rescue some captive Indian children from the curse of life-long slavery." At some point during this conversation, Porõ returned unnoticed. Now he's found something in the corner of the *óga* and begins digging and showering dirt in our direction. Yema goes over and picks up the dog, settling him in her lap much as Bishop Damião used to do.

"This is truly fascinating," Orlund says. "I knew some of this, but not this much."

There is a tone of understanding in his voice that I find most reassuring. I continue. "So I succeed with the Indian children, but it never stops. Next I struggle with you and Kwasi over the same subject. Regardless of any success, God puts me in greater peril—Fr. Tristamo and Juan Girona. In this latest trial, I suppose my *Tsorekh Goral* has become clear: To stop the Inquisition on these shores. In this little corner of nowhere, I suppose I have. What frightens me, Lars, will it ever stop? What's next?"

He gives me a hearty laugh. "God only knows. But what I do know, Sister Leah, is that you will be up to the task."

I get to my feet and take Porõ from Yema, handing him to Lars. "Here's your dog, sir. We have to get some sleep."

"Thank you Doçura for a delightful dinner and conversation. I will see you senhoras in the morning." He lights a torch from the fire and hands it to me. "So you can find your way back."

It's only a short ways, but the torch is helpful. As we walk to our hut, Yema asks, "Why didn't you ever tell me about this?"

"About the *Tsorekh Goral?*"

"Yes."

"Well," I sigh, "it's a Jewish belief. Not much room for it in the Catholic way of thinking. So much has changed since we've been on the run. And now with our isolated locale and the appearance of these tolerant Europeans, maybe I can be both Jew and Catholic. For a little while anyway. I still eagerly wish for Bishop Damião and Fr. Julian's return, but there's not much hope of me being both in their presence. However, just as they did at Luís, I think those two will tolerate at least some of the African traditions here."

"Is that why I almost never see you pray anymore?"

I say nothing as we prepare for bed. First I lean the torch on the fire ring and adjust my pillow. Both of us are using pillows made from flour sacks—gifts from Captain Vincent and stuffed with soft, dry grass. I extinguish the torch and climb into my hammock.

"Are you going to answer my question?" Yema asks.

"It's very personal, sweetheart. Let me think about it. Perhaps tomorrow."

* * *

The Sunday following our dinner with Orlund, four of us gather in front of the altar to conduct an informal service at the Capela de Tristamo. Our service has an interesting flavor, and I find it most refreshing. Standing in front of the congregation, I explain that while the Mass is conducted solely in Latin, our service will be conducted in several languages. First I welcome everyone, then recite 2Corinthians 9, verses 6-11 in Portuguese, blessing those who till the soil and sow bountifully. Yema stands next to me, translating for the Indians. Next I cite Kwasi as the bountiful planter, "The one who gives us two seeds from one, more than doubling our acreage."

Kwasi gives a brief talk in Guinea, praising his workers. Following him, Lars Orlund provides further praise for the workers, and thanks God and the Tupi for the gift of land.

Previously, Yema and I had discussed what she would sing at the service. With the exception of the African women who've been teaching her their songs, this will be the first time anyone outside that group has heard her sing. Regardless, the plantation and Tupi settlement have been rife with rumors about her voice. I assume that is why the chapel is full with all the benches occupied, and more people standing at the back and along the walls. I recite the brief *Plenum gratiae et veritatis* as introduction, and Yema sings the *Glória.* Everyone is spellbound by her voice, and I see they are eager for more. I can only assume that next Sunday we will have an even larger crowd.

Knowing that Yema will finish the service with another song, I recite Deuteronomy 7, verses 12-15, portraying God's promise to provide abundant crops and protect us from sickness. If we are to avoid plague sweeping through this settlement, surely we will need His protection.

Yema stands, announcing she will sing a tribal song. *"Agụ owuru na-enweghị,"* she says, "A boy and His Leopard." But when she sings, ♪ *"Enyi n'ihi na ndụ ...,"* the child does not use the Guinea word for leopard, instead she uses *"jaguarete,"* the Caeté word for jaguar. No one objects, and by the second verse all the Africans are standing and singing with her. It is a very festive way to end the service. Everyone applauds.

Lars Orlund smiles and says to me, "In the history of Christendom, I'd wager there's never been a church service like this one."

Chapter 24

We're nearing the end of October, and my thoughts return to Lisbon and the beautiful fall seasons we had there. The locust trees will be shedding the last of their golden leaves as the first chill winds from the Sierra de Gredos sweep through our streets and alleyways, herding clusters of leaves before them. Here, the seasons seem to hardly change, raining almost every day, or every other day depending on the time of year.

This morning it's threatening rain, but so far none has come. The sugarcane has an infestation of green bugs about the size and shape of one's thumbnail. We're stripping them from the stalks and leaves, grinding the insects underfoot. It's hard to tell if they are doing damage to the crop, though no one is taking any chances. These cane plants—now more than a foot high—have been in the soil a short six weeks, and they are far ahead of any crop I'd seen on São Tomé. If this growth continues, Lars and Kwasi will have a harvest in less than a year. It's time to consider a pressing mill and drying house.

Low clouds from the bay have swirled in around us, and we're shrouded in fog. We take a break from work and rinse ourselves in the Ribeiro da Lojurã, the name Yema and her friend gave to the little stream that runs through the plantation. The friend Lojurã is Pavê's daughter who shared our *óga* back at the Tupi village.

We're startled by a loud boom from the direction of the bay and the surrounding hillsides echoing the sound back to us. The Indians around us show considerable alarm. "What is that?" Yema asks. "It's not thunder."

"It's a ship's cannon," I say. "We have visitors."

The group of us troop down the hillside, soon joined by others from the fields below, including Kwasi and Lars. The fog thins as we descend towards the bay. We can see the ship now, a large four-master flying the Spanish flag. She's dropped anchor, and there are several men climbing down rope nets to a waiting boat. "Only one boat," Orlund says. "Not a raiding party. Could it be your comrades from Luís?"

My heart leaps into my throat. For some reason I'd not considered that when I heard the cannon. I take Yema's hand. "Wait," I say. "We can't let those Spaniards know we're here." Then to Lars and Kwasi, "You gentlemen do understand that?"

"Of course," they both say, and continue ahead of us.

Yema and I sit down to watch. We're a few hundred feet above the beach and perhaps a quarter-mile away from the landing site. We continue watching as people assemble on the shore awaiting the boat. It's too far away to identify individuals, but certainly Porõ will let us know if Bishop Damião is among them. The dog is easy to spot, a small speck dashing back and forth along the shoreline. I imagine he's barking his head off. As the boat draws closer, a man stands up and begins clapping his hands. Porõ jumps into the water and swims the short distance to the boat. The man almost topples over the side as he scoops up the dog, saved only by someone grabbing him from behind. It has to be the bishop. Even at this distance, we can hear him whooping with pleasure.

I'm overjoyed, and so is Yema. She's jumping up and down, shouting, "We've rescued those people! I can't believe it."

"Indeed we have," I say. "God has answered our prayers."

We watch the activity on the beach, and I believe I can see Orlund or Kwasi pointing in our direction. I can only hope they've remembered not to disclose anything about us. Not yet anyway, not until the other men in the boat return to their ship. I assume this Spanish vessel is bound for Colony Luís or Fortaleza.

It seems to take forever as the men confer on the beach. There's little movement except for a few Indians coming and going. Finally the group exchanges handshakes, and the ship's boat departs. With great excitement we see the five men start in our direction, Porõ dashing frantic circles around them. As Yema and I descend the hillside trail, my concern gets the best of me. I wonder, *They'll be grateful for our help in freeing them, but will they blame the two of us for what happened?* Regardless, the die is cast.

My thoughts are cut short by Porõ running up to us, barking, then zooming back down the trail. "I hope our reception is as friendly as his," I say. When we round a corner on the steep trail, we see the men by the Capela de Tristamo a hundred feet below. Yema takes off running, sprinting at breakneck speed. So typical of this child, she has likely read my thoughts—If any animosity resides in the three men, she is the one to charm them out of it.

I arrive at the chapel to find everyone inside, Yema sitting quietly on a front bench, Dr. Cardim beside her. Lars Orlund and Kwasi sit nearby. Bishop Damião and Fr. Julian are kneeling in front of the altar.

When they see me, everyone stands up. The bishop is the first to speak. "Oh dear Mãe, you and the child have rescued us. We cannot thank you enough." He embraces me, something I'd never imagined happening.

I say, "It was Captain Torres, more than I who made this happen. I am so pleased the three of you are safe and here with us." There are generous thanks and embraces all around. The men look tanned and in good health. All three wear the common dress of Spanish seamen, black pants, white shirt, open black vest, and felt cap.

Porõ, exhausted from his running, lies on the floor panting, his tongue lolling on the floor. Bishop Damião gestures to him, tears coming to the man's eyes. "I've been so worried about my little dog. You even saved *him.*" He pauses to compose himself, then turns to Yema. "I adore the name Porõ, Yema. I am so grateful to you. The dog is lucky, and so are we."

"As for his rescue," I say, "we have another captain to thank, Captain Eider Vincent of the Corajoso. An Indian child at the Luís settlement had the dog. She knew he was yours."

We talk for over an hour, me catching them up on our exploits, the uncertain conditions at Luís, and the Yema obsession at Fortaleza. The men are shocked when we tell them about Agato.

"We will conduct a memorial Mass for the boy," the bishop says. "I always thought he was a clever child." Next they tell us about their imprisonment and escape. "As soon as we left this bay," Bishop Damião says, "Captain Torres told us he'd found a safe harbor. He said nothing of you and Yema. We were due to be tortured in Lisbon. In case his plan failed, he didn't want the inquisitors to have the truth.

"A few weeks later, he smuggled us off the ship at Isle Hispaniola. It was in the middle of the night, and the Vitória left immediately. I have no idea how he handled it with Girona and Bishop Boeyens. All we know is they were very drunk the night we escaped."

Fr. Julian takes a letter from his pocket. "Captain Vincent gave this to Captain Torres of the Vitória. It explains your situation here. This could only have been done with God's help, Sister Doçura." He crosses himself. "Vincent also provided money for our passage, but we still have it. Instead we volunteered to work as seamen on the Spanish vessel. So here we are, well fed, free, and with a few coins in our pockets."

Dr. Cardim speaks up, briefly holding open his vest. "I'm keeping the money for these noble clergy. Their vows of poverty remain unblemished." Everyone laughs.

The African women have brought in quite a feast, laying it on benches behind us, maize and yam cakes, black syrup, fresh guava, dried fish, and spiced *ka'apetãi* greens. While Kwasi and Orlund tell Dr. Cardim and Fr. Julian about the plantation, Bishop Damião takes me aside. Yema tags along. "I want you two to understand," he says, "we do not blame either of you for what happened at Luís. In a way, this unfortunate circumstance was a product of Fr. Girona's foul intentions. Almost every night he'd get drunk and come down to our cell on the Vitória. He bragged about how he suspected corruption at the settlement and his intentions to expose it."

The bishop gets down on his knees, taking little Yema by the shoulders. He looks intently into her eyes. "I am truly sorry, little cantora. The death of Janaína and your father just played into Fr. Girona's hands." He lets go her shoulders, but continues his contrition. "I still think, dear child, you are indeed God's miracle."

I'm shocked at what the girl says next. "What about my mother, my little brother, our Caeté village?"

"Yema!" I say, "that is not—"

The bishop raises his hand. "She's right," he says. "That attack should never have happened. But it was not my doing. Do you understand? We were held prisoner in the stockade. It was that fellow Diego, Fr. Girona's henchman, who led the raid."

Yema reaches out and touches the bishop's cheek. Then she turns and walks over to the food. She takes a yam cake, dribbles black syrup on it, and goes outside. The bishop stands, tears again in his eyes. "I see she's as intense as ever," he says.

***

In the six weeks or so leading up to Christmas, much has happened. Our two priests have conducted frequent services, including a lovely Mass where we honored Agato and also christened Pavê's newborn son of the same name. Bishop Damião wants to be called Fr. Mateus, his given name. Both he and Julian admit they can never return to Europe or any port on this side of the ocean. "We will gladly spend our days here," they both say. To my pleasure and surprise, both have accepted the African Candomblé display in the chapel, and also welcomed Yema's singing both sacred and tribal songs. They still conduct the Mass in Latin, but have asked me to do a scripture reading in Portuguese at each service. It seems their brush with the Inquisition has enlivened them to challenge Church dicta in a variety of ways, and this includes their frequently calling me "Sister Leah."

Most pleasing of all, Yema often concludes the service with an African song, and many of those assembled join in. The first time Frs. Julian and Mateus experienced all this, they both appeared stunned, but any displeasure quickly disappeared when they saw how much people enjoyed the singing. No doubt they were also thinking about their growing congregation.

Dr. Cardim has set up a hospital in a large *óga* at the base of the hill. He sees plantation workers, and lately, more and more Tupi. There is always plenty of injuries to deal with, as well as an occasional woman giving birth. So far we've seen very little sickness, and as yet the coryza has not assailed us.

The doctor is intrigued with the Netherlands, and he and Lars Orlund talk about the region for hours. I believe, if given the chance, he would travel there. "I'd fit right in," he says. "The Inquisition will never find me." Orlund, plus a couple of seamen who stayed on to work the plantation, are teaching him Dutch.

Frs. Julian and Mateus—It's taking me forever to get used to calling the bishop by that name—are pleased with the rate of conversion among the Indians. The two have been slow to learn Tupi, so Yema and I provide instructions for those natives who wish to embrace Christ. Just as we did at Colony Luís, we often have baptisms after Sunday Mass, and then a festival.

I'm amused when Julian confides in me that the bishop still complains about the lack of clothing on the Indians and the bare-breasted African women. He quoted Fr. Mateus who called it, "A spectacle of nudity." And I must admit that our little capela is probably the only place on earth where naked people take communion. Our communion is another example of the adjustments we've made in this *"achterland"* as Lars calls it, which I think means a land of nowhere. We use small yam cakes for the sacramental bread and a foul-tasting beer made of black syrup and maize for our wine offering.

Both priests spend part of their days helping to build the pressing mill and drying house. Obviously they've benefitted from toiling on the Spanish ship, and they appear to enjoy the physical labor. Kwasi is the one directing the projects and demonstrates a full knowledge of cane production, seeding, growing, and processing. His grinding mill is of a different design from the ones I saw on São Tomé. There's no way to know if it's superior to those until I see it in operation, but I get the impression that his plantation on Cape Verde was quite productive because of this mill design.

Many Tupi also work at the plantation, both in the fields and the building projects. Kwasi and Orlund have many casks of black syrup which Captain Vincent brought from Fortaleza. They use it as currency to pay the Indians who find the stuff almost addictive. The Tupi provided an interesting twist to the refining process. They got wind that ants are a major problem in cane farming and sugar production. In this climate, there are ants everywhere, but never in the native huts, and now never in ours. The Indians harvest a low-growing plant that smells a bit like camphor. All dwellings have a shallow trench around them which is layered with this plant called *tyakuã*. The ants refuse to go near it, and Lars says he can make a fortune importing the plant to Cape Verde and São Tomé, and selling it along the Brazilian coast. As for our production he says, "Can you imagine the price we can get in Europe for sugar without ants?" Yema added that she's never seen the plant, so apparently the Caeté didn't have it.

* * *

It's mid-week with Christmas only ten days off, and Yema and I wash our morning dishes in the Ribeiro da Lojurã. Then we head to one of the middle cane fields to work, today hoeing and pulling weeds. The crop has grown incredibly fast, and is now almost three feet high. Yema has grown too. She seems to be thriving. As close as I can figure, the girl is eleven years old. It's difficult to fathom all we've been through given the short time we've known each other.

"The Caeté didn't keep track of birthdays?" I ask her.

"No. Everybody's was celebrated around the time they were born, at the beginning of a particular season, or the end. We really didn't keep track of days and years like you do."

"So shall we pick a birthday date for you?"

She gives me a shrug. "Sure."

"Alright, your eleventh birthday will be in a little more than two weeks, on January first, the first day of the new year. That way we'll never forget."

"When's your birthday?" she asks.

"March seventeenth," I say.

"When is that?

"About three-and-a-half months after yours. I'll be twenty six."

The child grows thoughtful and says, "I'm worried about my singing on Sunday. I've been rehearsing the *Confiteor Deo* with Fr. Julian, and it doesn't feel right. I'm just not sure why."

"I think you'll do fine," I say. "You sang it two weeks ago, and sounded great."

"I keep thinking about when I sang it at Colony Luís. Having Fr. Julian here brings back all those memories." She begins to cry and walks away from me, head down, her shoulders slumped forward.

I catch up and hug her from behind. Her tears are wet on my

arms. "Yema, I love you," I tell her, my face pressed into her hair. "If you don't want to sing tomorrow, Fr. Julian will understand."

***

At last Sunday morning rolls around, and my little cantora says she's ready to sing. I dress in my black skirt and muslin top. These days my hair is long, and Yema weaves it into a thick braid, securing the end with a ribbon she made from my sewing leftovers. I comb her hair and tie it back with a thin band across her forehead. She doesn't remember, but that's how I fixed her hair the first time she met the *Consilium de populi.*

By the time we get to the chapel, it's beginning to fill. If this Mass turns out like last Sunday's, there will be many of the congregation standing outside, peering through the open spaces around the building. The growing attendance has prompted Mateus and Julian to talk about enlarging the structure. It's raining, so the two priests stand just inside the back entrance, welcoming people. Next to them is an Indian boy about fourteen years old, and the closest person we have to an acolyte. He's interested in the Church, and has become quite fluent in Portuguese. Today the youngster is serving as translator, repeating the priests' greetings in Tupi. He will also translate during the Portuguese segment of the Mass.

This boy's name is Laãro, and he and Yema have become friends. She greatly appreciates his language skills, because more and more he's been standing in for her when translations are needed.

The Mass begins, and we're just a minute or two into Fr. Mateus' Sunday greeting when a commotion at the back of the chapel erupts with people screaming and running out the rear entrance. I look there to see Pavê's wife—baby Agato's mother—standing alone, cradling her child. Everyone around her has fled. I rush up the aisle, stopping when I'm about ten feet away. I'm horrified at what I see. Pointing to a bench, I say, "Sit right there, and don't move!"

I immediately go back to Yema near the front of the chapel. Fr. Mateus asks me what's wrong, but I'm too panicked to respond. I drag the girl outside through the front entrance. It's pouring rain and we're immediately soaked to the skin. "No questions," I say to her. "Go to our *óga* and take enough food for several days. Move into that abandoned hut at the top of the plantation and stay there until I come get you."

"Why?"

"We have plague, that's why." By now Laãro has joined us. He starts to speak, but I cut him off. "Go with Yema and help her," I tell him. "She'll explain." They both hesitate. I push them in the direction of our hut. "Now!" The two children hurry away.

Dr. Cardim runs up to me as I skirt the throng of Indians clustered outside the chapel. He points at the rear entrance. "Keep everyone away from her," he says. "I've got to talk with Mateus and Julian."

All at once, like a wave ebbing from the beach, people around the back entrance retreat, the circle widening in fear. The woman has stepped through the entrance into the rain, holding her baby. The child is wailing, and so is she. "Oh my God," I say when I'm able to get a closer look. The little bumps could have been raindrops, certainly as numerous as a mist of rain on a person's skin. But these are not raindrops. The woman and her baby have smallpox.

Chapter 25

Dr. Cardim returns and takes the woman by the arm. "Come with me," he says, "we'll take care of you."

I follow them over to the hospital *óga*. My head is pounding, and despite the rain, I'm sweating profusely. The smallpox could kill us all. Just as we arrive at the hospital hut, Frs. Mateus and Julian emerge, helping the other patients out the door, taking them to a nearby *óga* where they will not be exposed to the plague. A large group of Tupi and Africans have followed us, but at a distance. I notice the Africans are clustered to the rear of the group. I can only assume they have some knowledge of smallpox. The Indians have no understanding of this plague, or any plague for that matter. It makes no difference—This illness could spell their doom.

I wait outside while the doctor gets the woman settled. In a minute he comes to the door. "It's the white pox," he says. "More than half will die. Thank God it's not the red pox. Then nine out of ten would perish. Do you know the difference?" he asks me.

"Yes," I say. "I saw it in Lisbon. We lost a brother and a sister to the red pox. I had white smallpox and survived. Is it true I won't get it again?" I pull up my sleeve and show him the round scars on my arm.

He nods. "That's my understanding. One never catches it

twice. I had it too." For a moment he looks bewildered. "I think it's the goddamnable pigs."

"What do you mean? I've never heard you curse like that."

"They carry some kind of demon. Every time we bring pigs into an Indian settlement, sooner or later the pox breaks out."

"It didn't at Luís," I say.

"I know. Like everything in doctoring, there are more puzzles than answers." He looks to the south. "Are you going to tell Pavê? It's his wife and child."

I'm in a state of disbelief, and I've got to come to my senses. Also, I'm close to vomiting. "Yes, I'll tell him. I'm sure he knows. She came over here sick."

"She was looking for you or me, Doçura. That's what she told me."

By now Kwasi, Orlund, and the two priests have joined us. All of them look stricken. "Senhores," Cardim says, "I will leave the details up to you, but here's what we need to do. Send people to gather *jehe'a,* and bring it here. Boil up a whole pot of the stuff, as thick as you can make it. I'll use is as a palliative. Load all the swine into boats and dump them as far out in the bay as you can. Cut their throats so they can't swim back."

"Why the pigs?" Kwasi asks.

"They carry some kind of demon," the doctor says. "Where they go, the pox follows." Then he turns to me. "When you talk to Pavê, tell him we'll come over for the pigs. I know they still have several at the village. God only knows what else is going on there."

"I'll go now," I say, and start off. I'm only a few yards away when Fr. Mateus calls to me.

"Where's Yema?"

I gesture towards the hillside. "I sent her to that topmost hut," I shout. "Hopefully she'll be safe." The bishop crosses himself. I turn and head down the path to the beach.

The rain is falling even harder now, and I decide to take the trail through the jungle where I'll have some protection from the downpour. Upon nearing the lake, I run into Pavê, his second wife, a few warriors armed with spears, and a number of people trailing behind them. I've never seen the chief look so grim. He's heavily painted, as are his companions. Because of the rain, the paint is running in garish streaks down their bodies. I'm shocked when I get a closer look at the group behind them. All of them have smallpox.

One of the warriors points his spear at me. Pavê nudges it aside. "We have been cursed," he says. "And this curse is yours. It is because of that ceremony you had for little Agato, the 'christening' as you called it."

"I —"

"You see those people back there? I'm sending them to you so you can remove their curse. That's why I sent my wife and baby over this morning."

"I can't remove the curse, Senhor Pavê. Only God can do that."

He grows angrier. "I do not believe in your *guero'yrõ* god! He is a devil."

I point back the way I came. "Have those who are sick wait over there. I'll take them to Dr. Cardim. I must speak further with you."

He instructs his people, then says to me, "You are no longer my daughter. I do not want to hear more of your lies." The sick Tupi pass by me and stop a short ways down the trail. A few of them can barely walk.

"I have never lied to you, sir. And I will not lie now. Please hear me out." He nods, and I continue. "I think more of your tribesmen will get sick. If they do, send them to see Dr. Cardim. As soon as they appear ill."

"Three people are already dead," he says. "We buried them this morning. In the settlement, there was a black man living with a Tupi woman. She is one of those who died. We drove the man into the river this morning. The piranha killed him." Pavê takes a spear from one of his men and points it at my middle. He makes a short feint, but I do not step back. "If you," he continues, "or any of your whites or blacks come near us, we will kill them."

I say, "Two more things sir, please."

"What?"

"We must come over and take your pigs. We believe they carry the pox demon."

He glares at me as if I'm insane. "You can't blame this curse on your food animals. It is your fault, and the fault of those priests of yours. We will keep our pigs." He spits on the ground near my feet. "What else?"

"What shall I tell the Tupi at the plantation?"

"Return to our village," he says with a shrug, "or stay there. I'm certain they will die. You have corrupted them."

The situation has grown more threatening, his anger ready to spill into violence. I turn and walk to the group of waiting Indians. I'm sick at heart when I look them over. One of the worse off is Pavê's daughter Lojurã, Yema's friend. "Come with me," I say. We trudge slowly back towards the plantation.

We haven't gone far when Lojurã sits down, pulls her knees to her chest, and hugs them against her. "Sister Leah," she says, "I can't go any further. Leave me here." An older woman settles next to her, saying she will wait until we return with help. I assure her we will, and continue on. I doubt I can get anyone to fetch these women.

By the time our group gets to the hospital, I've lost two more, both sitting in the jungle by the side of the trail. I tell the remaining five to wait outside the *óga*. Mercifully, the rain has stopped. The doctor comes out and looks over the group. I tell him what's happened, but he doesn't seem to hear. "This is an absolute disaster," he says. "Three of these Indians have red pox."

***

Three days have passed, and the plague grows worse. A dozen people at the plantation have become sick. Four have died. The afflicted are mostly Tupi, but there are also three Africans and one white man, a sailor who stayed to work at the plantation. It wasn't until late afternoon on the first day that I was able to persuade four of our plantation Indians to go with me and retrieve the sick tribesmen we left along the trail. We found Lojurã dead, as was one other—the woman who stayed with Lojurã. In a brief ceremony, we buried the woman and girl a little ways into the jungle, then helped the two remaining natives to the hospital.

About a half-mile distant from our little colony at the base of the hill, we've dug a mass grave. I'm sure we will need another. A few Tupi returned to their village, but sick or otherwise, none came back. So we have no news from there.

I'm crazy with worry about Yema, and will go to see her this afternoon. Right now I'm helping with the sick, trying to make them comfortable, rubbing their bodies with the *jehe'a* mixture. Besides Dr. Cardim and I, there are only a few of us willing to touch them, Orlund, Kwasi, Mateus and Julian, and three African women who claim to have had the pox years ago. As for the Tupi around the plantation, all appear terrified, hiding in their *ógas*. Kwasi's Indian woman is one of those afflicted, so he takes particular care of her. He's never had the pox and I fear he will catch it.

We've got full sun today, and it's about straight overhead when I go to my hut and eat a quick meal, my first of the day. I'm exhausted, having tended to the sick long before daylight. I gather maize cakes and whatever else I can find, and start up the steep trail to the top of the plantation. I'm so unbelievably tired that I have to rest a few times along the way.

When I get to the topmost field, and in sight of Yema's hut, I call out. No answer. I go inside where I find her sitting by a dead fire. She's filthy from head to foot, and hardly acknowledges my presence. "Where's Laãro?" I ask. He's nowhere to be seen.

She points vaguely toward the entrance. "Gone," she says. "He's got the pox. Didn't want the demons near me."

This is terrible news. It means she'll likely get it too. I say a quick prayer, then ask, "When?"

"Two days ago." Her voice is dull, devoid of feeling. There's an animal look in her eyes. "He's probably dead," she adds.

"Why are you so dirty?"

"I'm rolling in the dirt. I am dirt. I caused this." She points to a corner of the hut. "See, I'm pissing there. I shit there. In my own house."

"Have you eaten?"

She shakes her head.

I set the basket down. "I brought you some food." Her behavior makes no sense. "You are not dirt," I say at last. "And Yema, you did not cause this. Let me take you to the stream. I'll wash you."

"'The stream?' How is Lojurã?"

My heart sinks. "Let's get cleaned up first."

The girl stands up and screams at me. "She's dead, isn't she? Lojurã came to me in my dreams. She told me!"

"Yes, she's dead. So is little Agato and his mother. There are many dead, and there will be more."

"Why? Why did you people ever come here?"

Sympathy hasn't worked— Perhaps anger will. I am so worried about this child. "Damn it, Yema, we've been over this before!" I pull her to her feet, and drag her outside. "We'll both feel better once you get cleaned up." The girl is limp as a rag as I wash her in the stream. I set her on a rock. I've nothing to dry her with, so I take off my muslin top and use it as a towel. She's seen me like this before, but never outside, not in broad daylight. To my delight, she begins to giggle, then breaks into a hysterical fit of laughter. I join her, both of us laughing and crying at the same time. I hug the child and stroke her hair. "This is not your fault, sweetheart. I'm so sorry it's happened."

She jerks the muslin top from my hand and runs off with it. "You're halfway there," she yells. "Now take off your skirt."

I walk her way, removing my belt, reaching for the tuck that holds the skirt around my middle. I partly undo it. Yema is mesmerized by my actions. She lets me get close enough to grab my top.

"I knew you were going to do that!" she says, and points to the hut. "What did you bring to eat?"

I get the basket, then come back and settle next to her. "Let's eat here," I say. "We can clean up later." With just this brief moment of rest, my fatigue overcomes me. "After you're finished, please tidy up your hut. Heap some dirt over your mess. Alright?" I fold my arms and let my head slump forward. "I've got to take a nap."

She stands up and touches my cheek. "Sure." She walks away as I close my eyes.

I sleep only a short while, but I do wake up somewhat refreshed. I wash my face in the stream and pull my damp top up to dry myself. Yema is sitting a distance away, eating a yam cake and poking a stick into the water. I sit down next to her. "How are you feeling?"

She gives me a wry smile. "I want to stay angry at you, but I can't."

"It takes practice."

The girl remains quiet for a few moments, then says, "Once in a while I hear you talk about penance. What does it mean?"

"It means contrition for one's sins. But you already know that."

"Do you ever do penance?"

"Not lately. Why do you ask?"

Her look turns serious. "I'm afraid to stay up here alone. I want to come back and help with the sick. I must do penance."

"I'll send somebody to stay with you. We'll alternate, change people every few days, bring food."

Yema shakes her head. "If you and the priests think I'm a miracle, then let's try it."

"What on earth do you mean?"

"If God considers me a miracle, He will also protect me from the smallpox. Put Him to the test."

"What you just said is blasphemy, dear child. Only in this wilderness could one say something like that. No one ever tests God. He tests us."

"You Europeans consider this a wilderness, we do not. Perhaps in this *wilderness,* God will permit such a test."

"And if you get the pox and die, what then?"

Yema stands in front of me. She tries pulling me to my feet. "Let's go," she says. "I have to do this for Lojurã, for Agato and Agato, for Laãro. For—" She picks up a rock and splashes it into the stream. "For everyone," she says.

"We should try to find Laãro first," I say.

"He was heading back to the chapel. If you haven't seen him by now, he's dead."

***

Christmas came and went without celebration. The same for Yema's New Year's birthday. If we survive, we'll celebrate it next year. It's nearing the first of February, the hottest time of the year. In another month the rainy season will start. The smallpox may be abating, and so far God has spared Yema and almost all of us Europeans. The poor Africans have not fared as well. Kwasi fought the pox for nearly two weeks. He finally succumbed after a valiant struggle. We did not bury him in the mass grave—sadly we're working on our third one—and had a funeral Mass for him at his own burial spot instead. His grave is marked with a sturdy cross and a wooden memorial with his name on it.

Of the thirty or so Indians who worked on the plantation, more than half have died. The rest disappeared back to the Tupi village. Only three healthy Tupi remain with us, two men and a woman. All the children have perished, blacks and Indians alike. It is tragic beyond words. This disease seems particularly hard on young ones. In our vicinity, dear Yema is the only child left alive.

Orlund and Fr. Julian went to the Tupi settlement a week ago. They found it abandoned. It's rumored that Pavê and his wife did not catch the pox, and that the surviving Indians took refuge upriver with their sister tribe, the Támoioj. Orlund described the village as a scene from hell. "No telling how many died," he said. "There are corpses everywhere. It looked like they gave up burying them."

The plantation is a mess. The jungle is beginning to creep into the pressing mill and the rough beginnings of our drying house. The cane is choked with weeds, but despite this, the stalks are over six feet high. There's no one to weed, much less harvest. It makes no difference since we have no way to process the canes.

Our single bright spot is that Dr. Cardim has five patients— two Indians, two Africans, one white—who appear to be recovering. Their sores are drying up, and they are eating regularly. We were all surprised at Yema's determination to help during the past six weeks. Every day she toured the three hospital *ógas*, dutifully rubbing *jehe'a* on each patient, seeming to disregard the bloody sores and their frightening deliriums. She cleaned up after the sick, fed the patients, and never complained. If she wasn't a miracle before, she is certainly regarded as one now.

"I think the demon is gone," she tells me at our meal this morning. "The doctor says if we can go another week without anyone getting sick, the plague is over."

I cross myself. "That would truly be a blessing. Everyone admires how hard you've worked. Perhaps we can relax a little today. Let's go for a walk. Dr. Cardim can look after the sick this morning. Is that all right?" She nods. "Go tell him."

She returns in a few minutes with Fr. Mateus and Porõ in tow. "I hear we're taking a walk," the bishop says.

"Yes indeed," I answer, and get to my feet. "Let's go."

As we walk along the beach, Yema picks up a long piece of kelp, tempts Porõ with it, and takes off running, the dog fast after the seaweed's bushy end. Fr. Mateus watches the girl for a moment, then appears so overcome with emotion, he can barely talk. He takes my hand. I'm surprised, and I pull away in reflex. "Sorry," I say, and put my hand back in his. He gives it a squeeze and lets go.

"May I confide something with you?" he asks.

"Of course."

"When I'm in the presence of that child, I feel I'm in the

presence of a saint. How can she be so joyful at a time like this?"

"Well, you've certainly seen her when she's not joyful."

"I know. But she seems to have the strength of an adult. I don't know how she does it. And she's the only child who survived the pox. I believe God spared her for a reason."

"I've thought that too," I say. "Maybe Fortaleza's *Santo de Yema* obsession has some merit. She *is* astonishing."

We look down the beach and see the her perched on a log looking out to sea. Porõ is scampering back to us, dragging the long strip of kelp. The child is pointing and yelling, but she's out of earshot. She jumps down and runs breathlessly back to us. "I see a ship," she says.

Indeed the child is right. Beyond the distant edge of surf at the bay's entrance, I can see a sail barely peeking above the horizon. "Do you think it's Captain Vincent?" Yema asks.

"We'll know soon enough," Fr. Mateus says. "I believe she's headed this way."

I'm excited at the prospect, and pose a question without thinking. "What are you going to do if it is, Father? I think Yema and I will depart this coast of sorrows."

"I don't know," he replies. "I was so pleased with our prospects here." The priest looks down and shakes his head. "Now, Sister Leah, I've no idea what to do." He calls to Porõ, "Come on little pup." Then to us, "If you ladies would please excuse me." He leaves us and heads back to the plantation.

Chapter 26

For a while, Yema is silent. I know she's thinking about what I said. She's probably shocked at the possibility of leaving. We continue down the beach a ways, and both of us stand on the log from where she first spotted the ship. It's closer now, and obviously inside the breakers at the bay's entrance. A few people are straggling down the hillside from the plantation. For certain, they've also seen the ship. We trudge back towards the hill to wait with the others.

Finally I say, "All right, little one, what's on your mind?"

"If we leave, where will we go?"

I shake my head. "We can't stay here. If the vessel is the Corajoso, Orlund and I have talked about going to the Netherlands.

He and Vincent say Almere's a friendly port. There's not much of an inquisition there."

"Maybe for them. What about us?"

Ever since the smallpox broke out, I've pondered this question. It's much broader than inquisition. I could hide myself by blending in, but Yema looks so foreign. If Portugal were possible, I could pass her off as a Moor—my adopted daughter or a slave. There she would attract little attention. The opposite would be true in the light-skinned provinces of the Netherlands where she would plainly stand out. And then there are her face tattoos and scars. She's not old enough to wear a veil. Regardless, that would be the best method of hiding her. But knowing Yema, the child likely won't tolerate having her face covered. If I'm to save us both, I must come up with something.

By the time we join the people at the base of the hill, there is no doubt the ship is the Corajoso. I take Yema's hand and pull her against me. I say, "And here we are at a crossroads again, dear child. Where shall circumstance take us this time?"

The girl lets go of my hand and runs to Fr. Mateus. She gathers up Porõ and begins whispering in his ear, then wades a short distance into the water. Captain Vincent has been absent from this coast for almost six months, and when he rows ashore, the first person to greet him will be Yema.

***

So far the Corajoso has been here four days with very few of the crew willing to set foot on land. Finally Dr. Cardim and Captain Vincent persuaded them it was safe, and most streamed ashore, eager to be free of the ship's confines. We've gone for over ten days now without another case of smallpox. I can only pray this marks the end of the epidemic.

Today we're touring the cane fields. Since Vincent has a financial interest in the plantation, he and Orlund must decide what to do. The two of them agreed to the demands from the remaining Cape Verde Negroes—five in all—that they receive Kwasi's share of whatever can be salvaged from the plantation. In addition, Orlund and Vincent offered to return them to Cape Verde.

The cane continues to grow despite the weeds and lack of irrigation. The rains of late have been sufficient, and there will be more in the next three months. "Here's what we hope to do," they tell the blacks. "When we get to Fortaleza, we'll try to find a reputable sugar processor who will harvest the cane and pay us a share of the profits. This plantation appears so productive, perhaps he'll want to buy the grower's license."

There's quite a discussion among the Africans. Some want to stay, demanding the grower's license as full payment and somehow making the plantation work again. Others want to take the promised payments and return to their home island. This latter argument won out, though with one shocking exception. That came just now as we prepare our evening meal. Frs. Mateus and Julian arrive at the entrance of our *óga* accompanied by a gigantic black man who everyone calls Carloso since no one can pronounce his African name. This is the man I first saw as Kwasi's bodyguard. Carloso stands over six feet tall, with broad shoulders, large hands and feet, an immense head, and a face endowed with a perpetual scowl. He's actually quite an agreeable fellow, his unhappy countenance the result of a childhood injury.

Fr. Mateus is carrying Porõ like a baby, cradling him belly-up in his arms. The dog's feet are relaxed and folded against his chest. Both Julian and Mateus have been weeping. The bishop speaks first. "Doçura and Yema, I've come to let you know that I will not be joining you on the return voyage." He sets Porõ down. The dog sniffs around the hut as Mateus continues. "I'm a marked man, and returning to Europe, even the Netherlands, is out of the question. I have decided to go upriver with the remaining Tupi. They want to join their sister tribe."

"That's dangerous," I say. "How do you know the Támoioj don't have the pox? Pavê went there with the swine and— "

"I'll take my chances. I do not intend to hide in Europe and remain a fugitive for the rest of my life. If the Támoioj do have the pox, perhaps I can help them. After all, I didn't catch it." He nods to the African. "Carloso's going with me."

"That's right, ma'am Leah," Carloso says. "I will keep him safe."

This is very upsetting. Even Yema and I haven't decided for-sure what to do, but we had assumed that the two priests and Dr. Cardim would go with us.

"Carloso, why are you doing this?" Yema asks. She and the man have worked together many times, helping the sick and working in the cane fields.

"The reverend father is my friend," he says, "and I like the Indian way of life." He gives us a tortured look, his scowl more intense than ever. "There is nothing left for me on Cape Verde. My dear wife and children are buried here. This is now my soil. Our soil."

For a while, everyone is silent. I return to my cooking chores, saddened beyond measure. Yema finally speaks up. "Fr. Julian," she says, "you're going with us, aren't you?"

"Yes I am, dear child. And Fr. Mateus is doing the right thing. Porõ would make him stand out even more. No one has pet dogs in Portugal, and Lars told us it's the same in the Netherlands. Only the nobles have dogs, and those are hounds for hunting."

After our meal, we go to the *óga* where Lars, Captain Vincent, and his navigator are staying. The navigator is a new fellow, not the same man from last fall, a Portuguese gentleman named Enzo Henry. They greet us warmly, and we settle by their fire.

"Are you surprised by Fr. Mateus' decision?" Vincent asks.

"I'm too sad for words," I answer. "I was hoping we could all find a productive life somewhere." I am not at all shy when talking around Enzo Henry. He is a Converso whose previous surname was de Hedeva.

"I've never seen such devotion to a pet," Orlund says, "but Mateus would certainly have trouble hiding with Porõ. With Boeyens' cathedral just across the bay in Amsterdam, his spies are everywhere. He and Fr. Girona must be furious about losing—"

"Are you inviting us to live on your farm?" Yema asks.

Captain Vincent and Orlund react with broad smiles. I'm embarrassed, having to remind myself that Indian children say whatever's on their mind. I guess I should be used to it by now.

"Matter of fact, I am," Lars Orlund says, "but on one condition, child."

Yema's taken up sparring with this Dutchman, and she's become quite good at it. "What?" she asks, a note of defiance in her voice.

"You'll have to wear clothes. Dutch children don't go around in their birthday clothes."

Yema has never heard this expression before, and she thinks it's quite funny. "And what if I want to wear my birthday clothes?" she asks.

"Well, little lady, if you don't wear clothes, you will freeze your behind in the wintertime, and you'll have to live with the chickens in the summer."

For once Yema's at a loss for words. She looks to me for help. "I hear they have very colorful clothes in Almere, Yema. You'll like them, and you're going to have to wear a veil when you go outside." There, I finally said it. It's the only solution I've been able to come up with.

"What's a veil?" Yema asks.

"You know that gauze we had over our hammocks? It's like that. It covers your face. You can see through it."

"Why? I don't want to do that."

I take her arm and put it next to mine. We've only the firelight, but it's sufficient to show the difference in our skin color. "You see how dark your skin is? Unfortunately you will look very foreign there. And that attracts attention. There are a few dark people in the Netherlands, and they are Moors. We will pass you off as a Moorish girl, my adopted daughter. All their women and young girls wear veils. It's a tradition."

She gives me a look of great skepticism. Fortunately we have plenty of time to work this out on our trip across the ocean. In the meantime, nothing has been settled about our move to the Netherlands. "Will you take us in?" I ask Lars Orlund. "We'll work in the fields to earn our keep."

"That's my plan," he says. "You can stay in the main house or a tenant house. Whatever you prefer. My farm is surrounded by smallholders. We have quite a community there."

"What about Dr. Cardim and Fr. Julian?" Yema asks.

"Julian is going to work on my farm and minister where he can." Orlund responds. "The doctor is going to sail with Vincent. He'll be one of his officers."

"My voyages will be more productive with a physician on board," Vincent adds. "As you suggested once before, Leah, Cardim is excellent company. A man of accomplished conversation."

Enzo Henry gathers some small sticks from a pile in the corner and stokes the fire. The coals jump to life, the flames dancing up the thatch walls. Yema's found a piece of cloth somewhere, and is dangling it in front of her face. She asks for my dagger so she can poke eyeholes in it.

"Gentlemen," I say to Lars and Vincent, "no one has bothered to explain this air of jollity that seems to pervade you two. This immense venture, this plantation, has failed. Why do neither of you seem concerned?"

Lars Orlund turns serious. "We are of course concerned about all the people we've lost, but financially it is not a problem. Dyewood is selling at a generous premium in Amsterdam. Vincent sold the last boatload for a fortune—the expense of the plantation many times over."

"Is that why you carry no westbound cargo?" I ask Vincent.

"Correct. With the money we made, I could afford to sail back here with only supplies for the plantation and a few contract items for Fortaleza. I'll have no problem selling the plantation supplies when we make port there."

I stifle a yawn, as does Yema. This has been a long day, and we're both tired. Orlund lights a torch and walks us back to our *óga*. On the way, we see the fire still high in the nearby hut occupied by Julian, Mateus, and Dr. Cardim. Yema claps her hands, and Porõ comes running. She picks up the dog and carries him back inside. We hear her say, "Good night, dear senhores." When she comes back out, I can see tears glistening on her cheeks.

Lars stays long enough for us to kindle a fire, then bids us a good night. In a few minutes we're side-by-side in our hammocks, the fire fading to embers.

Yema's crying, using the cloth with the eyeholes as a handkerchief. But she does not sound sad when she asks me, "Are you going to marry Lars Orlund?"

"Mother of God," I respond, reaching out and giving her hammock a shove. "I guess I should never be surprised at anything you say."

"You know he fancies you."

"You know he probably has a wife."

"He's never mentioned that, or children either. Why hasn't he said anything about them?"

"Men are like that, Yema. I think he's married."

"Marry him anyway. You can be wife number two."

"People in Europe only have one spouse at a time."

"Why?"

I give her hammock another shove. "Go to sleep, little

daughter."

***

The weather is quite agreeable the next morning with a cool breeze blowing from the Atlantic. The hot season is coming soon, and our voyage south and then across the ocean should provide a refuge from the stifling period ahead. Despite the fact that in a month it will be raining every day, the temperature will remain hot and steamy.

The Corajoso's crew is in no hurry to return to the sea. They've found the sandy shore of our bay a delightful place to rest after their long journey. Their leisure is cut short when Orlund and Vincent put everyone to work removing debris from the irrigation ditches. The weeds in the cane fields are so thick, they decide it would take too long to clear them. But since the flow from the Lojurã continues to provide water the fields, cleaning the irrigation ditches makes sense.

Yema and I work alongside Fr. Mateus, Julian, and Carloso. Our few Indians survivors have gone to the Tupi village to pay homage to their dead and retrieve canoes for the journey upriver. They return in the late afternoon, and the upcoming departure of Fr. Mateus begins to really take hold.

We eat a quiet meal of farewell that evening with Orlund, Vincent, Dr. Cardim, and the two priests. Yema is sitting next to Fr. Mateus. She's holding Porõ, rocking him back and forth and cooing.

"So Yema," Mateus asks, "who are you going to miss more, me or Porõ?"

"I'm going to miss you both, Father." She turns silent. It's obvious she's struggling to say more, though not quite sure if she should. At times like this, everyone wonders what strange things we'll hear next from her. Yema looks to me for approval.

"All right missy," I say. "You're among friends. Out with it."

She gulps and rests her hand on top of the priest's. "Well, Fr. Mateus," she says, "when you were bishop at Luís, I was afraid of you. But you've changed. Now we're just friends. Good friends. I like that much better."

I'm choked up and so is the bishop. In a moment he recovers and says, "I like it better too, sweet child." He puts his arm around her shoulder, drawing Yema against him. "This strange country has changed us all. Only God knows, perhaps we'll see each other again."

***

In the morning we have a community breakfast in the chapel. Fr. Julian leads a prayer service wishing "his comrades safe journey." Yema stands and sings an African song, first lamenting that she does not have her teacher to sing with her. The woman died of smallpox a month ago. Fr. Mateus gives a brief speech, thanking everyone for their friendship and encouraging us to hold true to our faith.

After the service, we trail down to the beach to say our good-byes. The Indians have three dugouts, paddling two and towing one behind loaded with provisions and belongings. Fr. Mateus positions himself on the middle seat in one of the canoes, Carloso behind him, manning the back paddle. Porõ next to the priest, peering over the side, his chin resting between his forepaws.

The farewell is as not as sad as I'd imagined. It seems we all have accepted this departure, and now it is at hand. Perhaps Fr. Julian is the one most affected. He and Yema stand together at the water's edge, the water lapping over their feet as the craft paddle away. We wave and call, then wait as the canoes grow smaller and smaller, finally disappearing behind the spit of land that marks their turn upstream.

"Well," Orlund says as we climb the hillside trail, "I guess we'd better make plans to also depart these shores."

***

The following two days are filled with activity. We salvage what we can from the pressing mill and drying house, taking only those items deemed saleable in Fortaleza. These include miscellaneous troughs and nozzles, the crushing wheel and supports, filter racks, drying tables, catch bins, and stores of nails, screws, and clamps. With the exception of the stone crushing wheel, we transport everything to the beach by hand or skidded on trundles.

The crushing wheel arrived in four parts and was assembled on a spindle inside the mill. Since it's round, Vincent elects not to take it apart. Instead he decides to muscle it down to the beach along the trail, holding it in check with restraining ropes. The thing proves too heavy for the men to hold, and it breaks free, gathering speed as it thrashes its way down the trail, the loose ropes throwing dirt and chaff in every direction. We're screaming to the workers below. People scatter in all directions. At last, almost comically, the thing launches off a bend in the trail and sails over the side, smashing onto the rocks below. It lands with a tremendous thud and breaks in half.

For some reason, Yema finds this so funny that she's paralyzed with laughter, falling by the side of the trail, barely able to catch her breath. Captain Vincent stands nearby and looks over the edge, presumably relieved that no one was hurt. "I guess we should have taken it apart," he says. The workers start disassembling what's left and move the parts to the loading area.

I'm standing next to Yema, and I give her a nasty look. "It's not funny," I tell her. "Someone could have been killed."

She's unrepentant. "No one got hurt," she says, "and that was the craziest thing I've ever seen."

"Let's go help," I say. "I'm glad you find everything so amusing."

"It *was* funny, and I think you're grouchy because you don't want to leave."

As usual, the kid understands me better than I do myself. Strangely, I did not considered this before. "You are mostly correct, little lady, though what I mainly fear is what lies ahead for us; as to departing this failed plantation, we have no choice."

"You know what I fear?" she says. "Is leaving all those ghosts behind. They will be angry we didn't stay and look after their spirits. That's what Indians do."

"We can't stay. You know that. We'll say a prayer for them tonight, and every night you want. Will that help?"

"I'll see what Lojurã and Laãro have to say," the girl tells me. "They visit me in my dreams."

***

By the week's end, the Corajoso is loaded and ready to sail. Captain Vincent takes us on a tour of the ship, showing us the quarters he's prepared for us. Enzo Henry has kindly vacated his cabin and moved in with the purser. There are four hammocks strung in the cabin—for Yema and me, and the two African women. "You can take your meals in here," Vincent tells us, "or I'd be delighted to share meals with you in my quarters." We assume the African women will eat with the crew since the two male Cape Verde survivors will bunk with the sailors, and there are several blacks among the ship's crew. They're an unruly lot, and I imagine the women—who themselves tend to be rather boisterous—would prefer their company.

Yema remains dissatisfied with the prayers we've been saying for the departed. There's just a half day left for us on this shore, so we decide to visit Lojurã's grave.

"May we take a candle?" Yema asks. "I want you to show me the *Nahala* again."

"That's a fine idea," I say. "Orlund has a lantern from the Corajoso. We'll borrow that." We go to his hut, ignite a stick from his smoldering fire, and light the tallow candle inside the lantern. When we get to the base of the hill, we spot Lars working with the loading crew. I hand the lantern to Yema. "Go ask him if we can borrow this."

The girl's back in a minute and says it's all right.

Walking along the beach to the lake trail brings back many memories, most vividly the impossible situation between the Africans and Europeans when they first landed here. It's hard to believe so much has happened since then. We pass the outcrop along the trail where we took refuge from the waterspout. From there, it's a short walk to Lojurã's resting place.

The girl takes the lantern and places it on the grave, then kneels and crosses herself. "All the Tupi spirits are here," she says, "in their beloved jungle. And I think they are at peace. They prefer not being near the plantation." She has collected a handful of stones, and places them in a line along the mound of earth, then ponders the assortment of plants growing from the fresh soil. Yema pulls them out, rearranging the stones as she goes along. She gets to her feet and stands next to me, dusting the dirt from her hands.

The child moves the lantern to the edge of the grave, and we both kneel in front of it. I make the v-shaped *baraka* with my hands, and she does the same. The child does it so quickly, I have to assume she's practiced it. I say Kaddish just as I did at Agato's grave, first in Hebrew, then in Portuguese. She follows along, repeating some phrases, staying in unison with me on others. I'm surprised at how much she remembers.

I've just started the third verse, "May He give reign to His kingship in—," when Yema breaks her pose and gives me a penetrating look.

"I have a question about this prayer," she says.

I put my face in my hands. "Yes?"

"If I remember correctly, this prayer only mentions God, never the dead. Isn't it supposed to honor those who died? At least mention them?"

"It's a traditional prayer, Yema. We're praising God who

gives the gift of life. We're praying *over* the dead. It's the Jewish way of—"

"I think it should mention the dead."

I'm torn between exasperation and humor. The child has a point, but prayers are not supposed to be literal. I don't think I can explain that to her. "Then you must want a different prayer?" I ask.

She positions her hands in the *baraka,* and closes her eyes.

I say first in Portuguese, "Blessed be these departed souls. May they find peace in the kingdom of heaven," then repeat it in Hebrew, *"M'vrakh' hayah eleh met n'shashot. Yakhl ..."*

Yema lifts the lantern glass from the bottom, careful not to burn her fingers. She blows out the candle and gets to her feet. "Thank you, Sister Leah," she says.

We return to the plantation where we find everyone gathered in the *Capela de Tristamo* for a final meal. Surrounded by many lively conversations, we eat a hearty dinner, then retire to our *óga.* Tomorrow is a new day, and a new beginning.

Part III

Chapter 27

The Corajoso set sail around noon the following day. Captain Vincent wanted to leave earlier, but it seemed everyone had something new to bring, or an item suddenly remembered. Once underway, Doçura, Yema, Lars Orlund, the doctor, and Fr. Julian stood at the rail as the beach and plantation hill receded from view. By the time they passed the line of surf at the north edge of the bay's entrance, the hillside could not be distinguished from those around it.

"As if it never was," Doçura mumbled under her breath. Yema stood next to her and began to shiver. *Oh God,* the nun thought, *either she's getting sick, or it's the breeze. I hope it's not—* then cut herself off mid-thought, refusing to consider the possibilities. "Come on child, let's get warmed up."

The girl followed her down the gangway into their quarter. Each hammock had a blanket to cover the open mesh. Doçura shook one open and wrapped the child in it, then boosted her into the hammock. She tucked a pillow under the girl's head. "If you're going to spend time on deck, either wrap yourself in a blanket, or I've got to make some clothes for you."

Yema turned on her side and looked at Doçura. "I hate being cold. It reminds me of when I had coryza."

"What say I make a robe for you? Like the daughters of the Moors wear."

"I would like that."

"Warm up," the nun said. "I'll go look for some cloth." In a short while she returned carrying a brown blanket, a pair of heavy shears, and a short length of rope knotted at each end. "Captain Vincent says there's no cloth on board. We'll try to find some in Fortaleza." She laid the blanket on the table. "In the meantime, I'll make an abbot's robe out of this."

With the hole in the center for her head, two for her arms, and the rope around her middle, Yema walked into the sunlight for the first time in many days wearing something rather than nothing. When Fr. Julian spotted her, he called out, "You look like a Franciscan friar, Cantora. The first female in our history."

The child stood in front of the priest, crossed herself and said, "Bless you Father," her words accompanied by peals of laughter from all who heard. Maintaining her imperious manner, she walked to the nearest shroud and climbed within reach of the mainsail's lower yard. Just as she settled there, the Corajoso came about, leaving her dangling on the shroud's underside when the ship slanted starboard. Above her head the massive yardarm made a resounding thump as it swiveled into place. Yema caught her feet in the netting so she wouldn't fall, but could not figure out how to get back on top of the shroud. Doçura steadied herself beneath the child, arms outstretched, expecting her to drop at any moment.

"Yema," a voice shouted from somewhere above, "if you're going to be a sailor, you must pay attention to what is going on!"

To the child's surprise, she spotted one of the Cape Verde women high in the mainsail's forward shroud. "What are you doing up there?" Yema asked.

"My boyfriend is in the crow's nest. I'm paying him a visit." Before Yema could respond, the woman yelled, "Listen to me, *Cantora menina!* Only at anchor do you climb the center of a shroud. At sea, you always climb on the edge. That way, when the captain calls 'Come about!' you move to the upside of the net. *Entende?*"

"But what do I do now?" Yema yelled.

"I'll catch you if you want to let go," Doçura said from

beneath her.

"I'm afraid to fall," the girl replied. She was swinging from side-to-side as the Corajoso worked through the oncoming swells, steeply mounting up the crests, then descending into the troughs.

"Climb to the other side. So you're on top."

"It's too far, Leah. I can't climb when I'm upside down."

"If a sloth can do it, so can you." When the girl did not move or respond, Doçura worked her way to the wheelhouse to talk with Captain Vincent. "What do you think of our little tree-monkey now?" she asked.

"I'm enjoying the show."

Orlund, who was standing beside Vincent, said, "I'm glad you moved. She's about to get sick."

Doçura looked back in time to see Yema spew a stream of vomit that splattered across the deck. The second mate called to a couple of seamen, "Go clean up that mess."

"How long are we on this tack?" the nun asked Vincent.

He glanced at his hourglass. "Another half-hour. Do you think she can hang on that long?"

"No! Of course not."

The captain shook his head and spun the wheel. The ship came upright for a moment, rolling violently in the sideswell, sails slack and flapping. "Go get her down," he said.

Before Doçura returned to the shroud, Yema was already on the deck, hanging onto the netting, spitting every few seconds. "Why am I sick?" she asked. "This is awful."

"You're seasick," the nun said. "You'll get over it." The ship slanted again, resuming its tack. Seawater sloshed across their legs and feet as the two seamen, seemingly oblivious to the deck's steep pitch, threw buckets of seawater across the wood planking, trying to come as close as possible to the two women without directly hitting them. "Alright, gentlemen," Doçura yelled, "That's enough!"

Both smiling, they touched their caps. "Yes ma'am," one of them answered. The two returned to their stations.

Doçura took Yema's hand. "What say we go to our cabin and work on reading lessons?"

The girl did not respond. Instead, she pulled away and climbed up the shroud, this time staying on the forward edge. The nun went to the rail and looked towards the coastline, just a low, dark line on the west horizon. She'd hoped to see the lower half of the plantation bay where Agato was buried, but the wind had not cooperated. Since the breeze came from the southeast, the Corajoso had tacked many miles into the Atlantic, then back again, zigzagging its way south. No sense worrying about Yema. The child had a mind of her own. Doçura went looking for Julian and Cardim.

***

By the time the Corajoso neared Fortaleza, Doçura and Yema had worked their way through the first part of Ludolphus de Saxonia's *Livro de Vita Christi,* borrowed from Captain Vincent's library. The nun helped Yema read a page until she could do it without prompting, then recited the page aloud while the child wrote the words.

When they got to the second chapter, Yema said, "Don't read it to me, I think I can do it from memory." To Doçura's amazement, the girl wrote the hundred or so words with only a few omissions and misspellings. Upon starting the third chapter, they agreed to give a demonstration to the men at dinner that evening.

During the restful sipping of port wine that concluded their evening meal, Doçura addressed those assembled, "Gentlemen," she said, deciding a little showmanship was in order, "Yema will now read a page from *Livro de Vita Christi.* One she's not seen before. Then from memory, she will write out what she's read." With a flourish to the girl, Doçura said, "You may proceed."

The adults enjoyed their port while Yema read, the men nodding with approval at her skill. Once she began with her quill, Captain Vincent took up the subject of Fortaleza and his intentions for commerce there.

Yema finished writing, blotted the page, and handed it to Orlund. He examined her work, then passed it around. Fr. Julian, the last to look at it, gave it back to Yema. He spoke for everyone when he said, "Cantora, you never cease to amaze us. Most females in Europe cannot read, and have little interest in doing so."

Yema replied with a nod to Doçura. "That's because no one teaches them."

Everyone looked to the nun. "My mother taught me at home," she said. "My entire family could read, even though the rabbis forbade women to do so."

***

The two women put lessons aside when the ship made port next morning. Everyone worked loading three of the ship's boats with goods destined for the town. After the midday meal, Vincent, Orlund, Fr. Julian, and Dr. Cardim all left for shore. Doçura, Yema, and Enzo Henry looked on as they departed. Lighters of many sizes and shapes plied Fortaleza's bay. The girl asked about the lighters, and the navigator explained, "The water is not deep enough for us to get any closer. That's where those shallow-draft boats come in, and that's why we and the other ships you see around us are anchored so far offshore."

Yema peered at the docks that dotted the shoreline. Though the distance was almost a mile, she could clearly see stacks of dyewood being loaded onto the various craft. "Can we go visit the town?" she asked. The girl had missed the conversation on this subject after the morning meal. At that time it had been thoroughly wrung out.

Doçura spoke up. "The men want to find out if the wanted notices are still up, and if *Santo de Yema* is still going on. Then we'll decide."

"Can we go in disguise?" the girl asked. "I want to see this obsession." She made a wry face. "Anyway, I lost my Yema doll. I want another."

"We shall see," the nun said. She looked at the sky. "It's a beautiful day. Let's do a lesson here on deck before the men get back."

They'd finished just three pages when the lookout shouted that boats were approaching. One quick look, and Yema and Doçura retreated to their quarters. There were two boats, both about a hundred yards away, and each carrying strangers. They could hear the two groups clamber onto the deck as a variety of conversations began. After a while, the men assembled in the open wheelhouse, just above the women's cabin. With the windows open, it was easy to hear the conversation.

Several subjects were under discussion. The first, mostly with Orlund and a cane mill owner and his agent, went quickly, the latter two agreeing to purchase the plantation supplies. The conversation about the harvest and grower's license went on for a while, finally sounding as if nothing had been concluded. The next conversation, among the captain, a dyewood broker, and the owner of the lighter fleet—men, she concluded, who had worked with Vincent before—

sounded almost perfunctory. They quickly agreed on a delivery schedule and the total hundred-weights of dyewood. The men came down the gangway and into Captain Vincent's quarters next door. Doçura and Yema could hear contracts being signed and money exchanged.

As soon as the strangers were gone, the women hurried on deck. "Could you hear what was said?" Captain Vincent asked. He'd planned all along to have the conversations within earshot of Doçura.

"Yes, thank you. So what's the situation in Fortaleza?"

The captain smiled. "Just a second." He went to the ship's boat, which by now had been hoisted onto the deck, and came back with a several *Santo de Yema* dolls. "These are everywhere," he said. "For sale by vendors, in the branches of trees, stuck between bricks, in baskets of fruit, around children's necks, perched on rocks. Everywhere." Yema took a couple and examined them, finally taking the whole bunch from Vincent. "There are still wanted notices for you and Yema. It would be dangerous for you two to go onshore."

"I suspected that," Doçura said. "What else?" Disappointment showed on Yema's face.

"There are also notices for the two priests and Dr. Cardim. But no likenesses. So I think it's safe for Julian and Cardim. But the whole settlement is on edge because of the Yema craze. There's just one priest in town, and everyone says he's a firebrand. Inquisition through and through."

"What's his name?" the nun asked.

"Fr. Almeido."

"He must be new." Doçura said. "Not the priest from last year. I'd wager he's a Converso. Likely his Jewish name was da Almeida."

"He makes no bones about it. Claims he's found the true faith."

"I'm not surprised. Those Converso priests are usually the most zealous. But why hasn't he put a stop to the Yema business?"

"Oh he would like to," Orlund said. "I imagine he'd lose most of his congregation if he tried."

The nun said, "Yema and I will keep out of sight whenever strangers are on board." She paused to make sure she could not be overheard. "Can we trust the crew not to disclose our whereabouts?"

Vincent gave her a determined look and pointed to the

mainmast. "I've let it be known that any man who discloses even a hint of your presence will be hanged."

One of the Cape Verde men joined them and asked about the cane harvest.

"It's complicated," Lars Orlund told him. "There's no way to know if the miller can make money by bringing the cane here, or whether they want to buy the grower's license. They've got more work than they can handle in Fortaleza—three sugar plantations, and only one pressing mill. They need to build another mill. That's why we sold the equipment so easily."

"All operated by slaves?" the man inquired.

"Unfortunately yes," Vincent answered. By now the other Cape Verde Negroes had joined the conversation.

Lars Orlund spoke up. "Vincent and I have talked it over. We can't expect the mill owner to pay us in light of all the uncertainties. We're going to offer him a contract for the cane and grower's license for whatever he thinks is fair after he sees the plantation and decides what to do."

"But that could take a year," a woman said.

"Granted. And we'll be back here before then. When we get his payment, we'll give you Kwasi's share on our way home."

"What we most need is an advance," one of the men said. "We cannot arrive at Cape Verde without funds. We have to reestablish ourselves. Our seaman's pay won't be—"

"Enough!" Lars Orlund said. "We're taking the same risks as you."

The black man swept his hand around the ship. "You white fellows have all these assets. We have none."

Doçura broke in. "Captain Vincent, Lars, what is the maximum you might receive for the plantation?"

She could see the men were reluctant to respond. Finally Vincent said, "Two thousand gold reis."

"And what's more likely?"

"I'd guess a thousand."

"Twelve hundred?" the nun asked.

"Maybe. Where are you going with this, Leah?" He sounded angry.

Unperturbed, she continued. "So Kwasi's share of one-third might be four hundred gold reis?"

"Yes, but—"

She turned to the Africans. "So if he gives you half of that—two hundred reis—and the rest when the deal is paid off, will that satisfy you?" At first the Africans did not answer. She sensed they'd never supposed a sum that large.

One said, "Two hundred reis would do nicely."

"See," Doçura said brightly, "it's settled."

"Yes," said Orlund, "it's settled. A penniless nun giving away our money. Your charity is beyond measure."

Doçura took Yema's arm. "We'll see you gentlemen at dinner." She and the girl walked to the stern to watch the lighters unloading at a nearby ship.

"How did you do that?" Yema asked.

"Get those people to quit arguing?"

"No. With the money. How do you figure numbers in your head?"

She squinted at the sun. It would be at least an hour before their evening meal. "Come on, dear child, it's time to move from reading to arithmetic."

∗∗∗

At dinner, Doçura noted the absence of Dr. Cardim. Since no one offered an explanation, she asked.

Fr. Julian cleared his throat. "He's staying in the settlement for a few days." Silence followed.

"And?" the nun asked. More silence. "May I speculate, gentlemen? A liaison? His woman friend from Luís?" Still, none of the men said anything. Doçura said, "By the way, her name is Ẽukia."

Fr. Julian smiled in spite of himself. "He thought it was a secret."

"It still is," Doçura retorted. She wondered what Yema thought about all this.

Lars Orlund picked it up from there. "So as not to stray too far from the caustic nature of this conversation Sister Leah, how do you suggest we get our two hundred reis back from the Africans if the cane processor pays us nothing?"

Doçura stood and carved a piece of bullock from the roast on the table in front of her. Once settled back in her chair, she said, "You don't." Out of the corner of her eye, she could see Yema facing straight ahead, eating quietly. But it was easy to tell by the uneven way she chewed, the child was thoroughly enjoying this exchange.

For a while there was only the clinking of silverware, the ship's creaking, and the sounds of people enjoying their food. Finally Captain Vincent stood and poured wine for each of his guests. Raising his goblet, he said, "I propose a toast to a prosperous anchorage in Fortaleza, and a safe journey home."

Chapter 28

Shortly after dawn the first dyewood shipments arrived—two lighters with bundles stacked high on their decks. A thick fog clouded the harbor, so the appearance of the boats caught the morning watch by surprise. Sailors scrambled everywhere, opening hatches, dropping the climbing nets over the side, and preparing the cargo hoists. Of this last item, there were two, one fore and one aft. Three men operated each hoist, first lowering the heavy canvas slings—the same ones used to raise and lower the ship's boats—waiting as the lighter crews positioned dyewood bundles within the slings, then winching them onboard. Next, the hoist crews rotated their equipment over the open hatch and lowered the cargo into the ship's hold, the process repeated many times over until all the bundles were loaded.

One lighter headed back to port for another load. The second one bobbed in the water as the aft hoist crew began lowering the plantation equipment onto its deck. Prior to this, the mill owner's agent had climbed aboard the Corajoso to tally the equipment and supplies. Now he stood on the lighter's deck, again recording the items as they arrived and were stowed.

Sometime in the late morning, Lars Orlund announced himself at the entrance to Enzo Henry's cabin. Yema went to the door and welcomed him inside.

"Working on lessons?" he asked the girl.

"Yes. And I'm bored. I want to see what's going on."

He thrust a large, brightly colored package her way. "Maybe this will distract you. Compliments of Captain Vincent and me."

Yema took the package, a brilliant yellow cloth tied with string, and set it on the table. She ran her hand over the material. "I've never felt anything like this," the girl said.

Doçura reacted with great pleasure as she examined the package. "This is silk, Yema. The fabric I told you about." She looked to Orlund. "Thank you, Lars. What is this?"

He smiled and said, "Open it up."

It turned out the fabric was that of a woman's skirt, with more clothing revealed inside, several garments in all. Doçura laid some clothes on the table and draped others over the chairs. Yema remained speechless as she examined each one, two wraps of yellow, one for a woman, one for a girl, two long-sleeved blouses of the same color— one large, one small—and the same quartet in a deep blue, and four head scarves, gauzy material, two a brilliant red, two the deep blue.

"There's a Turkish trader in the port," Orlund said. "He's set up a little bazaar dockside. We thought you ladies would appreciate some new clothes. In the style of the Moors."

Yema held the yellow blouse by its arms, tucking it under her chin. "Thank you, Senhor Lars, these are beautiful." Still holding the garment, she pranced about the cabin.

Doçura stared at Lars Orlund. "This is truly thoughtful, Lars. Many thanks to you and Captain Vincent."

"I'll tell him." He jerked a thumb at the ceiling. "The captain's busy with the dyewood loading." His voice held some amusement when he said, "After our awkward conversations yesterday, we thought we'd pour a little oil on the waters."

Doçura shook her head. "It is *I* who must apologize. I surely could have chosen my words better."

Lars put a hand to his face, covering his nose and mouth, but unable to hide the mirth in his eyes. "Leah," he said, "you are the most damnable woman I've ever met."

"I'll take that as a compliment."

"Compliment intended." Orlund made a grand gesture as he left the cabin, pausing for a moment in the doorway. "I trust you ladies will dress for dinner this evening."

* * *

The night-watch sailor on the fore deck woke in time to ring ten bells. He inverted his hourglass and stepped to the Corajoso's rail to investigate the sound of merry singing. A light rain fell, and the fog continued to hold over the water. He first spotted the lantern, then a boatload of sailors approaching the ship. He recognized the man in the bow, a fellow seaman named Françez. Another of the Corajoso's crew stood behind him.

"Permission to board," Françez called out, stepping onto the climbing net.

"Permission granted, you drunken sot. Who are those strangers?" he asked. The second man joined his comrade on the net.

"Headed to another boat," Françez said as he came level with the rail. The onboard sailor extended a hand. Françez reached out, grabbed the man by the hair, shoved a knife into his throat, and pitched him over the side. The sailor from the aft watch emerged from the dark, only to suffer the same fate.

Within seconds all the raiders were on deck, each one moving silently to their tasks. Two of the men waited by the crew hatch, hammer and nails in hand. Seven men descended the gangway to the officers' quarters, three of them with hammers and wedges, the other four ready to seize their victims. A sentry posted on deck by the gangway waited for the signal. It came soon enough, the sound of wedges being pounded under the doors of Captain Vincent, the purser's cabin, and the cabin housing the first mate and Lars Orlund. The sentry signaled the two men over the crew hatch. They quickly put hammers and nails to work, sealing the hatch.

At the sound of the first hammer blow, two men burst into Fr. Julian's cabin, clubbing him senseless and cinching a rope around his hammock. One man hefted the priest's weight while the other unhooked the hammock. They dragged his body into the hallway where the men who'd hammered the wedges waited to drag him up the gangway stairs. Once on deck, they threw him overboard to the waiting boat.

The pounding woke Captain Vincent, and he immediately went to the door of his cabin. In the dim light of his lantern, he saw the wedge protruding through the threshold as the pounding continued. He could also hear the commotion next door and Doçura screaming. Vincent rushed inside his chart room and retrieved his pistols. Assuming the fellow on the other side had not yet stood up, he placed two shots through the door at a height of three feet, directly above the wedge. Both balls hit home, one piercing the man's shoulder, the other shattering the side of his face. Vincent grabbed his sword and threw his weight against the door. It did not budge.

When the two assailants entered Doçura's cabin, they had the same plan as they'd used for Julian. As usual, the African women were absent from their hammocks, spending the night with their boyfriends in the crew quarters. One man bound Yema inside her hammock and tossed her into the hallway. At the same time, the other fellow threw a rope over the nun's hammock and reached under it, intending to grab the looped end and cinch it tight. As he straightened up, the woman's dagger struck five inches deep into the hollow between his collar bone and neck. The man screamed and grabbed at the wound. Leah bolted for the door, slicing the assailant's face as she passed him.

The man in the hallway held Yema, trying to haul the struggling child toward the gangway stairs. Doçura caught up with him, stabbing the assailant between the shoulder blades and jerking the knife downwards until it hit a rib. To her amazement, he kept moving. Her dagger raised, she rushed him again, this time on the gangway. Someone pulled the nun's hair from behind, sending her tumbling down the stairs. The assailant stepped over Doçura, fleeing up the gangway behind his bleeding comrade, pushing the fellow ahead to keep him moving.

Just as the two men reached the deck, the purser and Enzo Henry broke through their cabin door and charged up the gangway, almost reaching the top before the hatch slammed shut. The two assailants waiting there moved quickly, one standing on the hatch, the other nailing it shut. The man carrying Yema staggered his last step, then collapsed on top of her.

Heavy pounding and the sound of splintering wood came from the foredeck hatch. "Grab that kid!" one of the men shouted. "The crew's breaking out." They heaved Yema over the side and climbed down the netting into the waiting boat. Someone reached over the gunnel and pulled Yema from the water, pitching her onto the floorboards.

Once loaded in, all four oars were put to use, the boat moving quickly away from the Corajoso. One raider held onto Fr. Julian who was still in the water, unable to move, trapped in his hammock. He regained consciousness long enough to realize he was drowning. If he could just say a prayer. Please. Enough breath for a single prayer … But there was only seawater to breathe, and no time … no time …

***

Captain Vincent, still in his nightshirt, raged along the deck, first one side, then the other. All four boats had large holes punched in their sides. A discarded fire axe lay by one of them. Two sailors followed the captain, holding lanterns so he could examine the damage. "Fix this one first," he said. "There's enough lath on there that you should get a patch to hold."

Doçura sat on the quarterdeck stairs, rubbing her hands together. They tingled at first, then grew numb. Numb as if telling her she was helpless. Lars Orlund came by and held his lantern next to her face, one entire side was bruised and starting to swell. He sat down next to her. "Sister Leah, are you all right?"

She reached to touch her face. "I don't think I'm hurt," she said. "They threw me down the stairs." Doçura looked at her hands. "I can't feel my hands, Lars. There's something wrong."

He took her hands in his, massaging them softly. "We're all scared. As soon as that boat's fixed, we'll go looking for them." He pointed to the body by the nearby hatch. "That sailor's from our ship, the man you killed. Ortiz. He betrayed us."

"Who are they? The others who attacked us?" The warmth of his hands felt reassuring, her feeling coming back.

"I'm sure they're after the reward. The man you killed in your quarters was dressed like a sailor but his belt has the emblem of the Portuguese militia. He's probably from the garrison. You made quick work of them."

Doçura felt for her dagger. "Not quick enough. Where's my knife?"

"Let's go look for it." He could see she needed to do something, anything. Her voice sounded as numb as her hands must have been, and the thought of Yema's fate filled him with dread.

As they stood up, two sailors emerged from the hatchway carrying the dead man's body. Her dagger rested on his chest. The sailor holding the man's legs gestured with his chin. "I think that's yours, ma'am."

Doçura took the knife and wiped it on the dead man's shirt, then reached back and sheathed it in her waistband. "I want to see that man's belt," she told the sailors. "Take it off of him." The sailors set the body on the deck and removed the belt, handing it to Doçura. She ran her hand over the emblem branded into the leather, trying to make out some details in the dim light.

The sailors left the body where it lay. "We'll go clean up your quarters," one of the seamen said.

"Don't bother," Doçura told them. "Help fix the boats. We've got to find Yema and Fr. Julian."

"Not in your nightclothes," Lars Orlund said. "Do you even wear your dagger to bed?"

Doçura patted her waist. "Always. I don't feel safe without it." She looked down at her bare feet. "Give me your lantern. I'll go get dressed."

"Let me come with you. Just to clean up a little."

"Thank you, Lars. I don't know what's wrong with me. I'm not thinking very clearly."

They proceeded down the gangway, the steps slick with blood. The bloody trail continued in the passageway, with more on the floor of Doçura's cabin. Orlund took a blanket from a chair and covered as much as he could. "Wipe your feet on this," he said, reaching for another blanket, then suddenly startled. "My God. This is Yema's abbot's robe. What—"

Doçura slumped into a chair and began to cry, beset with anguish that seemed to come from her very soul. "Oh Lars," she said in a strangled voice, "Yema was wearing that yellow blouse you gave her. She insisted on sleeping in it."

***

Finally the raiders hauled Julian's body into the boat, the bound hammock now his shroud. They rolled him next to Yema, his face just inches from the girl's. Despite being still confined inside the hammock mesh, she began to scream and thrash with such ferocity that one sailor pitched her over the back seat, separating her from Julian. There she lay on the floorboards and sobbed until she could barely catch her breath.

An hour after the attack, the boat pulled up to a dock at the edge of the harbor. A group from the garrison met them, everyone jolly and triumphant with their catch. "Well, we missed two of the devils," Françez said. "Vincent killed one man, and that damn nun killed Ortiz and one other. We didn't get her, and Cardim was not in his cabin."

A cart and driver waited at the end of the dock. They loaded Yema and Julian's body onto its wooden floor. The driver flicked his whip over the donkey's flank, and they set off, jolting along the cobblestone road leading through Fortaleza. Yema could see nothing except the rough sides of the cart and poor Julian at the rear, his head flopping against the floorboards with every bump.

At the garrison, Commander Diego met the procession as it

entered the gate. When he saw Yema, he stood her against the cart's large wooden wheel. She recognized her tormentor from Luís. "Well, *Cantora Diablo,*" he said, "it seems we've caught you again." She spit, but it fell short. Diego laughed. "We'll see how well you spit after we burn you alive." He looked at Julian's body which still lay in the cart. "Too bad the priest is dead, but we'll burn him anyway." He turned to his men. "Put her on a slave post, but don't let her strangle. I intend to keep her alive." He jerked Julian's body from the cart. It fell onto the ground, making a dreadful sound. "Hang him up too," Diego said as he walked off.

A row of slave posts stood at one side of the garrison. Two men dragged the priest's body to a post, held him up, and slipped an iron collar around his neck, clamping the thing shut. Julian's weight slumped against the collar, his face staring grotesquely upwards into the night sky. The men found one for Yema, the collar chained and bolted to the post at the height of her shoulders. Once they locked her in, they untied the rope and unwrapped the hammock from her body, the collar butting hard against her chin.

"Am I supposed to stand here forever?" she said. "I can't move."

"Not forever," a man answered. "Only a few days." They left her alone, standing in the dark, the only light a torch burning a hundred feet away by the compound's gate.

The child struggled, trying to find something underfoot that would take some of the pressure off her chin. After a while she put her hands between the iron collar and her chin. That helped a little, but she wondered, *how long can I stand this?* Her hatred for Diego became intense. *This hate must sustain me,* she thought. *He is the man who ordered my village destroyed, my family killed.* She hissed in Caeté, *"Che yvyra hecha uperire avo arapa'ũ!"* "I will see this man dead!"

Yema considered all she'd heard. So Vincent killed one man, and Sister Leah two? She must have used her dagger. *If I survive this, I will have my own dagger.* She again thought about the Caeté village, her family, Agato, the dead Caribs, all those taken by the smallpox, and now dear Julian. Death had become so commonplace, she seemed to fear it less. *Perhaps death at this stake would be welcome. So Diego wants me kept alive? I'll fool him. He'll find me dead in the morning.* Keeping her fingers inside the collar and the back of her hands beneath her chin, Yema let her weight sag until she almost hung there, her toes providing only the slightest support.

***

On board the Corajoso, the tarred patch on the first boat took until early morning to harden. When the first light came to the eastern sky, the three other boats were also repaired, but their larger patches would take a few more hours to dry. The fog had lifted, and the harbor front could clearly be seen. The docks stretched for more than a mile along the shore, and there was no way to tell where the raiders' boat had landed. The two sailors killed during night watch lay on deck, ready for burial, their bodies fished from the water an hour earlier.

About the time the bodies were retrieved, Captain Vincent called a council in his quarters with Doçura, Enzo Henry, the first mate, Lars Orlund, and the purser. His steward passed around hot tea, maize gruel, and cold bullock from the previous evening. No one knew what to do next, and no one offered even an inkling of a plan.

"I'm not leaving this port until we recover our people," Vincent said. "And I will set fire to the entire town if I have to."

"Can we bring the ship close enough to the docks to shell them?" Doçura asked. "Threaten the harbor?"

Enzo shook his head. "The lighter captains tell me this bay is less than fifteen feet deep in places. We can't get close enough."

"Let's assume," Vincent said, "that Fr. Almeido is at the bottom of this. He sent the militia, and the attack was well planned. We'll probably find Yema and Julian at the garrison. How we rescue them is the problem."

"They'll probably want to parade the two around first, then burn them," Doçura said. "That will be at a burning yard, not at the church or garrison."

"That's right," Orlund said. "There is a burning yard about a half-mile from the garrison. Right now they're using it for a slave pen."

Second mate Jozef appeared at the cabin door. "Sir. Two lighters approaching. Both stacked with dyewood."

Vincent looked out his window. "It's hardly light yet. You sure it's not another raiding party?"

"They appear to be the same rigs as yesterday's," said Jozef. "What do you want me to do? We've not dropped the boarding nets."

"I want to see for myself," Vincent said. "I'm not taking any chances."

On deck, the line of armed sailors parted, allowing Vincent to pass. He called to the lighters through his speaking horn. "More torches down there. I want to see who you are." After a bit of hesitation, additional torches on each boat flared to life.

Vincent could see the owner of the lighter fleet standing in the bow of the second craft. "What is the problem?" the man yelled. "We thought you'd welcome an early shipment." He gave a friendly wave. "And I will welcome an early payment."

Seeing the lighters gave Vincent an idea. He turned to Jozef. "How long did it take to unload the first two lighters yesterday?"

"About three hours, Sir."

"Very good. Unload these, and that will be all for today. If anything suspicious happens, let me know." Vincent picked up his speaking horn, again calling down to the fleet owner. "I'm afraid it's too early for visitors. And we can only handle two loads today. Perhaps more tomorrow. I will come into town later this morning with your payment."

The man looked puzzled, but Vincent didn't care. He went below decks before the conversation could continue.

Chapter 29

Fr. Almeido woke in a foul mood, angry at Diego for not capturing all the criminals. At breakfast, he decided to skip the Lauds devotion and directed his assistant to conduct it. His aggravation had started right after the midnight prayers when the garrison commander came to his residence and announced they'd caught Fr. Julian and the child singer.

"What about the other two?" the priest had demanded. "If Cardim wasn't on the Corajoso, where is he? And now they know we're after them. We'll never get that nun."

"Françez says Cardim is somewhere here in town with his mistress."

"Well then find him," Almeido said. "That's another two thousand reis. A thousand for each of us." The priest shook out his nightshirt. "Now please excuse me, Diego, I'm going to bed."

***

The first thing Yema heard the next morning: "Where the devil is Diego? The girl looks dead!" She opened her eyes to see a middle-aged priest, somewhat dark of skin, close-cropped wiry hair, and a very unpleasant look on his face. *Whoever you are,* she thought, *I'm not dead.* And that was a surprise. She had no sensation in her fingers, her chin and hands ached, and her neck was impossibly sore. She straightened up, shaking her hands to regain some feeling.

About then Diego showed up, half dressed and out of breath. He immediately received a tongue lashing from Fr. Almeido. "You stupid idiot. I've got to have at least one live person to burn. The girl could die strung up like this. Lower that chain so she can sit."

Diego brushed the hair away from his face, went behind the slave pole, and unlocked the metal shaft holding the neck collar. "Pull it through, Father."

As the shaft came free, Almeido pulled the chain upward, holding Yema as one would an unruly dog. She had intended to run; instead she was almost pulled off her feet. The intense pain in her neck and her bruised chin made the child want to scream, but she would not give them the satisfaction. They forced her to sit, then inserted the shaft in a lower hole and locked it in place. The girl's angry glare enraged Diego. He drew back his arm with the intention of hitting the child. The priest stopped him. "I don't want her injured. The fire will be punishment enough."

"I need food," Yema told them. "I need water."

The men ignored her and walked over to examine Julian's body, the flies thick around his eyes and mouth. When they moved off, Fr. Almeido glanced in Yema's direction. "Get her some sustenance."

A while later a soldier brought her maize cake and a bowl of water. By now the clouds had burned away, and the tropical sun was intense. She thanked the man and said, "Fr. Almeido wants me to stay alive. I'll burn up without some protection. Please get me something."

He appeared to take pity on her, returning a few minutes later with an oilcloth. Handing it to the girl, he said, "This ought to do. It will also help when it rains."

And it did rain. An hour later the sky broke open, flooding the garrison yard with three inches of water. In the midst of the downpour, soldiers brought in another captive and chained him in place. Yema, huddled under the oilcloth, did not see the new prisoner; the only sound was the steady drum of rain on her covering. When the rain finally stopped, she shrugged off the oilcloth to see Dr. Cardim chained next to Fr. Julian. He was sobbing uncontrollably, even more so when he turned to see Yema.

"Holy Mother of God," he wailed. "You too?"

"They attacked the ship, Dr. Cardim. Sister Lea killed two of them. I think she's safe."

We're not, he thought to say, but held his tongue.

The girl said it for him. "They're going to burn us at the stake."

***

Captain Vincent stood at the Corajoso's rail instructing second mate Jozef and one of the Cape Verde Africans. The captain particularly liked this black man whose name was Obiike, "brave" in Guinea, the same name as his ship. Based on the fellow's appearance, Vincent figured he'd be a good man in a fight.

The captain waited until the second lighter had unloaded most of its dyewood, then called down to the fleet owner. "I'm sending two men into Fortaleza with you. Mr. Jozef has your payment for today."

Onboard the lighter, Obiike and Jozef found out what they needed from the fleet owner. When they arrived at the dock, they went to a nearby livery and rented a sturdy dyewood cart and a mule. The owner, a tall Sikh from India with a carefully trimmed mustache and white turban, spoke elegant Portuguese. "Why do you gentlemen wish to rent a mule? A donkey would serve as well, and is less expensive."

Obiike, playing the slave, said, "My master say 'get mule,' so I get mule."

The livery man took their money and sent them on their way. The two men went first to a lot that sold firewood and bought a cartload, stacking the bundles of six-foot sticks lengthwise on the wagon bed to a height of almost five feet. They also purchased a large oilcloth to cover the load. Just in time, it turned out, as the sky opened up with a deluge that made them run for cover, leaving the mule and cart to stand alone in the downpour.

After the rain stopped, they took a tour of the town, stopping at the church, garrison, and burning yard, offering to sell firewood to whomever they encountered. They sold several bundles to the soldiers guarding the burning yard, and two more to a fellow at the church. The soldiers at the garrison were not interested, and did not open the gates so they could see inside. Next, Obiike and Jozef went looking for Dr. Cardim.

They found the location near the edge of the Indian settlement described by Captain Vincent. There was nothing left but the sodden ashes of a recently-torched *óga*. The Indians were eager to tell the two men what happened, but no one could speak Portuguese, and the men could not understand the Indian dialect. Finally they located an Indian boy who spoke a little Portuguese and, for a few copper reis, got him to translate. The boy listened to the neighbors, then recited what he'd heard, that a white man had lived here with an Indian woman, four militia men taking him away this morning, and burning the woman's hut.

"Where is the woman now?" they asked.

"She go to docks looking for sea captain," the boy told them. "Very crazy."

Obiike and Jozef headed that way, spending more than an hour searching for the woman along the loading areas. Finally, when the sun was at about two o'clock— time to meet Captain Vincent— they took the mule and cart back to the livery, paying the owner for three more days' rent. "Just leave it stacked with wood," Jozef told the man. "If we don't come back, the firewood is yours. Sell it."

The owner of the livery judged the men to be somewhat peculiar, but gladly took their money. Obiike and Jozef walked in the direction of the lighter fleet's office, a shack set back a short ways from the docks. At two hundred yards, they could hear the woman screaming.

Obiike gave Jozef a toothy smile. "I think she found the captain."

"Glad to see you gentlemen," Vincent said above the din of the woman's screams. She spoke an Indian tongue that none of them understood. The fleet owner and one of his men sat at the far end of the room enjoying the drama; they too had no idea what the woman was saying. The only words anyone could understand were the names "Cardim," "Sister Doçura," "Yema," and "Captain Vincent." She had a *Santo de Yema* doll strung around her neck and kept thrusting it at the men.

Vincent put his arm around her shoulders. "We'll take you to see Sister Doçura," he said, repeating the nun's name again. The woman nodded as if her head had come loose, but she did stop screaming. "Is your name Êukia?" he asked, which calmed her further. On the way to the dock, Vincent told Jozef and Obiike, "She's from Luís and is speaking Caeté. That means Sister Leah can understand her."

At the dock, one of the repaired boats awaited them along with four oarsmen from the Corajoso. They loaded in and Vincent pushed off. The four rowers dug their oars into the water and headed back to the ship. As they neared the vessel, the woman spotted Doçura standing at the rail. She stood up and immediately began shouting. The nun answered in kind. "Excellent," Vincent said. "We're going to find out what she knows."

After talking with Êukia for a few minutes, Doçura explained what she'd heard. "They took the doctor an hour or two after sunup, then burned her hut. She followed the soldiers to the garrison stockade and saw them drag Cardim inside. She couldn't see much, but did glimpse a man and a child chained to slave posts."

"Yema?" Orlund asked.

"She thinks so," Doçura answered. "She also thinks the man was Fr. Julian."

"What else?" Vincent asked.

The woman blurted out a short burst of words. Doçura's face turned ashen. "She says Fr. Julian's dead. He was just hanging there."

"Merciful God," Vincent said. "This is terrible." He spoke to Jozef. "Dismount the stern rail cannon. Load it with grapeshot and stow it under a boat so it stays dry." Then added angrily, "We're going to put it to good use!" Jozef moved off and was soon replaced by the first mate who'd been supervising the dyewood loading. "How full are we?" Vincent asked him.

"Three more lighters ought to do it, Sir."

"Excellent," the captain replied. "We'll get filled up tomorrow. Good cover for us. Once we get our people back, we can flee this damned place with our cargo holds full." He took Lars Orlund by the arm and gestured to Enzo Henry. "Let's go see what else Sister Leah can tell us."

Doçura and the Indian woman had left the group a few minutes earlier and headed below decks. The men found them in the nun's cabin. Captain Vincent called for his steward and ordered hot tea, then settled himself in a chair. "All right, Sister, what more can you tell us?"

"It's pretty grim," she said. "Fr. Almeido conducts the Mass on Sundays. If there's going to be an execution, he announces it at the end of the service. The condemned are usually brought up to the church as the congregation is leaving. Following that, there's a procession to the burning yard."

"What kind of procession?" Enzo Henry asked.

"They use slave carts. When they get to the yard, they take the prisoner, slave post and all, and strap them to the burning stake."

The steward showed up and served tea. As if conjuring something, Vincent took off his hat and placed it in his lap with the brim facing up. He set his mug inside the hat and addressed Doçura. "Ask her if we can get help from the Indians."

The nun posed the question. Ẽukia's response surprised her. She stopped the woman and turned to Vincent. "First of all, the captain of the garrison is a man named Diego. He's one of Girona's henchmen. Fled here from Luís. He's the fellow who arrested me and Yema, Julian and the others. Secondly, the local tribe here is the Eimiõro, and the headman's name is Tendota. He's at odds with the clergy and Diego. They've put a price on his head. The Indian settlement is protecting the chief and keeps him hidden."

Orlund asked, "Will she take us to him? Will he help us?"

The Indian woman started talking before Orlund finished. Doçura listened and said, "She just offered to take us to him." The nun waited a moment longer. "But she's not sure if he'll help."

Vincent looked out the window. "We've got a little more than two hours of daylight. We'll go now."

* * *

Diego and Fr. Almeido sat in the church rectory and toasted the capture of Dr. Cardim. As they hoisted their metal cups, the priest said, "To our triumph over evil." The fiery local rum went down with ease. "We have an extraordinary opportunity here," the priest continued, "to rid this town of *Santo de Yema*."

Before the celebration could go much further, Fr. Almeido's scribe entered the room with his ink-and-quill box, and a folio of parchment under one arm. "Sir?" the man said.

"Ah, yes," the priest responded. "Please sit down." He raised the pitcher of rum. "Would you care for a drink?" The man declined, and the priest reacted with a brittle smile. "It seems we have fallen on some good fortune. We've captured three miscreants, Fr. Julian, Dr. Cardim, and the Indian girl named Yema. Please—"

"*A Santo de Yema?*" the man asked, his face bright with interest.

"The very same. But she is no saint. In fact she has caused great harm to our beloved Church." Almeido adjusted himself in his chair, put off by his scribe's reaction. He cleared his throat and continued, "Please prepare three documents of warranty, one for each captive. Then we must find three citizens from Colony Luís who can attest to their identity. Since we plan to execute them, we must— "

"*Santo de Yema?*" the scribe said again, this time with a look of dread.

Fr. Almeido stood and glowered over the man. He appeared ready to strike him. "This is the second time you've interrupted me. I will not have this Yema nonsense in my church! Do you understand?"

The scribe pushed his chair back and stood up, nervously retreating a few steps. "Yes, Fr. Almeido." He backed up a little more, then turned and left the room.

"Sir," Diego said, "I can sign the documents. Then we only have to find two."

"Not so. Since you are to receive a portion of the reward, you cannot also attest." The priest returned to his chair and remained thoughtful for a moment. After a sip of rum, he said, "I'm going to use these three captives as an opportunity to rid Fortaleza of this Yema insanity. A moment ago, you saw it on my scribe's face. I must put an end to it." Diego listened intently, delighted at the possibility of violence. "Tomorrow morning," the priest went on, "I want those three mounted in a slave wagon and paraded around town. We'll have the crier announce who they are, and invite everyone to the execution after Mass."

"A fine idea, sir."

"Well, there's more," Almeido said. "I want you and your men to accompany the procession and confiscate Yema dolls and any other Yema paraphernalia. The crier will further announce that such items will be added to the pyres when we burn the three. In my sermon, I will grant absolution to all those who comply." Diego moved to speak, but the priest raised his hand. "And, my dear Diego, you and your men will surround the church on Sunday. I will await the congregation in the greeting line. No one is allowed in unless they declare themselves free of Yema things. We will, of course, give them the opportunity to discard such trash before they are allowed inside our sanctuary."

"And if they refuse?"

"Then I leave it up to you and your men to deal with these troublemakers. It is my belief that a firm hand is the best policy." With these words, the two men drained their cups, parted company, and went about their separate chores.

* * *

Two boats set out from the Corajoso and headed for the south end of Fortaleza. The lead boat carried Vincent, Orlund, Obiike, Doçura, and the Indian woman. Vincent was the only person in the lead boat armed, and then just with a single pistol. The second boat carried eight sailors with muskets and swords. They planned to wait offshore in case Vincent's group needed rescue. Despite Vincent's and Orlund's trepidations, Doçura insisted on going along. After all, she was the only one who spoke Caeté. Ẽukia, as it turned out, also spoke the Eimiõro language. Vincent had no choice—He needed both of them.

About a half-mile out, it was easy to spot where the docks stopped and the Indian settlement began, the latter running a ways down the coast, the *ógas* coming nearly to the shoreline. In order to avoid any contact with Europeans, the boats continued towards the southernmost tip.

At about fifty yards from the shore, Vincent called to the other boat. "Wait here."

The Indian woman said something, and Doçura translated. "This is exactly what she wants us to do," she said. "We must not appear threatening."

When Vincent's boat pulled onto the sand, everyone stepped out except Orlund. He gave his hand to the women, helping Doçura and Ẽukia step over the gunnel onto the beach. Some Indian children from nearby huts immediately ran up. Moments later, a number of adults joined them. Vincent realized that his party appeared less threatening with the two women along, hopefully an advantage.

Ẽukia began talking with the natives, asking about the headman. It appeared they were suspicious of her since she had shown up with the Europeans, but after a few minutes of palaver, two of the men pointed inland. Ẽukia set off in that direction.

"Can you understand them?" Vincent asked Doçura.

She shook her head. "Hardly a word."

They had waited only a short while, when one of Vincent's rowers standing on the boat seat shouted, "Here they come."

Tendota and several of his warriors emerged from a cluster of nearby huts. The Eimiõro warriors carried spears with orange toucan feathers attached to the tips. Ẽukia appeared from behind them, distressed and crying. Then she ran forward, calling out to Doçura, almost as hysterical as before.

"What?" Vincent asked.

"They refuse to help," the nun said. "They have no interest in the white doctor, and claim to have a Yemanjá of their own. Mainly I think they're afraid of the soldiers."

"So why did he come?"

"He thinks you have gifts."

Perhaps I should just shoot this arrogant fellow, Vincent thought. He turned to Orlund. "Get the gifts, but wait by the boat. Maybe we can get a little further with this fool." Then he said to Doçura, "I want to hear it from him. Why he won't help. Particularly if we're able to defeat Diego and remove the threat to them?"

After a lengthy exchange, the nun said, "To sum it up, he doesn't think you have a chance against Diego."

Vincent turned to Orlund. "Give him the gifts anyway. Maybe—"

Three warriors strode past Vincent, threatening the Dutchman with their spears. Orlund handed over the gifts to the nearest warrior, a jug of black syrup and a felt sailor's hat. Tendota put the hat on his head and adjusted it just so. Then he smiled and pulled the stopper from the jug, sniffing the contents. The chief and his men turned, walked up the beach, and disappeared behind the cluster of huts.

Unable to contain her disappointment, Ẽukia fled up the shoreline, then wandered into the water, gesticulating and looking up, complaining to the heavens.

Vincent went to the boat and sat on its gunnel with his head in his hands. After a while he said, "Someone get Ẽukia, and let's head home." The two boats returned to the Corajoso, the sun setting behind them in the distant jungle.

Chapter 30

The next morning, and quite to their surprise, Yema and Dr. Cardim were each given a yam cake and a bowl of water.

"Why do you give us food," the doctor asked, "if you plan to kill us tomorrow?"

"Eat well," Diego said. "We want you to enjoy your execution."

"I will die before I take anything from you people," Yema said. She drank from the bowl, then dropped it and the yam cake onto the ground. The bowl did not break, so she kicked it aside and crushed the cake underfoot.

An hour later, a slave wagon entered the garrison compound, the town crier sitting next to the driver on the wagon's front bench. The soldiers unlocked Yema and Cardim's posts from the anchor stakes and carried the stakes alongside the prisoners while the two mounted a ramp onto the wagon bed. Once the posts were locked in place to stanchions bolted to the floorboards, the soldiers brought Fr. Julian's body onboard and mounted his rigored form at the rear of the wagon bed. With their vulgar display now complete, and under the watchful eye of Diego, the procession left the compound.

"I had the strangest thought," Dr. Cardim told Yema. "If I had not earlier escaped from the Inquisition, about now I'd be suffering this same fate in Lisbon or Madrid."

"There is a difference," the girl said. "The two Dutchmen and Sister Leah will save us."

"We can only hope."

The crier stood as the wagon bumped along. He steadied himself, holding onto a post that protruded through the seat. In the other hand he held the parchment with Fr. Almeido's missive. In a somber and forceful voice, he began his proclamation. For the citizens of Fortaleza, this was a familiar occurrence, although many people were unprepared for its taking place on a Saturday. A few townspeople took up stones and prepared curses for the condemned, but found themselves chastened at the unusual sight of a child in the wagon. When the crier called out the name "Yema," a gasp arose from the crowd.

A babble of speculation followed. Many thought, *How could this be The Cantora? A Santo de Yema? Certainly not this pathetic girl. And with a face so soiled, she could be anybody.* They began to chant and throw stones. Soldiers, both on foot and horseback confronted the crowd, trying to stop the mayhem. They had strict orders—The prisoners were not to be injured. Those in the crowd from Luís who recognized Yema, shouted, "This is Yema! This is Yema!" But they were few in number, and drowned out by the others.

Onboard the wagon, the girl and Cardim had their hands up trying to dodge the stones. The driver, in a panic—the stones also hitting him and the crier—drove the horse forward. The crier tumbled back into the wagon bed, and the townspeople scrambled to get out of the way.

The doctor shouted at Yema. "Sing. They don't believe it's you. Sing for God's sake!"

"What?" she shouted back. "The *Confiteor?*"

"No," he yelled, seeing all the Indians in the crowd. "What you sang the last time in Luís. When your aunt died. Yemanjá!"

And so Yema sang. Disheveled, bruised and bleeding, in her filthy yellow blouse, otherwise without clothes or any reason for hope, she sang:

♫ *Ixé téra Yemanjá, Tembireko pupé Paranã!*
Ixé 'am pu'ã japete
Me'ẽ paraguasu tata ...

At the sound of Yema's singing, the driver abruptly stopped and turned to stare. The crier righted himself and stared also. The crowd advanced, this time enthralled, curses replaced with silence. Some dropped their stones. Others kept them, eyeing the soldiers. The soldiers halted, confused as to what to do. A few knelt and crossed themselves.

Diego, who was following from a distance, saw the uproar and heard Yema singing. He ran back to the garrison and called for reinforcements, then saddled his horse and rushed after the wagon. He caught up just as they neared the church. There he saw Fr. Almeido and the soldiers dodging stones while the priest pleaded for order. His presence had the opposite effect—Everyone knew Almeido was responsible for this effrontery. A rock struck him squarely in the chest. Another grazed his head.

Diego charged at two of the rock-throwers with his sword, killing them, a young woman and a man, both Indians. The non-Indians in the crowd instinctively ran towards town, away from the melee. By now, more soldiers joined the battle. "Kill anyone with a stone or a Yema doll," Fr. Almeido shouted. The militia stampeded into the crowd, lances and swords thrusting and hacking, dispatching every person within reach. With the soldiers fast on their heels, the Indians retreated to their village. Now a wholesale slaughter ensued as the militia began setting the native huts on fire.

Cardim and Yema stood on the wagon bed stunned at the bloody spectacle. There were bodies strewn everywhere. Those wounded tried to crawl away, but were quickly cut down. Fr. Almeido called for a cadre of soldiers, jerked the town crier from the wagon, and seated himself next to the driver. "Head to the burning yard," he told the man. Thus surrounded by soldiers, the wagon bumped its way along the street, avoiding bodies in its path, weaving first to one side, then the other.

***

On that same morning, and as expected, two lighters arrived at the Corajoso just before dawn. By mid-morning, they were unloaded and the dyewood cargo stowed. A third lighter waited a short distance away, its load sufficient to fill the Corajoso's hold to capacity. The first and second mates managed the many tasks handily while Captain Vincent, Doçura, Enzo Henry, and Lars Orlund conferred on how to rescue Yema and Dr. Cardim. Ẽukia sat with them, understanding very little.

After returning to the ship the evening before, they ate a hurried dinner, then spent several hours struggling with the problem, concluding that the only option was to attack the slave wagon on its way to the church after Sunday Mass. Storming the burning yard once the prisoners were there, or the garrison at any time, was out of the question. They simply did not have enough fighters or weapons.

Now with the morning at hand, and having spent more time in the early hours again reviewing possibilities, a surprise attack along the slave wagon route remained the only choice. Captain Vincent went over the plans once more. "We'll park the firewood cart alongside the road and position it so we can kill as many soldiers as possible with the rail cannon. At the same time, we will take over the slave wagon and drive it to the docks. Our retreat will be the—"

"Sir!" The second mate stood in the doorway. "You'd better come topside. There's something happening in town."

On deck, Vincent found the first mate in shouted conversation with a man in the crow's nest. "What's going on?" he asked. Vincent could see smoke rising from the southern part of Fortaleza.

"It looks like about half the town's afire." The first mate

cupped his ear towards the settlement. "I can't hear it, but the man in the crow says he hears musket fire."

"I'll take a look," Vincent said, and climbed to join the lookout. Once he caught his breath, he too could hear muskets firing. "How long's this been going on?" he asked.

"'Bout a half hour, Sir. Didn't want to bother you 'til we saw it spread."

The captain looked down to the deck of his ship. The last two loads of dyewood were being winched aboard, and the lighter fleet owner waited on his deck, now curious at seeing Vincent in the crow's nest. Vincent shouted down to him. "Looks like there's a big fire in town." Next he called to Lars Orlund who, along with all the others from Vincent's cabin, were now on deck. "Get the man paid. We've got work to do."

Within minutes, and with payment received, the lighter and its crew headed back to port. Vincent assembled his most trusted men, Jozef, Enzo Henry, Obiike, and two others. He also selected his four strongest rowers and equipped them with muskets and swords. In addition, he wanted to send Lars Orlund, but the man's red beard and physical bulk made him an obvious target for spies. "Here's what I want you to do," he said. "First, locate an out-of-the-way dock where we can make preparations tonight. Second, Jozef and Obiike, go to the livery and make sure the firewood wagon and mule are still available. If conditions permit, take the wagon to the dock. Obiike, will you stay with it throughout the afternoon? It's likely to be quite dangerous."

The African responded with his distinctive smile. "With pleasure, Sir."

Vincent continued. "The rest of you go into town and find out what's going on. Most important, locate our people and figure how we might rescue them." He looked away for a moment, not willing to believe what he'd been told earlier. "And for the love of God, find out if dear Julian is alive or dead."

Next, he addressed the rowers. "Stay close to the dock, and keep your weapons hidden. You are there to cover a retreat if the others get in trouble." He squinted at the sun. "I want you back here at least three hours before sundown. We've a lot to do."

With everyone understanding their orders, the ship's boat set out.

***

Four hours later they returned, Jozef noticeably missing. "Where's my second mate?" Vincent asked.

"He's staying with Obiike," Henry told him. "But—"

"Damn it, those were not my orders!"

"Sir, if you'd let me explain. There's a good reason for him staying there."

"Go ahead," Vincent said, resigning himself to the situation.

Enzo Henry continued. "You can almost see it even from here. The native half of the town has been obliterated. Bodies everywhere. Mostly Indians."

"The militia did it?"

"Yes," he said, "under orders from Fr. Almeido. The rest of the town is sort of normal." He gave a shrug. "Although they've got soldiers stationed in various places. Yema and Cardim are being held in the burning yard. They've cleared out the slaves and have a number of soldiers stationed there. The execution is still supposed to happen after church tomorrow. And I'm sorry to report that Fr. Julian is indeed dead."

Doçura, who had been listening to the exchange, moved away, sitting on a hatch cover by herself. Still, she could hear what was being said. When the subject returned to Jozef, she rejoined the group.

"Jozef is going to see if he can get the Indians to help us," said Henry, "in the manner we discussed yesterday. The few Indians we found were talking revenge. Serious revenge."

"But he doesn't speak the language," Vincent said.

"He's got the gold reis you gave him. Says he'll figure something out."

"By damn," the captain replied, "there's a ray of hope." He made a broad gesture, sweeping his arm across Fortaleza. "Let's get busy."

***

Two hours later, all was ready. The captain insisted that everyone eat their evening meal. "It might be quite some time before you get another," he told them. Three hours after darkness fell, four boats set out, three for the docks, one for the remains of the Indian settlement. Included in this fourth boat, besides the rowers and two additional sailors—all armed with muskets and swords—were Orlund, Doçura, and Ẽukia, the women needed for communication with the Indians. No one in this boat held much confidence that Jozef had enlisted the natives' assistance. Nonetheless, they needed to find out.

The boats destined for the docks pulled up in total darkness, guided only by a hooded lantern which was unveiled at intervals by Obiike, its visibility limited seaward. "Welcome Captain," the African said quietly. "We are ready." He extended his hand.

Vincent took the offered hand and stepped from the boat. "Have you heard from Jozef?"

"No Sir, but I'm confident we will." Even the night could not fully hide the man's smile.

"I will attempt to share your confidence," Vincent said. "Is the firewood cart set?"

"Yes Sir. Just as you ordered." At the edge of the dock, one could hear the mule eating from a basket of feed.

Keeping as quiet as possible, and working in almost total darkness, the men prepared their assault on the burning yard. They retrieved the rail cannon from one of the boats and placed on the back of the firewood wagon. Several bundles of firewood, tied together in a V and also lashed to the wagon bed, were placed behind it, the arrangement designed to absorb the gun's recoil. A few sticks of wood set just back of the cannon's muzzle provided the correct elevation. The sailors made room among the firewood bundles for two men with muskets, one of which would fire the rail cannon when ordered. They would likely have only one chance with the cannon, although they brought powder and shot for three more rounds— Perhaps if needed on the retreat. The entire wagon bed was then covered with an oilcloth.

By the time they finished, Captain Vincent estimated it was an hour before midnight, the hoped-for time to connect with the Indians. Earlier, the captain had sent two scouts into the town to find the safest route to the burning yard, routes where they were less likely to be noticed. As he had suspected, the safest lay along the boundary between the town and the devastated Indian settlement. The scouts told him the area was nearly abandoned.

And so they set off. At first, Vincent found himself puzzled as to why the cart was so quiet. It thumped along the cobblestones on its wooden wheels, but without much noise. One feel of a wheel rim told him why. Obiike had cleverly nailed two strands of a one-inch hawser around the tread of each wheel and threaded them through the spokes. *I must give that man a bonus,* Vincent thought.

After a while the street gave way to a muddy track, easy going because the mud was mostly dry. If they rescued their people, the return trip would be quite perilous. Vincent wanted to return the most direct way, but that meant going right by the garrison and church. That would only be possible if the Indians joined the fight. He would know in another mile or so. By then they would be at the burning yard. The men could see better now; a sliver of a moon had appeared from behind the clouds.

Suddenly the sailors in the lead stopped, several of them leveling their muskets. Vincent rushed forward. He wanted no gunfire until they were in position at the burning yard. A figure appeared, talking quietly. The men shouldered their weapons and Jozef materialized out of the darkness. Vincent, a man not given to much emotion, gave his second mate a fierce hug. "Am I pleased to see you," he whispered. "Do you have good news?"

"Indeed I do. The Eimiõro are in a nasty mood. They like your plan. However, I believe they intend to take it much further."

"Where's Orlund and Doçura?"

"With the Indians near the burning yard."

"Is the gate shut? I'm counting on that."

"I don't know, Sir. We'll find out when we get there."

"Where's Tendota?"

"As you might expect," Jozef said, "he's the problem. The chief is hiding with his warriors near the garrison. He expects you to attack there first. I told him that's not possible."

For a few moments Vincent considered all that he'd heard. Finally he said, "I actually think this may give us an advantage. The garrison will come running when they hear us attack the burning yard. Tendota and his people will keep them tied up. Regardless, did you explain our plan to him?"

"I personally explained it."

"Very well," Captain Vincent said. "Stay with us, Jozef. Let's just hope Tendota follows through. When he hears our gunfire, he'll have no choice but to take on the garrison."

***

A half-hour later, most everything was in place. Vincent conferred with Orlund, Jozef, and Doçura, the three who had the most information about their objective. They were now hiding behind a low, mud-brick building, about fifty yards from the burning yard. Waiting nearby were a dozen Indians, a token force sent there by Tendota.

"Facing the gate," Orlund told the captain, "Cardim and Yema are about forty-five degrees on the right-hand side, and nearly at the back. If we set up the cannon at a left angle through the gate, our people should be safe."

Vincent peered around the corner of the building. He could see there was enough room in front of the gate to set up the wagon. The problem remained: How to lure a majority of the militia into one spot behind the gate when he fired the cannon. No one had any ideas. The captain searched through his pockets. Finally he said, "Does anyone have a piece of paper? Something that looks like a note?" They passed the word around.

A sailor came forward, offering a folded letter. "I have this, Sir. A letter to my parents. 'Case I get killed."

"May I have it, sailor?" Vincent did not reach for the letter right away. Instead he said, "I promise to give you all the paper you need when we get back to the ship." The sailor handed him the letter. "Good man," the captain said. "Thank you."

The seaman started to move off, but Vincent whispered for him to stop. "Sailor, I want you near the wagon when we get it in position. Keep your musket at the ready. You'll see your letter put to good use."

Over the next few minutes they brought the cart up and blocked the wheels with large stones. A man held the mule to keep him from bolting. Jozef notified the Indians and they took their places. The sailors did likewise. Vincent, his heart pounding, walked up to the gate holding two torches. He pitched one over the gate, waited five seconds, then threw the letter over, the parchment wrapped around a stone and tied with string. He moved quickly to the wagon where two sailors pulled back the oil cloth.

The captain waited another five seconds, jammed his torch against the rail cannon's fuse, stepped away, and drew his pistol.

Chapter 31

The loosely packed grapeshot blasted a four-foot wide hole in the burning yard gate, each deadly ball smashing through the wood with immense force, killing all eight of the soldiers examining the letter. Shards of wood, themselves deadly missiles, mortally wounded two more militia. Three healthy soldiers remained. They were shot dead the moment Vincent's sailors entered the compound.

The Indians came in behind, bows drawn, spears ready, no one left to kill. They drew their knives, intending to mutilate the dead. The sailors pushed them back while Jozef urged the natives on to the garrison. He cupped his ear and pointed. Everyone could hear musket fire from that direction. The Indians hesitated briefly, then rushed off.

As soon as Diego heard the cannon blast, he had his men form up. "No time to put on armor," he told them. "We'll go now." Most of his troops were dressed just in their underwear or nightshirts. They opened the gate and marched out, leaving a small force behind for defense. The Eimiõro warriors waited in the shadows. When the militia column was fully clear of the entrance, Tendota gave the signal. His warriors loosed a deluge of arrows.

Diego, at the head of his men, was one of the first to die. More than half the militia went down with the initial fusillade. A few were able to fire their muskets, but the shots went wild, the natives invisible in the darkness. As the wounded and able soldiers retreated to the garrison, Indian arrows cut them down, their poison taking quick effect. Next the Eimiõro rolled a loaded dyewood cart into the garrison entrance and set it ablaze, effectively cutting off any exit from the compound.

The flaming wagon was a signal to the Indians waiting behind the garrison. With a team of oxen stolen from a nearby plantation, they pulled down a section of the back wall and rushed inside. At the same time, several of them threw torches onto the thatch roof of the barracks. Within minutes, the garrison was completely aflame, and nearly every soldier dead. The few that were not, soon wished for death. The Eimiõro dragged the living ones out of the flaming compound and began to mutilate them.

With the garrison defeated, Tendota led a group of warriors the short distance to the church. They were disappointed to find the place abandoned, the occupants of the rectory and surrounding buildings having fled. The Indians set fire to everything and returned to the garrison.

At the burning yard, Doçura, Orlund, and Vincent ran to

Yema and Cardim, quickly releasing them from the slave poles. By now, everything except the cannon had been thrown off the wagon. Obiike stood holding the mule's halter, talking quietly to the terrified animal. Dr. Cardim was strong enough to climb onto the wagon bed without help. Doçura picked up Yema and set her next to Enzo Henry on the front bench, shuddering at the sight of her bruised and bloody chin and throat.

The girl pointed back to the slave posts. "We've got to get Fr. Julian."

"We can't," the nun said. "We're not out of danger and—"

Doçura flinched away from the wagon as Enzo Henry snapped the reins, sending the mule on his way. "We've got to get out of here," he shouted.

The nun ran alongside, ready to catch Yema if she jumped, and despite her weak condition, it appeared the child was considering it. As quickly as they started, they stopped. Vincent ran forward and grabbed the mule's halter. "Hold up," he said. "I want protection around this wagon. We're going right by the garrison and there may be a fight." The sailors quickly formed around the wagon, and they started again, this time with the mule at a trot, everyone running to keep up.

Vincent sent Orlund and Obiike sprinting towards the garrison. "Tell me what's going on there," he shouted. Everyone could see the flames ahead.

The two men ran down the road. Minutes later they were back, Orlund the first to speak. "The Indians have overrun the place. It's finished."

Earlier, Captain Vincent had expected to make a perilous charge through a pitched battle at the garrison, losing half his men in the process. The current state of affairs was completely unexpected. "Stay in formation," Vincent shouted to his men. "We have as much to fear now from the Eimiõro as we did from the militia."

"Not at the moment, Sir," Obiike said. "It looks like they're busy just cutting people up."

The scene at the garrison rivaled anyone's vision of hell. There were dead militia everywhere, many of them hacked to pieces. Tendota stood in the middle of the street swinging Diego's severed head by its hair. Dressed in nothing but a loin cloth, covered head-to-foot with vertical red stripes, he looked like devil himself. Enzo

Henry pulled the mule to a stop.

"Where the hell is Ẽukia?" Vincent roared, looking around for Jozef. "I need to talk with this crazy man."

Jozef, who'd been trailing behind the wagon and commanding the rear guard, ran forward. "I've not seen her since this evening when she helped us translate. I've no idea where she is."

"For the love of God," the captain shouted. He looked over to the nun. "Sister Leah, can you talk to this fool?"

"I'll try," she said.

"Tell him he now has what he wanted. Diego is dead and the threat is removed. I expect them *not* to attack the town."

Doçura addressed the man slowly, first in Caeté, then in Tupi. Tendota stood grinning like an imbecilic lout, swinging the severed head from side to side, his feet and legs covered with blood from his trophy. "I might as well be talking to a fish," the nun told Vincent. "Either he doesn't understand, or doesn't care to."

"All right," the captain said, "at least we're in less danger for now." He pointed toward the harbor. "Proceed."

Yema stood at that moment and almost threw herself from the wagon. The nun reached up and caught her just in time, forcing the child back onto the seat. Enzo Henry, sitting next to the girl, put his arm around her. Despite her weakened condition, Yema struggled as if possessed. "We've got to go back for Fr. Julian!" she screamed. "We can't leave him!"

Vincent looked up at her. "It makes no sense, child. You and the doctor are safe, and Fr. Julian's dead. We—"

"Get him!" she snarled, jabbing both hands at the captain, her voice so intense it shocked everyone into silence. "Get him," she said again with a look full of malice, "or what you see here will happen to us all."

In this setting, a night of crazed Indians dancing with severed heads, dismembered bodies strewn about, buildings ablaze—the fire at the church now evident to everyone—a prophecy like this could not be ignored. Vincent looked up at Henry. "Go back and pick up the body." Then to Jozef, "Just in case, take your rear guard."

Orlund and Doçura walked alongside the wagon as it turned around and headed up the street. Dr. Cardim began laboring to remove his neck collar, the heavy chain hanging down his back. "Doctor," Orlund said, "we have no way to take that thing off until we get back to the ship. Please endure." Cardim slumped forward, steadying himself with his hands as the wagon bumped along.

At the burning yard, they pulled within a few feet of Julian. The corpse looked ghastly in the torchlight, impossible to recognize who it had ever been. Doçura studied Yema. Would the child look away at this frightful sight? She herself could barely look.

Yema stood and directed the men, the girl holding her chain in both hands to take the weight off. "Pull the pin," she told them, "and let him down." The body, stiff and grotesque, thumped onto the ground. No one wanted to go near the thing.

Orlund walked up, dragging the discarded oilcloth. "Wrap him in this," he told the men. When none of the sailors moved to help, he spread the cloth next to the body and pushed the corpse onto it with his foot. "Now," he said, "roll it up and put him in the wagon." The men did as told, two of them vomiting immediately thereafter, the stink from the corpse nearly overwhelming.

Before the wagon could leave, Dr. Cardim stood up. "I have to get down," he said. "I can't stand this."

"I can," Yema said, defiant as ever. She got to her feet and stepped over the partition into the wagon bed. The girl pointed to the driver's bench. "Sit there," she told the doctor. They traded places, and the wagon headed back to the garrison. As soon as they arrived, the crew of the Corajoso formed up, and everyone set out for the harbor front.

A short distance down the road they encountered the burning church and outbuildings. A moment later the church roof collapsed and sent a shower of sparks into the night sky. For some reason it reminded Yema of Girona coming to pray outside her cell in Luís. She remembered him saying the flames at the burning stake would cleanse her soul. She paid no attention to his words at the time, but perhaps now they had some merit. She had nothing to cleanse, and the hateful priest from Fortaleza had much to cleanse. Thus God had spared her, and burned the priest's church. But why then had He taken dear Fr. Julian? A noble friend and teacher if there ever was one. And the deaths of so many precious others in her life; why had God taken them?

Despite any recompense at seeing the church on fire, Yema decided she owed God a cleansing—One that might protect those dear souls who remained in her life. With cleansing came pain, intense pain, that much she knew. The child focused on the still form of Fr. Julian under the covering and prayed for pain impossible to endure. Sore as they might be, Yema let the iron collar rest on her shoulders. Then she stood, first adjusting the chain behind her back, next sitting on the length of it, bringing her full weight to bear against the collar. It hurt, but not enough, so she reached down and pulled on the chain, leaning back against it until she could feel the collar cut into her flesh—more so each time the cart wheels jolted across a rut or over cobblestones.

The pain was indeed intense. Yema shut her eyes and gritted her teeth, fighting to keep the wealth of tears sealed behind her eyelids. She imagined the solitary Christ with his crown of thorns, blood running down his face. She felt for her own blood along her collarbone. When she sensed none on her hands, the child straightened further, jamming the collar against her flesh. This was the pain of Christ. This was the pain of cleansing. This was the pain to keep all those she loved safe.

When they arrived at the harbor, Doçura reached up to help Yema from the wagon. Since she sat at the front of the bed near the center, the child was out of reach. "Come on Yema," the nun said. "We'll get in the boat." In the poor light, she could barely see the girl, and Yema did not respond. Doçura climbed into the wagon and reached for her. Her hands came away bloody. Even in the dim light she could see that. "Oh Lord in heaven," she cried, "what happened?"

Lars Orlund ran over with a torch. "Good God," he said, "get her down." By now, the sailors had removed the cannon and Julian's body, the two lying side-by-side to the rear of the wagon. Doçura laid the girl on the wagon bed, examining her while Orlund held a torch.

The nun saw two gashes across the child's shoulders. "Yema," she asked, "how did this happen?"

"I must stay with Fr. Julian," she said weakly. "It is my penance."

"This is insane, Yema. You owe no penance!"

When she said nothing, Doçura gathered the girl in her arms and carried her along the dock to the nearest boat. Lars Orlund walked beside them with his torch, holding the chain to take the weight off. "She needs help," the nun said. "Can Cardim do something?"

In a short while Dr. Cardim showed up, aided by Enzo Henry

and Obiike. They helped the physician into the boat, seating him across from Doçura. He handed the nun two neckerchiefs. "Tie these together, then under her arms and over the wounds," he told her. A sailor, at Vincent's direction, sat behind them, holding a torch.

While Cardim and Doçura tended to Yema, Captain Vincent reflected on their situation, his thoughts suddenly interrupted when the mule muttered and shifted itself in the harness. The captain called for Enzo and Obiike. "Take this noble animal to the livery. We'll be ready when you get back."

They selected a few sailors for protection and headed out. Vincent eyed the oilcloth holding Julian's corpse. He briefly considered leaving it there, but quickly decided otherwise. After doing a rough count of his men, he turned to Jozef. "Put that body and the cannon in the boat at the end of the pier. We'll tow it to the ship."

Next, the captain considered how to keep the Eimiõro from overrunning Fortaleza. When Jozef returned, he said to him, "At dawn, I'm sending you and the purser to call on every ship in the harbor. We must protect our interests. You will alert the captains that the local garrison is no more, and that the Indians have free rein. Almost all of these gentlemen have commerce here, so they'll send forces to protect the town." He peered into the darkness, looking for his men coming back from the livery. While he couldn't see them, the captain was pleased to see the church still burning, and there were no torches advancing their way. He continued with Jozef. "You should be finished by nine bells. We will have everything ready by then, and we'll sail for home."

In a minute, Henry and Obiike returned. With everyone accounted for, they set off—Three vessels loaded with officers and seamen, each with a torch in the bow, a fourth boat towed behind in darkness. They had won the battle and rescued all their friends but one.

***

Once aboard the Corajoso, the ship's carpenter removed the collars from Dr. Cardim and Yema. A painful process as it turned out because he was unable to unlock the things. He had to file through each lock's metal shaft, a tedious process that further irritated their already damaged skin. Sitting on chairs in the captain's quarters, Yema and the doctor sat facing one another while the carpenter and his assistant filed away. Several of the crew steadied the collars with their hands, isolating metal from flesh as best they could.

When Yema asked about Fr. Julian, Doçura went on deck to find out. Two boats had been winched onboard, one turned over and secured, the other resting upright with Julian's body wrapped in the oilcloth. Since dawn was only a few hours away, two boats remained in the water, ready for their visits around the harbor. Everyone was exhausted from the night's labors, but the thought of sailing from this hated port kept all hands active.

Finally, after nearly a half-hour of filing, both collars came loose. The doctor was greatly relieved. Yema remained somewhat bewildered. Her neck, chin, and especially her shoulders looked terrible. When Captain Vincent came into the cabin, Cardim asked for a bottle of rum. "Doctor," Vincent said, "isn't it a little too early to imbibe?"

"For medicinal purposes of the flesh," the doctor answered. "I've discovered that wounds heal more quickly if one applies a mixture of rum and salt." He looked at Yema. "I must tell you though, it's the devil's concoction, and quite painful.

A little life returned to Yema's eyes. "You first, Dr. Cardim."

With the paste of rum and salt mixed in a cup, Cardim had Doçura apply the grainy substance to his neck and chin. When she merely dabbed it over the wounds with a cloth, he said, "No half measures, dear Leah. Slather it on." As she did so, tears came to his eyes and he gritted his teeth, finally saying, "That really hurts!"

Remembering how she withstood the pain during her journey from the burning yard, Yema said, "I'm ready, and I promise not to scream." Not the case. At the first touch, the girl shrieked in pain. Two people held her while Doçura finished the application. For a minute or so, Yema danced insanely around the room, tears streaming from her eyes, her arms outstretched, fingers splayed as if trying to fly.

When she did settle back to her chair, she inquired again about Fr. Julian.

Doçura said, "I talked with Captain Vincent. Once we leave the harbor, we will bury him at sea. It would be sacrilege to bury Julian in this harbor where he died."

***

Just after ten bells, the Corajoso sailed for open water. Because the wind blew due east, the ship first tacked north, then south, zigzagging its way up the coast. Jozef's visit to the ships anchored off Fortaleza had gone well, so perhaps the town's future would remain secure. All morning, commerce had appeared to go on as usual. Jozef speculated that if the Eimiõro were busy rebuilding their settlement, possibly they would find no time for war.

Inside their quarters, Doçura gave Yema a stand-up bath in a wooden washtub. The girl seemed surprisingly lively, given all that she'd been through. Once bathed and dried, she put on her friar's robe. "Fr. Julian liked this," she reminded Doçura. "I can't believe he's dead."

"I know, sweetheart. It's a terrible thing."

Yema picked her yellow blouse up off the floor, filthy, bloodstained and torn in several places. The child immersed it in the washtub, washed the garment thoroughly, and wrung it out. Holding the blouse up, she said, "Sister Leah, can you sew this?"

"Indeed I can, little one," Doçura said. "But in this case, since we are destined for a colder clime, I will show *you* how to sew. That's a skill you'll need in the Netherlands."

That satisfied the girl. She draped the blouse over a chair to dry.

A knock sounded at the door, and Yema opened it to see Lars Orlund. At that moment the ship came upright from its tack. The Dutchman grabbed the door frame to steady himself. He paused before speaking, obviously pleased at seeing the two women. "Ladies," he finally said, his voice turning somber, "please come topside, we're ready to bury poor Julian."

On deck, Julian remained rolled in the oilcloth. Two ballast stones had been added inside, and this sad bundle was now ready to go into the sea. Most of the crew were there, as were all the officers. Captain Vincent wore his dress uniform and hat, and since Julian was a man well loved by everyone, the captain asked for testimony. There was no shortage of good things to say about the priest, and a number of people gave thoughtful and heart-felt witness. When it was Doçura's turn, she recounted how she and Julian had traveled to the Caeté camp where they first met Yema, then described the joy she and Julian shared when they heard the girl sing at Mass.

The last person to give testimony was Yema, so affected at the moment that she could barely speak. "Fr. Julian was a good teacher and friend," she said through her tears, but could say no more.

All the while, the child had been holding a *Santo de Yema* doll. She stepped forward, kneeled by the oilcloth, and tucked the doll inside, then returned to stand by Doçura, taking her hand. Lars Orlund, reacting to the gesture, broke into wrenching sobs. He walked over and took Yema's free hand, struggling to hold his sadness in check. If the nun or Yema took notice of Orlund's unaccustomed behavior, neither gave any sign of it.

Captain Vincent removed his hat, placed it over his heart, and recited, "Unto Almighty God we commend the soul of our brother departed, and we commit his body to the deep; in sure and certain hope of the Resurrection unto eternal life, through our Lord Jesus Christ." He nodded to the three men on his right, Enzo Henry, Dr. Cardim, and Jozef, then to Orlund who had remained next to Yema. The four men picked up the oilcloth by its corners and balanced it on the rail.

Vincent recited the Lord's Prayer. When he reached the Doxology, "For Thine is the kingdom, and the power, and the glory, for ever and ever," he brought his hat away from his chest and extended his arm in salute to Julian. The men at the rail nudged the corpse over. It splashed almost silently into the water below. The captain recited, "Amen," and everyone remained in place, seeming afraid to move. Many crossed themselves.

After some quiet moments, the captain spoke up. "All right, gentlemen," he said in a firm voice, "we've a ship to sail."

Just as the wind began to move the Corajoso forward, the straw *Yema* doll bobbed to the surface, stirring in the ship's wake.

Chapter 32

After nearly two weeks of tacking against a due-east wind, and making little progress except north along the coast, Captain Vincent decided to head for the island of Hispaniola. Yema found the task of navigating vastly interesting, spending many hours in the open wheelhouse with Vincent and Enzo Henry as they plotted their course northward. Soon she was conversing in navigational terms as if she'd done it for years, "astrolabe," "sun quadrant," "moon quadrant," "horizon stick," "angle sighting," "celestial position," "longitude and latitude."

The two navigation aids that interested Yema most were the

index tables of sun, moon, and star positions, with their corresponding arrangement for points of latitude and longitude; and the magical astrolabe with its intricately carved surface, raised gold figures, and two pivoting arms. Enzo Henry gave the girl a demonstration one evening as the sun set, piquing her curiosity even more when he called the evening star a "planet."

"What's a planet?" she asked.

"It's a kind of a star that has a mind of its own," Enzo said. "Planet means 'wanderer,' a Greek word. That planet is named Venus."

The child had no idea what Greek was, but the idea of a star that followed its own rules spun her imagination. *Sister Leah and I are planets,* she reasoned. *That's what we mostly do. Wander.*

Yema wanted to know more about this strange star, but the navigator insisted on demonstrating the astrolabe before the sun's last glimmer faded below the horizon. He put the instrument on the navigation table, directed the short arm toward Venus, and moved the long arm toward the last glow of the sun. He then took his compass and set it into the recess at the center of the astrolabe, using the intricate degree markings on the compass to estimate the spread between the astrolabe's two arms. "Now you see, this is sixteen degrees," he said, indicating the different positons of the sun's glow and Venus. "So I can tell our latitude by looking up this spread in my book." He opened up his gigantic celestial index, and turned to the page inscribed February 3rd, moving his finger to the column labeled Venus. Indicating the top of the page, he said, "So here's today's date, and here is the spread between planet Venus and the Sun at ten degrees north latitude. It's fifteen degrees. We measured sixteen degrees, so that's close enough. That puts us right about here." Henry pointed to a spot on the map.

By now Captain Vincent had brought a lantern forward and set it on the table. Yema studied the map. "So here's Hispaniola," the girl said. "How far is that?"

"About three hundred miles," Henry answered. "We should be there in two days."

"Enough," the captain said. "Tonight's a special dinner, and we mustn't be late." He turned the wheelhouse over to his first mate and escorted Yema and Enzo Henry down the gangway to his quarters. When they arrived, his steward, dressed in an elegant white uniform, poured the newcomers each a steaming cup of tea laced with rum. They seated themselves among the other guests. The list included Dr. Cardim, Lars Orlund, Sister Doçura, Obiike, Jozef, and the sailor, van Hoff, who had provided the letter thrown over the burning yard wall.

Captain Vincent led off the evening with a prayer remembering Fr. Julian. When finished, he invited everyone to sit at the dining table, indicating a vacant chair reserved for the spirit of "Our dear Fr. Julian." It reminded Doçura of her Seder dinners at Passover in Lisbon. Her mother always reserved a place at the table for the Prophet Elijah, and her father opened a window—since they lived on the second floor—to allow the prophet his entry.

As the dinner progressed, the captain offered a series of toasts to the honored guests. "To Max van Hoff," the captain said in his first tribute. "For providing the letter which lured the militia into place behind the gate." Everyone raised their glasses as Vincent presented van Hoff with a sheaf of paper, and added, "Please write your parents and let them know you are safe and appreciated." Applause followed.

A short while later, Vincent recognized Obiike for, "...his service onshore the day of our raid, and into the night." Next came Jozef's, Doçura's, and Orlund's turn. For this tribute, the captain stood up, first honoring Jozef for the same service as Obiike, then adding, "And to Sister Leah, Lars Orlund, and again Jozef, for saving many of our lives by encouraging the Indians to join the battle."

Doçura waited for the applause to fade, then raised her glass and looked to Dr. Cardim. "And also to Ẽukia," she said. "She made it possible for us to communicate with the Eimiõro. I can only hope she is safe in Fortaleza."

The doctor cleared his throat. "I also hope for her safety," he said quietly. "One can only wish she had come with us."

While the steward and his assistant cleared the dinner plates and began serving brandy and dessert, the captain asked Dr. Cardim and Yema to say a few words. Doçura looked down at Yema, sound asleep in her chair, and decided she shouldn't wake the child. There was no telling what she might say. The nun turned to Dr. Cardim. "It seems our little girl has consumed a few too many toasts. Perhaps the doctor could speak for the both of them."

Cardim rose to his feet, raised his glass, and said, "To all of you for saving our lives. I, and I know Yema, will be forever grateful." He paused and placed his hand on the girl's head. "I think there is something no one knows. The day before we were to be burned at the stake, Girona and Fr. Almeido paraded us around town in a slave wagon to let everyone know we'd been captured. But the townspeople didn't believe Almeido's claim that the child was Yema, and they might have stoned us to death right then and there. In a panic, I told the girl to sing. When she did, it changed everything. The crowd turned on the militia, throwing stones at them. When that happened, the soldiers shot into the crowd and everyone fled. Killing people wasn't enough for Girona, so he ordered the Eimiõro settlement burned. So in her way, our little Cantora rallied the Indians to our cause."

* * *

Because of unfavorable winds, it took three full days for the Corajoso to make its way to Hispaniola. When they finally sighted the beautiful Bahía del Sol, the large bay on the east end of the island, it was near evening. Vincent decided to drop anchor and enter the bay in the morning. He posted the watch and went to dinner.

Near the end of that evening's meal, Yema reminded Enzo Henry, "Remember you promised to tell me about planets. How about tonight?"

"Sure," Henry said. "Let's go."

Captain Vincent, wanting to see if the child picked up this new knowledge as quickly as most everything else, took a lantern and followed them topside to the open deck of the wheelhouse. The three of them settled into chairs around the chart table.

"Besides Venus," Enzo started out, "there are four other planets, Saturn, Jupiter, Mars, and Mercury." He pointed to a spot just above the main mast. "There's Saturn or Jupiter. They look very much alike. I don't see Mars right now, but it's easy to spot because it's red."

"What about Mercury?" Yema asked.

"It's pretty hard to find. And it's very shy. I've seen it a few times near the horizon at sunset."

The girl held the lantern over the open page of Henry's celestial index. "I don't see columns for any other planets except Venus. Why is that?

"That's because Venus has a relationship with the sun at sunset and sunrise that we can use for navigation. The other planets just wander around."

Yema thought for a moment, studying the bright spot that was Saturn or Jupiter. "How do they wander?" she asked. "Don't they move right along with the other stars?"

"That's what makes planets so strange," Enzo said. "They *do* move with the other stars each night, but change position throughout the year."

The breeze was cool enough that Yema drew her cloak around her. "I don't understand," she said.

"Humm," speculated Enzo Henry, "maybe I can show you best with the astrolabe." He set the lantern next to his instrument and said, "Here are two stars, Vega in the constellation Lyra, and Centauri in the constellation Centaurus." He showed her the stars on the astrolabe's surface, then pointed into the night sky. "And there they are," he said, taking her small hand and pointing it at the two stars, one near the east horizon, the other overhead. "Now," he went on, "I'll move the arm of the astrolabe to just below Centauri. That's the east horizon. The other arm is on the right side, that's the west horizon. I want you to hold both arms while I trace that Centauri star across the sky, just as it will travel tonight." He rotated the face of the instrument to the right, and said, "See how Centauri rises in the east and will set in the west sometime near early morning?"

Yema kept her hands on the astrolabe arms and said, "Do that again, please."

Enzo Henry turned the face of the instrument to the left, then back again. "So the interesting thing is," he went on, "all the stars and planets will move from east to west during the night, just as the sun does in the day." He pointed to the bright planet overhead. "So that one, whichever it is, will set in about three hours. But guess what?"

The child put her chin in her hands, staring at the face of the astrolabe, touching first one star point, then the other. "You're going to tell me it wanders, but I don't know how."

"Here's how," Henry answered, delighted the child had it partly figured out. "Tomorrow night and every night, Centauri and Vega will always be the same distance apart. Always. But the planets do not stay in the same location compared to the stars. Each night they are in a slightly different location. Over a year, they can migrate thirty degrees further to the right, sometimes thirty degrees to the left. That's how they wander."

"Why?"

Enzo shrugged. "No one knows except God. I bet He knows."

"I think they don't like wandering," Yema said. "I think they're unhappy, and that makes them restless." The child stretched her arms into the night air and yawned.

Vincent pushed his chair back and stood up. "Yema," he said, "you come up with the most surprising ideas. Now to bed with you. We've a busy day tomorrow."

When the girl entered her cabin, she found Doçura writing in her journal.

"Sister Leah," Yema asked, "may I tell you something?"

"In a minute," the nun answered without looking up. "Let me finish this line." When finished, she blotted the page, closed her journal, corked the inkwell, and rolled the point of her quill into a cloth to clean it. "Yes?" she said.

"Do you know there are stars called planets, and they wander around the sky?"

"I've heard of that. Why do they wander?"

"No one knows. But I think they're looking for a home. Just like we are. Wouldn't that make sense?"

"Only to someone with an imagination like yours, sweetheart." Doçura found the idea intriguing. "So what will they do when they find their home?"

"They'll move in with the rest of the stars and stay in one place. Maybe I'll ask Enzo Henry tomorrow. He knows a lot of stuff."

***

The next morning broke clear and beautiful, the sea sparkling in every direction. Before them lay the emerald waters of Bahía del Sol with its many reefs and small islands. Yema and Doçura stood in the bow of the Corajoso taking in the sight. In the distance they could see several large ships in the harbor, and immediately beyond, the settlement of Puerto Príncipe. Further inland, across the east horizon, a line of mountains extended their green flanks into the sky.

Yema seemed most intrigued with the mountains, having never seen anything like them before. "What are those called?" she asked the nun. The girl continued to find it peculiar that the whites had names for almost everything.

"Those mountains are called La Reina del Cielo. It's Spanish for Queen of the Sky."

"'Queen of the Sky,'" she repeated. "I like that name."

A gang of sailors showed up and asked them to move so they could weigh anchor. The two women walked to the stern and stood just outside the wheelhouse railing, listening to the men as they discussed the morning's business. There was a favorable west breeze, and Captain Vincent studied the bay's obviously incomplete chart, trying to decide how best to proceed, first calling up to the man in the crow's nest. "All right, sailor," he shouted. "We're going to take her in slow at your direction." The crew unfurled just one sail, the aft trysail, allowing the ship to maneuver without an excess of forward motion. The first mate stood at the wheel, while Jozef supervised the sounding crews, one on each side of the ship, a few feet back from the bow.

With everything in place, the Corajoso began to creep forward. The first mate brought the ship around, allowing her to sail downwind and directly at the port. All the while, the sounding crews swung their lead plummets, calling out the depths, always in cadence, first from the port side, then from the starboard, "Port, six fathoms!", "Starboard, six fathoms!" and so forth. The captain kept his eyes focused on the lookout in the crow's nest, telling his first mate to direct the ship one way or the other.

After about ten minutes of due-east travel, the crow called for an immediate change of direction, a swing of thirty-five degrees. "Shed wind!" the captain shouted to the sailors manning the trysail. The crew let loose the top halyards, allowing the sail to flap in the breeze. The boom swung over the wheelhouse. Once it settled in place, the crew hauled on the halyards, catching the wind and bringing the canvas back into play.

"Sorry Captain," the crow's nest man called down. "There's rocks aplenty."

Captain Vincent moved closer to Doçura and Yema. "I've never before been to this harbor, ladies. And as you can see, it takes a cautious hand."

As they moved nearer to the port, and the vessels anchored there became more distinct, the crow's nest called down to the wheelhouse. "Captain! Those two four-masters are Spanish warships. One with sixteen guns, the other with fourteen." While the crow continued his observations, Vincent, Orlund, and Henry stepped to the rail for a better look. "There's a lot of activity," the man shouted.

"Boats in the water, plenty of back and forth. There's quite a bit of smoke in the settlement. Maybe more than there should be."

Because they were at deck level, it was difficult to see the detail described by the lookout. Vincent called to his first mate. "Take 'er to a half-mile from those Spanish. I'll go over and find out what's going on." He turned to Jozef. "Put a boat in the sling and lower the net. Let's the two of us take a jaunt."

The Corajoso sailed a short distance further before it dropped anchor. Knowing the Spanish always appreciated ceremony, the captain donned his formal hat; then he and Jozef, along with four rowers, climbed down the net and into the waiting boat.

With Captain Vincent absent—likely for an hour or more—two of the African women decided to "go fishing," as they called it. Walking around completely without clothes, they had no trouble enticing the sailors, with the first mate's indulgence, to lower another boat and aid them in their fishing expedition. Yema decided to go along, and this odd group rowed off a ways to dive for lobsters. They paused over the first shallow spot, and the women went into the water. Yema followed them, but stayed on the surface. The African women, seeming as agile as dolphins, dove to the bottom and came up moments later, each holding two lobsters. They repeated this a few times, then moved to the next shallow spot. Within a short while, they had two large baskets filled with the dark red creatures.

"Boat ho!" the lookout called to alert the fishermen and onboard crew. The fishing boat returned to the Corajoso, arriving a full quarter-hour ahead of the captain's boat.

Captain Vincent and Jozef climbed up the net and over the rail, leaving the rowers sitting in the boat. With just a few nods in greeting, the captain called up to the crow's nest lookout, "What do you see behind us, sailor? It's too shallow to go forward, right?"

In response, the crow called down, "That is correct, Sir. Tide's out. But clear behind."

Vincent turned to his first mate and said, "Let's tow her backward. We've got two boats in the water. That ought to do it."

The rowers from the fishing activity returned to their boat. The two ship's boats moved to the Corajoso's stern, picked up ropes thrown over the side, and secured them to cleats. The onboard crew drew the ropes taught and made them secure to anchor blocks on the aft deck. With everything in place, the first mate ordered, "Surface the anchor." The anchor crew cranked the weight off the bottom and pulled it to a level just over the water's surface—a precaution to prevent drifting aground in the event a wind came up. The rowers dug in their oars, and slowly began to move the ship astern.

Vincent and Enzo Henry huddled over the Bahía del Sol chart. "The Spanish said there's a slave rebellion going on in Puerto Príncipe." He tapped the chart at a point on the distant south arm of the bay. "We can pick up supplies in Miragoâne." He called up to the crow. "We clear yet?"

"No, Sir. Another two hundred yards."

"Sailor, you see those ships due south?"

"Yes Sir."

"That's Miragoâne," Vincent shouted. "Once we get clear of these shallows, that's where we're headed."

The lookout answered in the affirmative, and Vincent gave sailing orders to the first mate before heading in the direction of the gangway. When he passed by the baskets of lobsters, he said, "We've got a busy afternoon ahead. Cook some up for lunch."

***

After two hours of cautious sailing, the Corajoso dropped anchor a quarter-mile off the port of Miragoâne. She was the only Dutch ship in the harbor. The others were mostly Spanish and Portuguese. Vincent put three boats into the water, each of them with two, fifty gallon water barrels. Since the Corajoso had sufficient stores to sail northeast across the Atlantic from Fortaleza to the Cape Verde Islands, a voyage of about three weeks—a distance of eleven hundred miles—the quartermaster estimated it would require only four barrels of fresh water from Hispaniola to replenish the ship's cistern. To be on the safe side, they would also store six additional barrels filled with water lashed around the mainmast. Throughout the first half of the afternoon, until the cistern was full and the barrels stowed, boats ferried back and forth between the ship and harbor front.

The watering activity continued without problems, so Vincent, Enzo Henry, Dr. Cardim, and Lars Orlund ambled through the port looking for additional stores that might make their journey more pleasant. Besides purchasing a few bags of ground maize and five kegs of black syrup, they bought ten goats, two crates of chickens, and enough feed to maintain the animals until they became table fare.

Once their purchases were delivered to the port, the three men sought out the settlement's church, planning to offer prayers for a safe voyage. Before they entered, the men paused at the entrance to read the several announcements posted there, and immediately spotted a wanted notice for the two clergy and Dr. Cardim. They turned and headed for the harbor. When sufficiently away from the church, Lars Orlund said to Cardim, "I'm not surprised. This bay is where you three escaped."

"We never saw it in daylight," the doctor commented.

"There's too many Spanish military around here for my taste," Captain Vincent said. "We sail tomorrow. Early as possible."

Chapter 33

The crew of the Corajoso spent most of the afternoon and into the evening readying the ship for departure. They stowed the few stores purchased in the port, erected a pen on the foredeck to contain the goats, and cleaned out their long unused chicken cages. Vincent assigned one of the African women and Yema to take care of the animals. Within an hour, the child had named three goats and several of the chickens. She took a particular liking to a surly rooster whom she named Porõ, explaining to the struggling bird that being named Lucky might protect him from the cooking pot.

Captain Vincent found it impossible to sleep that evening, despite an excellent dinner of lobster left over from the afternoon, beet greens from a vendor's garden in Miragoâne, and roast bananas from of all places, Cape Verde.

By the roll of the ship, the captain knew a strong east wind blew topside, a fine breeze for exiting this bay. The shouted conversation with the Spanish warship's captain the previous morning kept running through his head. The man had sounded suspicious from the start, demanding that they come aboard for a visit. Vincent declined, citing his need to resupply. Because of his distrust of the Spanish, he did not give the captain his true name, nor that of his ship, nor the names of his companions. The Spaniard would find out soon enough from the merchants in Miragoâne.

At three bells, Vincent gave up any attempt to sleep. He woke his steward and had him bring tea. While waiting, he turned up his lantern and studied the charts laid out on the table. *Too many shallows,* he thought. *Can't risk it in the dark.* When the steward arrived, the captain said, "Wake Henry and bring him his tea here. Wake the officers and have them roust the crew. Give them an hour to finish breakfast. Sails up before first light."

***

Five hours later, just past eight bells, the Corajoso cleared the west end of Isla de Guijarros, the large landmass at the mouth of Bahía del Sol. Two Spanish military boats came into view as they rounded the island's north shore. Though nearly a hundred yards astern, the brightly uniformed soldiers with their muskets bristling at port-arms were clearly visible. The Spanish captain from yesterday stood in the bow of the nearer boat, hailing the Corajoso with his his speaking trumpet.

Captain Vincent said a short prayer, thanking providence for weighing anchor at such an early hour. If they'd left just a few minutes later, the Spanish boarding party would have intercepted them as they came abreast of the island.

The first mate stood at the helm and addressed a smiling Captain Vincent, "Your hunch was correct, Sir. I assume you want me to hold course."

Vincent responded. "We'll give 'em a smell of our bilge, Mr. Jansen." He called down to the second mate. "Mr. Jozef! Run out the spinnaker. Let's see if those rascals want to chase us all the way to the Verdes."

Within minutes, the giant foresail came into play, the canvas straining with each gust of wind, the thump of it reverberating through the ship. Snubbed twenty degrees to starboard, the sail caught the full force of the east wind. The Corajoso appeared to leap through the waves, now heading southwest, directly away from the Spanish. At the sight of the spinnaker—like a giant white flower bursting from the Corajoso's foredeck—the Spanish captain threw down his speaking trumpet and ordered a warning shot. The rail cannon, mounted in the front of his boat, was tiny, intended mostly for signaling. At this angle, their only choice was a shot directly into the fleeing Dutch vessel or alongside, the equivalent of a shot across the bow. Whatever their intent, the Spaniard's aim was faulty. The cannon ball poked a three-inch hole through the mainsail.

"Mr. Jozef!" Vincent called again. "Round up some slops and dump 'em. Those buggers need a dose of last night's dinner."

"Yes, Sir," Jozef shouted back. "With pleasure."

The captain glanced at Orlund who'd been keeping an eye on the Spanish. "Lars," he said, "I'll wager five gold reis that he doesn't fire again."

"You would win that bet, Captain. They've broken off. Just rested oars."

"Very good," Vincent responded, calling again to his second mate, "Shift the spinnaker twenty degrees to port, Mr. Jozef, and we're going to come about." Then to the man at the helm, "Put her on a north bearing, Mr. Jansen. We need to find that west wind."

In a few minutes everything was set. The Corajoso heeled into its new tack, surging northward through open water.

***

By mid-afternoon, eighty miles north of Hispaniola, nearly twenty degrees north latitude, the west wind won out, the pennant at the top of the mainmast giving the first indication, the sails following as they shifted into the freshening breeze. "There's our tropic, Mr. Jansen," Vincent exclaimed. "Bear east."

Yema, who'd been sitting in the animal pen with the goats and Porõ, joined the crew on the quarterdeck. "Have we finally turned east?" she asked. "Is that right?"

"What do you think?" Orlund said to her. "You tell me."

She studied the compass in its cradle on the chart table, then the chart. "Ninety degrees right of north. I'd say that's east."

"So where are the Cape Verde Islands?" Vincent asked.

There were several island groups on the map to choose from, the Canaries, the Cape Verdes, São Tomé and Príncipe, and Madera, none of which had labels.

Without a pause, the child pointed to the Cape Verdes. "Right there," she said. "Same latitude as us."

"How do you know that?" Enzo Henry asked.

"What?"

"Same latitude," he said.

Yema returned her gaze to the chart. "Well ..." she mused. She knew the answer, but wanted to tease the men a little. "Here's Hispaniola. We sailed north, so I think we're about here. And right across the ocean is Cape Verde."

Captain Vincent shook his head. "Yema, how do you know how far we've sailed? Amazing for a ten-year-old."

"I am pleased to inform you gentlemen," the girl said, "that I am eleven years old." She made a mock curtsey and a quick departure.

When Yema returned to the animal pen, she found Doçura sitting on a nearby hatch cover, mending her yellow blouse. "I thought you were going to teach me how to do that?" the girl said.

"We've plenty of time for sewing lessons," the nun responded. "We're headed east, and this weather's beautiful. I decided to sew a little and enjoy the sunshine."

The girl plopped down next to Doçura, running her hand over the silky fabric. "Why do you think they bought the clothes for us?" she asked. This was her way to get Sister Leah to talk about an uncomfortable subject, Lars Orlund and his interest in her.

The nun was equally adept at deflecting the subject, this time stretching the collar of the girl's tunic so she could examine her wounds. "I'm proud of how you've let us treat you after Fortaleza," she said. "I know it was painful, but you never complained. Now you're almost healed. More quickly than Dr. Cardim, I'd say, even though your injuries were worse than his."

At that moment, Doçura would have found herself surprised— She was not the only one considering the remarkable nature of the child. From the wheelhouse deck, Captain Vincent could see Yema and Leah sitting together near the animal pen. At the sight of the two women, the captain became reflective, first considering Yema who had been showing off her navigation talents just moments before. For quite some time he'd felt a strong affection for the girl, and he paused now to examine his thoughts. He'd never married; the sea had been his wife. *More a demanding mistress than a wife,* he told himself. And this Indian youngster, despite her scarred face and dark skin, felt like a daughter to him. By spending these months with her and Leah, he'd begun to yearn for children of his own. He would want boys of course, smart young captains to accompany him on voyages. But what about girls and their curious ways? And Leah? *Sister Leah,* a Jewess at heart, what about her? What a delightful and confounding woman. These two females were now part of his family, his ship's family. For His own reasons, God had put these strangely dissimilar creatures in his path, a native child and an irascible Jewish nun, females as perplexing as their lineage.

For a while he'd puzzled over Lars' peculiar behavior when it came to these two, but any confusion was put to rest after buying clothes for the ladies in Fortaleza. As they rowed back to the Corajoso, his friend confessed he was in love with Doçura. Vincent guessed Orlund's feelings came from losing his wife Greta three years ago—thus Lars understood and missed the joys of marriage. Though for Captain Vincent, Sister Leah felt like a true sister. Beatrix, the oldest of the children in his family, and his favorite person in all the world, had died ten years earlier from the plague. Since he and Orlund had grown up together, Vincent's parents considered Lars part of their family, and thus he was as close to Beatrix as anyone. And just like Doçura, Beatrix never tolerated nonsense, challenging both young men at every turn.

Orlund, sensing Vincent's thoughts, nodded in the direction of the women. "You know," he said, "those two have changed me in ways I never could have imagined."

"How so?" the captain asked. "They are an unusual pair."

"I took notice of it back at the plantation, sometime while you were away. Weeks before the plague hit, the two of them fixed dinner for me one night, and somehow the subject of my melancholy came up. It must have been Yema's asking. She's always posing questions that lead elsewhere."

Vincent smiled and nodded. "I know. Doçura does the same thing."

"I told them I keep busy to escape my sadness. I did not mention my wife's death, although I think that had a lot to do with it. Anyway, since that evening, my association with those two seems to have enlivened my moods. Settled my mind, so to speak. Even the failure of the plantation did not affect me that much. Can you believe it? I just figured things would work out somehow. Well, they didn't, but I don't seem to care. Maybe I've lost my senses? I think that evening is when I began to consider Leah for a wife."

The two men watched as Yema reached into the animal pen and picked up an orange rooster. As the child soon found out, the creature must have been drowsing. When the bird suddenly awoke, it flapped and pecked at the girl so furiously that she dumped it back into the enclosure. The girl dusted her hands in disgust.

"That kid's really something," Orlund said. "After all she's been through, her spirits are still high. She has more fortitude than most men I know. Opposite of a poor fellow back home in Almere. In his case, the local inquisitor questioned him about a Jewish merchant who came through town. As far as I know, he wasn't harmed and they didn't keep him overnight, but the gentleman turned so fearful, he became addled and eventually took his own life. So here's Yema, none the worse for wear despite being imprisoned twice by the Inquisition, *and* mistreated."

"Interesting you say that," Vincent commented, but did not continue. He eyed the pennants at the top of each mast, then turned to the helmsman. "We've a shift of wind, Mr. Jozef. How's she holding?"

Jozef rocked the wheel a half-quarter turn each way. "She's pulling, Sir. Was going to give it a few more minutes. Maybe we should adjust now."

Vincent called down to his first mate who stood just below them on the main deck. He was also watching the pennants. "Mr. Jansen! Haul sails to port. Line up this new breeze."

"Yes Sir," Jansen answered, and began shouting orders.

It pleased the captain to see his men work the riggings. Two gangs ran the halyards, first loosing the starboard lines to prescribed marks on the ropes—fifteen degrees in this instance—then snubbing each sail in its new position to port. They started with the foresail, first the top canvas, then the middle, lastly the course sail nearest the deck. The gangs moved on to the mainmast where they repeated the activity, then aft to the mizzen from which hung just two sails.

"That's a damned lovely sight," the captain said to Orlund and Jozef as the wind bowed the canvas straight out. The late afternoon sun scattered golden reflections from the sea onto the sails. He went to the quarterdeck rail and spoke to his first mate, loud enough so that everyone could hear. "Fine work, Mr. Jansen," he said. "Fine work."

The captain walked back to the men in the wheelhouse and cast an appreciating glance at Lars Orlund. This red-bearded friend had made it possible for him to buy the Corajoso, making Vincent one of the few captains who owned their own ship. When Orlund financed their initial dyewood foray to Brazil five years ago, it brought wealth to them both. Returning from that voyage, they sold the ship's cargo for an immense sum. With the proviso that the captain run two more dyewood expeditions for him, Orlund generously paid Vincent half the profits, more than enough to purchase the Corajoso, thoroughly refit her, and add armaments sufficient to keep pirates at bay.

While the captain, Jozef, and Lars Orlund continued to admire the scene, Enzo Henry emerged from the gangway and climbed the quarterdeck steps to the wheelhouse. He'd been in his cabin studying the Cape Verde charts when the ship's movement signaled their change of sail. Now he needed to check the compass heading. "Good afternoon, gentlemen," he said in greeting as he bent over the chart table. After a moment of study he said, "We're right on course, Captain. Let's pray this wind continues to favor us."

Vincent stole another look at the Doçura and Yema, then took the wheel from Jozef. "If you gentlemen would please excuse us, I need to confer privately with my imbecilic friend Lars Orlund." He gestured towards the foredeck. "Perhaps go entertain the ladies." The two men exchanged knowing smiles and trotted down the steps to the main deck.

"So you still want me to talk to her?" Vincent asked Orlund. He tested the ship's wheel, pleased to feel the rudder cutting water evenly under the ship.

"Absolutely," Orlund answered. "Not now, though. When we get closer to home."

"Why not ask her yourself?"

"That's not our custom, and I assume not hers."

"Leah's an uncustomary woman, Lars. Perhaps?" He let the question drift into the air.

Orlund said, "Usually a brother or uncle does the asking, so you are the closest." He looked very determined.

Vincent shook his head. "All right," he answered, "I'll do it. But give me a week's notice so I can figure out what to say."

* * *

Yema had taken to climbing into the shrouds before dawn to watch the sun come up. How the light played with the mainmast pennant, then worked its way down the canvas until she had to shield her eyes from the glare. How the edge of dawn shone on the sails as the ship rolled along, lighting the whole of the rigging, then fleeing to the topmost point, before again lighting the full canvas as the Corajoso tipped through the ocean troughs and swells.

The child often woke at four bells and went to the galley where she drank tea with the cook and ate a breakfast of whatever was available. Then she'd return to her cabin, turn up the lantern, and go over her schoolwork from the day before. If it happened to be a writing lesson, she might copy the whole thing over, making sure each letter was perfect, and sometimes adding little flourishes to the letters, or as sentence punctuations.

Doçura would awaken to find the girl bent over the cabin table hard at work, repeating the previous day's lesson. "Yema," she'd ask, "why are you doing that?"

"I didn't like what I did yesterday." Holding up the new copy, she'd say, "See, isn't this better?"

"It's better, sweetheart, but not necessary." The letters were indeed perfect, as perfect and well formed as any scribe's. They continued to use Vincent's copy of *Livro de Vita Christi*, sometimes taking two days' sessions to work through a single page. For Yema it was an exercise in reading, understanding the story and its writing, and copying the text. It turned out the child had a flair for the artistic. As time went on, her flourishes took on the character of the story. For the Sermon on the Mount and Jesus's admonitions to mercy, airy thistledown and rays of sunlight-through-clouds graced her sentences. For the crucifixion, flourishes resembling lightning bolts, and artfully disguised eyes—presumably God's—stared daggers at the reader.

When Leah and Yema first started *Livro de Vita Christi,* they found an elaborately illuminated pamphlet tucked into the volume's back cover. The ten-page tract described the life and teachings of St. Francis of Assisi. Yema was fascinated with the illuminations, having never seen drawings in color before. Taking notice of the child's interest in the goats and chickens, Doçura suggested they use the pamphlet for lessons, explaining to the girl that St. Francis was the patron saint who loved animals.

"I can't love my animals too much," the girl said. "Sooner or later they'll all be killed for food. The cook's already taken several chickens and a goat. But there's one nanny that's going to have babies. I've got to figure out a way to save her."

On the morning after they began working with the St. Francis booklet, the girl took on a new task. Using her written page from the day before, she began illustrating her own text. She'd never seen a hare or a sheep before, but the pictures were easy to duplicate from the tract— too easy in fact. So she took the rather placid images and added action, hares running or scratching their ears, sheep grazing and lambs nursing, birds circling a nest of hatchlings. What she really wanted were colored inks and paint, then she could truly illuminate her work.

Yema had almost finished her first nanny goat drawing when she heard the call to watch, remembering that Obiike was the morning's lookout. An hour earlier it had been chilly on deck, so she put on her brown friar's robe and hurried topside. Today from the crow's nest, she would be the first to touch the sunrise.

Chapter 34

When Yema emerged on deck, she saw Obiike coming towards her from the bow. The girl trotted over to the mainmast shroud and waited for him.

"Well little princess," he said, "are you going to be my assistant today?"

"Yes, if that's all right."

The two often teased each other, and this seemed like an opportunity. Obiike pointed up the shroud. "You go first. When you fall, I'll catch you."

"Maybe I don't want to go first," she said, her hands on her hips.

The African copied her stance. "When you're with me, I'm the boss." He again pointed upward.

The child turned on her heels. "Maybe another day."

Obiike took hold of the shroud and put a foot in it. "See you later," he said.

Yema scrambled up the net and waited a few feet above him. "How did you know I was going to give in?"

"Ah, little princess," he answered, "I can read minds. Girls are the easiest."

As they climbed together, she said, "Why are you calling me princess? You never did that before."

He reached up and patted her foot. "If you were a little black girl, Yema, we would make you our princess. The women think you have magic."

The girl continued upward. She knew Obiike meant this as a compliment, but him saying it made her sad. "I am not magic," she said at last. "I've just been lucky. So many others have not."

The two of them finished the climb in silence, entering the crow's nest through the small, square hatch in the platform's floor.

As they settled into the watch, the eastern horizon blushed pink and silver, announcing the sunrise. Venus, this day the morning star, preceded the rising sun, summoning the light.

"Do you know that star is Venus?" the girl asked. "It's called a planet. There are five like that."

"Ah," Obiike said, "we call such stars *pondo ekporpu.* It means stars that stare. Other stars we call *pondo itabi,* stars that wink."

"I don't understand," Yema said.

He opened his hand to the dark edge of the western sky. "Look there," he said. "See how the stars wink on and off. Venus does not do that. That makes it a *pondo ekporpu.* "

The child looked west to the stars, then east at Venus. "You're right," she said. "Why do some wink?"

"Because they are dangerous tricksters. Very dishonest fellows. And most stars are *itabi* stars. They cannot shine without winking. Stars like Venus keep them from misbehaving by staring at them. Otherwise they would take over the heavens."

"And do what?"

He shrugged. "No one knows."

Yema pondered this as the morning brightened.

Except for a heavy squall line holding over the ocean just north of where the sun would come up, the morning promised to be clear. As the sun climbed above the edge of the sea and began to light the earth, Yema stretched her hands high into the air, intending her fingertips to touch that first, precious light. Indeed they did, but for only an instant. The ship's roll pulled the light from her hands, then immediately thereafter made it shine on her and half the sails below. Yema grasped the crow's rail as the Corajoso rolled hard to port. She found herself suddenly fearful, looking straight down at the deck.

Obiike reached over and took the back of her tunic. "You're safe, little singer," he said. "I won't let you fall."

The ship righted itself, but Yema kept her eye on the deck. "It's still nighttime down there," she commented. "Why is it day up here, and night down there?"

"Not for long," the African answered. The Corajoso took another roll, this time with the bow high in the air as it rode through an oncoming wave. Yema lost her grip, ending up on the floor, then rolled against Obiike's legs as the ship returned to center. "It's daylight down there now," he said, helping her up. "You missed it."

"How do you manage to stay upright?" she asked him. "This is scary."

"Well, smarty girl," he said, "I'm pleased you don't know everything. Let me show you." He turned her shoulders so she faced towards the bow. "Now watch the waves," he said, "both coming at us, and from the sides. Feel how the ship moves with each wave and learn to expect that. Hold yourself accordingly."

With her feet wide apart, hands on the railing, it took the child only a few minutes to anticipate the ship's movement and make the adjustments in her stance. "This is easy," she said, releasing her hands, suddenly gripping the rail again as a wave broke over the foredeck. She watched it wash back to midships. Yema found herself looking down at the open sea a hundred feet below. Even Obiike was holding on.

"Is this rough enough for you?" he joked. The sun dimmed out as the Corajoso advanced into the weather. The African knew they were in for a very rough time.

"How do I get down from here?" she asked. "I've had enough."

They could hear orders being shouted from the deck below, the wind making the words impossible to understand. Yema announced she was climbing down and reached for the hatch. Obiike put his foot on it. "You can't go now," he said. "They're reefing the sails."

The two looked over the side to see many of the crew in the rigging, most of them hanging on for dear life. Some men were even perched along yardarms seventy-five feet above the deck. Others hung in the shrouds, freeing the canvas and feeding it along to the men straddling the yards. Still others manned the halyards, securing the sails into their rolled-up position.

A thunderous rain came with the wind, soaking everyone in an instant. The men on the yards had it the worst, straddling the heavy wooden beams, trying to keep from falling and gathering canvas at the same time.

A sudden gust knocked two of the crew from the mainmast yard just below the crow's nest. These two were prepared, having done this before in rough weather. Both had their legs hooked over the lines that stretched under the yardarms. When they were thrown loose, they hung upside-down for a moment, suspended by their knees. Almost as quickly as they'd been dislodged, the two hoisted themselves back onto the yard and continued their work. None of the crew in the rigging appeared particularly frightened. Apparently they enjoyed the challenge of working in the worst of conditions.

In a moment everything changed. The halyards holding the foresail's middle canvas broke loose, and the sail—now held only by the yard line—rapidly slid to the lee end of the yard. It began to flap dangerously close to the water. Pulled by this massive, rain-soaked canvas, the Corajoso tilted leeward, seawater surging through the port rails and along the deck. Another few degrees, and the ship would capsize.

The men on deck held on to anything that kept them from being swept overboard, many clinging to lifelines, praying for their lives. Captain Vincent remained at the wheel, secured in place by a harness bolted to the wheelhouse deck. In desperation, he spun the helm, turning the Corajoso's bow straight leeward. For a moment the ship righted itself, giving the man mounted in the foresail time to scoot along the yardarm to its end. Vincent was pleased to see it was Max van Hoff, the young fellow who had provided the letter during the attack at Fortaleza. "Van Hoff's a steady lad," Vincent said to first mate Jansen, also harnessed in place and standing next to the captain. "He'll get it done." Ever since they'd left Brazil, Vincent had considered promoting young van Hoff to ensign. He decided he'd do it for certain after this storm.

Once van Hoff reached the end of the yardarm, he freed the canvas with a hand-axe clamped in place on the spar's end for just that purpose. As the sail came fee, the loose halyard ran through the steel thread-eye at break-neck speed. The thick rope slammed into Max's head, knocking him unconscious and bloodying the side of his face. The young man hung briefly by his knees, then straightened out, catching a foot in the yard line for a second before he plunged into the sea and disappeared. The loose sail, now completely free in the wind, cartwheeled over the water, twisting away as if carrying Max van Hoff's soul with it.

As Obiike and Yema looked on in horror—the African with his eyes wide, a hand over his mouth, the girl screaming, her tears mixed with the rain—a bolt of lightning struck the foresail mast and splattered onto the deck, a radiant carpet of dazzling blue that poured over the Corajoso's sides and into the sea. Though stunned by the thunder clap and lightning flash, the several men in the foresail shrouds appeared unhurt. The crew on the deck also registered no injury, as did the livestock in the animal pen. Yema was most fearful for the animals, but evidenced by the goats panicked running and the chickens flapping and squawking, they also appeared unhurt.

"We're in danger up here," Obiike said. "We've got to get down." The crow's nest rocked so violently that he could barely remain standing. Knowing that Yema might not be able to hold on to the shrouds as she climbed down, he made a loop in a lifeline and snugged it under her arms. Then he opened the hatch in the crow's nest floor. "Hold onto the shroud," he told her. "If you break loose, I've got you with this rope."

If she looked straight down along the mast, descending to the deck did not appear that difficult. But then she looked to the side. Either side, it made no difference. As the Corajoso rocked in the heavy sea, the motion of the ship was such that most of the time the crow's nest was over the water, and only briefly over the deck. She froze, unable to put her foot through the hatch and step onto the shroud.

"Don't look to the side," Obiike told her. "Keep your eyes glued on the mast. Look only at the mast. Then just climb down." Though also frightened at the situation, he found her inability to move a little humorous. "Sing to the wind," he said. "Sing to Yemanjá. Tell her to calm the sea. The mast is attached to the deck. When you get to the bottom, you will be safe."

Yema sang, but not to the Sea Goddess— just some mother's nursing song that came to mind. She finally put a foot into the net and began to climb down. Obiike snubbed the rope around a cleat on the crow's nest rail, letting it slide as the girl moved downward. After descending about thirty feet, and still sixty feet from the deck, she came level with the upper spar of the middle canvas.

Though Yema held onto the wet shroud as firmly as she could, and had her feet solidly planted in the net, a gust of wind whipped the shroud into the child's face, knocking her loose. As she came free, Obiike could see that Yema was frightened out of her wits, or perhaps stunned. Regardless, she made no attempt to grab the shroud as she swung just inches from it.

Each time the ship rolled, the child rolled with it, her length of travel exaggerated by the thirty feet of rope above her. Most of the time she found herself over the sea, either past one side of the ship or the other. Obiike decided it was best to lower her further. In another twenty feet or so, near the top of the course sail, the shroud fanned out and Yema would simply run into it.

Captain Vincent stood at the wheel, struggling to keep the Corajoso headed into the wind, the only safe bearing in this kind of sea. He felt heartsick beyond words, blaming himself for Max van Hoff's death. *If I'd only reefed the sails earlier,* he told himself, *when I first spotted the squall. It's a tragedy to lose this young man.* Since Max's father was a smallholder near Orlund's farm, he would have to tell the boy's parents himself. Perhaps he'd offer them a compensation. He didn't know. But saving Yema was now his immediate concern. He turned the wheel over to his first mate and said, "I should have called them down sooner."

The captain, intending to climb the shroud and help Yema, had to struggle against the wind and torrents of rain just to reach the quarterdeck stairs. Before he could set foot on the main deck, Vincent saw Dr. Cardim emerge from the rear hatch and claw his way along the lifeline to the base of the shroud. Once there, the doctor climbed into the netting and advanced upwards towards the girl. By now, Yema was resting face-first against the shroud's skirt, three feet below the course sail's upper spar.

"I've got you," Cardim said when he reached the girl. Since she was still suspended by the rope, he climbed under her until she could reach around his neck. "Hold on to me," he said. "We'll climb down together." Though her grip was weak, Cardim felt it sufficient. The doctor went down the net while Obiike played out the rope from above. In a few minutes he delivered the girl to Doçura.

The nun stood in the pouring rain, holding the shroud for support. "Is she hurt?" Doçura asked.

"I think she's just scared," Cardim said. "Doesn't appear injured." They removed the rope and took her down to Doçura's cabin, exchanging a dry blanket for her wet clothes.

The nun put the girl in her hammock and tucked the blanket around her. "Yema," she said, "talk to me. Are you hurt? Say something."

The girl blinked her eyes open and looked up at Doçura. After a moment she reached up and touched the nun's face, running her fingers along the woman's cheekbone. She said, "I'm tired of being scared, Leah. It's been happening too much. I just want to sleep."

***

Yema stayed in the cabin for several days, doing nothing but sleeping, eating very little, and reading the St. Francis booklet and *Livro de Vita Christi*. Doçura put up with the girl's behavior for nearly a week, then became fed up, and quit bringing her food. "You're not hurt," she told her, "and I'm tired of your hiding here. If you want to eat, you'll have to join the rest of us."

"I'm afraid to go out," Yema said. "I don't know what happened to my nanny goat and that stupid rooster." She pulled the blanked up to her chin and stared at the ceiling. Finally she said, "I named the goat Venus because she's white. Anyway, the Africans think I'm magic. Maybe I don't need to eat food."

"First of all, you are not magic. And when you spout nonsense like that, I know you're not sick. Now, I've got good news for you about Venus and Porõ, or whatever you call him."

The girl brightened a little. "What?" she asked.

Doçura put on a resolute face and laced her hands together. "I'll only tell you if you'll eat dinner with us this evening and resume taking care of the animals. In fact, you should go on deck now. It's a beautiful afternoon." She pointed towards the door.

"I think I agree," Yema said. "Please tell me the good news."

"Lars and Captain Vincent agreed to spare Porõ and Venus from the cooking pot as your payment for taking care of the animals. And you can keep them at Orlund's farm when we get to the Netherlands."

"What about Venus's kids? She's going to have babies, you know."

"I imagine you can keep her offspring too," Doçura said.

Yema headed for the door, pausing in the threshold. "You coming?" the child asked.

"In a minute," she answered, and did not mention the second surprise waiting for her at the top of the gangway. At least she hoped the child would be surprised. Pleasantly surprised.

When Yema came on deck, Nanjala, the Cape Verde woman who helped her tend the animals was waiting. She said, "Say, young singing girl, would you do me a favor?"

"What's that?" Yema asked. She liked this African woman,

full of mischief and always helpful.

"You know that Guinea song you sang in church back at the plantation, A Boy and His Leopard? We'd like you to sing it at the celebration tomorrow night."

"What are you celebrating?"

"That we will be halfway across the ocean. Next stop, my home." Nanjala pointed to the mainmast. "In case you haven't noticed, the wind has been straight from the west for almost a week."

The woman carried a little drum unlike anything Yema had ever seen, a wooden ring with a skin stretched across it, and with small brass plates attached to the perimeter. When she pointed with the drum and said, "Let's go practice in the bow where no one will hear us," the brass plates made a rattling chime.

The two of them stood next to the rail at the very tip of the Corajoso. Yema suspected that Sister Leah had put Nanjala up to this, but she didn't care. Singing at the celebration would be fun. "What is that little drum?" she asked.

"It's called a tambourine," the woman answered. "Sing your song, and I'll provide rhythm and harmony."

The girl sang the leopard song while Nanjala accompanied her with the tambourine, thumping the instrument for cadence, and rattling it with emphasis at the end of each verse. As the woman sang with Yema—a full two registers below hers—the child felt Nanjala's voice resonating inside of her, somehow reinforcing the song. When they finished, Yema said, "I've never sung with anyone before, not in a harmony like that."

"We make a good pair," the woman said. "Now I'll teach you the Fire Song. It's about our home in—" She stopped when Yema broke into tears. "What's wrong?" she asked.

Memories flooded through Yema's thoughts, of the pleasant days in Colony Luís rehearsing hymns for the Mass with Fr. Julian and Sister Doçura, her beloved family listening from the back of the chapel. And then there was Fr. Paulo accompanying her on the lute from time to time. The girl so wished she could return to those days. She brushed away her tears with the back of her hand. "I'll be all right," she said. "Just remembering how I sang at the Mass when we lived in Luís."

Nanjala decided this was as good a time as any. She said, "Before I teach you the Fire Song, there's something important I want you to hear. Something all of us Africans agree on." When Yema said nothing, she continued. "We think you are a magic girl. So when we get to our Brava Island in the Cape Verdes, we want you to come live with us. Think how nice it would be, to bathe in the ocean every day, and not be around these smelly Europeans."

The idea was so foreign to Yema, it took her a moment to respond. "We're going to live in the Netherlands," she said, "Sister Leah and I."

"Sister Leah is welcome to live with us too," Nanjala continued. "You will not be accepted in the white-man's world. They will hate you because of your skin color." She pulled up her sleeve and held it next to Yema's arm. "Don't you see, child, you are much closer in color to me than to the whites."

Yema didn't know what to say, and continued to find the idea confusing. Instead of responding to Nanjala, she walked over to the animal pen and counted the goats. Two were missing, including a wine-colored ram she'd named Mars. At least Venus and Porõ were still there, the latter perched on the fence nearby, daring anyone to come near him. Yema grabbed the bird and hugged it to her, forcing his head into her tunic so he couldn't peck. He tried to scratch her with his claws, but she held his legs tight with her other hand.

The seed that Nanjala had just sown grew into a real fear, and she wondered, *Will we still be in danger in the Netherlands?* Yes, she understood that. *But perhaps even worse in the Cape Verdes which were completely controlled by the Portuguese? Or was it the Spanish? It didn't make any difference.*

The girl leaned over the fence and dropped Porõ inside, then put her arms up as the rooster flew at her in a rage. She batted it back into the pen and turned to Nanjala. "I'll ask Sister Leah about this. Now please teach me the Fire Song."

Chapter 35

"Why is there blood on your arm?" Doçura asked the girl when she walked into their cabin.

"It's nothing," Yema said, pulling her sleeve over the cuts. "Porõ tried to scratch me."

"Looks like he succeeded," the nun said. She pulled up the sleeve and dabbed at the wounds, the girl flinching a little as she did so. "Let's dress you up for dinner tonight." She gestured at the girl's blue clothing laid out in her hammock. "It's your first night back with the living. I'll wear my blue outfit too."

Quite off the subject, Yema said, "Do you think we will be safe in the land of the Dutch?"

It was a topic they'd discussed many times, and Doçura wondered why it had come up again. "Why do you ask? We've already—"

Yema broke in, her words tense and anxious, telling Leah about Nanjala's suggestion.

Doçura listened carefully, then said, "Nothing has changed. We're better off in the Netherlands with Orlund and Vincent to protect us there. We might be safe on Ilia da Brava for a little while, but the demand for slaves is growing. Sooner or later our African friends will be taken again." She lifted Yema's tunic over her head and sponged off her arm in the washbowl.

"Making people slaves is not right," the girl said, drying her arm.

"Right or wrong, we're better off in the Netherlands." Doçura picked up the blouse and helped Yema into it, carefully buttoning it down the back, wondering at that moment if the child knew how much she loved fussing over her. She kissed the girl on the top of her head. "Let me tell you something," she said. "If you hadn't missed the service we had for van Hoff, you'd have heard something quite extraordinary from Captain Vincent. He actually admitted he was at fault for Max's death, that he should have anticipated the storm and acted sooner."

"Why is that important?" Yema asked.

"Because Captain Vincent, and I believe Lars Orlund too, are unique men. There's not one man in a thousand who would admit to a mistake like that. Particularly a ship's captain. Of all the people in this world, above all others, Yema, we can depend on them to protect us."

Doçura shook out the blue wrapping skirt and knelt in front of the girl. "Here," she said, "hold it up. I'll wrap it around you." No matter how tight she made it, the skirt kept slipping down. "You need a bigger *katesh*," the nun said.

"What's that?"

"Hebrew for backside. I'll find you a belt."

While she was searching, Yema said, "Nanjala thinks I won't

be accepted in the Netherlands."

Doçura found a length of rope and again knelt in front of the child. "If you want to call it that, neither one of us will be accepted. We are fugitives. We'll hide our identities, and always have to do so." She had the girl pull the wrapping skirt a little higher, then put the rope around her waist and tied it in place. "Now," she said, folding the rim of cloth over the rope belt, "does that settle it?"

"Not really," Yema said. "Anyway, please get dressed. I'm hungry."

***

Early the next morning, Yema went to see the ship's cook, a large Portuguese fellow with a gruff manner and a florid complexion. But on this morning he was all smiles when he saw the girl. "I've missed you, little one," he said. "Would you care for a cup of tea?"

"Yes," she said demurely, "with a touch of black syrup if you please."

He prepared the tea, then held the mug out of reach above the girl's head. "Only if you promise to not stay away any more."

"I promise," she said, and took the mug, holding it with both hands and blowing the steam away. She loved the warm feel of it in the morning. "Has anyone talked to you about that white nanny goat and the orange rooster?" she asked the cook.

"They have indeed," he said. "Captain Vincent himself told me not to harm them. So harm them I won't. But that rooster has extremely bad manners."

"His name is Porõ, and he can't help himself."

"Porõ must mean stupid," he said. Then, with an uncommon twinkle in his eye, he asked, "And what's the name of the white nanny?"

"Venus."

"What are you going to name her kids?"

"I don't know. It depends on whether—"

The cook could contain himself no longer. He broke into fits of laughter. "You better go check. She had twins last night."

Yema handed the mug to the cook and ran for the gangway stairs.

***

That evening, with the moon overhead, the Corajoso creaking eastward under a light breeze, and everyone gathered around the open brazier, the African celebration began. There was drumming, singing, a prayer offered by Captain Vincent, and a generous portion of rum for all. Yema drank very little, recalling how the strong drink often put her to sleep.

Earlier in the celebration, an English sailor had played the hornpipe. His lively tunes inspired many to get up and dance. When it came time for Nanjala and Yema to sing, the two women stood in front of the flaming brazier. Standing to one side was Obiike with the tambourine and the sailor with his hornpipe. The women started with the Leopard song, and the scene took on a dreamlike quality, everyone listening in spellbound attention—Nanjala's low-pitched and darkly serious voice providing a soulful contrast to Yema's vivid soprano.

The second offering was a child's tale, of a brother and sister discovering magical creatures in the forest. Nanjala, as if one of the creatures herself, recited the fable with manic gestures, while Yema, Obiike, and the hornpipe player accompanied her in muted tones.

Nanjala and Yema concluded with the Fire Song. And as they sang, their hands suggested fire, moving between them, rising and falling, their fingers magical flames that floated through the air. The crowd watched with fascination as the two women—now seemingly possessed by the music—circled each other in front of the brazier, their blending voices casting high into the night.

When they finished, a few people applauded, most sat stunned, and many crossed themselves. Yema walked over and sat down next to Doçura. "That was wonderful," she told the girl, and handed her a cup of rum. "I've never heard you sing like that. Any moment I expected the goddess Yemanjá to rise out of the sea and sing with you." Yema thanked her and handed the cup back, then put her head against the nun's side, making herself as comfortable as she could ever be.

***

Ten days later, accompanied by excitement and much trepidation among the Africans, the Corajoso arrived at the Cape Verdes and dropped anchor in the Bahía del Sintra at the north end of Ilia da Brava. No other ships were in the harbor, and as far as anyone could tell, no military presence. And surprisingly, no one ventured out to greet them. A scattering of huts dotted the hillside above the shore, a few dugouts rested on the beach, but not a single person could be seen.

Captain Vincent ordered two boats put into the water while he and Obiike watched from the rail. If the shores proved safe, he intended to take on supplies. "What's your guess?" Vincent asked the African. "Why no people?"

"They're hiding in the hills," Obiike answered. "They think we're a slaver."

On the previous evening, the captain had called Obiike to his quarters. "You're a hardworking and able seaman," he told him, "and I'd like you to consider staying on. When we arrive home in the Netherlands, there will be some promotions. Additionally, I plan to purchase another vessel, and make my first mate Jansen her captain. Jozef will be promoted to first officer on this ship, and I'm offering you the second mate's position, either on the Corajoso or with Jansen."

This greatly pleased Obiike, though he also found it perplexing. He said, "With all respect, Captain, do you believe white sailors will take orders from a black man?"

"By Christ they will," Vincent responded, "or they can sail with the bloody Portuguese."

The African removed his hat, and shook Vincent's hand. "Sir, I am honored by your offer. I would like to think about it overnight. The answer's likely 'No,' but I'll have a firm decision in the morning."

"And what if you can't reclaim your plantation?"

"Then my people will need me even more. And I still may have some family on Brava, or at least tribesmen. That island is our home. We will somehow endure."

That ended it until the next morning when Obiike told Captain Vincent, "I want to live on Brava. If we can't regain the plantation, we'll start a new one with the two hundred reis."

"There will be a little more," the captain said. "Three gold reis for each of you. Your seaman's pay."

"Thank you, Sir. We never expected to get paid. We assumed our passage and board was enough."

"Well," he said, "you assumed wrong. And perhaps a year from now I will see you with an additional sum from the Brazil plantation."

By now, two boats were ready to depart, both with three

empty water kegs, a compliment of four rowers, and three additional sailors in each boat with muskets. Jozef, Obiike, and the other Cape Verde African man, a fellow named Uduak, were the last to climb down to the boats.

As they set off, Nanjala called down to Obiike. *"Jisie enyi 'm,"* she said in Guinea— "Good luck my friend." She turned to Yema and Doçura who stood close by. "If we find a welcome here," she asked, "will you ladies come ashore and see our island?"

"Of course," the nun replied. "By all means."

Nanjala continued to stare over the side as the boats moved away. She called to the other African women. "There's our lovely bonito. Let's catch some." Doçura and the girl looked also. Sure enough, right next to the Corajoso the waters teemed with the sleek fish, some nearly as large as Yema. The creatures darted everywhere, often breaking the surface in a flash of silver and rainbow as they chased smaller fish.

Captain Vincent ordered a boat lowered, and the three black women scampered down the net and prepared to fish. They used a stiff wooden pole about six feet long with a heavy line attached. The line was about the same length as the pole, and had a large fishhook tied to one end. A chicken feather was threaded through the eye of the hook.

The moment the lure hit the water, a fish grabbed it. Nanjala hefted the thrashing bonito into the boat where it was clubbed senseless and gutted. Soon the water boiled with fish as they fed on the bloody offal. Within ten minutes, the three women had a half-dozen large fish covering the bottom of the boat. Ten minutes more, and they had no place to stand. Sailors dropped a cargo net and the women began loading the bonito into it. Suddenly the boat lurched sideways. Several large sharks appeared in a frenzy of activity, feeding on the bonito and offal.

"Get out of there," someone yelled. The women climbed onto the net ladder just as the boat took a direct hit from a charging shark. The sailors retrieved the cargo net and, since the winch lines were still attached to the boat, hoisted it from the water. Everyone went to work, scraping out the guts and slicing the fish lengthwise. Soon there were fresh bonito pieces hanging from every shroud, and the deck slippery with fish blood and slime. Yema went around counting them. "Thirty-seven fish," she announced.

The African women, in typical carefree fashion—and seemingly unaffected by the encounter with the sharks—stripped bare and doused each other with buckets of seawater, then rinsed off their clothing and rung them out, hanging the garments over the animal fence to dry. The three disappeared down the forward hatch and emerged a few minutes later dressed and eager to sample the morning's catch. By now the decks were clean, and several bonito sizzled on the brazier. During the next few hours, they cooked the entire catch, thus preserving it for days to come.

Yema, not caring whether the fish was cooked or not, borrowed Doçura's dagger and cut strips of raw bonito, offering it to anyone who wished to try. The Europeans were reluctant until Doçura demonstrated her liking for it. "Raw fish and shellfish kept us alive after we fled Luís," she told everyone. "It's better cooked, but we had no fire."

One of the last to try was Lars Orlund, and only because Doçura and Yema teased him. He took a small bite, then handed it back to the women. "I'll leave eating raw fish to you natives," he said. At that moment, seeing these two females smile back at him and shake their heads in mock disapproval, he desperately wanted to say how much he loved them both. But he said nothing, fearing these sentiments would make him sound like a fool.

***

The two boats returned sometime after mid-afternoon. Even at a distance—riding low in the water—it was easy to see they were fully loaded. As the rowers drew closer, the onlookers on the Corajoso's rail were surprised there were no new people in the boats. Most everyone had assumed that at least a few Brava residents would come to visit.

For the first quarter-hour or so, the crew toiled to bring the new cargo onboard, eight kegs full of water, a great number of delicious-looking yellow melons, and a dozen clusters of date fruit, each bunch weighing more than ten pounds.

The African women began asking questions, mostly in Guinea. When Obiike and Uduak climbed over the rail, the two men looked very glum, and answered in Portuguese, purposely addressing their answers to Vincent who stood nearby. "Captain," Obiike said, "of the few members of our tribe who might have remained, none are left. And no one knows what happened to them. We found some

Africans from a tribe called the Kindiña." He made a futile gesture. "They're from the mainland, north somewhere. We've never heard of them."

Nanjala brought a slab of cooked fish, and the two men ate hungrily as they talked. "These fish are welcome," Udauk said. "At least our bonito have not vanished."

Obiike picked up the conversation about the Kindiñas. "They think we're slavers, and that's why none came back with us. There are no more than eight families living on this end of the island. Most of their people live to the south, by the Baía do Sul. All of them are refugees from a slave ship that ran aground about six months ago. They killed the slavers and burned the ship. Supposedly there are about twenty families living at Baía do Sul, enough to work the plantation if I can persuade them to move to this end of the island."

"So are you still going to stay on Ilia da Brava?" Vincent inquired, still hoping the Africans might change their minds.

"We'll talk it over," Obiike said, "but most likely." He nodded at the distant shore. "Our plantation was up the valley where that stream comes out. Most of it's still there, including the drying house. The grinding mill is in shambles, and the wheel's gone, but the cane situation is amazing. The fields are choked with weeds, but the cane's kept growing and spreading. It's covering an area half-again as large as when we left it.

"I think things can work out with the Kindiñas," Obiike continued. He pointed to the melons and date bunches. "They gave us this food in exchange for a promise that we would not bring any more white men on shore. They are afraid of disease, or maybe being kidnapped. If they've got muskets, we didn't see any."

Jozef spoke up. "We only got as far as the beach. They made us whites wait at the tree line. I can't complain. Look at all the food they gave us."

Tears welled in Obiike's eyes. "You'll have to excuse me, Captain. I feel very at home on this ship, and it truly pains me to leave." The other Africans nodded in agreement. Obiike turned and walked towards the bow. Yema and Nanjala followed him.

"I feel awful about you leaving," Yema said. "Just awful. Why don't you stay on the ship?"

"We can't stay, little one," Nanjala said. "We are people of the land, and no land will take us except perhaps here. All of us want to have families. That's not possible on the ship."

Yema took Nanjala's hand, and when they caught up with Obiike, she also took his. "You've been such good friends," the child said, and began to weep.

Obiike picked Yema up and set her on his shoulder. He pointed at the island. "What do you think the name of that mountain is?" he asked.

"I don't know," the girl sniffed. "But I wanted to explore it with you."

"It's called Pico de Fontes, Peak of Fountains."

"Fountains?"

"Yes. You see that dark cloud over the mountain? It's almost always there, and it's almost always raining. And all that rain makes rivers and streams that run everywhere on the island. So it's a very special mountain."

Nanjala took Yema from Obiike's shoulder and set the child in front of her. "Listen, little one," she said, "I will climb that mountain and think of you. And I will sit in the rain at the very top, and think of you. And at night when you dream, we will climb the mountain together." She paused and touched a finger to Yema's nose. "In fact, any night you want to dream of that mountain, I will climb it with you."

***

The next morning was one of good-byes. The Africans loaded their few possessions into the cargo net and had it lowered to the single boat that awaited them. A line of well-wishers said their farewells, and Captain Vincent embraced each African as they prepared to leave, giving the promised purse of gold coins to Obiike.

Earlier, Vincent and Obiike had prepared a list of supplies the Africans might need—including a grinding wheel—and Vincent promised to bring everything in about six months on his return voyage. Obiike offered to pay in advance, but the captain waived him off and said, "If you can't use the supplies, I can sell them for a solid profit at any sugar port in Brazil."

Now the boat was loaded and began to pull away, the five Africans sitting in the bow, the four sailors rowing, and Jozef steering from the stern. Nanjala cupped her hands and shouted at Yema. "All right, singing girl, think of me sitting in that cloud atop Pico de Fontes. That's where I'll be tomorrow."

Chapter 36

After a month of fair sailing, the Corajoso dropped anchor in the port of Los Llanos off Isla Santa Cruz, the most seaward of the Canary Islands. Since Los Llanos was controlled by the Spanish, Doçura decided it would be unwise for her and Yema to go onshore. Captain Vincent sent three boats into the town for supplies.

Although there were several ports-of-call available to merchant ships in the Canaries, Vincent knew the governor of Santa Cruz Island was the most tolerant of all. He had resupplied at Los Llanos twice before without incident after a small gift of cash to the harbormaster. Additionally, since there were no warships in the harbor, he did not expect the Corajoso to undergo the routine inspection that often took place when a Spanish military captain spotted a Dutch merchant. He'd undergone such searches before, but never with fugitives onboard. In the past, a cash payment to the inspecting officers usually put to rest any concerns they might have possessed.

Yema and Doçura hoped to explore the town with its colorful buildings, wide streets and, according to first mate Jansen, many parks with fountains, green lawns, and stately trees. Yema was also intrigued by the mountain spine that traced the entire length of the island. "Sister Leah, do you think Nanjala really climbed to the top of the cloudy peak on Ilia da Brava?"

"I'm certain she did," Doçura said as they watched the three boats pull away. "That's what she promised."

"Then why haven't I dreamt about it?"

"I don't know. Perhaps you will tonight." Nearly everyone aboard the Corajoso missed the Africans, and they were often the topic of conversation, many of which included speculations as to their fortunes, favorable or otherwise. Several times over the past month, people had asked, then pleaded with Yema to sing the Leopard or the Fire song, but the girl refused, saying she couldn't sing without Nanjala. Though Doçura knew this was foolery, she chose not to pressure the child about it.

A shout from the lookout drew everyone's attention seaward. "Captain Vincent, Sir, there's a large three-master heading this way. Mediterranean rigged. I think it's a Turk. Maybe the Rasuul Karim."

Vincent squinted at the approaching ship. "Run up the Netherlands flag," he shouted. "If it's Zaver Bariş, he'll know it's me." Then he turned to Enzo Henry who stood next to him on the rail. "I haven't seen Bariş in over a year. I wonder what that rascal's up to?"

As the ship came within a quarter mile of the Corajoso, she ran her red-crescent flag partway up the mainmast, then immediately back down. There was no doubt now; the visitor was the Rasuul Karim. At about a hundred yards out, the Turkish ship hove to, reefed its triangle foresail, dropped anchor, and made preparations to put a boat in the water. In the meantime, Doçura and Yema had moved to a position on the far side of the quarterdeck, out of the visitor's sight.

"Captain Vincent," Doçura called, "what do you want us to do?"

Vincent thought for a moment. "The captain is a friend, but a terrible gossip. Go to your quarters and stay by the window. We'll have our meeting up here, and you'll be able to hear us." The two women hurried to the rear hatch, stepped down a few stairs, then peered along the deck and through the rail. The side of the Rasuul was clearly visible as the rowers and officers climbed down the boarding net into their boat. The most conspicuous was a large figure dressed in a flowing red kaftan. The man also sported red boots and a turban of the same color.

"Is that him?" Yema asked.

"I assume so," Doçura said. "That's typical Turkish garb, at least for nobles and people of importance. If he's really rich, there will be gold threads woven through every inch of his clothing."

"Even his undergarments?" the girl asked. Yema assumed she was making a joke.

"That's what I hear."

The two women went down the stairs, into their cabin, and seated themselves by the window.

They could hear shouted greetings as the men came onboard, then formal greetings as Zaver Bariş introduced his officers. Captain Vincent did likewise, introducing Enzo Henry, Dr. Cardim, and his purser, and apologizing that his first and second mates and Lars Orlund were absent in port gathering supplies. The men took seats around the chart table next to the helm. Their voices could be heard clearly. Sounds of tea being served and sweet cakes passed around accompanied a lively discussion.

Bariş had a booming voice, and seemed to be dominating the conversation. While his speech was thickly accented, his Portuguese was quite cultured. Doçura concluded the Turk must have lived in Portugal prior to the Moors' expulsion. In that case, he would likely be sympathetic to the Jews. She next wondered if he was headed for Gibraltar, and then east into the Mediterranean. If so, she had a letter ready for her parents. *How nice,* Doçura thought, *to avoid the peril of my letter being on a Christian ship.*

After listening for a while, the women lost interest and moved on to other things, Doçura occupied with bringing the letter to her parents up to date, and Yema with her lessons. An hour later, they could hear the men leaving. A few minutes passed and Captain Vincent knocked at the door. "Your meeting sounded rather routine," Doçura told him, then nodded in Yema's direction. "So we turned to lessons and letter-writing." She pointed to the two parchment sheets on her table. "If Bariş is going to the Ottoman, I'd like to send my letter with him."

"Indeed he is," Vincent said. "He's going to resupply here, and then we'll convoy to Tangier. Safer than sailing alone. Many pirates between here and the Spanish coast. You can give him the letter there."

"Tangier? I thought our next port was Gibraltar?"

"Bariş told me that port is shut down. A Moorish rebellion of some sort. Only Iberian shipping allowed in. It won't be a problem, we can supply in Tangier."

"I heard him talking about dyewood. Did he say the price was 'sky-high?'"

"Yes. He's taking a load directly to Naples. Bariş says the price there for the red is fifteen gold reis per hundred-weight. That's likely more than I can get anywhere in Spain, Portugal, or even in Amsterdam."

Yema spoke up. "Then why don't we go to Naples?" Any new place sounded like an adventure to her.

Before Vincent could respond, Doçura asked, "Where is Bariş going from there? Istanbul?" Her heart skipped a beat. The pulse rushed in her ears.

"Yes," the captain said.

Almost breathlessly the nun asked, "And after that? South to

Antalya?"

Yema looked up from her work. Something had suddenly changed. Captain Vincent looked stricken. "Leah, please!" he said. "I didn't ask him."

At this moment, all three of them knew what this meant. Doçura's family lived in Antalya. Possibly she would take passage on the Rasuul Karim and sail for home. After an oppressive silence, she said, "Have Lars Orlund come and talk to me, and—" She looked at Yema. "No, come talk to *us.*" Doçura shook her head. "I'm sorry, dear Captain. I know Lars cares for me, but we need to have a conversation. I'm sure his hopes, and my plans, are very different."

To the women's surprise and the captain's too, tears brimmed in his eyes. In his entire adult life, he'd shed tears only three times before, when they buried his dear parents and his sister Beatrix. He said, "We all care for you, Leah. You and Yema. You've become our family."

"I know, Eider,"—She rarely used his first name—"but a family who can't show their face in public? Or even go out? What kind of life is that for us?"

"And will your family in Turkey accept Yema?" he asked.

Doçura felt a flash of anger, but it ebbed quickly when she looked at the child. Yema stared back and said, "Don't think I haven't thought that too."

The nun raised her hands in resignation. "Please, Captain, have Lars come and speak with us."

"I'm supposed to speak for him. His *oom.*"

"His uncle? His second?"

"Yes, that's our tradition. Is it not yours?"

"Similar. An uncle or a brother, but it's a bit of a sham."

"Sham?"

"That's because almost all marriages in the Jewish community are arranged by the families and a marriage broker. The couple-to-be has little choice. A man can only hope his bride is not too ugly or a shrew. The woman hopes the husband is not a tyrant of some sort." Leah did not tell the captain that she considered Lars Orlund quite handsome, and expected he would be a kind and thoughtful husband. But saying so would be misleading in the extreme, and much too forward.

At this point Leah found the conversation somewhat

humorous. "Except that my father is supposed to have a dowry to present." She put an arm around Yema. "This child is my dowry."

Yema made a face. "What's a dowry?"

Doçura reached out and took the captain's hand. "We are on the high seas. I have no country, and neither does Yema. Eider, we are fugitives. Traditions be damned. Tell Lars you've spoken to me, and I wish to hear from him directly."

Vincent dabbed his eyes with the back of his sleeve, smiling a little as he did. "Why am I not surprised to hear this?" he said. "I will indeed tell Lars."

***

Two days later, the Corajoso and Rasuul Karim unfurled their sails and headed into the open sea. They gathered a steady west breeze that brought the vessels close to the African coast. From there they hoped to pick up southerlies that might sweep them north along the rim of Africa to Tangier. The winds did not cooperate, so the going remained slow, each ship burdened with lengthy tacks and making only slight northern progress.

The frequent comings about, resetting sails, and the steeply slanting decks weighed heavily on both crews. One of the most affected on the Corajoso was Lars Orlund. He needed to talk to Doçura, but lacked the confidence to do so. The specter of Captain Bariş's ship, almost always in sight, became a painful reminder that arriving in Tangier might forever end his connection with Doçura and Yema. And Leah didn't make things any easier. She remained as friendly and agreeable as ever, almost as if saying, "I know this is difficult, so take your time." Or did her behavior indicate indifference?—As if she might say, "I know you wish to discuss marriage, but I am not interested."

The winds gradually shifted to the southeast, allowing the convoy to take a more direct route northward. With the shift of wind came a bountiful harvest of flying fish. The "little angels," as everyone called them, leapt in droves from the waters around the ships. The wind swept many of them onto the deck where sailors collected the fish by the dozens. Soon there were long strings of flying fish hanging from every shroud. Most would be left to dry for a few days, but there were plenty for eating right away—skewered on thin poles and roasted over the brazier.

A few of the seamen knew that flying fish eggs were the

tastiest of all. They carefully squeezed the roe from the females as they held the fish just so, directing the stream of orange-colored eggs into their open mouths. Yema joined in eagerly. Soon she had fish eggs plastered all over her face, clothing, and hair.

Orlund, Leah, and Dr. Cardim sat on the quarterdeck stairs sharing a basket of roasted flying fish. The three of them watched Yema's antics as she continued to squirt fish eggs into her mouth and went on joking with the sailors who were also eating the fish roe. Cardim stood and excused himself, saying as he left, "No amount of civilization will ever take the native out of that child."

For some reason, the remark made Leah glance over at the Rasuul Karim which sailed three hundred yards to port, and slightly ahead of the Corajoso. Lars Orlund noticed the glance. He swallowed hard and said, "People wonder if you're going to the Ottoman on that ship after we get to Tangier."

"I've thought about it some, Lars. But to put any speculation to rest, we're going to the Netherlands." Orlund started to respond, but Leah raised her hand and said, "Let me explain."

"Please," he said. It was just as well that Leah continued to talk. At that moment he felt such a strong sense of relief, he wasn't sure he could say anything.

"Last fall, when the captain was returning to Amsterdam, I gave him a letter for my parents. I told them about Yema and what the two of us had been through. Perhaps there will be an answer waiting when we get to the Netherlands. Who knows? Half these letters get lost or stolen." She looked up to see Yema coming their way. Hurriedly she said, "Lars, I've no idea if my family will accept her. At least I know where I stand with you and—" She stopped when the girl arrived.

"Out of fish roe," the child said, brushing the eggs off her tunic.

Orlund patted the stair tread next to him. "Come sit with us. You smell like a fish market, but I'll put up with it." Yema plopped down next to him. He made a face and scooted away. "Just don't touch me."

"Yes, Senhor Orlund."

"Actually it's *Meneer* Orlund. I hear you're going to the Netherlands, so you'd better learn Dutch."

The girl looked at Leah. "Is that true?" she asked.

"Of course it's true, Yema. I've never said otherwise."

"It's just that I've heard talk. I mean... That Turkish ship and all. I know how much you miss your family." The child smiled at Orlund. "Meneer Lars, I can't wait until we get to your farm. I can tend the goats and chickens, and you can teach me Dutch."

Orlund picked some fish eggs out of the girl's hair. "We can start today if you want, but first I have something important to say to you both." He paused and took a deep breath. "I've grown very fond of you, Yema, and of Sister Leah as you call her. I once had a wife. Her name was Greta, but she died a few years ago. We had no children. I've been very melancholy since she died, so I traveled a lot, and worked hard in an effort to shed this sadness. But it has followed me like a terrible ghost, always lurking in the shadows."

He reached over and took Leah's hand. She let him do so, responding with a mild squeeze and a glance that pleased him. "When I first met the both of you at the plantation, I began to feel less sad. And as I got to know you, my sadness ebbed further. Do you remember that evening when you two fixed dinner for me? When Porõ ate that lizard in my óga?"

"I remember," Yema said.

"Well, after that night, my ghost of sadness went away. Vanished. I hate to say it, but I felt it coming back when I thought you might leave us at Tangier." He released Leah's hand and made the sign of the cross. Then he stood and seated himself to one side so he could look at them both. "I would like to give up my travels and stay at my farm. I want to have a family. I would like you to be my family, if you will have me."

Leah glanced at Yema who was smiling and on the verge of saying something. The woman put a finger to her lips. "Yema, give me a minute to gather my thoughts." When the girl again started to speak, she motioned a second time for her to stay silent. Finally, Leah said, "Lars, I am flattered beyond words, and honored too. Since we're not going to vanish to the east, let's give this some time. Yema and I need to see the Netherlands for ourselves."

***

Two days later, the Corajoso and the Rasuul Karim sailed into the crowded North African port of Tangier. Since there appeared to be mainly Turkish, Portuguese, and Spanish ships in the harbor, and with no Dutch vessels in sight, Captain Vincent and second mate Jozef went over to the Rasuul. After a brief conference with Bariş, they decided to go ashore with the Rasuul's resupply crew to determine if there would be problems for Dutch merchants.

"You can't visit the port looking like Dutch officers," Zaver Bariş said in his expansive manner. His steward and an assistant brought forth two brilliantly colored kaftans, wide-brimmed hats of matching colors, red for Captain Vincent, and olive for Jozef, and matching malakī shoes with turned-up toes. "Now," Bariş said, "you will look like proper officers in the service of the caliph."

Vincent thought to say, "We'll look like clowns," but held his tongue. Once they arrived at the harbormaster's office, everyone stayed in the boats except Bariş and his purser, the latter along to offer the expected bribe. Although the purser was a Muslim, he dressed himself in Spanish garb since, as Bariş explained it, "Men of Allah do not soil their hands with bribes."

"And fish do not swim," Jozef mumbled under his breath when he heard this.

After a half-hour, with everyone waiting in the boats and sweating in the hot sun, Bariş returned from the harbormaster shack. "Well," he said, "it seems there is a prohibition against Dutch traders. Not only here, but across the strait in Gibraltar, and all along the Portuguese and Spanish coasts, whether the Atlantic or east into the Mediterranean."

"Why?" Vincent asked.

"They claim you northern folk are involved in illegal trading of some sort. But what they're really trying to do is break the back of the Dutch dyewood business. Corner the market for themselves."

"Can we resupply here?" Jozef inquired.

"I'm afraid not," the Turk said, "but nonetheless, I have good news. Number one, I will resupply for the Corajoso; and number two, the French port of Gujan-Mestras, a little ways north of the Spanish border, will accept your dyewood. Apparently the price is as high there as I can get in Naples.

"I enjoy commerce much more," he continued, rubbing his hands together, "when there is a little intrigue. In this case, it seems the French are quite eager to undermine the Spanish embargo, and the Basque smugglers are equally happy to sell purloined dyewood to Spanish and Portuguese millers."

Next, the Rasuul's captain had a short conversation with his resupply crews in the other three boats, then sent the fourth boat back to the Dutch ship. "Dear Captain," Bariş said to Vincent before they left, "Give my purser your list of supplies, and we will get them. I assume you'll need water as well. Bring your ship next to ours on the seaward side, and we can load the barrels after dark."

"I am most obliged," Vincent said as they departed. "If ever I get the chance, I'll repay you ten-fold."

"Two-fold will be quite sufficient," Zaver Bariş said with a grin.

Chapter 37

During the late afternoon—their third day in Port Tangier—and with the resupply nearly finished, Captain Vincent sought out Leah. "I've invited Captain Bariş and his officers to dine with us this evening. They've been quite helpful, and it's the least I can do. I'd like you and Yema to attend."

"Why now? Ever since being here, we've kept out of sight."

"You're in no danger," the captain said. "Tomorrow we sail north, and the Rasuul to the east." He realized his answer was not truly relevant. After a pause, he said, "All right, I'm being selfish. Women are almost never allowed on Turkish ships, and I want to twist his tail a little. It's a game that he and I play. Will you go along?"

"Have you given his purser my letter yet?"

"I will right after dinner, along with settling my accounts. I still owe them for supplies. The letter will just be another matter of business. It will draw less attention that way."

Leah looked out her window at the Turkish ship floating just fifty yards to starboard. "I'm sorry Captain. No. Yema and I will be under great scrutiny, and I think it's unwise."

"Perhaps you're right," he said. "Though it's going to be an excellent dinner. I'll have the steward serve you in your quarters."

"That will do nicely," she replied. "Thank you."

The meal was indeed excellent, all the ingredients fresh from the port, roast bullock, yellow squash with bacon and black syrup, beet greens, and to Leah's delight, oranges slices dusted in sugar. "I've not tasted oranges in five or six years," she told Yema. The child was equally impressed, having never tasted the fruit before.

The dinner activity next door concluded with rounds of brandy. Although the Rasuul officers were devout Muslims, and prohibited by the Koran from drinking spirits, they imbibed without hesitation. Zaver Bariş explained, "We will sample your strong drink, dear Captain Vincent, as our salute to your hospitality."

Since the evening remained balmy and the seas calm, the group of men moved to the open wheelhouse just above the women's cabin. Their several conversations, story-telling, and conviviality continued. Leah listened casually, then suddenly became attentive when she heard the Turkish captain say, "Captain Vincent, the letter you gave my purser earlier, did you say it was addressed to Antalya?" She heard Vincent answer in the affirmative, then Bariş request the letter from the purser. For a short while, neither captain spoke. She concluded Bariş was studying the address in the weak lantern light.

The next words from the Turk brought her to her feet. She moved as close as she could to the open window. Bariş said, "I've heard of the family Saulo. They are quite prosperous I think. Jews from Lisbon. It seems to me I delivered some bricks of theirs to the Sultan of Izmir."

Lars Orlund asked, "How long ago? Did you meet them?"

"No, never met them," the Turk answered. "It was three or four years back, a small consignment. Just sent in on a lighter."

"What kind of bricks?" someone asked.

"I did not see them," the captain answered. "They were packed quite carefully. Only a few hundred pounds. I think they were for decorations of some sort."

At hearing this meager, but so heartfelt scrap of news about her family, Leah bent double, unable to stand or catch her breath. She lay down on the floor, crying so hard it felt as if her eyelids were turning inside out. Yema brought a pillow and put it under her friend's head, weeping as well, puzzled by her own feelings of sorrow.

***

The Corajoso weighed anchor at nine bells. An hour earlier, the Rasuul Karim had left their side and sailed east into the Mediterranean. Lars Orlund joined the two women on the rail as they watched the Turkish ship depart. Without looking at him, Leah told Lars about overhearing the previous evening's conversation. She knew her eyes were red and swollen from crying.

"I thought you might have heard," he said. "If not, I was going to tell you."

"Should I have come on deck and introduced myself?" she asked. "Maybe he would visit my family?"

"I don't think that's likely," Orlund said. He sensed she was highly upset, and wished to ease her discomfort. "My understanding," he continued, "is that Bariş plans to pick up olive oil in Naples after he sells his dyewood. Then he's going to Istanbul. From there, he'll bring silks to Brazil, and return to Europe with dyewood. He said your letter would be given to a coastal trader for delivery to points south."

Leah looked at him briefly, then turned away, her hair blowing a little in the wind. She detested feeling vulnerable, and even more-so when she couldn't hide it. In hopes of making a further connection with her, Orlund said, "I'm confident your letter will get there. The name of the Turk's ship, Rasuul Karim, means Generous Messenger. That has to be a good sign."

Leah felt a strong sense of relief, not because of what he'd just said, but that the Dutchman understood her mood. This time she did not hesitate to look at him, and said, "That's thoughtful of you, Lars."

At that point he excused himself, citing a need to help store the last of the resupply goods.

When the Corajoso left the harbor, Leah and Yema found themselves surrounded by activity as the ship gathered the wind and came under sail. Sailors on deck toiled everywhere, securing the vessel for the journey, many of the men perched in the rigging adjusting canvas and hauling sails into place. The two women moved to the port rail and looked east, the Rasuul Karim appearing now as just a speck of sail on the horizon, and almost even with the Gibraltar promontory that loomed gigantically to its north.

"If we climbed to the crow's nest," Yema asked, "could we see Antalya?"

"No, sweet child. It's two thousand miles distant. At least two weeks' travel."

"I didn't know the world was so big," said Yema. "How far have we come from Brazil?"

Leah counted on her fingers as she considered the question.

"Oh, I think twice as far. Four thousand miles. Probably more since we didn't come directly here." The women continued to stand at the rail as the Corajoso moved into the Atlantic and turned north. Soon, even the great hulk of Gibraltar began to retreat below the horizon.

Enzo Henry joined them, commenting on the beautiful sailing weather.

Yema said, "I think we're heading west as well as north. Why is that?"

"I see you've not lost your sense of direction," Henry said. "And you are right. As long as Spain and Portugal are on our flank, we'll remain far out at sea. Both the Spanish and Portuguese have coastal patrols that imperil us. We hear their so-called embargo has expanded to seizing Dutch and French ships."

"So how long until we get to the Netherlands?" the girl asked.

He gazed up at the mainsails. "If this wind keeps up, I'd say less than three weeks. Maybe a little longer. In ten days or so, we'll stop at Gujan-Mestras on the French coast. It will take two days to offload the dyewood if we can sell it there."

"Then another week or two to Almere?" Leah asked.

"Yes," he answered. "Again, it depends on—"

Yema interrupted him. She gave Enzo Henry a devilish look. "Sister Leah needs to know so she can decide whether to marry Lars Orlund or not."

Leah was horrified. "Oh Mother of God, Yema, how could you say such a thing?"

"It's important," the girl said. "I want to know."

"Enzo," Leah said, "I apologize for this foolish girl. She has no sense of propriety."

The navigator could not suppress his laughter. "Believe me," he said, "it's all right. Everyone wants to know."

Leah stared daggers at Yema and said, "When I decide, I'll have Miss Big-Mouth here announce it from the crow's nest." She took Yema's arm. "If you would excuse us, Enzo, I must have a chat with my adopted daughter. Or should I say my former adopted daughter." She led the girl towards the bow, and settled herself on the forward hatch cover. Taking Yema by the shoulders she said, "Never in my life have I ever been angry at you. But I am now. I am angry and upset. How could you have said—"

"I'm sorry," the girl answered. "It just slipped out."

"Do you understand that some things are private between people?"

"Not really."

Leah closed her eyes and thought. "In your Indian community," she said, "this would be an open subject. Right? I don't believe there is a word for 'private' in the Caeté language, or in Tupi for that matter. Is that correct?"

The girl nodded.

"Well in Europe, some matters are private. It's something you've got to learn."

"But Lars asked both of us."

"And why do you think he did so?" Leah asked.

Yema shrugged. "I don't know."

"Because he sees us as a family, Yema. Me as his wife and you, if we get married, as his daughter. It's an honor, and he's very unusual. Most men don't even want stepchildren."

The girl seemed puzzled, not knowing what next to say. Finally she said, "What's a step—?" Still struggling for the right words, she asked, "Am I a stepchild?"

Leah drew Yema close and hugged her, stroking the girl's hair as she did so. "Oh sweetheart, you are my daughter always. And if I marry Lars, you will be his daughter."

"So are you going to marry him?" the girl asked, her words muffled in Leah's clothing.

"I don't know. I've got to collect my thoughts." She pointed to the animal pen. "Go fuss with Venus and her babies. We'll talk about this later."

***

After a week's sailing, the Corajoso rounded Spain's Cabo del Norte and headed northwest into the Bay of Biscay. The French port of Gujan-Mestras lay a few days ahead. Leah and Yema had talked about their new life in Almere until there was nothing left to discuss. Once everything was wrung out, all that remained was a list of overwhelming uncertainties. While life with Lars Orlund might be a blessing, neither of them wanted to live in secret. So Leah decided to tell him that they were determined to wait and see what faced them in the Netherlands. When Yema inquired as to her love for Lars, she said, "I care for him, but cannot love him. At least not now. Our lives ahead are too uncertain."

The next day they asked Lars to join them for dinner in their quarters, having arranged with the cook to prepare a special meal. After doing so, Leah realized the invitation might give Orlund the wrong impression; so keeping this in mind, she and Yema asked him to sit with them in the afternoon sun on the foredeck by the animal pen. With the dinner scheduled that evening, he sensed the discussion of important subjects was at hand.

Lars—rarely at a loss for words—thought of a sailing question to ask Yema. He knew this would, at least at the start, prevent things from getting too awkward. As they sat down on the hatch cover, he said, "Yema, see how the sails are full of wind. If that's so, why isn't it windy down here?"

The child put her hand in the air. "It's a little windy down here, but not that much."

"Now look at the waves," Orlund said. "The wind's really blowing out there." The Corajoso was heaving through yard-high rollers, the wind catching foam and spray at their crests and rolling the froth across the sea. "You can see the wind is quite—"

"I know!" she shouted, jumping to her feet. "I know!"

"Well?"

"It's because we're below the rail and it's protecting us from the wind."

Lars shook his head. "Nope." He combed his fingers through his beard, then said, "Look at that rag in the shroud. It's way above the deck and it's barely moving. You could climb up there, and you would still feel hardly any wind."

"Well then, I don't know," the girl said. "Anyway, we want to talk to you about our life in Almere."

"No," Leah said, *"I* want to talk with Lars about our life in Almere. When I'm through, if I've left anything out, then you may ask him."

"Yes, Sister Leah," Yema said with obvious exaggeration. The girl sat down, arms crossed, and stared straight ahead, a trace of lunacy in her eyes. If there was going to be any awkwardness for the three of them, Yema had quickly put an end to it.

"You know, Lars," Leah said, "I may just leave her with you in the Netherlands and continue north." She reached over and took his hand. *Nothing is as it should be,* she thought, *and for the past nine years, any possibility of my life having some semblance of order has been dashed by events no one could have ever foreseen.*

"Lars," Leah continued, "as I said before, your offer to make us part of your family is flattering and an honor. More than we ever expected." She avoided the word marriage because he had not used it. "But we want to wait. Let's see what our life is like in Almere. If we have to always stay indoors and out of sight, or in disguise if we go out, what kind of life is that?"

"That's pretty much what I expected you to say. There's a cottage a short distance from the main house, and you ladies can stay there."

Leah squeezed his hand and said, "Thank you Lars. You are a unique man to show such understanding." She turned to Yema. "Anything to add?"

The girl shook her head and sighed. "I guess not, but I'll have an answer to the wind question at dinner tonight."

"Excellent," Orlund replied. He stood and stretched, feeling intense disappointment, and some relief too—Leah had not completely closed the door to his offer. "Until dinner then, ladies. And thank you."

The two of them watched Lars work his way aft along the tilting deck. As the ship churned through the waves, and the Dutchman grabbed a halyard for balance, Leah's thoughts turned to darker notions. Notions that had haunted her ever since Yema suggested Orlund might have an interest in her. Leah doubted she could ever tell Yema about them, and certainly not Lars. She really didn't want to marry. Not ever. The idea of bringing more children into this world frightened her. Any girlish ideals she'd once entertained in Lisbon about a husband and family had been buried, or torn apart, or sundered in some other fashion, by the Inquisition, the frightful behavior of the Spanish and Portuguese, the Church, and even the Indians for that matter.

Well, at least there was one thing she could tell Yema. To introduce the subject in an indirect manner, Leah said, "I don't think Lars considers me a nun anymore. He certainly wouldn't have—" She stopped when Yema turned and gave her what appeared to be an almost insolent look. "What now?" she asked.

The child shook her head and, as if instructing a four-year-old, said, "No one considers you a nun anymore. Not since we left Brazil. Or maybe even before."

"That's news to me," Leah said. "Now, may I continue?"
Yema nodded.

"I no longer consider myself Sister Mãe da Doçura. I am Leah Anna Saulo, neither Catholic nor Jew, but perhaps some of both."

Something in what she said struck Yema deeply. Her intense, dark eyes shone with tears. "May I still call you 'Sister Leah?'" the girl asked. "Even though you're my mother, 'Sister Leah' just sounds right to me."

Now it was Leah's turn to be struck. She hugged the girl to her, more fiercely than she'd ever done before. "You've never called me mother until just now, and I love you dearly for it."

***

Early the next day, the Corajoso cautiously approached the port of Gujan-Mestras. Captain Vincent put his two best lookouts in the crow, and listened to their every observation. The only warships they spotted were French, and these vessels appeared to be patrolling at the outer perimeter of the sizeable merchant fleet anchored inside the shallow harbor.

"Give me a flag count," the captain called to the lookouts.

The two men in the crow counted. After a pause, one of them called down, "One Portuguese, three Dutch, two French, two Spanish, three I can't identify, and one Turk."

Leah and Yema stood on the quarterdeck next to the wheelhouse. What they saw in the harbor was unlike anything they'd ever seen before. There were five, large floating platforms—"barges" Enzo Henry called them—and each had a ship moored along its side. One actually had two ships docked there, one on each end. All the barges were stacked with trade goods as crews actively unloaded the ships. Outsized, oar-driven boats with six rowers each were ferrying the merchandise toward shore.

"Why are there Spanish and Portuguese ships in the harbor?" Leah asked. "I thought they were banned."

"Gold talks," Henry answered. "If they can get a better price for their cargos here, they pay a bribe to the commander of those French warships."

From what they could see, a great variety of things were being offloaded, casks of sugar, stacks of dyewood, covered bundles of cloth or wool, or perhaps rugs from the Turkish ship, and cattle, sheep, and goats.

As the Corajoso moved closer to one of the French frigates, an officer—apparently the ship's captain—in a fancy red-and-black uniform called over to them. "Greetings, Captain, from the French Crown and the port of Gujan-Mestras. What do you carry, Sir?" Leah was surprised the man's accented Portuguese was so precise. She had expected to hear French.

Captain Vincent picked up his speaking trumpet. "Thank you, Captain, for making us welcome. We carry dyewood. What is the price today?"

"Fourteen gold reis per hundred-weight of red. Nine for orange. Five for black."

Vincent conferred with Lars Orlund and his purser while Leah explained to Yema what she understood about the goings-on. "As you can see," she said, "Portuguese currency and the Portuguese language dominate commerce everywhere." Leah turned again to Enzo Henry. "Why so little ceremony?" she asked.

"I guess they've got more business than they can handle," he answered.

In the meantime, the French captain directed the Corajoso to one of the barges. "There's a dyewood broker there, *Messieurs*. He will handle the details."

As the ship—driven only by its aft trysail—moved slowly towards barge, Captain Vincent ordered a boat readied. He turned to Leah and Yema. "Put on your fancy clothes, ladies. After we get docked, let's visit the port and see what we can find."

Chapter 38

Once moored alongside the dyewood barge, the business of selling and unloading began. After the terms were settled, Vincent left his purser and the first and second mates to supervise the activity. The rest of the officers and the two women departed in a ship's boat for their excursion to Audenge, the small town at the head of the Gujan-Mestras estuary.

As the group neared the entrance of the estuary, they were met by a French military craft who provided an escort to *"Le quai pour les visiteurs, "* as the officer in the boat called it, "The dock for visitors." Once there, the escort disembarked from his boat and introduced himself as *"Offiucer* Jérôme." He was a rotund gentleman, about fifty years of age, with carefully groomed gray hair, a long mustache, and a friendly demeanor. When introduced to Leah and Yema, he made an awkward bow and, in hesitant Portuguese, expressing his delight at meeting, "Such charming ladies of the sea."

To everyone's surprise, Leah answered Jérôme in French, explaining to him that her great-grandfather Marcel was once a citizen of France, then to everyone else, "Because of my great-grandfather, that was a second language in our home." She left out the fact that Hebrew was also spoken in her household, information that no one needed to know.

While they trudged along the stone-lined path to the village, it became obvious why only boats of commerce were allowed inside the upper reaches of the estuary. Officer Jérôme pointed to the many craft ferrying goods to the offloading stations that lined the waterfront at the foot of the town. "We are so busy these days," he said, "there is no room for anything but boats with trade goods. And as you can see, it is faster to walk." Indeed, portions of the narrow estuary were clogged with boats, those loaded heading inland, and those empty heading back to the bay. Captain Vincent and crew also knew that having an escort was a way for the French to glean information from visitors.

Once the group arrived in Audenge, Officer Jérôme excused himself, saying that he would return in two hours with, *"un délicieux déjeuner,"* "a delightful luncheon." They found the small town bustling with activity, mules and donkeys loaded with supplies— coming and going—the same for carts heaped with goods, and visitors and townspeople browsing among the many stalls set up to sell almost anything imaginable. Captain Vincent bought a keg of fragrant red wine and another of syrupy rum that tasted of almonds. Not to be outdone, Lars Orlund purchased two kegs of the most expensive brandy. These heavy items were set aside to be picked up later on the way back to the dock.

At the next stall, Leah selected three headscarves for herself, one red with an embroidered black design, one a plain yellow, and the third, a brilliant green, also with black embroidery. "Pick out three for yourself," she told Yema. The child did so, taking her time with a dozen or so, asking the group for their opinions. The third one the girl selected, a yellow scarf similar to Leah's, but with a brown design, she looped over her shoulders, tying it neatly, and adjusting it in place like a decorative shawl.

"You are a lady of fashion," Leah told her.

In the midst of their shopping, Captain Vincent spotted two men dressed in gold caftans, obviously officers from the Turkish ship in the harbor. Taking Enzo Henry along, he strode over and introduced himself. With tightly reserved manners and more than a little condescension, the Turks accepted the introductions. Their behavior changed abruptly—as if the captain and Henry were old comrades—when Vincent said, "I am good friends with Captain Zaver Bariş of the Rasuul Karim. We were together in Tangier less than two weeks ago."

After exchanging a few yarns about Bariş, the conversation turned to commerce. Vincent disclosed they were selling dyewood and intended to return to Amsterdam mostly empty. The Turkish captain recounted his rather difficult voyage from Istanbul with a cargo of silk garments, ornamental rugs, and olive oil purchased in Sardinia, "Goods now being offloaded as we speak." When asked about his return voyage, the Turk replied, "We'll take on wine, spirits, and cork here, sell the wine and spirits in Palermo, and replace them with olive oil. Then it's straight back to Istanbul."

Vincent remarked that they had seen loads of cork being ferried out to the bay this morning. "Yes," the Turkish captain said, "That was ours. Cork is so bulky and lightweight, we'll not stow it in the holds, just stack the slabs on deck and cover it with oilcloth. We'll only be two-thirds full when we leave here, so we'll pick up something else in Tangier, or Gibraltar if it's open. I'd like to get my hands on some of that fine Spanish leather, and silver jewelry if we can find it."

With the pleasantries concluded, Vincent and Henry went looking for Leah and the others. They found them in front of an apothecary, everyone waiting on Dr. Cardim who was inside the little shop purchasing remedies of various sorts. The doctor emerged looking quite pleased with himself. He said, "This shop has more medicines than I've ever seen before. Stuff from all over the world. I'm going to have several large bundles. Let's pick them up on our way back."

At the very end of the street, they found a seller of jewelry, a Gypsy man and woman working out of a cart with baubles displayed on every surface. They had a small monkey dressed like a Spanish nobleman. The animal sat atop the cart gesturing and making chittering sounds at everyone.

Orlund insisted on buying the ladies gifts, telling them to, "Pick out whatever you find pleasing."

Leah, somewhat embarrassed by the offer, agreed after a brief hesitation. Yema, as usual unperturbed by any thought of propriety, yet polite to a fault, said, "Thanks, Meneer Lars. You are so very kind." Then she turned to Leah and said in Caeté, *"Peẽ hecha che japo hai Úva- úva,"* "You notice I did not call him Papa."

"You do," she responded in clear Portuguese, "and I'll sell you to these Gypsies. They'll dress you up and put a collar around your neck like that monkey."

"What did she say?" Orlund asked.

Leah glared at Yema and replied, "The child said, 'I must learn to keep my mouth shut.'" Her glare swept to Dr. Cardim who she knew understood Yema.

He backed away with his hands in the air. "I didn't hear a thing," he said. "Not a single thing."

Yema disappeared to the other side of the cart, while Leah stood in place, collecting her thoughts. The child trotted from behind the cart followed by the Gypsy woman who complimented Yema on her, "Wonderful taste in jewelry." Indeed the piece was tastefully pretty, a dark blue, moonstone pendant flecked with silver highlights. The stone hung on a delicate silver chain that added to its appeal. Leah watched the girl closely, wondering if the piece would remind her of Agato and his shell necklace. If it did, Yema gave no indication of it. But Leah felt a brief wave of sadness. For just a moment, she held her hand against the gold chain beneath her garment and said a quick prayer for Agato.

Leah selected a filigreed silver wristband with a polished orange and brown agate in an oval setting. Lars Orlund appraised the choices as "Exceptional," and happily paid for them. After thanking Lars, she turned back to the cart and purchased two silver combs, one for herself, and one she presented to Yema. The child could not miss the admonition in Leah's eyes when handed the gift.

A few minutes later, Officer Jérôme appeared, and announced, *"Messieurs et madames,* luncheon is served." They followed the Frenchman to the edge of town, into a small park with a scattering of oak trees. In the shade of one of the larger ones, there sat a cart with a donkey grazing nearby, the cart's driver resting a little ways off, and a broad table covered with a white tablecloth. At the end of the table, two Negro attendants—a man and a woman in starched white livery—stood at attention awaiting the guests. Leah considered asking if they were slaves, but reminded herself, *You're back in Europe. Get used to it*, then found herself wondering if Lars had slaves on his farm. *Oh well*, she thought, *we will find out soon enough.*

The luncheon was indeed impressive. As the guests seated themselves in cushioned wicker chairs around the linen-covered table with its elegant place settings—rose-decorated dishware, polished silver cutlery, and napkins with gold stitching, they viewed a remarkable display of food: Heaps of roast partridge, a fragrant carrot-and-raisin salad, goblets of white wine with the scent of peaches and hazelnuts, pickled beets done with vinegar, nutmeg, and black syrup, and a saffron-egg custard in individual silver cups crusted with caramel glaze.

Just as Captain Vincent finished the first toast, "To *Offiucer* Jérôme. For his generous welcome and delightful lunch," the ship's purser and First Mate Jansen came striding toward the table. After being introduced to the French officer, the two men seated themselves, and in turn saluted Jérôme with raised goblets.

"Gentlemen," Vincent asked, "how did this morning's commerce go?"

"Very well," the purser said. He lifted his leather shoulder bag onto the table. "Four hundred and twenty-five gold reis. Somewhat more than we expected."

"Excellent," Vincent exclaimed, and raised a toast to *"Le commerce de Français."*

The luncheon continued for almost an hour, with animated conversations and many goblets of wine consumed. The two attendants circled the table, serving food and replenishing the wine. The many toasts finally got the best of Yema. She mumbled an excuse, then left the table and sat down for a nap, dozing with her back against a nearby oak tree. A short ways off, the cart driver had a kettle of tea boiling on a small fire.

While the tea was being served, a noisy disturbance broke out at the far edge of the park. Everyone looked to see a ragged assembly of people, men, women, and children, being escorted by a cadre of

French soldiers who urged the group forward with curses and threats. The loudest voice came from an elderly, white-bearded man in a tattered black robe and knitted blue cap who was arguing with one of the soldiers. The soldier jammed his musket against the fellow's chest, thrusting him back into the arms of his comrades. Obviously hurt, he fell to his knees, unable to catch his breath. The procession halted for a short time while the old man, helped by his friends, struggled to his feet.

There was no mistaking who this bearded Spaniard was. By his garb, Leah knew he was a rabbi. The people with him had to be Jews.

Before she could say anything, Vincent asked Officer Jérôme, "What is this about?"

"Those are Jews from Spain," the Frenchman said. "Fleeing the Inquisition. There were caught crossing the border."

Vincent continued, "What will happen to them?"

"We've held the Jews in a camp a short distance from here," Jérôme said. "We're just moving them elsewhere. Our border guard was supposed to be here a week ago and take them back." He paused and rubbed his chin, at last saying, "They are just riffraff, and we're tired of feeding them."

Leah, struggling to keep a level voice, said, "Officer Jérôme, if they're forced back to Spain, won't they be tortured and killed?"

"But of course," Jérôme said. "As it should be for all heretics."

Despite her disgust and shock at the plight of these Jews, Leah sensed there was something in the Frenchman's manner. She couldn't be sure. Perhaps in the way he phrased his words. But she was much too drunk to give it much thought. On impulse she said in Hebrew, "*T'h vmt l mtchvvn lzh,*" "You really don't mean that."

Officer Jérôme's face registered a mixture of fear and surprise. He blurted out, "My allegiance is clear." He stood up and moved away from the table, quite uncertain as to what he'd just heard.

Leah bade him stop. "You are among friends," she said. "My great-grandfather Marcel Saulo was a Jew. Many believe he was a Saddiq." She turned and addressed the others. "A Saddiq is a Just Man, one who risks his life to save others."

Jérôme stopped and slowly approached Leah. In a quiet voice he said, "My grandparents on my father's side were Jews. I do not hate the Hebrew race. Quite the opposite. But in the current situation, there is little I can do."

Lars Orlund spoke up. "Officer Jérôme, you just said you were tired of feeding them. How much would it cost me to buy the whole lot?"

The Frenchman blinked several times, obviously perplexed by the question. "Monsieur Orlund," he stammered, "what do you mean?"

"I require workers for my farm. I'll buy those people and take them with me." Orlund had no intention of taking them to the Netherlands, but felt a need to do something. Staying in Leah's favor demanded it.

Officer Jérôme said, "I cannot make that decision. I must talk to my commanding officer." Still standing, he picked up his mug of tea and took a drink, then moved to seat himself again at the table.

Feeling the full effects of the wine, and holding onto a chair for balance, Lars Orlund rose to his feet. "Let's go now," he said. We're hoping to weigh anchor in the morning." Next, speaking in Dutch, he rattled off several quick sentences to Vincent. The Frenchman did not stand and appeared frozen in place. Orlund strode forward, took Jérôme by the arm, and walked off, dragging the man with him.

As soon as the two were out of earshot, Captain Vincent began giving orders. "Jansen, come with me. We're going to find that Turkish captain I met this morning. If he's not in the village, we'll row out to his ship. How many boats do we have at the visitors' dock?"

"Two, Sir."

"That will work," the captain said. Next he addressed the purser and Enzo Henry. "Take two hundred gold reis for Orlund and give me your shoulder bag with the rest." To Dr. Cardim and Leah he said, "Hire the donkey cart and pick up our goods in town. Meet me at the dock." As he and Jansen left, Vincent gave Leah a smile. "And don't forget to take the kid."

Dr. Cardim offered the cart driver ten copper reis to hire him for the rest of the afternoon. After conferring with the two attendants, he agreed, and proceeded to harness the donkey. Leah looked into the cart, and seeing nothing but the bare wood floor, took the table cloth and folded it into a pillow. Stuffing the cloth into a front corner, she picked up Yema and laid her on her side with the cloth under the girl's head. They set off for town.

***

An hour later, with their purchases loaded into the cart, and Yema finally awake and dragging along with Cardim and Leah, they arrived at the dock. Lars Orlund, Enzo Henry and the purser were waiting for them by the one remaining boat.

"Any luck?" Leah asked them.

"They're thinking it over," Orlund said with a shrug. "That's so typical of the French."

"Do you really want to take those people to the Netherlands?" she asked. They moved to the shore end of the dock, while the Corajoso's rowers and the cart driver loaded their purchases into the ship's boat. Yema walked over to a nearby grassy slope, lay down, and was soon fast asleep.

"No. Just an excuse. If the Jews agree, we'll send them on to the Ottoman with the Turk. If he won't do it, I think I can talk Vincent into taking them back to Tangier. I'm confident we can find more cargo there to sell here, or in Amsterdam."

"Lars," Leah said. "I can't thank you enough for doing this." She wanted to kiss him on the cheek, but as usual felt it would give the wrong impression. "Where's Jansen and the captain?"

"They went out to the Turkish ship. If their captain goes along with us, and the French also, we'll take the refugees out to the Turk. Let's wait for a while and see what they decide. Jérôme knows we're waiting for him."

Dr. Cardim paid the cart driver and sent him on his way. Leah looked over at Yema who lay snoozing on the grass. She suddenly felt an urgency to get away and go back to the Corajoso. She knew what the fear was— *That bearded rabbi will show up and, regardless of any appreciation he might feel, will take a look at Yema and spit.* She remembered the old rabbi in Lisbon who was always intolerant of persons he deemed unworthy.

Since they had only one boat, Leah could not ask to be rowed back to the ship. Instead, she retrieved her yellow headscarf from the package in the boat, and went over to Yema. She seated herself in the grass next to the child. Pulling the girl into her lap, she undid Yema's headscarf, tying it across her chin and over her forehead, leaving only the eyes visible.

Half awake, the girl asked, "What are you doing?"

"We're practicing our disguise," Leah told her, remembering her thoughts about the old rabbi. She could only hope the child would not catch on.

"Why now?" Yema asked.

She ignored the question and tied her own headscarf in the same way. "This is how we look," she said. "What do you think?"

Yema stretched and yawned. "I think we look stupid." She rolled onto grass, staring at the brilliantly blue sky. After a few moments, the girl pulled the scarf over her eyes and returned to sleep, mumbling a little nonsense as she did.

Leah saw Orlund and Dr. Cardim leave the dock and start walking towards the village. She spotted Officer Jérôme coming down the trail accompanied by another officer, a tall fellow who carried himself in an imperious manner. Though they were too far away to hear the conversation, it was obvious that the French greeted Lars and the doctor in an unfriendly way.

Chapter 39

Enzo Henry and the purser were lounging on the grass with the rowing crew a few yards from Leah and Yema when the French officers appeared. They followed Orlund and Cardim up the trail, but stopped when they saw that things were not going well. At the conclusion of the brief exchange, and in a clear disregard of protocol, neither Jérôme nor the other man offered a hand to Lars or the doctor.

The Frenchmen started back towards the village, while Henry and the purser waited for their comrades to join them. As the two approached, Enzo asked, "What in God's name happened?"

"Quite a change from earlier," Orlund said. "That tall fellow is the captain of the border guard. Apparently they showed up just after we left. I'm suspicious that Jérôme knew they were coming. Probably wanted to get some money out of us before he turned us down."

"Did either of them say why?" the purser asked. "Are they open to some kind of offer?"

Cardim shook his head. "Not a chance, and no reason given. They threatened to arrest us if we even suggested it again."

"How about Jérôme?" Henry asked. "Can we get to him?"

"I don't think so. He's pissing in his boots."

The four of them turned and started back towards the dock. Someone asked, "Who's going to tell Leah?"

Orlund raised his hand as if to say, "I guess that's me."

***

The next morning, the Corajoso left Gujan-Mestras bay and set sail for Amsterdam. Leah and Yema watched from the rail as the ship's canvas gathered wind and moved out of the harbor. Leaving the refugee Jews behind was tragic, made even worse since the Turkish captain had agreed to take them to the Ottoman.

Dr. Cardim and Lars Orlund stood with the two women. Orlund said, "I'm truly sorry, Leah. There's nothing we could do." In the distance they could see the Turkish ship still moored by one of the barges and taking on cargo.

"Those people are doomed," Leah said. "The Spanish will break up the families, send the girls to convents, the boys to monasteries, and the adults will be killed or forced to convert. Things were so different before the damned Inquisition." She sighed and turned to Yema. "Go tend your animals. I'll catch up on my journal; then we can start your lessons."

A while later, when Yema entered their cabin, she found Leah sitting by the window staring out at the open sea. Orlund sat in a chair a few feet away, his hands folded in his lap. "Hello Yema," he said. "I guess it's time for your lessons. I'll be going."

"You can stay if you want," the girl said, looking over at Leah. It was evident she'd been crying.

"Try one of those cinnamon sticks," Leah said. "A gift from Lars. I guess Dr. Cardim bought them at the apothecary yesterday."

There were several laying on the table, and Yema picked up one. "What do I do with it?" she asked.

"Just chew it lightly," Lars said. "It has an interesting flavor."

Yema did so, then smacked her lips and grinned at Orlund. "Thank you, Meneer Lars. I've never heard of cinnamon."

"It comes from Egypt. That's a country at the east end of the Mediterranean, directly south of Turkey." He walked over and put his hand on Leah's shoulder. "Please try to cheer up," he said. "We'll be home in less than two weeks." Without thinking, he bent down and kissed her on top of her head, something he'd never done before. If Leah and Yema were surprised, Orlund was shocked. He mumbled something and made for the door.

Leah looked at him and smiled. "Thank you, Lars," she said, then repeated in Dutch, "*Dank je, Lars.*"

Lars Orlund left the cabin a happy man.

***

On the last day of July, five-and-a-half months since they had left the *Costa do Tupi* plantation, the Corajoso's lookout spotted Den Helder Inlet, the passage into Amsterdam Bay. From his position at the wheel, Captain Vincent could see the narrow slit of land beginning to show itself on the eastern horizon. The ship and crew had been away from their home port for almost ten months, and they could only speculate as to the current state of affairs.

What Vincent heard next from the lookout was reassuring. "A dozen or more fishermen, Sir. That's a good sign."

"Thank you, ensign," he called back. It was indeed a good sign. Fishermen rarely ventured out if there was conflict onshore, or anywhere in the nearby countryside. Since they had just two hours of daylight left, Vincent decided to anchor and enter the bay in the morning. Once through the inlet, it was still four hours of slow sailing to Almere at the bay's south end.

About a mile off the Den Helder Inlet, and right in the middle of the fishing boats, Vincent ordered sails furled and the anchor dropped. Shouted conversations started with the two nearest fishing boats, everyone eager to catch up on the news. Leah, Yema, and Dr. Cardim listened intently from the rail, trying to understand as much Dutch as they could. Orlund soon joined them and helped translate. As several boats pulled in nets brimming with silvery fish, it was clear the fishermen were there for the herring run.

Lars called down to the nearest boat. "If you're selling, we'll take three baskets of those herring. How much?"

"Two coppers per basket," the fisherman called back.

"That's cheap," Orlund told those around him. "Must be a big run this year."

Soon there were three baskets of squirming fish on deck, and the cook put everyone to work skewering them onto long sticks. Within minutes, many stringers of herring roasted over the brazier. As quickly as a stringer was cooked, it was replaced with another. Everyone feasted on herring, spitting out the bones and throwing the remains overboard to the waiting gulls.

Orlund bought three more baskets for the morning, then cupped a hand to his ear when he heard someone yelling. It turned out the shouts came from a boat quite some distance away. "I think that's somebody from my farm," he remarked. The distant ship put a small dinghy in the water, and the single occupant rowed quickly towards the Corajoso. Within minutes, the tiny craft came alongside. Leaving the boat tied to the boarding net, the tall, rather thin young man climbed aboard and gave Lars Orlund a hearty hug.

"This is Jorrit Winard, the son of my foreman," Orlund explained. "Jorrit, is my farm still there?"

"Indeed it is, sir, and productive as ever. The vegetables are doing well, the berries are about gone, we'll have apples and pears in a week or so, and the grain crops look good. We've had ample rain."

"The vegetables are selling?"

"Oh yes," Jorrit said. "The women take a cartload into town at least twice a week."

"And how is that maize doing? The grain we brought from the New World. And the yams?"

"The maize came up, then died. We don't know why. We just ate our first yams last week. They're particularly good with black syrup and butter."

Orlund, meaning to introduce Leah and Yema, looked for the two women. Curiously, they were nowhere in sight. A minute before he'd seen Yema feeding herring scraps to the chickens. Now all he saw was her basket abandoned by the animal pen and a few chickens pecking around it.

Inside their cabin, Leah explained to the child why she had abruptly taken her below. "These Dutch are strangers," she said. "Until we find out if that wanted notice has made it here, we must be cautious."

Yema, always eager for anything new, glumly accepted this. "I guess you're right," she said. "I never again want to go through what happened in Fortaleza." She ran a hand around her collarbone and under her chin, feeling the scars left by the slave yoke.

"We still don't know what became of the priest there," Leah said, "Fr. Almeido. If he survived the Indian attack, then he's likely implicated the Corajoso. There must be some survivors who knew it was us."

The girl went to the window. Craning her neck and looking

aft, she could see the dinghy bobbing alongside the ship. "That fellow's still here," she said.

Leah did not respond. At this moment, her mind was so cluttered with competing fears, she struggled to put them in some kind of order. Was there a letter waiting for her? If so, had her parents accepted Yema? Were there wanted notices posted in Amsterdam and Almere? To her, it felt impossible to stay in this land of the Dutch. Sooner or later they would be discovered. Why had she ever assumed they would be safe in the Netherlands? At least she found one thing reassuring—Travel to Tangier and then to the Ottoman was possible. Perhaps in Tangier, they should have taken a ship to her parents in Antalya. If they rejected the girl, then the two of them could live apart from them.

Yema became uncomfortable with the silence. "What?" she asked.

"I'm trying to figure out what we should do, sweetheart."

"Maybe we could just live on the ship," Yema suggested. "Like Dr. Cardim."

"I don't think he's going to live on the ship while we're here. Just travel with Vincent on the next voyage."

"Well, he's on a wanted notice too."

"You're right," Leah said. "We'll talk about it at dinner this evening."

***

Around noon the following day, the Corajoso neared the south end of Amsterdam bay, the city visible to the west, the small settlement of Almere to the east. On their way south, the first thing that had caught Yema's eye were the several windmills they passed. Leah explained what they were used for, and that they also had them in Portugal. "Windmills pump water and grind grain," she told the girl. Closer to Amsterdam, the bay became crowded with ships of various kinds, lighters, fishing boats, small pleasure craft with one or two rowers and occasional passengers, boats carrying produce, several open-sea traders like the Corajoso, and two impressive Portuguese military craft, each displaying mainsails with large orange and black crosses emblazoned across their board canvas.

The two women paid even more attention to the brown granite cathedral that loomed over the north edge of Amsterdam, the archdiocese of Bishop Adrian Boeyens. Having discussed their concerns about Bishop Boeyens and the possibility of wanted notices the night before, Captain Vincent decided to make some cautious inquiries. In addition, he wondered if the Corajoso had become a pariah due to the events in Fortaleza. At the conclusion of the evening's conversation he remarked, "Who knows? Maybe we all are fugitives."

Vincent brought his ship within a half-mile of Amsterdam and put a boat in the water. He sent Enzo Henry and second mate Jozef into the city to investigate, instructing the two, "Have the rowers take you to our mooring when you're finished." Then he dropped anchor and called for an assembly of all hands. Once the sailors were in place, Vincent stood on the quarterdeck and addressed them.

"Because of our actions in Fortaleza, we share a common danger. All of you fought bravely, and I am grateful for our success. But we must tell no one of our exploits in Brazil. Even a hint of our activity there, or our rescue of the hostages, and we will feel the full force of the Portuguese Crown. Each of us will experience torture and death. And an equal fate awaits your families and loved-ones."

Vincent paused, waiting for this uncomfortable truth to sink in. "So hear me now!" he said. "As Mr. Jansen calls your name and so records it, I want each man to step forward and give me an 'Aye' in agreement."

First mate Jansen positioned a small lectern to one side of the assembled men. He opened the ship's log and placed it there. Poised with ink and quill, he waited for Vincent's order. At the same time, the purser came forward carrying a basket heavy with the crew's pay. No one lost the significance of the two activities happening together.

When the two officers were in position, the captain continued. "As each man pledges, he will receive his pay for our profitable voyage. So profitable in fact, that I have added one hundred and fifty copper reis to each sailor's earnings." With these words, the purser picked up a cloth pay bag, jingling the little purse with its coins inside.

A cheer went up from the crew, and the pledging and pay activity continued until all thirty seven men had pledged and received their purse of coins.

The Corajoso weighed anchor, and moving under short sail, soon pulled alongside Vincent's Almere moorage. Meanwhile, Leah, Yema, and Dr. Cardim stayed in the captain's cabin and awaited the news from Amsterdam. The ship's crew spent the rest of the day securing the ship and preparing for the extensive refit scheduled to take place the following week. They also unloaded the remaining goats and chickens, the small amount of cargo, and the officers' baggage.

Enzo Henry and Jozef returned in the late afternoon, and reported finding a wanted notice posted for the fugitives at the Amsterdam cathedral. Displaying the notice, they joked how they had paid a street urchin two coppers to steal it from the posting board. In the meantime, Lars Orlund, accompanied by many friends and townspeople eager to hear their most prominent citizen's exploits in the New World, strolled into Almere and discovered no wanted notice at the town's gray stone church. The elderly town priest, Fr. Willemsen, showed no trepidation or hint of concern when he greeted Orlund, but it took until the next morning for Lars to persuade Cardim, Leah, and Yema to venture onshore.

***

By the week's end, everyone had settled into a daily routine. After breakfast in the main house, Yema, along with several other children and Migle, the foreman's wife, went to the pens to look after the many animals. Once finished, the child would join Leah working in either the orchard or one of the numerous vegetable plots. On the day Jorrit brought Leah the letter from her family in Antalya, she was working by herself in the orchard. In a panic, she tore open the lappet and quickly scanned the letter, worried that Yema might show up at any moment. Looking around, she saw the girl playing with some children quite a distance away, so she read the missive more carefully, her panic turning to bitter disappointment. The letter— written in her father's hand—was unusual, since it was her mother who normally wrote. Obviously they'd received hers months earlier from Brazil, yet there was no mention of Yema. Not a word. Her father hoped she would make it safely to the Netherlands, and encouraged his daughter to someday join them in the Ottoman.

Leah's panic returned when she saw Migle and the children working their way towards her, picking up fallen apples and gathering dry pruning cuttings for firewood. She quickly folded the parchment and shoved it into her waistband, then pulled her muslin blouse over it. Making the excuse that she needed to return to the cottage, she left the children to work with Migle and hurried away. Leah looked back several times, fearing that Yema—as she so often did—had read her thoughts. Once in the cottage, she read her father's words again. With tears streaming down her face, she hid the letter under a pile of sacks in a storage shed behind the cottage.

After Leah regained her composure, she returned to the orchard. As soon as Yema spotted her, she up and said, "Migle's going to sell vegetables in Amsterdam tomorrow. May we go with her? She said we could." When Leah did not immediately respond, the girl said. "I want to see Amsterdam. We can wear our veils."

"Excellent idea," Leah answered, relieved that the child appeared to suspect nothing.

***

Early the next morning, Leah and Yema, wearing veils and dressed like Moorish women, climbed aboard a large two-horse wagon driven by Migle's son Jorrit. The wagon was piled high with harvest baskets full of cabbage, turnips, apples, red plums, carrots, yams, beets, and several kinds of squash, at least three of which appeared to be the same sort grown in Brazil. Migle sat with Leah and Yema behind the driver's bench on a flat wooden plank. Two farm workers, burly men wearing black aprons with pockets for coins, sat next to Jorrit as he maneuvered the heavy wagon down the farm lane to the dock.

"Good morning, Mistress Leah," Migle had said in greeting when the two women climbed onto the wagon.

A few days after she and Yema had arrived in Almere, people began calling her "Mistress." Leah found it puzzling, and was unable to determine why people had titled her thus. Perhaps because she and Yema supped at Orlund's table, and that made her the mistress of his house. Certainly no woman of position lived in the main house, except housekeepers, and even the most senior of them deferred to her. More likely, since Lars favored her and Yema, he expected others to show respect. Though another possibility infused the title with a hint of disquiet: That she was Orlund's paramour.

As the farm wagon continued along its way, Migle picked up her long braid and coiled it into her lap. Almost all the local women wore their hair in this fashion, a long, single braid, often extending below their waists. Leah and Yema's hair was now long enough to weave into such a braid, but theirs only reached to just below the shoulders. For the Dutch women's hair to be this long, surely most of them had never before, even once, cut their hair.

Despite the accepting nature of nearly everyone on this Dutch farm, more and more, Leah felt she and Yema were out of place. So many of the Netherlanders looked the same, blond hair, blue eyes, and skin so fair they had to shield it from the sun. Indeed there was a smattering of women with red hair, and men like Orlund with red beards, but no one had the dark skin of Yema's, nor the brown eyes of the two of them, and none had Leah's light olive skin with its Mediterranean tone.

Oddly, even Orlund's kindly attention to her and Yema did not generate feelings of kinship. She hoped this was a passing discomfort— Perhaps a consequence of the poisonous letter from her father the day before.

At the moorage, a lighter with eight oarsmen awaited the wagon's arrival; and a short distance out in the bay, the Corajoso lay at anchor, its rigging and deck bustling with the refit activity. Just as the wagon neared the moorage, two groups of farm workers appeared, trudging up the road from the south end of the bay. The nearest group were Gypsies, replete with two wagons, several mules, and a great number of children. Close on their heels was a ragged assortment of families, perhaps thirty people in all. Many in this second group appeared to be Jews. Most of them, except the smallest children, carried bundles or pushed wheeled trundles stacked with personal belongings.

Without Leah asking, Migle offered an explanation. "These folks come each season and camp in the woods. They work the fields and we pay them a little. Mostly we let them glean crops after harvest. They dry most of it for the winter ahead."

"Are those people Jews?" Leah asked. "It looks like they're carrying everything they own." She studied Migle for a reaction. She had no idea if the woman knew she was Jewish.

"Yes," Migle answered matter-of-factly. "They're from Maarssen. In a day or two there will be much violence in that place. They flee it every year. Lars Orlund is a man of courage. He, like his father before him, gives them refuge each year."

Before Leah could ask for details, Jorrit turned and handed Migle two polished wooden slave yokes. "Please show Mistress Leah and Yema how to put these on," he said. "I don't want to raise suspicions among the lighter crew."

The Dutch woman passed one to Yema and snapped the other

open, placing it around her neck and latching it shut, demonstrating how to wear it. Then she removed her yoke and handed it to an astonished Leah. "Please put this on, Mistress," she said. "It's just a formality. The only Moors allowed in Amsterdam are slaves."

"Why didn't someone tell us about this before?" Leah asked.

Migle shook her head in apology. "Sorry, Mistress. I thought Meneer Orlund told you. Without a slave yoke, you will attract attention and could be arrested. You will likely see a number of Moors in Amsterdam today, and all of them will be wearing yokes. I'd venture to say only a few are slaves."

As Leah adjusted her veil and positioned the yoke, Migle continued. "This is how we Dutch accommodate to having these foreigners in our land." She smiled and gave a shrug. "In a way, wearing these silly yokes makes sport of the damned Portuguese."

Yema set her yoke on the wagon seat and said, "I'm not wearing that thing. If I have to, then I'm staying here."

Several times Migle had noticed the scars on the child's neck, throat, and shoulders, and she knew only an iron slave collar could make such scars. The Dutch woman picked up the yoke and handed it back to Jorrit. "You don't have to wear it," she told the girl. "Just stay close to Mistress Leah. Her wearing one is sufficient."

Chapter 40

Moments after the lighter set out for Amsterdam, Captain Vincent shouted, asking them to come alongside the Corajoso. He clung halfway down the boarding net and waited. As the lighter eased next to the ship, he climbed down the rest of the way and jumped onboard.

Very good, Leah thought, concerned over asking Migle about the Jews and the mentioned violence. *Now I can ask Captain Vincent.*

Once the captain finished with his greetings and introductions, he, Leah, and Yema retired to a bench on the lighter's stern. "What made you decide to join us?" Leah asked.

He glanced at the Corajoso. "Our refit is coming along quite well, so it's time to look for a second vessel."

"A while back," Leah continued, "you said Mr. Jansen will be her captain. Is that still so?"

Vincent nodded. "Yes, and I still wish Obiike were with us. He'd be an ideal second mate on either ship."

"Interesting," Leah said. "Yema and I continue wonder about Nanjala."

Suddenly the captain had a broad smile on his face, and Leah could almost guess what was coming. "You wonder about Nanjala and Obiike?" he asked. "We'll probably head back to the Verdes in about two months. Marry Lars Orlund, and that can be your nuptial voyage."

"For the love of God, Eider, is nothing ever private with you Dutch?"

"Not between Lars and me. Marry him. I want to see my friend happy."

"And if I don't?"

"Then he's going to find a sultry temptress who will make you insanely jealous."

"Jealousy is not my nature."

"I told him that was likely. But if you don't marry him, he's going back to the New World with me."

"Captain Vincent," Yema asked, "why have you never married?"

He gave them another smile. "Now you two are ganging up on me."

But more pressing subjects were at hand, and there seemed no opening to ask; so Leah just blurted it out. "Does Migle know I'm a Jew?"

"Yes, of course." He appeared surprised by the question. "Why do you ask?"

"Everyone on the farm knows I'm Jewish?"

"I assume so," he said. "In the grand scheme of things, it's not all that important."

"Well," Leah said, "I guess I am truly among friends."

The captain shook his head with amusement. "When did you ever think you were not? Make friends with Migle. You can trust her."

"Did you see the Jews coming up from Maarssen? Migle mentioned violence. What did she mean?"

By now they were halfway across the bay, and Amsterdam sparkled in the mid-morning sun. "I did see them," Vincent said quietly. He made a face and looked toward the city. "This is not the best week to visit Amsterdam. But we have produce to sell, so there's no choice. Today is the second day of the *Krüisiging oogst dans.*"

"A Crucifixion harvest dance?" Leah asked.

"Yes, from Groningen, a town north of here. It happens about this time every year. It's very hard on the Jews. There are these fools—" He paused, searching for words. "It's these ignorant peasants from the countryside. The parish priests work them into a frenzy and demand recompense for the Crucifixion. So they go after the Jews."

"Don't they hide or flee? Like the ones from Maarssen?"

"Yes, of course. But the Krüisigingers always catch a few. Some Christians try to hide them, but if they're caught, the dancers burn the Christian homes."

"I guess this is never going to stop," Leah said.

"I'm afraid not," the captain replied. "Unfortunately you'll see some of it today at the market. It's really a shame." He put a hand to his forehead, shielding his eyes and looking east. "Well, look at that," he said. A short distance behind the lighter, three Portuguese warships were coming into port, the nearest just fifty yards astern. "I wonder what those thieves are up to?" Vincent said.

"Pull harder," the lighter captain ordered his rowers as the Portuguese ship drew closer. "I want to dock before those *klootzakken* block our way."

"What's a *klootzakken?*" Yema asked.

"You don't want to know," Vincent said.

He was about to say more when the captain of the Portuguese vessel called to them through his speaking trumpet. "Ahoy farm scow!" he snarled. "What produce do you carry? Is it for sale?"

The man's insulting tone was not lost on Migle. "You can buy it at the market this afternoon," she shouted back. "Like everyone else."

"Then I'll confiscate the whole lot of you," he shouted, "the wagon, the scow, you blond witch, and those two Moorish slaves. We need women on our ship." Leah reached under her tunic, feeling for her dagger.

Not wishing for a confrontation, Jorrit spoke up and recited their list of produce.

The captain conferred with an officer next to him, then ordered his boarding net and a boat lowered. "I'm sending my purser and cook over," he said. "They'll select what we need and pay you. Consider yourself lucky that I'm in a generous mood today."

The lighter captain cursed under his breath and ordered his rowers to hold the boat in place. A few minutes later, the Portuguese purser, cook, and three crewmen came onboard, strutting around and poking into the baskets of produce. Yema and Leah glumly watched the goings-on. Yema commented, "I've lost interest in seeing Amsterdam. Can we go back to Almere?"

"You'll be safe with Jorrit in the market," Vincent said. "I'll stay there with you if you want." Two Portuguese seamen approached, curious about the Moorish women. Vincent stepped in front of them, right hand resting on the hilt of his sword. "Turn away," he whispered to Leah and Yema.

"Stop!" he said to the sailors, purposely making his Portuguese thick with his Dutch accent. "These females are the property of Graaf van Orlund. They are not to be approached." The sailors hesitated for a moment, then returned to the produce wagon.

"What's Graaf?" Yema asked.

"It means nobleman," Vincent said. "The Portuguese are easily intimidated by titles."

Despite all the previous bluster, the exchange of goods and money went smoothly. The lighter pulled next to the warship and the sailors loaded the produce into a waiting cargo net, finally standing aside as it was winched onboard. Jorrit called a "Thank you" to the Portuguese captain, and the lighter proceeded to the dock area reserved for the town market.

"Well," Migle said as they waited for the crewmen to secure their boat at the pier, "we sold almost half of everything without lifting a finger. It's a good start for today's commerce."

The Amsterdam market stretched out along the waterfront in both directions. The wagon pulled off the lighter and moved slowly along the cobblestone street to a space reserved for *Orlund Pachthoeve*, Orlund Farm. Once in place, both sides of the wagon were unlatched and propped level, with the harvest baskets displayed along their length. The business of buying-and-selling went on all around them, and the bright sunshine gave a festive quality to the scene.

Vincent and Jorrit led the women around the marketplace, while Migle and the two farm workers busied themselves with customers. It seemed that anything imaginable was for sale, farm animals of all kinds, cows, goats, chickens, sheep, pigs, noisy geese and ducks, as well as songbirds in reed cages, a great variety of fish, both fresh and dried, and stands with bread, honey cakes, and biscuits, many of them decorated with colorful flowers. In addition to the multitude of food items, there were rugs from the Mediterranean, Spanish and Italian olive oils, silk fabrics from Turkey and points east, wines from France, many kinds of spices, leather goods, harnesses and Spanish saddles, wood and stone carvings, ornaments, women's and men's clothing of every size and color, apothecaries with a myriad of remedies, farm implements, and jewelry of gold, silver, and brass, many set with jade, black onyx, or precious stones.

As they neared the south end of the market, the street became crowded with people leading, holding, or dragging their trussed-up animals, each waiting in line at the butcher stalls to have their purchases slaughtered and dressed. At this point, Leah suggested they turn back. She continued to find the killing of animals distasteful.

On their return, they passed a gaggle of well dressed Moorish women, all of them wearing slave collars and escorted by fierce-looking Dutch soldiers. "I'm certain none of those ladies are slaves," Vincent commented. "It's the locals' way of thumbing their noses at the Portuguese. Likely those aren't even militia, just mercenaries hired by the Moors so their women can go to market." Once back at the Orlund wagon, Leah and Yema helped with selling produce, although they avoided any conversation with customers.

At first the sound mixed with the market noise, and was barely audible; minutes later it could not be ignored. There was a cacophony of drums, cymbals, and pipes, all coming from north of the marketplace, the direction of the Boeyens Cathedral. Many in the crowd paused, looking up the street. Preceding the noise, two criers appeared, one dressed in a bizarre, mostly-black clown's outfit, the other in Portuguese Military garb, the clown heralding the advent of the *Krüisiging oogst dans,* the military crier announcing the presence of a refreshed Portuguese garrison, "Three hundred new recruits, brought today by His Majesty's warships in service of The Holy Inquisition; to root out subversive Jews and other dangerous criminals."

Right behind the criers, the first military contingent marched into view, five abreast, regimental pennants flying, led by their officers, three impressive groups of a hundred each. Then the Krüisigingers appeared, first the musicians with their infernal music, then the dancers—all festooned in vivid regalia and waving sticks with colored ribbons attached—and lastly a group of wretched looking Jews prodded along by men in devil's costumes.

Each captive had a wooden cross strapped to their back, some so heavy that, particularly in the case of the children, they could barely walk. The devils viciously prodded the slower ones with their iron pitchforks, not allowing the adults to help the struggling children.

This spectacle of mistreatment displeased the market crowd, many of them booing and shouting catcalls. One young fellow, tall and thin like Jorrit Winard, shoved a devil aside and helped a child to his feet. The marcher retaliated by jabbing the Dutchman with his pitchfork. The thrust sent the good fellow sprawling, bloodying his side, the devil continuing to jab him as he crawled away. An angry shout erupted from the crowd and someone threw a cobblestone. The stone missed its mark, but the ones following did not. A few marchers went down. Most fled for their lives. In the midst of the riot, the Jews were quickly freed of their burdens and disappeared into the crowd.

The Portuguese troops, who were now directly in front of the Orlund Farm wagon, reversed their march and charged the sullen crowd. Since the soldiers were not armed, they grabbed anything they could to use for weapons. In only a few minutes, the troops overwhelmed the rioters, leaving a number of bloody dead and wounded in the street. The regimental commander appeared and walked among those injured. Unsheathing his sword, he methodically killed any citizen not obviously part of the *Krüisiging* dance. Three of the dancers lay immobile on the cobblestones, one of them in a devil costume. The commander directed several of his men with stretchers to cart them away. Then he turned and glared at the remaining crowd. "This disorder will not be tolerated," he shouted. "Now collect your dead and behave yourselves like worthy Christians."

Fortunately the group from Orlund Farm was some distance from the riot which had taken place at the north end of the market, so none of them were directly affected. Nonetheless, Vincent, Jorrit, and the two farm workers rushed to the scene to help the Dutch citizens gather up their dead comrades. All the stands and carts within a block of the riot were tipped over, their contents scattered across the square, the merchants scrambling to salvage their goods.

Migle, Leah, and Yema attended to the few hurried customers who completed their purchases and fled into the city. Though there was fair amount of produce left, no shoppers remained in the marketplace. The women tidied up what remained while they waited for the men to return. Migle filled two harvest baskets with vegetables and set them in the street. "For the poor," she said.

"What would have happened to those Jews," Leah asked, "if the crowd had nor freed them?"

"The dancers usually take the poor souls they catch to the edge of town and crucify them."

"Even the children?" Yema asked.

"I'm afraid so," Migle said. Obviously disturbed by what had happened, she busied herself stacking baskets before she spoke again. "Despite the bloodshed," she continued, "this riot could be a good thing. Maybe the Krüisigingers are so disorganized, they won't go on to Maarssen. Perhaps they'll turn back to Groningen."

A little while later the men returned, their hands, arms, and shirts smeared with blood. They knelt by the livestock watering basin and rinsed themselves. "What a mess," Vincent said. "I've never seen our people so restive. Sooner or later we Dutch will drive the Portuguese out of our land." He sighed and sat down on the wagon tongue. "Let's head back," he continued. "I'd planned to inquire about ships for sale at the harbormaster's office, but the man's a Portuguese sympathizer. I can't go there looking like this."

* * *

The riot was the main topic of conversation at dinner that evening. Leah complimented Lars for protecting the Maarssen Jews.

"It's been common knowledge around here for years," he responded, "but there could be a problem with these new Portuguese troops. All that talk about enforcing the Inquisition."

After a while, Leah felt they'd fully wrung out the subject, so she excused herself and took Yema with her. They walked outside into a balmy and pleasant night lit by a newly risen moon. "Let's go visit the worker camps," the girl suggested. "Those people look interesting."

"All right," Leah said. "We'll visit the Gypsies. I'm not ready to visit the Jews quite yet."

"Why not?" Yema asked.

"Because they're from the Roman province to the east. They are very different from the Jews of Iberia."

"How?"

"Their customs are different, and to some extent, we don't worship in the same manner. I am a Sephardim. Those Jews are the Ashkenazi." She did not tell Yema that the two groups detested each other, often viewing their counterparts as inferior miscreants.

"Well then," Yema said, with a note of doubt in her voice, "let's go visit the Gypsies."

They discovered the air filled with the sweet scent of wood smoke and fruit as they approached the Gypsy camp. The two women heard singing and merriment, and saw many fires smoldering with fruit and vegetables on drying sticks suspended in the smoke. The Gypsy leader, Gunaro, a pleasant looking, stocky gentlemen in his fifties with curly gray hair and a closely trimmed beard, greeted Leah and the girl with great ceremony, thanking them for the surplus of produce— Orlund had distributed a goodly portion of the leftover market produce to the worker camps.

A woman offered Yema and Leah a place to sit on a rough wooden bench next to the campfire, then handed them each a cup of beer. "We make this from dried fruit," she explained. The beer had an odd, but pleasing taste, a little sour like vinegar, a little sweet like fruit. As soon as the visitors settled, many conversations started, most in the Gypsy's strange sounding Rodi tongue, although the people around Leah and Yema continued to speak in Dutch out of courtesy to the newcomers.

As usual in her typically inquisitive mood, Yema got up and began to wander around. She noticed most of the drying fires were attended by children who kept the coals stoked and at the right level, cutting and skewering fresh fruit and vegetables onto sticks, and stripping the dried fruit into waiting baskets. It briefly reminded the child of her time with Agato and the dreadful Carib tribe.

She had just knelt by a fire to work alongside the children, when the figure of a large man, led by a young Gypsy boy, came out of the darkness. The man, though truly immense, appeared quite old and stooped. He had long unkempt white hair, a halting gait, and was obviously blind. Yema followed the two as they moved in the direction of the main campfire. As they got closer, she ran ahead, seating herself next to Leah, curious to see the old fellow in a better light.

When he appeared, the Gypsies murmured their greetings, and made room for him on one of the benches. Someone handed him a

mug of beer. He raised his cup in salute to his invisible friends. "Who
is he?" Yema asked the woman next to her. He looked so different
from the Gypsies, very florid of complexion, and much larger than
any of the other men.

"He is named Helgen," the woman said. "From a tribe so far
north that his land has no trees."

"How can that be?" Yema asked.

"It is too cold for trees. Now, he says, all his people have
vanished. Swallowed up in years past by the winter snow."

A young woman appeared with a lute, sat next to the man, and
whispered something in his ear. Helgen smiled and straightened up a
little. The woman strummed the lute, then began to pick out a tune.
The old fellow commenced to sing, sing in a deep, resonant voice, a
lovely song that stirred the air like an unseen and graceful bird.

At the beginning of the second verse, Yema, not knowing the
words, began to sing the melody with Helgen— Not in her full voice,
but with sufficient tenor that most everyone paid attention. As the old
fellow neared the end of the verse, he let his voice drop so the girl's
last few notes were clear to all. "Come sit by me," the man said,
patting the bench next to him. "Tell me who you are." Yema walked
over and settled beside him. He reached to touch her, running his
immense hand along the girl's shoulders and down her back. "Are
you a child?" he asked with surprise.

"Yes," Yema said. "I'm eleven years old."

"My goodness," Helgen said, touching her face, lingering a
hand over the scars on her cheek. "A child who has been through
many terrors. Is that why you sing so beautifully?"

"I sing because I love to."

"That's the best reason for anyone." He turned his head
towards the lute player. "Please start again."

Chapter 41

After their first visit to the Gypsy camp, Yema and Leah's daily
routine changed. They worked in the fields until the hour of noon,
then walked with the Gypsies who labored around them to their camp,
and ate their noon meal around the campfire. Helgen was always there
waiting for them. He and Yema sat together, ate whatever was
available, and sang until the bell at the Orlund house signaled the start

of the afternoon's work. Their repertoire grew a little each day, he teaching her ballads from the Gypsy and Norse traditions, she teaching him the African songs she learned from Nanjala.

Leah made a point to toil alongside some of the Jewish workers in an effort to get to know them. They were not particularly friendly, but tolerated her presence. Even though the farm provided a temporary refuge, Leah understood why they remained circumspect— the typical Jewish fear of strangers. Any strangers.

Sometime during the second week after they began taking their noontime meals with the Gypsies, Yema asked, "When are you going to tell them you're a Jew?"

"I may never tell them," Leah said. "It serves no purpose."

"But don't you want to be with your own people? I'd love to spend some time with the Tupi or—" She didn't finish the sentence. The regret over her lost Caeté tribe made the child unable to continue.

At the time, the two of them were working in one of the vegetable plots, hoeing weeds from long rows of carrots and onions. Leah put an arm around the child's shoulder. "I'm sorry, sweetheart. As far as the Maarssen Jews are concerned, they're not my people. To me, they feel as foreign as the Portuguese, or for that matter, the Dutch.

This puzzled Yema. "Did you ever feel comfortable around the Portuguese?" she asked. "You must have known some Catholics when you lived in Lisbon."

"Not many, though my father's brickyard did most of its commerce with the Portuguese community. Even some clergy. Once the Inquisition started, everything changed. I was in the convent then, but we heard that Jewish businesses were burned, and people being forced to convert. Either convert, or expelled or killed." At that moment, remembering her father's letter, Leah experienced a rush of despair. She pushed ahead of Yema and began hoeing in front of her. Without looking back, she said, "That's when my parents fled to Turkey." The girl found Leah's behavior curious, though she chose to ignore it.

After the noon meal that day, Helgen taught Yema the song he had sung that first night. "It's called *Kaunis Revontulet,*" he told her, "The Beautiful Northern Lights."

The tune was simple enough, but the words—sung in the Rodi language—were difficult to pronounce. This song was familiar to the

Gypsies, and many of them sang along, although in muted tones so that Helgen and Yema's voices stood out. After a couple of times through, Yema asked, "Is this something made up, or are the northern lights real?" She wished she could understand the words.

"They are both," the girl who played the lute said. "On the very coldest nights of winter, they shower the northern sky with radiant curtains of green, orange, red, and yellow."

"What are they?" Yema asked.

"No one knows for sure," Helgen said. "Though most people believe they are torches leading lost souls to a new land of warmth and plenty. As a child, I was not blind. So I saw them."

Yema gave Leah an uncertain look. "Did you ever see them?"

"Yes," Leah said. "But just a few times in Lisbon. You see them more often if you're further north."

"Are we far enough north?" Yema asked.

"Ah, wait until this winter," one of the men replied. "You will see them most every night."

Off in the distance, the farm bell rang. "Time for work," someone said.

"I don't think I can wait until winter," Yema remarked as they headed into the fields. As they went about their work, the child continued to ask Leah questions. "Tell me more about the northern lights. Are they curtains or fog? Do they fall like rain?"

"What I saw," Leah said, "were more like ribbons. As if someone was waving ribbons in the sky. Across the sky, not up and down. And they were green. Not so much red or yellow."

"Were they ever blue?"

"I don't think so."

"Well then," Yema said, "I think they are forests. Jungle forests without rivers. The sky is sad because there are no jungles up north, so it makes its own."

"And are there jaguars in this forest?" Leah asked.

"Yes, of course. But the jaguars are hiding. That's why you don't see much yellow or orange." She appeared overcome with excitement. "I can't wait until wintertime. I've just got to see those lights!"

***

Most of the talk at breakfast the next morning focused on Vincent's absence and his efforts to acquire a second ship. "He intends to stay in Amsterdam until he finds a new one," Orlund said with little enthusiasm. To him, the thought of a second vessel brought departure from his farm ever closer. Fall harvest would be nearly finished in about six weeks, and the refit of the new ship would be completed at almost the same time. Then of course, his friend Eider Vincent would be eager to set sail for new adventures and commerce. And there sat Leah across from him, blithely chatting about the new ship and occasionally the blind Viking, while he pined away, wondering if she would ever marry him. He wanted a wife again, and children this time. A family to whom he could pass on his farm and shipping business. And Yema, what a fine and clever daughter she would be. In a few years, he'd find her a husband, and he would have grandchildren.

Because many of Vincent's crew were now laboring as farm workers after the Corajoso refit, most of conversations in the vegetable plots that morning were also about Captain Vincent and the possibility of a new vessel. In addition to the sailors, a number of the smallholders surrounding Orlund's farm took to working the fields. Migle had explained when they left after breakfast that morning, "The smallholders work on the farm. In return, we sell their surplus goods at the market for them. It works out for everyone."

When Yema and Leah left their chores in the orchard and moved to the task of hoeing, they found themselves working among a group of smallholders. After a while, one woman whom Leah had seen a few times before introduced herself. "I am Lynne van Hoff," she said.

"Oh my goodness," Leah responded. "Are you Max van Hoff's mother?"

"Sadly I am." She turned to the man working next to her. "And this is my husband, Linder."

"I'm so sorry about your loss" Leah said. "Max was a lovely boy. And a hero too."

"That is what Captain Vincent told us. He's such a kind man. He gave us Max's pay, and a compensation also. It was very thoughtful." Lynne paused, then asked, "How was Max a hero? The captain never gave us details."

Leah thought about the question for a moment, not sure how to answer. Finally she said, "Max helped us win a battle in quite an unusual way. Unfortunately I can't tell you any more. Captain Vincent and Lars Orlund want to keep the details secret. But your son died in service to the ship, not in a battle. It was during a terrible storm at sea."

"Yes, that's what the captain told us," Lynne van Hoff said. "I just wish we knew more."

"And I wish I could tell you, Mrs. van Hoff. But suffice it to say, your son was a true hero."

The noon bell rang from the farm house, and each group went their separate ways. Several sailors walked with the two women to the Gypsy camp. More and more, various people, including these seamen, went to the camp at lunchtime to hear Yema and Helgen sing. So as not to tax the Gypsy's supply of food, everyone brought something edible to the camp, either in the morning for cooking that day, or at lunch for the following day. Because of this, the noontime fare usually consisted of a thick vegetable stew of unpredictable content. Occasionally someone brought bread, or the strange Dutch confection called *koekjes,* small spice cakes made from mashed turnips, apples, and wheat flour. "Once they're ripe," one Dutch woman explained, "we use pumpkins instead of turnips. The *koekjes* come out orange, and taste quite differently."

A few Jews had joined the luncheon activity, though they stayed grouped together and talked mostly among themselves. Because of their dietary laws, they always brought their own food. Leah had not kept kosher—nor had she been able to—since her days in Lisbon, and she found herself surprised at her reaction. At first she had missed the kosher rituals, particularly the companionship of preparing meals alongside her mother, but after all these years, the dietary laws now seemed foolish, almost a little amusing. Yet the thought of again spending time in the kitchen with her mother brought tears to her eyes. That opportunity would be so welcome.

As they settled for lunch that day, the sailors—all of whom Leah and Yema knew quite well—suggested that Yema and Helgen sing one evening at the moorage. "We can invite the people from Almere," one said. "My parents would love to hear them sing." Another added the thought, "From the deck of the new Corajoso."

The girl deemed it a splendid idea, but Leah did not. "We'll consider it," she said, directing a piercing look at the seamen. The child's singing had become too well known. There was significant peril in that, and Leah told them as much on their way back to the fields.

"Well," one sailor said, "we could lower a sail, and Cantora could sing from behind it."

Leah thought the suggestion absurd, but she know how much these men admired Yema, so she again told them she would consider it.

A few nights later at dinner, after Vincent had returned with a new merchant vessel, and the excitement of that had worn off, Yema brought up the subject of her singing from the deck of the Corajoso. At first, everyone thought the idea was hilarious. "Sing from behind a sail?" Enzo Henry asked. "So where will Helgen stand? In front? As if he had two voices?"

"No," the girl said, "he would stand with me behind the sail. And the same for the lady who plays the lute. It would be kind of a mystery."

"Is the hornpipe player around?" Dr. Cardim asked. "We can bring him in too."

Yema was so pleased with the idea, she could barely sit still.

"Please Sister Leah," she pleaded, "it will be safe. We can do it after dark, and no one will know it's me."

"Everyone from the camp will know it's you, Yema. Do you really think it's safe?"

"We can trust them," the child added. "It's been safe so far."

Lars Orlund spoke up. "I agree it's not a good idea. As much as I love your singing, child, it puts us all in danger." He paused for a moment, knowing what he said next would hurt her feelings. "I'm sorry, but I want you to stop singing at the Gypsy camp."

Yema put her head down and said nothing. She did not like being defeated in this manner. Yet, when her memories returned to the slave cart and the riot in Fortaleza, she knew Orlund's decision was wise.

As it turned out, a knock on the door later that week brought Helgen and his singing back into the girl's life. The before-dinner custom at Orlund's was to meet in the sitting room and share a glass or two of wine while going over the day's events. That evening, just as they settled in—Leah, Yema, Lars, Captain Vincent, Dr. Cardim, Enzo Henry, the new captain Jansen, foreman Pieter Winard, wife Migle and son Jorrit, and a few others—someone rapped on the front door. The housekeeper opened it to find the leader of the Gypsy band waiting there.

"Meneer Gunaro," the housekeeper said, "come right in."

Orlund went to see who it was. The man stood, hat-in-hand, just inside the entrance. "Ah Gunaro," Lars said, "please join us for a glass of wine, or perhaps stay for dinner? You would be most welcome."

The Gypsy leader had never been inside the Orlund house before, and was awed by the surroundings. "No thank you, Meneer Orlund. I've just come on an errand. If you would please hear me out sir."

It was obvious that the fellow was quite ill at ease, so Lars did not repeat his invitation. Instead, he turned to the housekeeper and said, "Please bring our friend a glass of wine."

In a minute the woman returned with the wine and handed it to him. Fearing he was so nervous he might drop the glass, Gunaro set it on a nearby table. He cleared his throat and said, "All of us want to thank you for your generous employment this year. In a few weeks the harvest will be over and we will be heading north to find more work. In the meantime, I have a great favor to ask."

"Of course, Gunaro, what is it?"

"Well, that girl Yema, the one that sings so beautifully, we miss her. In particular Helgen misses her. We see the child working in the fields, but she told us she cannot sing anymore during our lunchtime. So in a way, I'm here on Helgen's behalf."

"Please," Orlund said, "tell me more."

"Meneer Helgen is old, and he believes he may not live through the winter." Gunaro paused and crossed himself before continuing. "The old man needs someone to teach his songs to. We all know the songs, of course, but he feels Yema has an unusual gift with her grown-up voice, and it would be a blessing to teach her some of our special ones; songs that have the most meaning to us, both Viking and Gypsy. He would like to arrange a time to meet with her. Is that possible?"

"I think so," Orlund said. "Why not do that here? Does he want to come each day? As you said, there are only a few weeks—"

Gunaro seized Orlund's hand with both of his. "Oh thank you, sir. Thank you!" He hesitated for a moment and said, "May the boy who leads him come too, and the lute player?"

"Yes of course. This will all be good news to Yema. They should come after the evening bell. That will give them at least an hour before our meal. And I want everyone to stay here for dinner. I'll have places set for them in the kitchen."

Gunaro poured out his thanks again, and excused himself rather abruptly, leaving his wine on the table without ever tasting it.

When Lars Orlund returned to the sitting room, he said, "Yema, I have a big surprise for you."

***

The following morning after breakfast, Migle told the children to fetch sacks from the shed behind Yema and Leah's cottage. "We're going to change the bedding for the chickens," she told them. "I want you to collect straw from the field that was cut last week. Two sacks apiece."

Yema was second in line. She grabbed her two bags and ran back to Migle. The other children did the same, and when one little boy came to the letter, he examined it for a moment, then stuffed it under the bottom of the pile. An hour or so later, Leah saw the children working in a nearby field gathering the straw. Her apprehension was almost overwhelming when the sight of the bags registered with her. She rushed back to the cottage, pulled open the shed door, and saw the pile at only a fraction of what they had been previously. *So Yema or someone must have found the letter,* she thought. In a panic, and confused as to what to do next, Leah picked up the remaining bags, intending to restack them. And there at her feet lay her father's letter.

Thoughts raced through her mind. *If Yema found it, she can't read Hebrew, but the address is in Portuguese. Clearly the letter came from Antalya, and it would not be hidden unless it contained bad news. The girl would surely know that.* But thinking back to the children in the field, she remembered spotting Yema working with the other kids, and the girl had appeared her merry self. Leah took the letter into the cottage and hid it inside the chest where she kept her clothes.

***

Once the singing lessons started, Helgen and Yema's practicing became the before-dinner entertainment. On the third evening, the girl moved into the kitchen to sup with the Norseman, the boy who tended the old man, and the lutist. After a few more evenings she convinced Lars to let the visitors sit at the grand table in the dining room. An excellent choice as it turned out—Helgen was a gifted storyteller, weaving fascinating tales of the distant North and his adventures in that strange land.

It was during this second week that after-dinner entertainment was added. As with many things at the Orlund farm, the lessons and dinner turned into a routine. Everyone listened to the before-dinner activities, which included Helgen teaching songs and Yema singing along, the girl writing the words into a bound volume, and the two of them practicing. Then everyone sat down to dinner to hear the Viking's new tale of the great North, or the continuation of his story from the previous evening. Shortly after the meal's conclusion, and to the delight of everyone, Helgen, Yema, and the lute-player gave a performance. The Viking's voice had a rich quality at least three registers below Yema's, quite extraordinary for a man his age. The two of them singing together created an atmosphere of rapturous music that transfixed the audience, an audience that expanded to include many in the Orlund household, cooks, housekeepers, anyone who wanted to listen, all of them crowding into the sitting room after dinner.

Chapter 42

Most people in the little settlement of Almere considered Foygen Belye to be insane, or at least possessed in some manner. Even a stranger might consider him thus simply by his appearance. Foygen was a small young man, barely five feet tall, thin, and heavily freckled. His head was larger than most, and covered with a thick mat of wooly, red hair. So wooly that many people referred to him as *de rode schaap jongen*, the red sheep boy, or more frequently, Sheep Boy.

A few years earlier, Foygen might have died at the hands of some town ruffians—young men almost as dimwitted as Sheep Boy—when they decided to burn him at the stake just for the sport of it. Fortunately the town priest, Fr. Willemsen, saved Foygen before the heap of flaming sticks crackling around his feet consumed him. Though Sheep Boy survived, he would forever be a cripple, although in his case not a slow one. Before the incident, Foygen had been a fast runner, having much practice fleeing the town bullies. After his feet healed, though his gait was truly painful to watch, he learned to run almost as quickly as before. Unfortunately he again became the object of ridicule due to his inability to walk or run in a normal manner. This time Fr. Willemsen stepped in and thrashed the bullies so severely that they left Almere for good.

Belye had been a relatively quiet fellow, and stayed out of people's way; but after the burning incident, he became obsessed with visions of holy events which he frequently shared with Fr. Willemsen. Whenever the priest got wind of Sheep Boy's most recent obsession, the good father took him aside, patiently listened to his wild tale, and tried to convince Foygen not to badger the townspeople with his latest vision. After the first few of these "revelations" as Sheep Boy called them, followed by angry threats from the local citizenry, it became obvious that the young man would not survive without more protection from Fr. Willemsen. So the priest arranged for Foygen to sleep in the woodshed at the rear of the churchyard, and made sure that his new ward received at least one good meal each day.

For all his twenty-three years, Foygen Belye had never experienced even a crumb of kindness until Fr. Willemsen took him under his wing. In return for the priest's meager charity, Sheep Boy kept the little Almere church and its grounds spotless, cleaning, sweeping, polishing, and gardening from sunup until sundown.

During the last week of September, when the priest heard Foygen regaling people with his latest revelation—one that Fr. Willemsen knew was partly true, and held substantial peril for those involved—he instructed Sheep Boy to stop spreading the rumor, and threatened to withhold meals if he did not comply.

"But Father," Foygen said, "people have seen this girl. They've heard her sing."

"So I've heard, son," the priest said. "Perhaps there is some truth to this. However, one must be careful with these—"

"No, no, Father. Not only is it true, but it has been revealed to me who she is. This is a revelation come true."

Fr. Willemsen decided to humor the simple fellow, and asked him to describe his revelation.

"Well," Foygen said, trying to add some authority to his high-pitched voice, "she is either the miracle child singer from Brazil that people talk about, or another possibility." His eyes darted around as if others might be listening. Then his voice dropped to a whisper. "I think she's really a witch. Not a bad one, you see, but a witch with great power. She is not a child at all. She is a grown woman who has turned herself into a child."

"And why would she do that?" the priest asked.

"Because she is Nestoria, the secret wife of Prester John, the Christian ruler of the Orient! From *De Stad van Jezus!*"

Fr. Willemsen considered this. *What nonsense,* he thought. *There is no Prester John, or City of Jesus. These are just stupid myths.* But perhaps agreeing with Foygen might convince him to keep his revelation secret.

"Foygen," the priest said, "I want you to give me your word that you will not discuss this vision with anyone. Anyone! Do you understand?"

"But Father—"

"No, no. You listen to me, Foygen Belye. This may be an important revelation, the presence of the Ruler of the Orient among us. I'll look into it further, and tell you what I find. Do you agree to keep quiet? To tell no one?"

"Yes, Fr. Willemsen," Sheep Boy said. "I swear in the name of the Blessed Jesus. I swear."

"Thank you, Foygen," the priest said, and crossed himself. "Now go finish your chores."

Fr. Willemsen had known the truth for quite some time, shortly after the Corajoso arrived in Almere. A month earlier, a messenger from Archbishop Boeyens had delivered the wanted notice to his church. Because the notice mentioned five people Willemsen had never heard of, including an errant nun and an Indian girl from Brazil, he gave it little thought, and did not post it for public view. Then, when he heard the Corajoso carried a woman and an Indian child, he burned the notice. Fr. Willemsen did not want either of his good friends, Lars Orlund and Eider Vincent, implicated. After all, the Orlund family had been the largest church contributor, was always generous with the poor, and regularly provided employment for the townspeople.

The priest first heard details about the Indian girl from Vincent's seamen during confessions. They described her beautiful singing voice and magical nature, and several referred to her as a saint. If she was a fugitive, then so be it. But the girl and the woman—he assumed this was the errant nun—were a Portuguese problem, not his fugitives, nor Dutch fugitives for that matter. Besides, nearly every citizen of the Netherlands considered Archbishop Boeyens a lackey of the Spanish Inquisition and Portuguese Crown. Now the girl's singing at the Gypsy camp had become too well known among the townspeople, and sooner or later the rumors would make their way to Amsterdam and the archbishop. Fr. Willemsen's greatest regret was that he had not heard the child sing.

***

The first week in October brought an end to the harvest, and Lars Orlund announced there would be a celebration at the moorage on Friday. "Our celebration," he said, "will include a feast starting at noon for all workers, smallholders, and migrants. In addition, Captain Jansen and I have named our new merchant ship. We will christen our vessel that day, and make public her name."

When Helgen got wind of the announcement, he knew his lessons with the precious girl singer were coming to an end. He felt she was indeed ready to learn the most difficult song of all, *Hvem Kan Seile*. So on that last Wednesday before dinner, he began teaching it to her. "This will take both evenings," he told the girl. "It is really quite a simple song, and I'm going to teach you first in Dutch, and then tomorrow night in the old language. It is much more beautiful in the ancient tongue, but the pronunciation does take some time to master."

Lars Orlund had not paid much attention to this early conversation, but when he heard the lutist play the introduction, his heart pounded and he felt that familiar, overwhelming sadness at the death of his wife Greta. Three years earlier, *Hvem* was the song sung at her wake, and he had not heard it since that most difficult time. Without a word, he rose from his chair, went to the sitting room doorway and listened from there. If he were to break down and cry, at least he could turn into the hall so no one would see him.

"We usually sing it twice through," Helgen said. "It is a lament of leaving. The song is short, and the words are not fancy, but I think the melody is heart-wrenching." And he began...
 ♫ Who can sail without the wind?
 Who without oars can row?
 Who can leave a best friend behind?
 Without tears falling as you go? ♫
 When they started the second verse, and for the very first time to the delight of the listeners, the lutist also sang, her voice blending beautifully with Yema's.
 ♫ I can sail without wind
 I can row without oars
 But I cannot part from my friend
 Without shedding tears ♫
 Leah took notice of Orlund facing away from them in the hallway, his shoulders hunched and shaking. She went to join him, putting a hand on his shoulder. "What, Lars?" she said. "Tell me."
 He explained about the song, then said, "Leah, I'm surrounded by riches and success, but I'm lonely. If only—"
 She put a finger to his lips. "Shhhh. I care about you, Lars. I truly do. But do you really think we can stay here? Where Jews are hunted like animals? Please, let's give it more time."
 Orlund pulled a handkerchief from his vest and wiped his eyes. "I don't think you understand," he said. "Just now. That simple touch." He raised her hand to his lips. "*Your* simple touch, and my heart is glad again. Don't you see how much I love you?"
 "I know, Lars," she said, "and I'm honored. But I must consider my safety and Yema's." She thought briefly about her father's letter. *There's no safe place for Yema and me. None.* "As I said, Lars, please give it more time." Right then, the housekeeper called for dinner. Leah took Orlund's arm as they headed for the dining room. "Lars," she said, "do you want me to ask Helgen and Yema to sing something else after dinner, a different song?"
 "No, I'll get used to it. I guess they will be singing again tomorrow evening. I've never heard it in Norse before."
 Practice continued after dinner until the trio sang *Hvem* perfectly. When they finished, Yema saw Helgen, the lute-player, and the young boy to the door. As she bid them good-night, Helgen reached out and picked up the girl. He kissed the child on the cheek

and whispered something in her ear.

As the two women retired for bed that evening, Leah asked, "What did Helgen whisper?"

"I'm not sure," Yema replied. "I couldn't understand him. Maybe it was in that old language. I'll ask him tomorrow."

***

Practice started anew the following evening. This time Helgen recited the words slowly, while the lutist sang them, using her hands for emphasis with the unfamiliar language.

♫ *Hver getur róðið þó gefi ei byr?*

Hver getur ...

At the start, Yema had her ink and quill poised, planning to write down the song as she had done many evenings before. But no one could spell any of the Norse words, so she set the writing aside and concentrated on singing. She worked through the first verse, line by line, repeating each several times to get the pronunciation just right.

Leah watched the child closely. She had not seen Yema this engaged in a song since her days learning the *Glória* back at Abby Luís. At first the girl seemed frustrated, but on the fourth or fifth time through, she warmed to the task. When they began the second verse, Yema seemed to have the pronunciation mastered, singing it completely through on the third try. The trio just had time enough to sing *Hvem* together before the housekeeper called them to dinner.

Much of the talk around the table involved tomorrow's celebration and the christening. Captain Jansen announced that Fr. Willemsen from the Almere Church, "... will bless our new ship. And we've nearly completed the Avontuur's refit." The new captain put a hand to his mouth. Everyone laughed. "Oops," he said. "The name was supposed to wait until tomorrow."

Lars turned to Leah. "You like the name 'Adventure?'"

"It's fine," she said, "but I'm concerned about this Fr. Willemsen."

"Oh," Lars said, "he's been a loyal friend of our family for years. You've nothing to fear from him."

She gestured to Yema who sat across the table from them. "Should we stay away tomorrow?"

"I'll leave it up to you," Orlund said. "Personally, I think you will be completely safe."

Yema, sitting between Helgen and the lutist, turned to the old man and said, "What did you whisper to me last night?"

The Norseman took on a wistful look. "That was my way of explaining why *Hvem* is so special to me. Did I say, *'Ég hef skilið svo mörg lönd mér'*? It means, 'I have left so many lands behind me.' I should have translated it."

"Just like me," Yema said. "I have left so many lands."

He reached over and took the girl's hand. "That's why I said it, dear child. We are kindred in song and experience."

She leaned against the old man, resting her head against his massive shoulder. "I will miss you, Meneer Helgen."

"I will miss you too," he replied. "But tomorrow is not goodbye. We won't leave for another day or two. We'll have time to say our farewells."

After dinner, everyone returned to the sitting room. The trio sang the song through in muted tones, working together on the cadence and perfecting the pronunciation, including the language's strange combination of broken syllables, guttural sounds, and abrupt consonants.

At last they were ready for the full song. The lutist played the introduction, and they began to sing.

♫ *Hver getur róðið þó ...*
Hver getur ...

As the powerful melody and mysterious words swept over the audience, Leah realized that something had changed about Yema. It was as if she had gone into dinner a child, and emerged a young woman. She carried herself differently, moved her hands in a different manner. *What is this?* Leah asked herself, and looked around. Was it the force of this music? All the listeners seemed enthralled, many with tears in their eyes, and most resting their gaze on Yema.

When the trio finished the song, the entire room held its breath. "Again," Helgen said, and they returned to the beginning. This time Yema stepped forward and sang as never before, her voice soaring above the others, fuller and more mature than Leah had ever heard it.

Yema felt the change too, as if *Hvem Kan Seile* was inside her body, part of her very being, as real as the beating of her own heart. She could picture the words, etched in the agony of Jesus on the cross. As the girl sang, she turned her face upwards, tears streaming

down her cheeks, lacing along the scars and down her chin, onto her throat, her features radiant in the candlelight.
And after the last line,
♫ *Kvatt hann án skilnaðartára,*
Yema sang it again, this time,
♫ *Ég hef skilið svo mörg lönd mér* ♫
and then reciting for the audience, "I have left so many lands behind me."

***

"I don't know," Yema said as she and Leah prepared for bed. "It was if I were a different person. Someone outside myself."

Leah studied the girl as she changed out of her clothes. Over the past few months Yema had grown some, a little taller, a little thinner perhaps, though no sign of becoming a woman. Not yet. Her figure was still that of a child's. Still, there seemed to be something, possibly her carriage. *That's it*, Leah realized. The girl had displayed her usual confidence this evening, but it was no longer that of a naïve child; it was the confidence of a grown woman.

***

Everyone in the Orlund household rose before dawn the next morning to get ready for the celebration. After a hurried breakfast, Yema and the other children left with Migle, the cook, and two housekeepers to take care of the animals and select those destined for table fare. Inside the barn they found a rabbi and his assistant waiting for them. Yema and a few of the other children who'd never seen a rabbi before were startled to see these strangers with their long beards, black robes, and tall, cup-shaped hats.

Migle explained, "Since the Jews from Maarssen will be at the celebration today, the rabbi will ensure that the animals are slaughtered in their traditional way. Otherwise, none of our Jewish friends can eat the meat."

"And," the rabbi added, "I am here to thank the Orlund farm for giving us the opportunity to harvest food for the upcoming winter, as well as providing a refuge during this difficult time."

The children went about their assigned chores, but when the rabbi and most everyone else entered the goat pasture, Yema walked outside to watch. They had already selected a number of chickens and ducks, and three large geese which were now enclosed in a covered pen next to the barn. The girl did not check to see if Porð was among the chickens. She had not seen the orange rooster in several weeks, and assumed he'd wandered off or ended up in someone's cooking pot. The girl did take notice when the rabbi pointed to Venus and one of her kids, the latter now almost fully grown. A housekeeper slipped a rope around the neck of each goat.

Yema ran to Migle. "I don't want them killing Venus and one of her babies," she said. "Meneer Lars told me they'd be safe."

Migle took her hand and they walked into the pasture. "We'll ask them to choose some others," she told the girl.

They could see the rabbi's assistant kneeling by the two goats, feeling along their bellies. "What are they doing?" Yema asked.

"They select only the healthiest animals," Migle answered. "They also make sure the females are not carrying offspring or producing milk. If so, they are unfit for slaughter."

As they approached the group, Migle said, "Rabbi, please select some different ones." She gestured to the two goats and pointed to Venus's second kid which stood a few yards away. "These three are pets."

The rabbi gave the woman a sour look. "How can food animals be pets?" he asked.

"They're my pets," Yema said.

"And who is this strange looking child?" he asked.

Regardless of the man's stature, Migle considered the question rude. "She is a guest here, just as you are."

"Please forgive me. I meant no offence." He turned to his assistant. "Take off those ropes. We'll find other ones."

Migle said, "Thank you, Rabbi." She took Yema's hand and the two of them left the pasture.

Chapter 43

Just before noon, Leah, Yema, Lars Orlund, and several others headed for the Almere moorage. Along the way, the girl recounted the incident with the rabbi.

"Don't worry about it," Orlund said. "Regardless of their circumstance, the Maarssen Jews are very particular about their food. Because it's Friday, the rabbi's here to hold Sabbath services this evening."

"Is he also from Maarssen?" Leah asked.

"Yes. Sent me a note a week ago. He wrote that the Krüisigingers didn't make it south of Amsterdam. I guess the riot was a good thing." He paused for a moment, smiling as he did. "By the way," he continued, "we received a letter from the sugar merchant in Fortaleza. He wants to buy the plantation. When we set sail in a few weeks, that's where we're headed."

"How are you going to accomplish that?" Dr. Cardim asked. "Showing the flag there will get you arrested."

"You mean 'get *us* arrested.'" Captain Vincent added. "You're sailing with me, doctor, remember?"

"All I know," Orlund went on, "is that the merchant said the cane harvest was successful, and he thinks the plantation can be even more productive."

"Maybe it's a trap?" Cardim suggested. "The authorities might have put him up to it."

"Seems unlikely," Vincent said. "Hopefully we'll find him at the plantation. That's my first stop after the Verdes. If we don't find him there, then we will have to take our chances in Fortaleza."

While this conversation went on, Leah kept glancing over at Yema. *When are you going to tell her about your father's letter?* she asked herself. *All this talk about letters and sailing. The child must be wondering.*

When they were within a half-mile of the moorage, just past the grove of elm trees lining the road, the waterfront came into view. Groups of people could be seen gathered around cooking fires, the breeze carrying the delicious smells to anyone approaching. "There she is," Orlund exclaimed. Ahead, the three masts of the Avontuur tilted in the light swell, the Dutch pennant flying from the mainmast. "That pennant's a good sign," he went on. "That means they've got the mainsail rigged. She'll be ready for sea in less than a week." He glanced at Leah who was walking next to him.

"The ship's beautiful," she said. "I can't wait to see it."

Yema took off running, turning back for a moment to yell, "That food smells too good!"

The girl first spotted the cook working with several other people from the Orlund household, along with the Gypsy cooks and the rabbi's assistant, all of them busy carving meat, dishing out vegetables, bread, and measures of beer to whomever had a container. Yema had no container, so she grabbed a thick piece of crusty bread, plus a large drumstick—probably from a goose, she decided, walked over to the beer keg, and dipped her bread into the open barrel. She'd never tasted wheat beer before, and found it quite delicious. The girl saw Helgen sitting in the grass a short distance away with a heaping plate of food in front of him. She plopped down next to the Norseman and greeted him.

"Ah," the old Viking responded, "it is my magical singing partner. Shall we sing for the crowd today?"

"I don't think I'm allowed to," Yema said, "but I'll ask."

When Orlund and his group arrived, the crowd responded with cheers and applause. "Thank you all," he shouted, and headed for the food. Those surrounding the serving tables parted, allowing him to pass through. In turn, he asked the ladies—Migle and Leah— to go first, and soon they all emerged with plates of food and flagons supplied by the housekeeper. Following a stop at the beer keg, the party seated themselves around the table reserved for the Orlund household.

Lars and his entourage ate lunch while people of all kinds began to line up near the table. Orlund turned to Leah, and said quietly, "Every year they have this thank-you ceremony. It gets a bit long, but they insist on doing it." When he finished eating, Orlund drained his beer, stood, and approached the head of the line. In a loud voice he said, "I know you are here to thank me, and I greatly appreciate it. So let's get our thanks over with; then we can get on with the afternoon's activities."

An hour-and-a-half later, the last thank-you was offered and accepted. It seemed the entire gathering had gone through the greeting line, some apparently more than once. By then, Lars had consumed several flagons of beer and found himself increasingly amused with each passing minute. Finally he returned to the table, drank hot tea, and ate pumpkin *koekjes.*

Now that most of the food was consumed, the crowd turned to serious drinking. The cook brought out a fourth keg of beer and shouted for the revelers to line up for their share. In no time at all, a goodly fraction was quite drunk, and many lay sleeping in the grass. Leah, who'd been sitting with Yema and Helgen, returned and settled next to Lars. "Interesting," he said, observing the people around them, "how drink enlivens people to mix beyond their own crowd." Indeed this was so. The lutist, and the hornpipe player from the Corajoso, along with a couple of Gypsy women keeping time with tambourines, played local tunes while many people danced and joked. The children—those reasonably sober—danced or played tag or hide-and-seek among the piles of ship's stores covered with brown oilcloth and stored along the wharf.

While all this revelry went on, Captain Jansen and Vincent's first mate Jozef toured people around the newly fitted Avontuur. The ship was a little longer than the Corajoso, and since it carried no cargo, rode high enough in the water that her copper flanks were exposed. "I don't know why the broker sold it so cheaply," Captain Vincent told anyone who would listen. "She was quite a bargain. A naval vessel only six years old, in some need of repairs, but not a lot. And they left us six cannons; three on each side. Enough to keep the pirates at bay. Our biggest problem now," he added, "is to find enough crew for both ships."

Fr. Willemsen, a latecomer to the festivities, arrived and greeted Lars and the others around the table. Orlund had earlier consulted with Leah as to how he might introduce her. He stood and presented her as, "My dear friend, Leah Anna." The priest seemed satisfied with that, and circulated through the crowd, chatting with his parishioners.

Captain Vincent walked over to the cook and asked her to prepare a plate for Fr. Willemsen. She returned with a meager portion of food and a flagon of beer. "Sorry, Captain," the cook said, "the locals have ate almost everything."

"It's all right," Vincent replied. "He's not one to complain. Go tell the good reverend we've a plate for him."

Willemsen returned and sat down across from Orlund and the others. "Quite a show," he said. "As with years previous, you always put on a good celebration." He spent a few moments looking at the Avontuur. "She appears to be a fine ship, Captain Vincent. I'm ready for the christening when you are."

"Jansen's showing people around right now," Vincent said. "As soon as he's finished, we can start."

Minutes later, the Maarssen rabbi strolled over accompanied by his assistant. He touched his cap and acknowledged the priest. "Good afternoon, Fr. Willemsen. It is always good to see you."

"And the same Rabbi Fröhlich," the priest said. "I'm pleased to hear the Krüisigingers didn't make it south to your village. Perhaps they'll starve on their way back to Groningen."

With this remark, Leah realized that, just as Lars had told her, Fr. Willemsen was indeed a friend. While she was speculating how much the priest might know about her, Yema showed up. She'd been playing with the other children and looked quite unkempt. The girl dusted herself off and addressed the rabbi, curtseying as she did. "Thank you sir for sparing my goats."

"You're quite welcome, child," the rabbi said. He then turned to Lars. "Meneer Orlund, I want to thank you ten-fold for your many acts of kindness, providing my people work and refuge, this fine feast which respects our kosher laws, and the generous harvest that will see us through the winter."

"You are most welcome, Rabbi," Orlund said. "I hope you noticed that we left the pigs back at the farm?"

Rabbi Fröhlich smiled. "Indeed I did notice, honored sir. And your thoughtful nature is not lost on me." He looked around at the throng of people. "In a little while, I'll take my flock back to our forest camp. It's Friday, and soon time for evening services." He again touched his cap and turned to leave. As he did so, he glanced at Yema and, with no change in his cheerful expression, said to his assistant, *"Hh l d msfk 'm zh frchch mchrd,"* "I've had quite enough of that hideous brat."

Without thinking, Leah jumped to her feet and responded in Hebrew, *"Ch sh m'z lkll s hld shl!"*, "How dare you curse my child!"

The rabbi stopped in his tracks, turned and glared at Leah. "If that child is your daughter," he said in Dutch, "then you have fornicated with the devil!" He took a step towards her. "And who are you to speak to me in our sacred language? You must be a Sephardim. No Ashkenazi woman ever speaks thus. It's not allowed." He made a dismissive gesture at her face. "And no head covering? What kind of Jew are you?"

"I am a Jew who adopts orphan children. That's who I am. And only a fool would judge me and my daughter as you have!"

The rabbi looked at Orlund and made a slight bow. He said, "I am here at your mercy, Meneer Orlund, but as a man of God, I cannot abide this company. I thank you for your kindness, and now I must leave." He turned, pushed his assistant ahead of him, and walked off.

"What did he say?" Lars asked. "Was that in Hebrew?"

"It was a curse," Leah answered. "I will not repeat it."

Orlund rose to his full height, looking as angry as Leah had ever seen him. He pointed at the rabbi and said, "Obviously he insulted you. I'll have him strung up and thrashed." Everyone within hearing turned silent, all staring back at Orlund, all wondering what had just happened. A few murmured questions.

Leah tried to calm herself. She realized this outburst could cause many problems. "Lars," she said, don't bother with him. I'm not insulted that easily."

"But—" He glanced at Fr. Willemsen.

The priest sat there peaceably, trying to appear as benign as possible. When he turned to Leah, he had just the slightest twinkle in his eye. "That's the most interesting exchange I've heard in some time," he said. Then he looked over the table at the Avontuur. "Here comes Captain Jansen. Let's get started with the christening."

Leah sat down, shaken to her very core. This was the worst thing that could happen—A rabbi cursing Yema. *What a problem,* she thought. *How will the girl come to terms with this?*

Rather than being upset, Yema appeared somewhat amused. She repeated her question, "What did he say?"

"Ashkenazi Hebrew is different from Sephardi," Leah said. "I may have misunderstood him."

Yema shook her head. She said, "I guess you're not going to tell me, Sister Leah," then giggled and ran off. The girl stopped a short distance away and yelled, "I'll just have to imagine the worst." From the way she carried herself, Leah knew—despite the child's feigned amusement—she was shocked by the incident.

Everyone except Orlund and Leah left the table to attend the christening. As they watched the procession move up the gangplank onto the Avontuur, Leah said, "Lars, I'm so sorry."

"I'm sorry too," Orlund said. "Sorry for the way the rabbi behaved. I've never seen him like this before. Usually he's quite amiable."

"I should not have reacted as I did."

"You reacted just as I would have. Did he really curse Yema?"

"Yes," she said, and laughed. "It sounds worse in Hebrew than it does in Dutch." Then she turned serious. "Lars, I don't see how we can stay here. I think we should leave when the ships are ready to sail. You have been a good friend beyond measure, but I just can't marry you. Our marriage would put you and your farm in jeopardy." She pointed to a group of young women dancing and laughing. "Look at all these pretty daughters of your smallholders. Marry one of them."

"I don't want a compliant farm wife. I want you. A woman with opinions. One that's not afraid to tell me what she thinks."

"After a while you'd grow tired of my opinions."

He gave her a look of complete anguish "It's not just you, Leah. If you leave, then I lose Yema too. I absolutely adore that kid. Just like you, there's no other like her on earth. He rose to his feet. "No more talk of this," he said. "I'm going to the christening."

***

Foygen Belye first heard about the Orlund Farm celebration early in the week when he eavesdropped on Fr. Willemsen and Eider Vincent discussing the christening. Very soon, Almere was abuzz with rumors about Friday's activities, and most all the residents looked forward to the celebration.

When Fr. Willemsen ate his morning meal with Foygen on Friday, and saw the lad eager to follow him to the moorage, the priest recited a list of chores for him. Sheep Boy begged Fr. Willemsen to take him along, arguing that he could do his chores the next day. "You will stay here and do your work," the priest told him. "If I see you at the moorage, Foygen, I will thrash you until you can no longer stand. And you can sleep with the pigs for a month."

In the early afternoon, Foygen waited a short time after Fr. Willemsen's departure and set out for the moorage. Instead of following the narrow lane leading to the Orlund farm, he traveled cross-country, through woods and along a boat canal that put him behind some bushes within a hundred yards of the moorage. There he waited, watching the festivities and trying to spot the witch-child. His hiding place was too distant, so once he saw the priest seated at a table, occupied with eating his lunch, he moved to a clump of bushes that was much closer. From this vantage point, he identified a few possibilities for the witch-child, Yema, a Moorish slave girl belonging to one of the smallholders, and three Gypsy girls of the appropriate age and coloring.

His hiding place was not very secret, since a number of the children had stumbled over him during their games. But most youngsters were afraid of Foygen—either because of his fearful appearance, or they knew who he was—so when word got around as to his whereabouts, the children avoided him. When Sheep Boy saw the angry exchange at the priest's table, and one of the dark girls first there, then running away, he decided she was the child witch. He wanted to confront the girl, call her by name, "Nestoria," but that was not possible with Fr. Willemsen sitting right there. He grasped the wooden cross that hung around his neck, certain that if he thrust this symbol of Jesus at her, she would materialize into the adult woman. At last he could declare the truth of his revelation to the world.

The afternoon's stress and fatigue finally got the best of Foygen, and just prior to Fr. Willemsen joining Captain Jansen for the christening, Sheep Boy dozed off. In his dream, he heard the priest calling him to worship. The lad awoke with a start, realizing that he was indeed hearing the voice of the Fr. Willemsen. There stood the good reverend on the deck of a ship, holding a cross to the heavens and pronouncing a benediction. And there was the witch girl, unguarded and standing with some children just a few yards away. He rose to his feet and ran at the child, breaking the strand around his neck and extending the wooden cross in her direction. "Nestoria!" he cried, "I am from the City of Jesus. I know who you are. Reveal yourself!"

"Holy Mother of God," one of the children exclaimed. "It's pumpkin head Sheep Boy."

To Yema, Foygen looked like a deranged scarecrow. She screamed and thrust her arms towards him, intending to push this crazy person away. A boy close to her threw himself at Foygen, knocking him to the ground just before he reached Yema. At the same moment, Fr. Willemsen stopped in mid-prayer, staring in disbelief at the scene.

Sheep Boy struggled to his feet and charged again. This time he screamed, "I know you're the secret wife of Prester John!" He intended to say more, but a man standing nearby bashed Foygen in the head with a pewter tankard.

Leah ran forward and stepped over Sheep Boy's prostrate body. She grabbed Yema and pulled her away. "I've had enough insanity for one day," she said. "Let's get out of here."

As soon as they left, Yema asked, "Who was that person? He really scared me."

"I don't know," Leah replied. "Some fool from the village. A few people seemed to know who he was."

They walked in silence for a while until Yema said, "Those ships will be ready to sail soon. What are we going to do?"

"My first choice is to go to Gibraltar and find a ship that will take us to Antalya."

"But I love it here," the girl said. "The farm people are friendly, and the Gypsies and Helgen, they're like a family. I think you should marry Lars." She appeared on the verge of tears.

Leah took the girl's hand. "And do what?" she asked, "Live on a ship for the rest of our lives? As comfortable as we are here now, our presence puts Lars in danger. Once we're found out, the Portuguese will seize his farm. Then we're all done for."

"But he and Captain Vincent are wanted too. Why haven't the soldiers come already?"

"I guess the news from Fortaleza hasn't reached here yet." Leah sighed and looked back at the moorage. "That's *also* only a matter of time."

With the sun low at their backs, Yema stopped and looked at her shadow. "My *kuarahy'ã* is long and pointing east. I guess we should go to live with your parents. I wonder why you haven't heard from them?"

Leah scooped Yema into her arms and said, "Now both our shadows are pointing east, dear daughter." Then the girl felt Leah trembling. The woman's next words came in a hoarse whisper. "Yema, sweetheart, I've something to show you back at the cottage."

Chapter 44

As soon as the two women entered the cottage, Leah went to her clothes chest and retrieved the letter. She handed it to Yema and said, "Let's go over to the main house. I'll read it to you there. I'll need to talk to Lars and Captain Vincent as soon as they get back."

They walked the short path to the main house, their shadows even longer in the late afternoon sun. Yema studied the address as they walked, then unfolded the lappet and pulled out the two parchment sheets. "I don't think this is your mother's writing," she said.

"You're right," Leah said, "and you are amazing. I can't believe you remember the writing on the letters I showed you at Abby Luís. It's been two years."

"You told me women weren't allowed to write. But your mother was an exception. That's why I remember it."

"Why are we having this conversation about hand-writing?" Leah asked. "You know if I hid the letter, it's not good news."

"I figured that," the child said. "After today and that crazy man, nothing surprises me."

The interior of the house was dark, so Leah lit two candles from the side table with the oil lamp that burned by the front entrance for just that purpose. She handed one to Yema and carried the other into the sitting room. They set the pewter candlesticks on a table between two heavily upholstered chairs, and sat down. "All right," Leah said, "the letter *is* bad news. And I'll read it in a minute. But I want you to explain your—" She stopped, searching for words. "Well then. The rabbi cursed the both of us this afternoon, and you seemed almost indifferent to it. Next, you find out about the letter, and you still appear indifferent. Why aren't you more upset?"

The girl got up and stepped over to Leah's chair. She knelt next to the armrest and ran her hand down the woman's arm, lacing their fingers together, resting her head against Leah's elbow. "I have learned from you," she said, "and I have learned from Helgen. Even from dear Agato, Fr. Julian and Fr. Mateus. One can endure almost anything." She straightened a little. "I'm ready, Sister Leah, read me the letter."

"It's from my father," Leah told her, and began to read.

When she finished, Yema remained looking straight ahead, her face stoic, tears on her cheeks. "What do we do now?" she asked.

"We will go to the Ottoman and live separately from my parents if they won't accept us. At least we'll not be persecuted there." She reached over and pulled Yema into her lap. "It's so strange," she continued, "my parents have adopted two children, ones they took in when their parents died. I wonder what's changed? Even my brother adopted children."

"Did you write them back?"

"No, I was too upset. Just didn't know what to say. Or for that matter, what to do."

Yema twisted and faced Leah, their eyes just inches apart. "You want my opinion?" she asked.

"Sure."

"You did know what to do. It's the two of us, you and me. We'll make it work."

Yema's words were far from the truth. In fact, she felt quite the opposite. Despite almost two years of struggle, nothing had worked. They'd survived by the skin of their teeth, and life shouldn't go on this way. She yearned to be back in Brazil, in her green jungle and on the open beaches, feeling the warm rain on her skin. What Lars had said this morning settled everything—He was going back to Brazil, and she would go with him.

"Speaking of Agato," Leah said, "Monday will be one year since his death. We'll say *Nahala* that evening."

When the rest of the household returned a few hours later, they found Leah and Yema sound asleep in the chairs. Leah decided the men were too drunk to have a worthwhile conversation, so she and the girl bid them good-night and headed off to the cottage.

The next morning after chores, the two women and a few others walked to the Gypsy camp to say their farewells. On the way there, they passed near the Jewish camp where the rabbi was just starting the morning Sabbath. Leah paused and told the rest of the group she'd catch up. Standing a good distance back so as not to be noticed, she watched for a few minutes as the rabbi unrolled a small Torah, held it to the heavens, and began to read. She then spotted a group of smallholders also observing the service and staying respectfully to the rear of the assembled Jews. She walked over and joined them.

This Sabbath didn't seem much different from the services she'd attended in Lisbon so many years before. Except for this congregation sitting on crude benches or on the ground, the gathering here looked much like those of her Sephardic congregation, the men sat apart from the women and children, the females with head scarves, the men with their black caps and prayer shawls. After yesterday— since everyone knew she was a Jew—she expected the smallholders to treat her differently. To her surprise, they did not. After a little while, listening to the rabbi chant familiar Hebrew scripture, Leah grew weary of standing there and moved on to the Gypsy camp. Once there, she helped load the wagons, wishing everyone a safe journey in the process.

An hour later, the caravan headed for the moorage. From there they would take the road north to another large farm like Orlund's. Yema rode in a wagon with Helgen, sitting next to the old fellow and trying to make light conversation. Leah walked alongside, occasionally joining in. When they arrived at the moorage, the caravan stopped to receive well-wishes from many from the boat crews.

Yema waited until the last minute to get down. As she hugged the old Viking and kissed him on the cheek, he reached into his pocket and handed her a rosemary sachet. "This will help you remember me," he said. "I made it myself." Then Leah reached up and helped Yema to the ground. Silently, and hand-in-hand, the two women stood there. The cart driver popped his whip, the horse strode forward, and the Gypsies were gone.

Everyone returned to work or went back to the farm except Yema. She used the excuse that she was going to roam around the ships. In truth, the girl wanted to talk with Captain Vincent. She found him in his cabin studying charts. He greeted her cheerfully and suggested she sit down. Once seated, Yema told him why she was there.

"Have you told Leah?"

"No."

"Lars?"

"No." The girl shifted in her seat. "I haven't told anyone except you."

"Why me?"

"Because you're a friend, and I need advice."

Vincent shook his head, running a hand over the charts on his table. "Your reasons for not going with Leah seem sound, but perhaps there's a compromise of some sort." With a shrug, he said, "So you asked where we're going after we leave Gibraltar? The Verdes. We'll stop first at the Canary Islands for supplies, then on to Ilia da Brava."

"Will you see Obiike?"

"That's my intention. I'll bring him the money and supplies we promised. I also want to see if he's established a sugar plantation there. If not, he's the expert when it comes to cane growing. Maybe he'll come with us."

"To the Brazil plantation?"

"Yes, but just to collect our funds from the Fortaleza merchant. Then we're going north to the Spanish coast. Somewhere where we're not fugitives."

"Is Lars going?" she asked.

"That depends on Leah." Vincent gave her a puzzled look. "Good God, Yema, this is a conversation you should be having with her." He sighed and said, "But enlighten me— What are you intending to do once we get someplace?"

"I might go live with Nanjala, and if that won't work, then I'm going upriver from the plantation to find Fr. Mateus. The Tupi are the closest people I have to a tribe."

"If you don't mind my saying it, I'm really exasperated with you. Why aren't we a tribe? Me, Lars, especially Leah, the whole damn bunch of us who care about you?"

She shook her head, seemingly unfazed by his reproach. "I don't know."

"Well you asked for my opinion, so here it is. An eleven-year-old girl doesn't make this kind of decision on her own. Get Leah's—"

"I'm almost twelve."

Vincent stretched and rocked back in his chair. "You've already decided, haven't you? This is one of those Yema decisions we've all come to expect. Right?"

She stood and nudged her chair against the table. "Please don't say anything until I find a way to tell Sister Leah. It's going to be difficult."

He thought to say, "You'll break her heart," but decided against it. Instead he rose to his feet and said, "All right, but use your head. Think it through."

Yema left Vincent's cabin without looking back.

***

The first hint of fall appeared Wednesday morning with cool weather and a light frost. Yema was fascinated by the tiny ice crystals, running her hands along the iron railings that lined the porch in front of the main house. How could this strange, white frosting be cold in her hand one moment, and turn to water the next?

Leah waited for her at the entrance, amused by the girl's behavior. "This is an example of the ice I told you about," she said. "When it gets cold enough, water actually freezes. Then it's in big pieces. Not those tiny crystals. Now come in to breakfast."

The conversation during the morning meal centered around Vincent and Jansen's efforts to recruit enough men for the Avontuur's crew. "We're twenty short," Vincent said. "Let's pair up the experienced men with the new ones, and sail short crew on both ships to Gujan-Mestras. We'll take on cargo there and hire a bunch of Frenchies. They make good sailors."

Lars Orlund remained silent throughout most of this exchange. From his point of view, nothing felt truly resolved between him and Leah. To Leah, it was indeed resolved—She and Yema were going to the Ottoman, and soon she would have to inform everyone. Orlund finally took part in the conversation when they began to discuss what cargo they could sell at the French port. "We only pledged half our wheat to the brewers in Amsterdam," he said. "Let's load the rest and sell it wherever we can."

"Then it's settled," Vincent said. "We'll sail a week from today. Jansen and I will visit the smallholders again. Maybe we can recruit a few more of their men."

When Leah, Migle, and Yema walked out the front door, intending to head for the animal pens and the morning chores, they paused to watch a wagon coming up the lane from Almere. It advanced at a fast pace, the horse alternating between a trot and a gallop. At that moment, Lars joined them. "That looks like Fr. Willemsen," he said. "I wonder why he's—"

"And that blasted Sheep Boy's driving," Migle cut in.

As the wagon drew closer, they could see that Foygen Belye had an iron collar around his neck, the end chained to a bolt on the wagon seat. They also noted that right side of his head and face was blue and frightfully misshapen from the abuse he'd endured the preceding Friday. At about twenty feet out, the priest suddenly grabbed the reins and pulled the horse to a stop. He reached behind him and produced a black cloth bag which he placed over Foygen's head.

"Sheep Boy has spread his last rumor!" Fr. Willemsen shouted. Then he got down and hurried in their direction. He had a parchment tucked under one arm. "Can we go inside?" he asked. "I need to talk with Captain Vincent if he's here. Also Dr. Cardim."

Once in the house, the priest unrolled the parchment and spoke in a hurried voice, nodding to Vincent and Cardim who joined them just as he began to speak. "A friend," he said, "stole this from the posting board outside the Boeyens Cathedral. He said it was put up yesterday. He also said there are others like it displayed at the other two churches across town."

The notice was similar to the ones posted for Doçura, Yema, and the others over a year ago at Colony Luís and Fortaleza. It offered substantial rewards for Vincent, Cardim, Orlund, Doçura, Yema, and Unnamed Others, For CRIMES AGAINST THE HOLY ROMAN CHURCH AND THE PORTUGUESE CROWN.

A deadly silence descended over the group. Vincent was the first to speak. "Why hasn't the militia come across the bay to arrest us?" he asked.

The priest said, "The archbishop sent the entire force south to Maarssen to harass the Jews. I'm sure there's a runner on his way there now. If the militia marches up this side of the bay, they could be here in a day or two."

"Then that's the end of this farm," Orlund said. "My parents, and their parents before them. And now I've lost it."

"Fr. Willemsen," Captain Vincent said, "I thank you for this warning. You've saved all of us." He thought for a moment before continuing. "I'm sending Enzo Henry back with you. Help him recruit as many young men from the village as you can find. We need to flesh out our crews. They should be at the moorage by sundown this evening. We sail tomorrow before first light." He turned to Lars. "You take care of everything here at the house and farm. Jansen's down at the waterfront. He and I will get the ships ready."

"The Avontuur doesn't have a navigator," Orlund said. "What—"

"We'll make do," Vincent replied, and headed for the door. He stopped in the threshold and looked back. "Can you get the wheat down to the dock by this afternoon?" he asked Orlund.

"I think so. What about the animals?"

"We'll set up pens for the goats. Bring a dozen or so. Crate the chickens. Everything else, give to the smallholders. I suggest giving the cattle to the van Hoffs, but bring that small bullock and all our winter stores to the moorage. We've got no furniture or galley supplies on the new ship, so bring anything you want from the house. We can use it." The captain broke into a smile. "And see if you can get your cook to sign on. She's a fine chef, and we'll see how our sailors like having a woman boss them around."

***

The news came as a shock to the farm and household workers, though somewhat lessened when they heard that most of the livestock would be given to the smallholders. Because many of those in Orlund's employ came from the surrounding farms, the animals represented a valuable windfall. Most everyone also assumed that by spring, since it appeared Orlund was abandoning the farm, they would have more land to till. In the end, only Migle, her son Jorrit and husband Pieter, the cook, and two workers who had no local family, agreed to sail in the morning. Orlund asked everyone to work all day, and into the night if need be.

On the way to the animal pens, Migle pointed to the many gleaners in the fields. "The cool weather," she told Yema and the other children, "is reminding everyone that winter is not far off. I want you kids to go tell those folks that they can come here at noon and claim some animals. Make sure you tell everyone, and tell them to let their neighbors know."

Instead of running into the fields with the other children, Yema shouted, "Back in a minute," and sprinted to her cottage. A short time later she returned with a length of blue ribbon and handed it to Migle. "Tag Venus and her two kids with this," she said. "I want them staying here. Any goats on a ship will end up as food." The woman took the ribbon. Yema turned and ran after the other children.

As the morning progressed, cart after cart of household items, farm stores, and animals headed for the moorage. Once there, almost everything was trundled up the gangplanks either to the Avontuur or the Corajoso. To the amusement of Captains Jansen and Vincent, two carts arrived with large wooden beds and straw-stuffed mattress from the main house. "Just leave those dockside," Vincent told Jorrit Winard who was driving the lead cart. "Obviously you've never been under sail before. We use hammocks. Otherwise you'll end up on the floor every time the ship rolls. Anyway, they're too large. We'll never get them below deck."

The problem with taking large objects below deck did not deter the captains when Jorrit later showed up with Orlund's beautiful dinner table and ten chairs. The ship's carpenter simply sawed the table in two, delivering one half to the dining cabin on the Avontuur, the other half to its galley.

Each cart's return trip to the farmhouse carried water barrels. Soon there were over thirty standing on end near the well, each waiting to be filled by the children. A little after noon, the cook laid out a gigantic feast for anyone who wanted to partake. It appeared she had cooked anything not already transported to the dock, boiled onions, wheat porridge too infested with weevils to take aboard the ships, stewed apples, an excess of pork—cooked because they had run out of packing salt, and a mountain of baked yams on the edge of spoiling. No one had any plates or utensils, so everyone ate with their hands.

While they ate, Leah and Yema watched as their two trunks of clothes and possessions were loaded onto a cart along with several full water barrels. "We've got a cabin on the Avontuur," she told the driver. "Please see they are unloaded there."

"Why aren't we staying on the Corajoso?" the girl asked. "In our old cabin?"

Leah let out a sigh. "Because Lars is just miserable thinking about our leaving him at Gibraltar. This makes it easier for all of us."

Yema turned away at this moment, her face clouded with uncertainty. *Am I really going with Lars and Vincent?* she wondered. *How am I ever going to tell Sister Leah?* The child's thoughts were interrupted when in the distance she saw Venus and one kid being led away by a smallholder family. She had no idea where the other kid was. She threw her half-eaten yam back onto the platter and ran in the direction of the smallholders. After a short distance, she stopped and turned around. *We're running for our lives,* she told herself, *and you're worried about goats? They're probably safer than we'll ever be.*

***

With the approach of evening, the last items were loaded aboard the ships, firewood for cooking, animal feed, a cache of blankets from the Orlund house—enough to provide one for each sailor, several large stacks of oilcloth which were folded, bound, and lashed on deck, whale oil for lamps, and six boxes of books from Orlund's library. Half of the books were placed on the shelves in Captain Jansen's cabin, the other half in Vincent's quarters.

As the October sun dropped behind the Boeyens Cathedral on the bay's distant west shore, Jorrit and the cook showed up with a wagonload of food for the crews. The entire meal, mostly leftovers from the luncheon feast, was contained in iron cooking pots. "Eat it all," the cook shouted. "These pots are going onboard the Avontuur. Anything left over, you'll see it again for breakfast."

While arranging things in their cabin, Leah and Yema heard the commotion and came on deck. Despite the arrival of food, neither had any appetite, the two of them shocked at the suddenness of tomorrow's departure. They watched as the large cooking pots were unloaded onto the ground. The sailors swarmed around them, every man impatiently hungry from the day's work.

Some distance up the lane, and partly obscured by the failing light, two figures appeared— Lars Orlund and Linder van Hoff. When they caught up with the now-empty wagon, the two men stopped and talked for a few moments. Then van Hoff embraced Orlund, climbed onto the wagon seat, turned the horse, and headed back in the direction of the farms. Lars Orlund, his shoulders slumped and head down, walked along the dock and up the gangplank onto the Corajoso.

Chapter 45

"I'm going to see Lars," Yema announced. "I'll be back in a while." As soon as she jumped onto the dock, the child shouted at him and ran up the gangplank. He stopped and waited for her at the foot of the quarterdeck stairs.

"Well, it's good to see at least one smiling face on a gloomy night like this," he said.

"It's not all that gloomy, Meneer Lars. It's clear. And the stars are shining."

"Take my word for it, child, it's—"

"I'm not going to Turkey with Sister Leah," Yema blurted out. "I'm going with you."

Orlund sat down on the bottom stair, hardly believing what he'd heard. "I don't understand what you just said. Explain."

"Things are too dangerous for me in this place, and probably the same in Antalya. It makes no difference how beautiful your farm is. Look what's happened to us. I'm attacked by a crazy man, that rabbi cursed me, and Leah's parents don't want me. Now we're running for our lives!"

"I heard Leah received a letter, but—"

"Her father wrote it! She read it to me. I can't go to Turkey." Yema broke into tears and sat down next to Orlund. "They don't want me," she wailed, "Don't you understand?"

He put his arm around the child and hugged her. "Yema," he said, "I love you like a daughter. If you went with me, I wouldn't miss Leah as much. But it's the wrong thing to do."

"I'm not going to live on the ship. You said something about the coast north of the plantation. The Spanish Coast? A plantation? Maybe I can live there?"

He turned her shoulders so she looked directly at him. "You haven't told Leah, have you?"

"No."

"That's because your heart is telling you it's not right." He stood and gazed over at the Avontuur. Little was visible except for the many lanterns in use by the crews preparing for departure. "Tell you what," he said. "Despite the fact that I'd love to have you with me, this is very upsetting news. After you've told Leah, and talked it through with her, then let's you and me talk again. Can you do that?"

The girl stood, but did not move to leave. "You think she'll forbid me. Is that what you think?"

"No, I do not think that. As I just said, tell her first, then we'll talk."

Yema gave Lars Orlund a brief hug and hurried down the gangplank. He stood looking after her, shaking his head in disbelief.

***

In preparation for the morning departure, both crews worked until eleven bells. At this point, and with everything ready, a goodly number fell into exhausted sleep on deck, many of them rolled into blankets from the Orlund house. As the night grew progressively colder, those sleeping on deck went below to their quarters. Leah and Yema slept well, each wrapped in quilts they'd brought from the cottage.

At four a.m., the ship's bell commenced ringing with an incessant call to assembly. Crews and officers alike struggled on deck. Onboard the Avontuur, the cook and her helpers brought two steaming pots up from the galley, one with porridge, the other with freshly boiled pork.

"I never liked those pigs very much," Yema said after drinking some of the pork broth. "This food tastes great."

The two women went to their quarters, put on their warmest clothes, and returned topside to help with the preparations. Since short crew meant short sails, they found little to do. Fortunately there was a fresh breeze from the east, allowing the ships to maneuver northwest into the bay using only the lower-third mainsails and the rear trysails, tasks easily managed by the limited crew.

The ships moved silently away from the moorage, first in tandem, then side-by-side as the wind shifted from east to south. Despite the early hour—pitch black and with no hint of dawn—campfires on the nearby shore and torches flickering atop the Boeyens Cathedral in far-off Amsterdam provided adequate navigation markers for sailing up the bay.

Interesting, Leah thought. *That vulgar monument to Archbishop Boeyens provides us a beacon for escape.*

A shout from the lookout interrupted her thoughts. "Captain Jansen! Big fire south," the sailor called out. "Looks about at Stichtsekant. I can hear cannon fire too."

Everyone stared southward.

After a short while, Leah and Yema moved to the quarterdeck and sat down on benches next to the navigation table. "What do you think?" Leah asked Captain Jansen.

"I think that Orlund and Vincent have again saved the day," he said. "I'd wager the militia's advance guard is already at the farm. It's lucky we left when we did."

"What do you make of the cannon fire?"

"Typical of the Portuguese. They likely ran out of Jews to kill, so now they're ravaging the countryside. When they find out we've escaped, they'll probably take it out on the smallholders. What a shame."

***

Shortly after eight bells—a dozen miles from the Almere moorage—braids of smoke began to rise from the Orlund farm and adjacent areas, the south wind bending the plumes towards the ships. The only structures visible at this great distance were a cluster of forty-foot-high hop frames a mile north of the moorage. They soon erupted in flame. Leah and Yema watched from the rail of the Avontuur. Several on the Corajoso were doing the same, including Lars Orlund.

Captain Jansen joined the two women, but said nothing. Everyone knew what the fires meant. "I guess it's our fault," Leah said. "Otherwise, none of this would have happened."

"I consider it destined," Jansen responded. "The farm's a terrible price to pay, but you saved us all from the Africans and made the plantation possible. If not for you, we would be enslaved in Brazil, or maybe dead."

Yema, who so far had remained silent, glanced at them both and walked away. By her stiff walk, Leah knew she was angry. Jansen noticed it also. "What's going on with her?" he asked.

"The child's too polite to say it around you, Captain Jansen, but she wants to tell us something like, 'If it weren't for you whites, I'd be living with my family in the jungle.'"

The south wind increased throughout the day, and the two ships made good progress, arriving at eventide just a mile below the Den Helder Inlet at the north end of Amsterdam Bay. Since neither ships' lookouts had spotted any perusing Portuguese craft, the two captains decided to anchor for the night. The next morning they would sail through the inlet and out into the broad Atlantic. A number of fishing camps could be seen on the bay's west shore, and shortly before dark, Captain Vincent called over to the Avontuur.

"Captain Jansen! Kindly send a boat over first thing in the morning. Let's see if we can tempt some of those fisher lads into becoming blue-water sailors." Jansen agreed, and ordered the ship made secure for the evening.

The next morning, having enticed only three fishermen into a year's sailing adventure, the two ships nosed into the ocean swells rolling through Den Helder Inlet. They emerged a half-hour later into the sun-dappled Atlantic. Since the wind continued from the south, they began a long series of tacks, first beating west away from the coast, then shorter tacks east, zig-zagging their way south only a few miles at a time. The wind shifted to the west by mid-afternoon, and progress improved.

With strong breezes, the majority of them favorable, and three days' sailing, Guernsey Island off the coast of northern France came into view. It was late in the afternoon, and since Captain Vincent had used this anchorage before, he led the way into the narrow passage between the east side of Guernsey Island and the smaller Île de Herm. The two islands, both with significant headlands, provided excellent shelter from the open sea.

With sails furled and everything settled well before dark,

Captain Jansen invited the Corajoso's officers over for the evening meal, the first time on the voyage that everyone had supped together. Greetings were warm, and perhaps a little effusive, but the dinner conversation turned stilted and quiet. Everyone around the table found their thoughts tortured by the many losses and uncertainties, past and future— Losing the Orlund farm; the smallholders' fate; the uncertain knowledge about Yema's intentions; Leah's unwillingness to accept Lars Orlund's offer of marriage and her likely departure to the east from Gibraltar; what they might find at the Gujan-Mestras port in the way of additional crew members, sale of cargo there and new goods for trade in Gibraltar, Tangier, or elsewhere; and lastly, were these two southern ports even open to Dutch traders? Particularly the Corajoso and Avontuur with their fugitive officers and passengers?

Thus sailing and cargo matters continued as the most frequent topics, and no one it seemed, wanted to discuss anything else. The dinner however, did not lack for excellence. The Orlund farm cook, remaining true to her reputation, prepared a fine meal consisting of a stew made from wheat dumplings and fresh-caught fish, carrots simmered in beef fat, roast bullock tongue in a sweet raisin sauce, pickled cabbage, and pumpkin *koekjes* to go with the after-dinner brandies. Near the end of the meal, Captain Jansen summoned the cook to the dining cabin for a round of applause, then led a prayer of thanks for "the fine food, good company, and favorable sailing weather," and asking God to bless them with continued safe voyage.

***

After two weeks with their short crews struggling against difficult seas, the ships neared Gujan-Mestras Bay, the last trading port north of the Spanish border. Leah and Yema recalled their visit nearly five months earlier and the delightful shopping excursion to Audenge at the east end of the estuary, but also remembering the sad turn of events right after the elegant luncheon hosted by Officer Jérôme.

"I hope we'll be more welcome here than when we left the last time," Leah said. "I still wonder what happened to those poor Spanish Jews."

The Avontuur, with Enzo Henry onboard, had taken the lead throughout this leg of the journey. When they left Guernsey Island, Henry stayed on the Avontuur to train one of the Dutch fishermen who had shown some aptitude for the science of navigation.

Just before noon, the lookout sighted the entrance to the

French port. His call to Captain Jansen came as a relief to everyone on board. Both ships were running low on food and drinking water. In addition, a few nights inside the bay with protection from the wave-tossed Atlantic would provide a welcome respite from the stormy seas and constant pounding.

With the wind at her heels, the Avontuur had just rounded the south-pointing peninsula into the bay's entrance, when the lookout called out in alarm. "Heave to, Captain. Three Portuguese warships inside the bay. Two miles ahead."

Jansen immediately ordered sails furled, and made the difficult turn into the wind. Then, using only the forward trysail snubbed hard to port, he maneuvered the ship south and away from the bay's entrance. The lookout, also on loan from the Corajoso—and one of Vincent's most trusted seamen—raised the warning pennant from the crow's nest, signaling the Corajoso to follow their lead.

Once back on the open sea, the two ships headed south as best they could, struggling through one rough tack after another, fighting the south wind throughout the rest of the afternoon. Near evening, the wind dropped first to a stiff breeze, then to calm. Neither captain was comfortable with the sudden change because of the ominous squall line on the south horizon. Both Vincent and Jansen wished to confer on the situation, to tally supplies and plan for some emergency port before they reached the Spanish coast, but the grim November seas remained too rough for the ships to approach sufficiently close for conversation.

"We're in for a difficult night," Captain Jansen announced. He ordered Jorrit Winard—newly promoted to second mate—to supervise securing the ship for the coming storm. He next sent Enzo Henry down the front hatch to the galley with instructions to have the cook bring a quick evening meal on deck for the busy crew. She and a helper soon appeared with baskets of cold biscuits and dried apples, and passed them around. Henry, now acting as first mate as well as navigator, took over the watch from a weary Captain Jansen and fastened himself into the storm harness at the ship's wheel.

Leah and Yema, each wrapped in a heavy quilt against the chill wind, stood by the quarterdeck rail, eating their cold dinner and watching the approaching storm. Before they could finish their meager ration, a massive wave slammed into the Avontuur, sending water across the weather deck, and also drenching those perched five feet higher on the quarterdeck. Both women had dropped their food and grabbed the rail a moment before the wave hit.

As soon as it passed, Leah took Yema's hand and said, "Let's get where it's dry." The two stepped over their sodden dinner scraps, went down the quarterdeck stairs, lifted the rear hatch, and descended the steep companionway to their quarters. Once inside, Leah braced herself against the damp bulkhead and stared through the foam-splattered window at the dark ocean, hoping to catch a glimpse of the Corajoso. And for just a moment she saw it. A bolt of lightning lit up the surrounding sea, outlining the ship in a vivid flash of blue-gray.

Then another large wave battered the Avontuur. Little spurts of seawater sprayed against Leah from the bulkhead seams. She immediately got down on her hands and knees, examining the hull area near the floor.

"Well," she said, running her hand along the wet bulkhead, "at least we're not leaking below the waterline."

"Do you think we'll sink?" Yema asked.

"No," she said. "The seams have loosened a little because of the weather. We'll be all right."

With the storm raging, sleep became impossible. The ship lurched in every direction, wave after wave slamming against the hull. Curtains of lightning flashed outside the window, and streams of water surged against the glass— seawater thrown up by the waves, and rain that came in torrents. Their sleeping hammocks usually provided some isolation from the ship's movement, but not on a night as violent as this. After a while, Leah tied the two hammocks together, which added a little stability, and the women fell into an exhausted sleep.

The wind and rain abated somewhat as morning approached, although the waves continued as powerful as ever. Hungry and wondering what conditions were like topside, Leah reached from her hammock and took hold of the window sash, steadying herself long enough to get a view of the outside. It puzzled her for a moment— all she saw was the ocean, ocean that somehow extended itself above the window. Then the immense wave hit the Avontuur, and a horrific cracking sound reverberated through the ship. The sound was followed by a deafening crash. Suddenly everything listed starboard at an extreme angle, and did not recover.

Both women had slept in their clothes. Now they got out of

their hammocks, quickly put on their shoes and oilcloth capes, stumbled through the strangely tilted passageway, clambered up the ladder, and pushed open the hatch cover. They found the deck in complete shambles. The mainmast lay splintered, wedged into a shattered portion of the starboard rail, the mast's upper third dipping in and out of the sea.

The entire crew—few as they were—struggled to deal with the damage. The two women could only hold onto a lifeline and watch as the sailors tried to free the mast and right the ship. Since the massive timber was impossible to move, Captain Jansen ordered the ship's carpenter to saw off the mast a foot or so from the rail on the seaward side of the hull. Leah and Yema held their breath as the crewmen took on this perilous task. The carpenter stood atop the smashed rail, one foot on the splintered wood, the other on the fallen mast. He had a rope around his waist, and two sailors held onto it, leaning back against the sloping deck, keeping the carpenter from tumbling into the sea that washed just below his feet. He progressed to a point where the mast was about two-thirds cut through. At that point the ninety-foot timber began to flex upward, jamming the saw within the cut each time waves lifted the submerged end. The carpenter adjusted to the problem, waiting until the mast flexed downward, sawing furiously each time the cut opened again.

After what seemed like an eternity, the mast cracked and fell into the sea. The Avontuur abruptly tilted upright, launching the carpenter onto the deck where he collided with the two sailors who had been holding him. The three men rolled around on the planks, playfully punching each other, gleeful they'd succeeded.

"All right, gentlemen," Jansen announced. "Good work. Now, secure those shrouds and lash the yardarms to the rail. I intend to salvage the sails once this sea settles down."

The sailors used grappling hooks to pull the mast next to the ship. The six yards on one side of the mast stuck straight up, the other six remained underwater, projecting straight downward. Because of the drag, the Avontuur began drifting sideways to the swells.

"Mr. Henry," Jansen called to the navigator who was manning the wheel, "can you hold her?"

"No Sir," Henry shouted back. "I've got the rudder full over and she still wants to yaw." The captain turned back to the crew. "Cut the halyards and saw off the yards. Bring those sails on board before we flounder. I want two men sawing, the rest of you haul sails. And salvage the crow's nest. We'll mount it on the foremast."

One man with a saw began to cut the lower yard, while five men clustered around the upper yard with its furled sail, one of them sawing, the others cutting the halyard lines and bringing the heavy, water-soaked canvas onboard. As soon as they finished this canvas— the mainsail—they moved to the topsail and repeated the work, and then on to the top gallant. By now the ship lay fully sideways in the rough sea, each wave boiling over the deck, driving the tethered mast against the hull, and making it impossible for the men to cast the thing loose so it could be turned over.

Jansen studied the situation. If they freed the mast and tried to rotate it, the yardarm stubs would smash through the Avontuur's hull. He called out to the crew. "Hold that mast in place. We'll get turned around." He gestured to Enzo Henry, and shouted. "One-hundred-eighty degrees, Mr. Henry." The navigator spun the wheel, and the Avontuur began to turn. Jansen again addressed the sailors. "As soon as we're on the lee side of the wash, loose that mast and rotate it."

The ship began to roll violently as it yawed sideways, the waves now impacting on the starboard side. Leah and Yema continued to hold onto the lifeline as they watched the sailors struggle to rotate the mainmast. They finally got it turned, lashing the port yards to the rail, the long timbers waving violently above their heads.

"Excellent work, gentlemen!" Captain Jansen shouted. "Now Mr. Henry, take her into the wind."

With the water's drag of the long yards and wet sails no longer a problem, the Avontuur turned into the wind and the deck roll stabilized. Immediately the sailors began to salvage the sails and crow's nest. Leah and Yema worked their way forward through the debris of broken fittings, ropes, and shrouds to the ship's bow. As they arrived at the place near the foremast where the animal pens had been, the cook joined them. No trace of the pens or their occupants remained.

"What a shame," the cook said. "I hope we can make the salt pork last." She pointed to the forward hatch. "Come below, ladies. Let's see if we can feed you."

Still steadying themselves with the lifeline, the trio started back in the direction of the hatch. They had to step aside when Jorrit Winard and four sailors dragged the wicker crow's nest past them towards the foremast. Winard stopped and let the seamen continue with their burden. He gave the women a wretched look. "No one's seen the Corajoso," he said. "Once we get the nest mounted, I hope we can spot her. Everyone who's dear to me is on that ship."

Chapter 46

A month later, on a sunny day in early December, the Avontuur arrived off the coast of Gibraltar. Once the storm had passed, the crew toiled night and day to clear the wreckage and repair what they could. When they finally hoisted sails on the two remaining masts, the ship made adequate progress despite the reduced canvas. The day before they arrived at Gibraltar—with the immense headland just emerging from the south horizon—they'd passed a Dutch merchant. The captain, a man whom Jansen knew slightly, told them the port was open to all ships.

"Did you see the Corajoso?" Jansen asked him.

"No," he said, "she's not there."

Sad news indeed. No one on the Avontuur wanted to give the ship up for lost. Jansen called back, "If you see her on your way north, let Captain Vincent know we'll lay over for at least three weeks. We're in great need of repairs."

"Better start with your mainmast," the Dutch captain joked.

Jansen set his speaking trumpet aside and cursed. The last thing he needed was someone making light of their situation.

In the month since the storm, and on their way south past the Spanish and Portuguese coasts, they'd seen a great number of ships, but none turned out to be the Corajoso. Jansen had conferred with the cook and his few senior officers, deciding they could make do for a month with the remaining foodstuffs and water, pointing out the danger of stopping at any of the possibly hostile ports along the way. Since they encountered rainstorms every few days, drinking water remained in supply. Food was another matter. In the last week before reaching Gibraltar, all hands were living on one ration a day of *geel brood,* a remarkably unpleasant, yellow bread made from ground pumpkin and wheat flour.

"We've nothing left to sweeten it with," the cook told all those who complained. "It's all we have. Eat it or starve."

***

As soon as the Avontuur dropped anchor in Gibraltar harbor, Jansen unloaded a half-dozen barrels of wheat and sent a crew into town to sell it. "Before we contract for the rest of it," he told Jorrit, "let's see what wheat's selling for. Whatever you get for this grain, use it to buy food. We'll worry about repairs later."

Worries upon worries—The majority of their funds were somewhere out at sea on the Corajoso. If Vincent and crew didn't show up soon, they would be stuck without resources in Gibraltar. The Avontuur carried over two hundred barrels of wheat, so they could sell them for sustenance, but the substantial funds needed to repair the ship were completely out of reach.

At dinner that evening, Captain Jansen reviewed their situation. Despite the much welcomed fresh food, there was little jollity in the conversation. "With the current price of wheat," he said, "we can feed the crew and ourselves for two months. But that does not solve the repair problem. We could sell all that grain, and still not have enough for a new mast and rigging." He glanced out the dining cabin window. "And then we need monies to purchase supplies and trading goods for Brazil, or wherever we end up."

Jansen raised his cup of wine in salute to Enzo Henry. "It is our good luck to have Navigator Henry with us. When Mr. Henry came onboard, he brought a proxy letter from Captain Vincent. In the event that—" Unable to speak for a moment, Jansen set the wine cup on the table and raised a hand to his face. At last he said, "In the event that dear Vincent does not show up, the proxy letter may allow me to borrow funds here in Gibraltar. Also, I am authorized to take payment for the plantation if we ever get there."

For a few moments, no one said anything. Finally the captain nodded to Enzo Henry, and said, "We've considered these eventualities as best we could. Enzo, please tell our esteemed company what we've come up with."

***

Over the next week, crew and officers alike worked to ready the ship for its eventual new mainmast. The stump of the old mast was chiseled out of its berth, then split and formed into wedges, these to be used to secure the new mast in place. Along with splitting the remaining timber and old wedges for firewood, the crew made every repair possible with the supplies on hand.

When the repairs were well underway, and leaving Jorrit

Winard in charge, Jansen and Henry took a ship's boat into the Gibraltar settlement seeking to borrow funds. The captain and navigator met with a half-dozen money brokers and, since neither the Avontuur nor Captain Jansen had any record of successful commerce, no one offered them a loan. Finally they sought out a supposed money lender, a scruffy, light skinned Moor from Tangier in the guise of a Jew. The fellow made an unreasonable collateral demand, saying, "I will loan you half the value of your wheat stores, but only after I see them, and after they are delivered to my warehouse for safekeeping."

Jansen had no intention of accepting the offer, but wanted to string the rascal along a little. So he said, "That's not what I had in mind, though I might consider it if the interest rate is reasonable."

"Certainly reasonable," the fellow said. "Only five percent a week."

Knowing the man was a Moor—a Muslim forbidden to loan money at any interest—Jansen gestured to a mosque and its adjacent minaret just a block away. He said, "Let me consult with the local imam about your interest rates."

At hearing this, the man became furious. "I will not be insulted in this manner!" he shouted. "In a different circumstance, I would kill the both of you."

Jansen and Enzo Henry raised the hems of their vests, each revealing a pistol stuck in their waistbands. The money lender, without saying another word, closed his ledger book and hurried away.

"Well, well," Jansen said, "let me treat you to a sumptuous lunch, Mr. Henry. If we make a show of it, perhaps we can attract an investor or two."

They sought out the settlement's most opulent inn and, while the luncheon was indeed excellent—generous servings of wheat beer, roast mutton, parsnips poached in buttermilk, beet greens with vinegar dressing, and cinnamon-and-ginger-spiced apples for dessert—they attracted little attention except from a couple of prostitutes who were promptly escorted from the premises by the inn's proprietor.

On the way back to the Avontuur, Jansen and Henry made a tentative plan. "We'll give it about two more weeks," Jansen said. "In that time, if we're unable to raise funds, or the Corajoso doesn't show up, we'll sail to Tangier and try our luck there." The two crewmen rowing the ship's boat were listening intently to the conversation. The captain looked at them and said, "I know what you gentlemen are thinking. What happens if we fail in Tangier? I don't know. But I'll make an announcement when I figure it out."

Enzo knew what the alternative was, but he did not say it. Instead he said, "So you'll supply the two women with funds for passage?" His question was purposefully deceptive, and he studied Jansen's reaction.

Obviously the captain knew as much as he did. Jansen said, "Don't be coy with me, Mr. Henry. The rumor was that Yema was going to the Verdes with Vincent. If he doesn't show up, I've no idea what either of the women will do."

The next day was Sunday, and Leah, at Captain Jansen's suggestion, led a church service of sorts. Late the prior afternoon, when the two officers returned from the Gibraltar settlement, Jansen had announced his intentions to the assembled crew and officers. Leah addressed these plans at the Sunday morning service. She stood at the top of the quarterdeck stairs behind the navigation table which had been moved there for the occasion. After introductory prayers— one thanking God for their safe arrival in Gibraltar, the second asking for His guidance in the two weeks ahead, and a relevant Scripture reading—she produced a lantern, along with a wooden box of candles. Extracting fourteen, she said, "We will light one candle tonight and another each night thereafter until we sail for Tangier. We'll protect it inside this lantern and leave it on the navigation table. This will be a beacon to our lost loved ones, and guide them to our side." Leah then reached underneath the table and set a lighted oil lantern on its surface. "I'm going to pass this around," she continued. "I want each of you to stand and call out the names of those dear to you on the Corajoso. Then tonight, and every night, we will use this lantern's flame to light our beacon candle."

She first handed the lantern to Captain Jansen, he in turn to Enzo Henry, next to Jorrit Winard, then to the cook, and on to each crew member. The recitations were many, the most-often named, Lars Orlund, Eider Vincent, Dr. Cardim, Pieter and Migle Winard, First Mate Jozef, along with other family members and loved ones on the absent ship. By the time they finished, nearly everyone was in tears.

Yema was the last to speak, again hoping for the return of their absent friends. She placed the lantern on the table as the hornpipe player mounted the stairs and stood next to her. He played a solemn introduction to *Hvem Kan Seile,* and Yema began to sing, her lovely voice resounding across the water. When the child finished her song, Leah offered a prayer of salvation to the sobbing crowd …and the service was over.

***

The possibility of salvation presented itself in a most unexpected way. For the two weeks after the Sunday service, and with hopes fading for the Corajoso, Captain Jansen made preparations to depart for Tangier. Still unable to borrow funds for repair and supplies, he made do with what they had, bartering a few barrels of wheat in exchange for items critical for the short voyage across the strait to Tangier. Except for her missing mast, the Avontuur was in excellent shape— decks, fittings, and rails repaired, cleaned, and polished; seams newly calked; barnacles and seaweed scraped from the hull; shrouds rewoven and stretched tight; and damaged hatch covers replaced with watertight seals.

It was midday Saturday, with both crew and officers relaxing on deck in the warm Mediterranean sunshine. While the cook and her helpers cleaned up after the noon meal, a sailor lounging in the crow's nest called down to Jansen. "Captain, Sir. I've spotted a ship. Appears to be that Turk who helped Vincent resupply in Tangier last summer. Heading in from the south."

Jansen abandoned what remained of his lunch and directed the crew to lower a boat. Charging down to his cabin, he donned his captain's hat, retrieved the proxy letter from his safe, and summoned Enzo Henry. In under five minutes, the two men set out for the Rasuul Karim, reaching her about a half-mile away and just as she prepared to steady her moorage by dropping a second anchor.

"Ahoy Captain Bariş! This is Captain Thomas Jansen of the Dutch ship Avontuur from Almere. We are the sister ship to Eider Vincent's Corajoso. May we come aboard?"

In a moment, the captain's florid, mustachioed face appeared at the rail. "Ah Jansen and Navigator Henry," he shouted. "I recognize you. Please come aboard." Immediately a sailor dropped a boarding net. The two Dutchmen climbed up the webbing and over the rail. Both received hearty hugs from Captain Zaver Bariş. "Where is dear Captain Vincent?" he asked.

Enzo Henry spoke first. "Missing at sea, I'm afraid.

"A terrible misfortune, gentlemen. I can only hope it's temporary. Details please." When the sad news was thoroughly wrung out, Bariş ordered his steward to bring tea, and bade the men sit with him in his open wheelhouse. They sipped tea and ate ginger sweets as they continued their conversation.

Finally, arriving at the distasteful subject of finance, Jansen said, "So you see, Captain Bariş, we need funds for repair and commerce." He produced the proxy letter from inside his vest, untied the red lappet string, and opened the flap. "Here is my letter of proxy from Captain Vincent. It authorizes me to—"

Bariş put both hands in the air. "No need," he said. "I cannot read Dutch, and I know you to be men of unquestionable honesty. If Captain Vincent has confidence in the two of you, then I am content with that surety. I will help with repairs, and we can talk about commerce later."

The Turkish captain squinted at the sun, then surveyed his deck which was busy with crewmen stacking trade goods for transport to the markets of Gibraltar. He stood and said, "As you can see, we've just arrived. There is much to do this afternoon. Bring your ship close to ours. Once we get situated, we'll help with repairs." He beckoned to his purser. The man rushed to his side and stood at attention. Bariş smiled broadly and said, "Give Captain Jansen one hundred gold reis. He's not a miscreant like the absent Captain Vincent, but start a ledger just the same."

After only a few minutes, the purser returned with a leather pay bag and handed it to Jansen. "I am elated," Jansen said. "We cannot thank you enough."

"It's as one should expect," the Turkish captain said. "Dear Captain Vincent would have done the same for me."

The three of them walked to the rail. Before climbing down to their waiting boat, the Dutch visitors paused and shook hands with Bariş. "Gentlemen," the Turk said, "I've no concern about repayment. I have the sense this investment will work out well for all of us."

***

With the supply of funds from Bariş, the deck of the Avontuur became a flurry of activity. The two vessels lay at anchor next to one-another, with seamen from the Rasuul working alongside the Avontuur's crew. The new mainmast, ferried out to the Dutch ship from the harbor on a narrow barge designed specifically for transporting long timbers, towered over the deck. Once the mast was seated and wedged true, then bound solid by ropes soaked in tar, the spars were hoisted and lashed in place. With that task finished, the sailors attached the fittings and shrouds, and threaded the halyards. Then with great ceremony, the sails were hauled in place and furled onto the spars.

Captain Bariş came over from the Rasuul to join the festivities. He stood on the quarterdeck with Jansen, Enzo Henry, Jorrit Winard, Leah, Yema, and the cook, all of them cheering each time a sail—accompanied by a lively tune from the hornpipe player—was hoisted in place. Though surprised to see women on the Dutch ship, Bariş held his questions until he could talk more privately with Captain Jansen.

The opportunity presented itself soon after the topside celebration. Bariş, his purser, Captain Jansen, and Henry retired to the dining cabin where they planned to discuss finances over the noontime meal.

Bariş had just introduced the subject, saying, "It is very rare that women are allowed onboard a Turkish ship," when the cook and her two helpers—the trio smartly dressed in white livery—appeared with the luncheon fare. As the fine aromas of the several dishes registered with the Rasuul captain, he found himself at a loss for words. The meal, served on elegant, blue porcelain from the Orlund household, included whole roast chickens; sliced cucumbers in a dressing of black syrup, lemon juice, and olive oil; beets coated in nutmeg butter; and bread pudding. As soon as the servers left the dining cabin, Bariş said, "I could certainly make an exception if that woman were my chef."

Captain Jansen, drumstick in hand, picked up the conversation. "Do you make exceptions for women passengers?" he asked.

"A woman traveling on my ship must be accompanied by a male relative, her father, husband, son, uncle, whatever. Females may not travel unaccompanied."

"Well," Jansen continued, "that woman and little girl you saw earlier may wish to travel with you to Antalya, or as close as you can get them. Is there an arrangement we can make?"

After a few moments of thought, Bariş said, "In this instance, no arrangement is needed. We are transporting three concubines from

Tangier for the Sultan of Izmir. Your females can house with them."

"They are prepared to pay for passage," Enzo Henry said.

"Makes no difference. The Rasuul is not a passenger ship. As I said, there will be room for them with the concubines."

"You say they're from Tangier?" Jansen said. "We've been here two weeks, and I've never seen them on deck."

Bariş made a dismissive gesture. "They are never allowed on deck. The three of them stay in their cabin."

"For how long?"

The Turk appeared irked by the question. "Dear Jansen, trust me. We take care of their every need." He stuffed a spoonful of bread pudding into his mouth and washed it down with hot tea. "Now, let us talk about financing your voyage to the New World."

Chapter 47

By the third week in December, preparations on the Avontuur were well underway for its journey across the great ocean. With the additional funds supplied by Bariş, Jansen and Henry had no trouble finding crewmen for the upcoming voyage. It seemed that many of the sailors looking for work in Gibraltar were eager to seek their fortunes in the New World.

The spirit of adventure infected most everyone onboard the Avontuur, and both crew and officers toiled diligently to get ready. One evening at dinner, Jansen explained the agreement he'd struck with the Turkish captain. "We expect to depart in about a week," he said, "right after Christmas. By then, if dear Vincent has not shown up to settle accounts with the Turk, here's what we've agreed to. He will receive one-third of all profits from trade sales and any plantation activity we take on. He'll receive this until we have paid him twice the amount he's loaned us. I have to say that Zaver has been very generous. He's provided sufficient funds for repair, hiring more crew, and purchasing the plantation supplies we promised Obiike. We've sold most of our wheat stores. With these funds, I plan to take on goods we can sell in Brazil or points north of there." He paused and took a sip of wine, then crossed himself. "It is by the Grace of God that our paths came together. Despite the Turk's heathen beliefs, he has behaved in a most Christian manner."

Early the next morning, in preparation for a new supply of

livestock, two crewmen, along with Leah and Yema, worked to enlarge the animal pens on the foredeck. One of the sailors, the hornpipe player, talked excitedly about the voyage ahead. Yema and Leah, both absorbed in the work and their own thoughts, paid little attention until he said, "So Yema, which rumor is true? Are you going with us to the New World, or to the Ottoman with Leah?"

The girl gave him a horrified look. "People know?"

Leah spoke up before the sailor could respond. "Yema," she said gently, "the secret's out. So tell us."

"How do you know?" Yema asked Leah.

"Lars told me when we were anchored between those French islands. The night we had dinner."

"It was supposed to be a secret. I was going to tell you first, Sister Leah. How does—?"

"Apparently he told more than just me," Leah said. "Anyway, I think Lars felt it was important that I know."

The girl sat down on a nearby hatch cover. She put both hands over her eyes. "Can we talk about this later?" she asked.

"I'm sorry if I caused a problem," the hornpipe player said.

"It is not a problem," Leah told him. "I've said nothing to Yema because she has to decide this for herself." Leah felt sick at heart, and struggled not to show it. *The days are running short,* she thought, *and I can't think of anything that will change the child's mind.* She reached over and touched Yema's cheek. "We can talk about it this evening, sweetheart."

When Captain Bariş came over from the Rasuul an hour before the noon meal—supposedly "to inspect my investment," as he told Jansen—it was obvious that he wanted a luncheon invitation. Jorrit Winard made a point to visit the galley, asking the cook to prepare a special meal.

"Haven't you noticed?" she said. "With all the new supplies, every meal is special."

"I'm well aware of that," he answered. "Please make this a little more special."

As soon as Leah saw the Turkish captain touring the ship, she decided to introduce herself. Jansen had previously told her about the proposed living situation on the Rasuul Karim, so this visit presented an opportunity to further explore the subject. Leah took Yema's hand, and they walked towards the stern. Zaver Bariş, Captain Jansen, and

Enzo Henry were standing at the base of the quarterdeck stairs when the two women approached. Jansen immediately introduced them, adding, "… and one or both of these ladies may be your passengers to the Ottoman." Then, not missing an opportunity to aggravate the Turkish captain a little, he invited Leah and Yema to lunch with them.

Despite Yema's upset feelings, she understood the nature of the invitation, remembering how Captain Vincent had done a similar thing last summer with Bariş. The girl pulled at the hem of her brown tunic and curtseyed. "Thank you, Captain Jansen," she said. "We will be most honored."

Leah suppressed a smile. *Here she is again,* she thought. *If Jansen wasn't charmed with Yema before this, he certainly is now.*

Once seated at the table in the dining cabin, and duly thanking Jansen for the invitation, Leah brought up the subject of living quarters with the Rasuul's captain. "The opportunity of traveling with a known, friendly captain from Turkey," she said, "is most welcome. Since we are prepared to pay for our passage, could we—"

"Are you the L. Saulo whose letter I took from Captain Vincent in Tangier last summer?"

"I am."

"And you wrote it?"

Leah knew what these questions implied. *It's obvious,* she thought, *Bariş is quite irritated that we're at lunch with him.* Realizing this was not going to be easy, and needing some time to think, she raised a finger and put a hand over her mouth, taking an extended time to chew and swallow a piece of bread.

Enzo Henry, recognizing the awkward nature of the situation, said, "We're wondering if a separate cabin could be made available for your passengers. Housing these ladies with the concubines does not seem appropriate." He gestured to Yema. "Particularly for the child."

"Rubbish!" Bariş said. "Two of the women have children. One an infant, the other about two years old. We have no other accommodations for females."

"But—"

"Let me be clear, Mr. Henry. On my ship, everyone follows my rules. And in the case of women, they also fall under the rules of the Koran."

Leah stood and motioned for Yema to do likewise. "I can see

our presence has made dear Captain Bariş uncomfortable. We will take our meal elsewhere."

Bariş immediately got to his feet. "Excuse me," he said. "I am guilty of bad manners." He bowed slightly. "Please stay. This is not a closed subject. I will see what we can do."

"Thank you," Leah responded. She reseated herself, and Yema did also. When Leah pulled the chair forward, bringing its back against her own, she felt the reassuring pressure of the dagger in her waistband. "Captain," she said, "you asked if I wrote that letter. Indeed I did. To my dear parents."

"It is forbidden for Turkish women to read or write," he said. "For Jewish women, I don't know."

"It is the same for Jews, but my family was different."

"Well let me tell you, Miss Saulo, we have great respect for the Jew. He is *Kanun vermek erkekler*. A loose translation would be, The men who give the Law. As for—"

Yema spoke up. "Do women have to wear veils?"

He appeared surprised by the child's question. "Turkish children do not speak in the presence of adults," he said. "Usually a parent speaks for them." Bariş looked at her curiously. "You are dark enough to belong to one of our desert tribes, although I am unfamiliar with your facial tattoos. Where are you from?"

"I am a Caeté Indian from Brazil."

With an air of disbelief, Bariş said, "Your Portuguese is quite polished. What is your age?"

"I will be twelve soon."

"I see," he said. "You look much younger. If you are indeed twelve, then on my ship, whenever you are outside your cabin, you must wear the veil." Bariş found himself increasingly unnerved by Leah's penetrating stare. He thought, *Maybe if I flatter this Jewess, she will soften a little.* He smiled at Leah and said, "And of course that also applies to Miss Saulo. My crew would find the presence of such an attractive woman without a veil quite distracting." His comment appeared to have no effect on her. *Alright,* he thought, *I'm outnumbered here, and a little outfoxed. It's a travesty these Europeans allow their women such latitudes. If and when these arrogant females end up on my ship, I will teach them some Turkish manners.*

Leah asked, "Do women on the street in Antalya have to wear

veils? Jews or otherwise?"

"I am not certain," Bariş answered. "In Istanbul, all women wear veils in public. The local sultan sets the rules. I'd guess it's the same in Antalya."

***

That evening after dinner, Leah and Yema sat on deck in the pleasant twilight and talked.

"You're not angry at me?" Yema asked.

They were sitting on a bench amidships near the new mainmast. The gentle swells caused the shrouds to sway, and the deck underfoot to creak. It seemed as if each passing wave made the planks beneath their feet shift a little.

Leah took Yema's hand. "Of course I'm not angry. I've turned everything over in my mind so many times. If I were in your shoes, I'd do the same."

"You're assuming I'm going with Jansen?" the girl said.

Leah felt a sudden upwelling of hope. She was almost breathless when she answered "Yes," but I've been praying for a different answer.

"Well I am," Yema said. "I want to live with Nanjala. If I can't, then I'll go upriver from the Brazil plantation and find Fr. Mateus. I'll sing at his Mass."

So here it is, Leah told herself. *After all these years, the two of us fleeing from here to there, and it all comes down to this.* Her thoughts were followed by a torrent of bitter tears. "I'm sorry, sweetheart," she said. "I've been dreading this moment ever since I read my father's letter to you."

"It's not just that, Sister Leah. That rabbi cursed me, and I think other Jews might also. And we're always running. I'm tired of being afraid."

"But don't you see," Leah said through her tears, "in the Ottoman, the damned Portuguese have no influence. They're not even *there*. We could live apart from my parents. They will learn to love you. Just as everyone else does."

"And what would we do?" Yema asked. "Work on a farm? It was easy for us at Almere because Lars favored us. But did you see how hard those smallholders worked? How miserable they were most of the time? I'd rather take my chances in the jungle." When Leah said nothing, the girl continued. "And I'm not going on that Turkish ship. You can just hear how they treat females. I don't trust that captain. He'll lock us in that cabin with those concubines, and it will be weeks before we see the light of day again."

Leah turned and stared at the massive Gibraltar headland, the evening sun fading to the very top of the granite peak. "I think Lars had a premonition about the storm," she said. "He wanted us to be safe. I suspect he had a hand in sending Navigator Henry with us."

"I really miss Lars," the girl said. "Do you think he's still alive?"

"I don't know," Leah answered. "I certainly hope so." She sighed and put an arm around Yema, pulling her close. "I miss him too, sweetheart. How different things might be if he were here."

***

Over the next several days, both ships rushed to prepare for their voyages and to take on trade goods. Though the Rasuul already had a considerable supply of textiles purchased in Tangier, they purchased many more bundles of decorated cloth from the Gibraltar markets. And though spirits of any kind were forbidden transport on Turkish ships, fifty casks of French wine were added to the cargo. Bariş planned to trade them for olive oil in Sardinia. Six dozen pallets of precious, New World lumber, mahogany, rosewood, lignum vitae, and wood from the Brazil nut tree, were the last items loaded into the ship's hold.

Plantation supplies made up the bulk of the Avontuur's cargo. While shopping for these items in the Gibraltar settlement, Jansen was delighted to find a beautifully crafted grinding wheel made of granite from a local quarry, a wheel far superior to the sandstone ones currently in use. "If Obiike doesn't want this," he said, "I can sell it for a fortune in Brazil."

"I have a second wheel almost ready to go," the quarry master told Jansen. "Do you want it also?"

"Indeed," the captain replied, and paid for both.

The Avontuur also took on a hundred barrels of Spanish olive oil purchased from an East Indian trader who seemed to have an unlimited supply. This man of impeccable manners and diction, and wearing a turban of lustrous gold cloth, promptly delivered the purchase the same afternoon. He did so in a barge he owned, one especially constructed for transporting trade goods to the merchant fleet.

As the trader supervised the unloading of the barrels onto the Avontuur, he noticed the bundles of cloth stacked on the Rasuul's deck. "Meneer Winard," he called out, "Do you want some cloth? I have a quality much superior to your neighbor's supply."

Winard consulted with Enzo Henry. "Sure," Henry said, looking over his ledger. "Let's buy ten hundred-weight. That's all we have room for." He paused, glancing around. "Go into town tomorrow and see what he has, and take Leah and Yema with you. I'm tired of looking at their long faces."

Next morning, the two women welcomed the opportunity to go into the Gibraltar settlement. They rode in the back of the ship's boat, while Jorrit Winard and the cargo ensign, a recently-hired, older sailor with many years of experience in the merchant trade, sat in the bow and talked commerce. A short half hour after they set off, and with the two oarsmen rowing in perfect unison, they pulled alongside the trader's dock.

The Indian gentleman appeared truly pleased at seeing the two "exotic female travelers," as he called them. He promptly served everyone scented tea from an inlaid silver urn that steamed into the morning air. Leah and Yema were equally pleased at the great variety of goods in his warehouse. When they finally got around to examining the many bolts of cloth, Leah helped Winard select lots which she felt would sell best in Brazil. "If you remember," she said, "there are numerous traders from the Far East selling silk cloth in the local markets. So I think these simple cotton fabrics will sell the best." She also had him select two hundred-weight of gauze. "Mosquito netting is in great demand," she reminded Winard.

While the Avontuur's ensign tallied the bolts of cloth, and the warehouse workers trundled them out to the dock and onto the transport barge, Winard and the two women toured the warehouse, poking through stacks of goods from every corner of the world. Within the hour and with accounts settled, they prepared to return to the ship. It appeared that the trader intended to follow them out in his barge.

"Ladies, ladies," the East Indian said, "I would consider it a great honor if you would ride to your noble ship in my pathetic little craft. You may sit under the stern canopy in the upholstered chairs placed there just for such lovely creatures as you."

"How can we refuse?" Leah said. She put an arm around Yema's shoulder, and the two of them strolled onto the barge.

The Avontuur's boat set out, immediately followed by the barge and its six rowers. The gentlemen trader stood in the bow talking with one of his men, so Leah and Yema had the stern to themselves. "I guess we'll be leaving in a few days," the girl said. "I'm still going with Jansen, but I feel terrible about it."

"You can always change your mind."

"Will you still berth with those concubines?" Yema asked.

Leah shrugged. "I may have no choice. Perhaps I can persuade Bariş to—"

"For how long?" the girl asked. "You know it's about three weeks to Turkey? I can only imagine how horrible that cabin will smell with four women and two children cooped up inside."

"What's your point?" Leah asked. She found herself a little irritated at the interruption.

"I don't have a point. You should just go with me, that's all."

After remaining quiet for a few moments, Leah said, "We still have a few days. I'll go over tomorrow and take a look." *For the love of God,* she thought, *my mission, whatever that used to mean, my Goral Tsorekh, has dissolved into a struggle just to stay alive.* "You do have a point," she told Yema. "It's that our lives have become an unending quest for safe refuge. That's it. Nothing more."

By now they were within a quarter mile of the Avontuur. At the sight ahead, the rowers backed paddled their oars and brought the barge to a stop. The ship's boat, only a few yards in the lead, did the same. The Avontuur now had sailing ships on both sides— the Rasuul on her port, a new vessel with Dutch colors on her starboard.

While they watched, two officers from the Dutch ship climbed up the boarding net and over the rail onto the Avontuur. Jorrit Winard ordered the ship's boat back to the barge. "Get in," he told the women. "We'll go over there and see what's going on." He asked the Indian merchant to wait, then they rowed for the Avontuur. As ship's boat nosed into the boarding net, the ensign took hold of it as the rest of the party climbed up. When the two women and Winard climbed over the rail, they were surprised to see a crowd of officers standing around the navigation table, Captain Bariş and two of his men, Jansen and Enzo Henry, and the two Dutch officers, one of them the new ship's captain.

"Winard," Captain Jansen called out, "come up here. You need to hear this."

Leah and Yema mounted the quarterdeck stairs behind Jorrit and paused outside the wheelhouse enclosure to listen.

Jansen introduced the Dutch captain to Jorrit Winard, explaining, "This is Captain De Holman of the Krijgsman. He just started telling us what's going on." He glanced at the visitor. "Captain, please start over."

De Holman cleared his throat and said, "There's a rebellion against the Portuguese authorities that started in Amsterdam. I've heard it's spreading. As one would expect, the Portuguese have allied themselves with the Spanish. Now they're seizing all shipping that's not theirs, French, ours, English, others I guess. They've assembled a big fleet at Cádiz. It's just fifty miles north of here."

"You saw them?" Bariş asked.

"My lookout did. At a great distance. When we were about three miles west of Cádiz, we picked up some French sailors in a ship's boat. They said the Spanish sunk their ship when they refused to surrender."

"What's the chance they're coming here?" Jansen asked.

De Holman looked over at his ship. "We're not taking any chances. This is an open port with a lot of merchant shipping. Just right for plunder. Since you were the farthest out in the harbor, we decided to let you know." He took off his captain's hat, ran a hand through his thick hair, and gestured towards the harbor. "Alert others if you want to. We need to resupply, but not here. We'll do it at Tangier." He replaced the hat and said, "Good day, gentlemen. Safe sailing."

Jansen said, "Thank you, Captain De Holman." Then he and Bariş saw him and his lieutenant to the rail.

Before they returned to the group, Bariş took Jansen's arm. "Let's get out of here first thing tomorrow. And I suggest not spreading the word. Those Iberian thugs can stay busy plundering this harbor and leave us alone."

"I concur," Jansen said. "You look ready to sail, and we're fairly close. I'm going to need help getting all our cargo stowed. May I borrow ten of your crew?"

"Certainly."

***

As they prepared for bed that evening, Leah and Yema traded a some items they most treasured, three scarves and a few pieces of jewelry. Following this, Leah packed her trunk. When finished, she said, "I'll have them take this over to the Rasuul in the morning."

"You won't be able to inspect the concubine cabin," Yema said.

"I guess I'll just take my chances," she said, then sat there, silent and looking perplexed.

"What?" Yema said.

"Before he left, Helgen gave me something for you. I was going to make it a birthday present in a year or two. But now your birthday's only a week away, and—" Leah made a sigh of regret and frustration. "And who knows? So here's a present for next year's birthday, or the year after that." She bent and opened her trunk, offering Yema an item wrapped in sheep's hide and tied with a leather thong.

"What is it?" the child asked.

"Open it. Something I hope you never have to use."

Yema untied the thong and opened the hide. For a moment she looked confused. Then she said, "It's a dagger," and drew it from its sheath.

"Careful, it's unbelievably sharp. It's Helgen's. He wanted me to have it. To protect you. When I told him I already had a dagger, he said to give it to you."

"It's beautiful," Yema said. "Fancy handle."

"Made from an antler of some kind."

Yema put her hand out. "Show me yours."

Leah reached to her waistband and withdrew her dagger and sheath. She handed it to Yema. The child laid the two side-by-side. "Why don't you take Helgen's," she said, "and I'll keep yours? Like we traded scarves."

"I thought about that," Leah responded. "I think there's a little magic about Helgen's. Perhaps his weapon will protect you better."

Yema handed Leah's dagger back, and set Helgen's aside. Leah stood and picked up the girl. She carried her over to the bench by the cabin window and sat down, setting Yema cross-legged in her lap. She ran her fingers through the child's hair, and said, "You know you'll always be my daughter. And I love you."

"And on this earth, you will always be my mother. But may I

still call you 'Sister Leah?' I've come to love that name. And you are also like a sister to me. A big sister."

With both hands, Leah reached back and took off her gold necklace. She put it around Yema's neck and fastened the clasp. "I want you to have this," she said.

Yema pressed the strand against her throat. "I can't take this."

"Yes you can, my daughter. It's yours. I once said it was my life's most precious gift, but you've become more precious, much more than a mere possession."

"I'll return it to you one day," Yema said.

"I'm confident of that," Leah said. "In the meantime, it will bind us through the coming years; just as it's done for my life up to now." She looked out the cabin window at the dark hull of the Rasuul Karim. "If I can convince my parents to accept the both of us, then I'll somehow find you and see if you want to return with me."

"And if they won't?"

"Either way, expect to see me climbing the hill to Nanjala's, or coming upriver in a Tupi canoe. After all this time, my parents won't want to lose me again. I imagine I can convince them."

Leah stood and carried Yema to her hammock, set her into it, and pulled the quilt up to the girl's chin. As she had done during the storm, Leah tied the two hammocks together. Then she got into hers and settled under the covers. She took Yema's hand and said, "Sleep well, sweetheart."

The child lay there crying softly, wiping the tears on her nightshirt sleeve. After a while she stopped, and said with a sigh, "I guess I'll never get to see those northern lights."

***

The next morning, and well before first light, crews and officers on both ships made ready for departure. At seven bells, sailors went aloft into the shrouds, scooting along the top spars and loosening sails. Onboard the Turkish ship, the second mate shouted a halt to the activity as the harbormaster's skiff pulled alongside. "Ahoy Rasuul Karim," the official called out. "Where are you headed?"

Captain Bariş stepped to the quarterdeck rail and looked down. "East," he called. "First Sardinia, then Istanbul."

"Excellent," the fellow shouted back. "I've got mail for transport. Will you take it?"

"Of course." Bariş ordered a line lowered.

The Turk and his first mate watched impatiently while a seaman aboard the skiff took his time attaching the leather mail pouch to the line. Just before the Rasuul's first mate began to pull it up, the harbormaster shouted again. "That Dutch ship next to you. Where's she headed?"

"West out of the straights, then south. Likely stop at the Canaries for supplies. I think Ilia da Brava after that."

"I don't recognize her."

"She's the Avontuur. Sister ship to Captain Eider Vincent's Corajoso."

Much to Bariş's irritation, the man took several minutes conferring with his assistant. Finally he called back to the Rasuul, "Interesting. I may have something for Vincent. Where is he?"

"We fear lost at sea."

The assistant walked over to a large wooden box resting in the center of the skiff. He opened it, revealing a sizeable file of documents. He quickly produced a letter and handed it to the harbormaster. The official studied the address for a moment, then shouted, "The letter's from your end of the world, Bariş. Antalya. It's addressed to an L. Saulo in the care of Eider Vincent in Amsterdam. I guess we need to find someone going north."

"Saulo's my passenger," Bariş called down. "She's over on the Avontuur right now saying good-byes. Put it in the pouch. I'll see she gets it."

A sailor aboard the harbor skiff held the pouch while his assistant put the letter inside. The Rasuul's first mate hurriedly pulled the pouch onboard. He untied it and handed it to Bariş. The captain hefted the pouch for a moment, then walked to the rail. "Harbormaster," he called, "a Dutch ship on her way to Tangier yesterday stopped here around noon. The captain said there's a sizeable Portuguese and Spanish military fleet that may be headed here from Cádiz. They intend to seize the port, and take it over."

The harbormaster, speaking quietly in Spanish, said to his assistant, *"Eso sí que es interesante. Si tuviéramos un buque de guerra aquí , me gustaría tener a capturar ese buque holandés. Hay probablemente una recompensa. Por lo menos ahora sabemos dónde va."* "Now that's interesting. If we had a warship here, I'd have them capture that Dutch vessel. There's likely a reward. At least now we know where she's going."

The official looked up at Bariş. "Thank you," he shouted. "I will let everyone know." He pointed to a distant vessel, gave an order to his rowing crew, and set off. He looked back at the Rasuul and called, "Safe voyage, Captain Bariş!"

Zaver Bariş turned to his second mate. "Mr. Uçar," he said, "proceed as before."

Onboard the Avontuur, Leah saw the Rasuul's sails begin to unfurl, each canvas snubbed short at half-open. She finished her farewells to Jansen, Winard, and Enzo Henry, then gave Yema one last hug, both their faces wet with tears. Leah climbed over the rail and down the boarding net to a sailor waiting for her just above the waterline. He reached over, grabbed the Rasuul's boarding net, and passed it to her. Taking hold of Leah's arm, he made sure her footing was secure before she started to climb. Once onboard the Rasuul, Leah mounted the quarterdeck stairs, walked past the wheelhouse, mumbled a thank-you to the captain, and stood at the stern rail looking over at the Avontuur. She could see Yema amidships talking with Jorrit Winard.

"Raise anchor," Bariş shouted. Even with the sails at half position, the ship strained at the anchor rope. Twelve men, three on each of the four turnstile arms, rotated the spindle and raised the heavy weight from the sea floor. The moment the anchor came free, the Rasuul Karim surged forward. At the helm, the first mate brought the heading to due south. The ship moved directly away from Gibraltar and into the Mediterranean passage.

Bariş gave the command, "Full canvas." One by one each sail thudded against its lower spar and the Rasuul picked up speed. Far out in the strait, the sun-swept whitecaps streamed towards the Atlantic from the North African desert, the east wind casting ribbons of spume across the wave tops. At this distance, the entire ocean appeared to be a river flowing westward.

Within minutes the Avontuur took sail, at first moving obliquely until she came free of the Rasuul Karim's wind shadow. Then the two vessels progressed in tandem, south into the strait. The Dutch ship, with her larger canvas and sleeker lines, gained a little on the Rasuul as they continued on. Yema and Jorrit Winard stood in the bow and waved to Leah. Leah gripped the rail, steadying herself as the Turkish ship plowed through the ever-larger swells. At last she raised a hand in salute to her darling Yema, and quietly said in

Hebrew, *"N fgvsh vtch shvv, hvt shl,"* "I will meet you again, my daughter."

Aboard the Avontuur, the crow called down to the wheelhouse. "Captain, Sir. There's at least two-dozen sails on the north horizon. Could be that military fleet we heard about."

Jansen turned to Enzo Henry. "It would appear," he said, "that dear Captain Vincent is still looking out for us. Another escape, and we're too far away for those bloody fools to catch us." He squinted at the mainmast pennant. "There's our wind, Mr. Henry. Take her west."

As Enzo Henry spun the wheel and the Avontuur made its turn, Winard and Yema hurried past the two officers, the young man and the girl standing together at the stern rail. Once the ships moved beyond Gibraltar's high thrust of granite, the east wind worked itself to nearly a gale and set the vessels on their separate journeys. The Avontuur, her sails full-out, bowsprit cutting through the waves and foredeck drenched in ocean spray, drove west before the wind. The Rasuul Karim shed that same wind and came about, tacking north, then south, hard-heeled at each leg, copper flanks exposed, scattering sunlight as she advanced into the Mediterranean.

On this sad and glorious morning, as the two vessels drew further apart and the figures less distinct, would it be folly to imagine the great ocean rising just a fraction from the flood of tears shed at this parting?

~End~

Acknowledgements

Extending many thanks to the following: My extraordinary editor Naïma Msechu whose great eye for detail and literary style provided the many needed changes and improvements to make *The Cantora* the best it could be. To my cover artist Nicole Brauch whose tireless efforts, infinite patience, and sensational artistry gave us the fine cover portrait of Yema and associated images. To web and book-layout designer Dan Gayle for providing both our creative website design and final cover layout. To singer Julie Larson whose lovely ballad *Hvem Kan Seile* captures the many moods of this novel and even that of Cantora herself—as the reader will discover in Chapter 42.

Additional and generous thanks also go to my business manager Lynda Makara for her publishing research and ongoing website activities. For the writing encouragements and content comments I received from my singer-songwriter daughter Jill Cohn and friend Natalie Msechu. To Ingram Spark Publishing for their excellent publishing, distribution, and promotional services. To Sonny Shaffer who spent many afternoons listening to me read from the text and provided insightful feedback. And lastly to Laurie Batchelor—Belated but thankful acknowledgements for her suburb editing for the digital version of *São Tomé* which also provided the text for the Portuguese publication *Rapto em Lisboa*.

A number of historians provided the much-needed details and backgrounds for this novel. These works include: *Colonial Brazil* edited by Leslie Bethell; *A History of São Tomé Island* by Robert Garfield, *Jewish Child Slaves in São Tomé* by Moshé Liba, *Chapters of Brazil's Colonial History* by Jão Capistrano de Abreu, *A History of Brazil* by E. Bradford Burns, *An Early History of the Portuguese Inquisition* by Ervin Kolbertz, and *Into the Rising Sun* by Luc Cuyvers. In addition, I would be remiss if I did not acknowledge and thank Wikipedia for their wealth of information and reference materials.

The Many Faces of Cantora

The cover artist for *The Cantora,* Nicole Brauch,
(http://www.nicolebrauchart.com) spent many hours preparing
black-and-white drawings and color layouts before we settled on
the final cover. What follows are some of the layouts she prepared,
along with two images that helped guide us through the process.
I've added comments for a few, and those are noted below the
images.

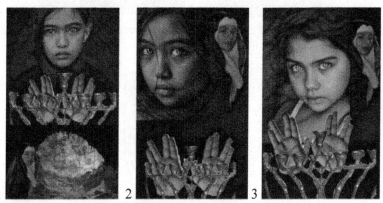

In images 1, 2, 3, and a few others, Sister Leah appears. With the nun's
image included, the cover art looked a little too cluttered, and the image
was distracting, so we left it out.

Image 4 set the face of Cantora, age, appearance, look, hand placement,
and forest colors. A little of image 6 was blended into the final cover.

7 8

We admired image 8, *The Book Thief* cover, because of the way Liesel appears to emerge from the painting.

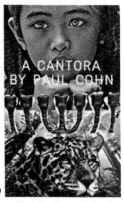

9

When I saw image 9, I immediately knew the jaguar, menorah, and forest were just about right and belonged on the cover.

 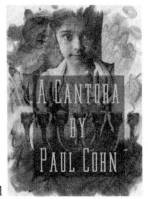

10 11

12

You will notice the *baraka* hand position in many of Nicole's drawings. This is the Jewish blessing for the menorah and other sacred objects. It forms the Hebrew letter *Shin*, **שׁ,** a word for God. We could never make the hand position work for the cover because it always appeared as if Yema was pushing the viewer away.

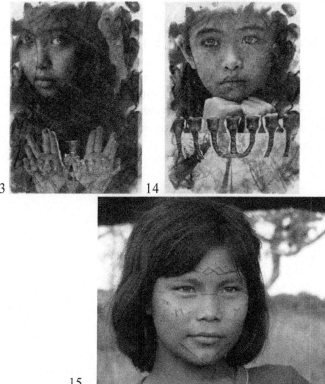

13

14

15

The above photo of a Brazilian native girl, number 15, was my original model for Cantora—for her appearance, age, and look of determination. And this is how I imagined her. But we decided to make her appear younger, vulnerable, and somewhat uncertain after several women ~consultants said the kid looks too much like a rebellious preteen. I figured there was no arguing with that.

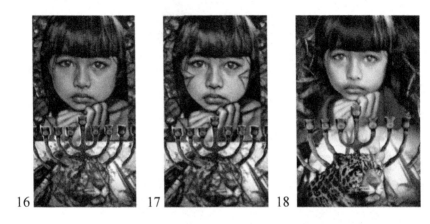

16   17   18

Images 16, 17, and 18 were the final layouts that Nicole used for the completed cover. She tried it both with and without tattoos, but we felt the tattoos were distracting, so we left them out.

If you would like to see these images in color, please visit our website at thecantora.com.

CPSIA information can be obtained
at www.ICGtesting.com
Printed in the USA
BVOW06s1755240917
495760BV00011B/179/P